THE NEXT VICTIM

The girl's limbs were spasmed, her head thrown back, the face contorted in a death scream. Joe's face reflected the shock I'd seen on Fitzy's face just a few days earlier in front of Aggie's B&B. Same picture of shock Aggie had seen on mine when I'd stumbled through her front door.

Rachel Shaw wasn't as naked as Dana. All the same, what clothes were left on her were in tatters. She had ripped them off, though not as completely as Dana had. Shreds of shirt were in her hands. Fitzy was looking at a sex crime even if it turned out no one had engaged in a sexual attack upon her that left evidence of such. Gave her something that so tormented her she tried to pull her clothes off.

And he watched.

He watched until she was dead and then he dumped her . . .

SHE'S NOT THERE

MARY-ANN TIRONE SMITH

PINNACLE BOOKS
Kensington Publishing Corp.
http://www.kensingtonbooks.com

PINNACLE BOOKS are published by

Kensington Publishing Corp.
850 Third Avenue
New York, NY 10022

All Kensington Titles, Imprints, and Distributed Lines are available at special quantity discounts for bulk purchases for sales promotions, premiums, fund-raising, and educational or institutional use. Special book excerpts or customized printings can also be created to fit specific needs. For details, write or phone the office of the Kensington special sales manager: Kensington Publishing Corp., 850 Third Avenue, New York, NY 10022, attn: Special Sales Department, Phone: 1-800-221-2647.

Pinnacle and the P logo Reg. U.S. Pat. & TM Off.

First Pinnacle Books Printing: March 2005

Illustrated map by Laura Hartman Maestro

10 9 8 7 6 5 4 3 2 1

Printed in the United States of America

With love and affection

I would like to dedicate this book to

Maryann, Susan, Joan, Nancy,

Amy, Nora, Melanie, and Kara.

1

I stood outside on the long wood porch. The morning sun had burned off most of the haze. The day would be warm but not muggy. Maybe the curl I had to my hair, far more fanciful than usual, would calm itself. Long spiraling tendrils sticking to my mouth are not as adorable as *Vogue* magazine would have people believe.

I could see Joe's cat, Spike. Actually, his fat, furry, marmalade tail, upright in the high grasses a few yards away. He was happy. Hunting. Then eating. He'd eat most of the game he snagged, leaving just the internal organs in a little pile for us right in front of the door. I'd been forewarned, so I always managed to step over the gift rather than in it. Joe has great respect for these acts of generosity so he doesn't mind the cleaning-up part. Joe is attached to this old tomcat, who yowled during our entire two-hour flight from Washington to Block Island. The yowling was nothing compared with the stench of the prodigious amounts of urine, doo-doo (Joe's term), and vomit Spike produced. Joe told me not to worry—

there was a guy at the landing strip who would clean his plane.

"Fumigate it too, hopefully."

No comment.

"Maybe you should add a little Dramamine to his kibble."

Joe put the plane into a steep bank.

I took one of the bikes leaning against the side of the cottage and walked it up the grass-matted path to the unpaved road. I was thinking, It's Bastille Day. This is the kind of thing I've had on my mind during the few days spent away from my FBI chores—*It's Bastille Day, how interesting*. When I'd admitted such a thing to Joe he said, "Told you so." I'd forgotten one of his many exhortations on the pleasures of his hideaway: "The best part of Block Island is its ability to turn your brain cells to mush," a sensation I was positive I could not experience. And I was surprised it could be true of Joe Barnow, chief field adviser for the ATF, a brilliant and aggressive fellow when it came to serving justice. I never dreamed he'd be right. But there I was, thinking about Bastille Day and not much else.

The sound of Joe's little Cessna replaced the stillness all about me. He was off for a few hours on an errand. I shaded my eyes and looked up. The sun was dazzling. Climbing into the sky, Joe tipped a wing at me. Spike raised his head above the weeds and looked up too. So maybe Joe was tipping his wing to his cat.

I got on the bike and bumped along till the track merged with Coonymus Road, which led toward the old harbor on the other side of the island. The first half mile of Coonymus wasn't paved. The rest of it was, but barely—a network of gaping fissures and a mass of potholes. Block Islanders don't patch the asphalt all that often unless the state of Rhode Island really pushes them.

They don't like tourists racing all over the place in cars. Tourists should walk. Joe bragged that you could walk the perimeter of the island in eight hours. That had me worried. I'm a city girl. Hearing that, I'd felt trapped before the plane ever took off from Dulles. But the sea did not trap me. The world seemed expanded, in fact, and I liked the place more and more each day, mushy brain cells and all.

I navigated through and around the obstacle course that was the road, guiding the handlebars with my right hand and holding a mug of coffee in my left. I took a sip whenever there was a smooth stretch. Look, Ma, no hands. Imagine that—me being giddy. At one point I stopped on a rise, one of the highest points on the island: a hundred and fifty feet above sea level. I looked north across the landscape dotted with restored farmhouses and new million-dollar vacation homes. Joe told me the natives had done the restoring and then sold off their surrounding acreage to developers for a ton of money. He said the only difference between Block Island today and Block Island twenty-five years ago—besides the fabulous new "cottages," including his own—was that the islanders no longer drove beatup red Ford pickup trucks with the mufflers hanging off. Now they owned Cadillac Escalade EXTs—"they come with leather upholstery and Bose sound systems"—silver being the most popular color, with gold detailing of their own design and the capacity to haul 8,500 pounds, though there was nothing to haul and no place to haul it. "This used to be an island of fishermen whose wives farmed their own food and raised cows."

"So what do they do now?"

"Whatever they want."

The low coast of Rhode Island lying almost flat on the horizon twelve miles across the Atlantic was blurred.

The haze still hung over the mainland. Washington was probably 97 degrees in the shade with a humidity just shy of rain. Ha-ha on them. Block Island was as remarkably beautiful as Joe had promised, hills and vales and young trees, none high or full enough to obscure the view. I would have to ask him where the real trees had gone. A tiny breeze blew one of the tendrils that had escaped my scrunchie out of my mouth. I got the bike moving again.

I passed the Pleasant View, a rickety farmhouse not restored but reconfigured into a B&B. The view from the front was the road to the town transfer station; from the back, "a stand of hoary willows and soggy bogs" was how Joe had put it. Then the poet had smiled at me. "There's always going to be the other side of the tracks, no matter your paradise." I thought, I suppose so.

No one was up and about yet. At this particular B&B, most tourists slept far later than I was able to; Joe said the Pleasant View clientele were heavy drinkers who missed the last ferry and had very little money left over after an evening at the Club Soda. They crashed there, four cots to a room, $25 per cot. "Block Island has many facets," he had said by way of explanation, when we'd driven by the first time and I'd asked, "What's that, a flophouse?" And so I learned that one of Block Island's many facets was a metaphorical railroad track.

Gulls were swarming a hundred yards past the Pleasant View at the corner of Coonymus and Center Street. (Not seagulls. I had learned from Joe, that the *sea* in seagull is redundant. "There are no gulls in Peoria," he'd said.) A cemetery was at the corner there, an Indian cemetery, mostly little rocks sticking up here and there to mark a body. No headstones in the traditional sense. Someone had put up a small sign asking those passing to remember the souls of these departed Narragansetts, the first inhabitants of Block Island, which they called Manissees.

"Then why is the road by that lighthouse called Mohegan Trail then?"

"Because that's the place where the Manisseeans pushed the invading Mohegans over the bluff and into the sea."

Oh.

When he showed me the cemetery, Joe said, "The Manisseeans are extinct, of course." Of course. Then, "There are a few slaves buried here too."

"Slaves?"

"They were leased."

Leased? I'd started to say, but he'd turned my attention to another point of interest. Many facets, indeed.

Now, gazing at the swirl of white birds, it took my mushy brain cells a few moments to recollect that bees swarm, not birds. There were dozens of them, and more were coming in from all directions. They made a god-awful racket, worse as I came closer. They did that kind of thing on the harborside when the fishing boats dumped out leftover bait. Just not this many. The gulls' wings were flapping so rapidly I could hear the beating over their raucous cawing.

They were circling above something lying in the crossroads in front of the cemetery. I slowed just enough to keep the bike from falling over. Where Center Street met Coonymus lay a lumpy mound. It was white, almost as white as the gulls, and it shone in the bright morning light. I couldn't make out what it was in the blinding glare of the sun. I came to a stop, put my feet down, and once again had to shade my eyes with my free hand. Then I got the bike moving again, pedaling closer, scaring off all but a few particularly brazen birds.

It could be a beached seal, I thought, its color washed out by the sun. Joe and I had come across one on a deserted west side beach. But how could a seal wash up here, so far inland? A good *mile* inland. Obviously, it wasn't a seal. The mush was clearing from my brain; I knew what I was seeing.

The mound was a body. Or was it two bodies, intertwined? I pedaled closer. No, it was not two bodies, it was an overweight adolescent girl, naked, her large limbs wrapped grotesquely around her torso. This was not typical rigor mortis: it was as if every muscle in her body had cramped and spasmed and then stayed spasmed. I stopped the bike. She was not entirely naked. A few shredded edges of her clothes—the waistband of her shorts, the collar of her T-shirt—lifted in the breeze. A very big girl—from the camp, I thought. Joe had mentioned something like that, not too far away. She was not one of the four campers we'd seen yesterday at the harborside, walking down the ferry ramp amid the daytrippers. This was a different girl.

Her long lovely strawberry-blond hair fanned out from her terribly twisted face.

I thought three things in a row: First, she was dead; second, Joe hadn't come upon her; third, the gulls hadn't drawn blood. The first meant there was nothing I could do for her. The second meant she'd been lying there for a very short time. The third, she'd been dead too long for the gulls to make a meal of her. Gulls do not hesitate when a fisherman tosses a fish he isn't interested in, but if he simply drops it at his feet, the gulls are out of luck. By the time he packs up and leaves, the fish is no longer suitable. Put it together and she'd been killed elsewhere—at least an hour ago, probably—and dumped here.

I got off the bike and let it fall, forgetting I had a coffee cup in my hand. It fell, too, and smashed. The gulls screamed and, disappointed to begin with, reversed direction. So did I. I ran back to the B&B and threw open the door. The proprietor was right there, about to go out herself. Joe had dropped in to say hello to her on our first day and to introduce me. She'd given him a big hug and ruffled his hair like he was five years old. Aggie.

Now Aggie smiled at me and said, "Hey, honey, c'mon in. I was just about to go see what the hell was perturbin' the gulls"—she squinted at me—"but first I'm goin' to have to ask what's perturbin' you? You seen a ghost?"

She wore a housedress, the kind I suppose you can buy only in a Wal-Mart. Instead of the top two buttons, a rhinestone brooch was holding the front of the dress together.

I said, "Don't go out there. Just call that cop in town."

"What cop?"

"The one from Providence. There's a body out in the crossroads."

She hustled to the window. "I don't see no body."

"Aggie, where's your phone?"

She pressed her face against the glass, craning her neck. "Whose body? Not one of ours, I hope."

"A girl. A girl from the camp."

"A girl? Dear God! What, was she hit by a car? Damnable tourists. I'm always the first to say—"

"I know. Aggie, the phone."

She came away from the window. "Don't you worry now, I'll call over to Tommy's. Forget about that state cop. Hung over at this hour." She was probably right. I'd met him the day before, on duty for the summer season. He was completely played out. Tommy was the island's constable.

Aggie picked up a table phone from behind her counter and set it in front of her. She dialed and waited. She looked up at me. "All bloody, was she?"

"No."

Then Aggie spoke into the phone, slowly and clearly, the way a person talks to someone suffering from dementia. "Jake? Now Jake, honey, this is Aggie . . . *Aggie*. You listen to Aggie very carefully. Get Tommy. Tell him to hurry up to my place. Pronto. We got an emergency. Tell Tommy it's an *e-mer-gen-cy*. So what did Aggie say we got, Jake?" She waited. "That's right. Good boy. An *e-mer-gen-cy*." She hung up. She said to me, "Jake'll understand enough to get him. Tommy'll come up here by way of the crossroads. Hope he don't bring Jake along." I'd met Jake. He lived with the constable. Jake was particularly deranged. *No*, Joe had said. *Autistic*.

The pitch of the gulls' cries had ratcheted up many decibels. Aggie headed toward the window again. "Buncha new gulls are headin' in. I was hopin' none of my guests would wake up for a while. That way I can tell 'em they missed breakfast. Won't sleep through this kind of racket, though." She glanced nervously at the stairs behind her. Again, she asked me, "Hit by a car, was she?"

I started to say no to her question. The body would have been far less gruesome if it had been hit by a car, if there were blood all over her. Blood is normal, a contorted musculature is not. So this time I said, "Yes." It worked. She cringed and pulled away from the view out the window.

My guess was that a drug or combination of drugs had killed the girl. There had been no wounds or any signs of asphyxia, nothing around her neck, no marks. Some drug—or else a mix of several—had devastated her central nervous system violently contracting every muscle. What drug or drugs might cause so tortured a death I had no idea. I depended on my crime lab to answer questions like that. I wished I was one of those people who could honestly say, Where do the kids get this stuff? I already knew the answer. They get it from hard-core addicts who sell drugs to make money to buy drugs for themselves. Where the addicts get the drugs from is always the more imperative question, one Joe Barnow is paid to figure out.

Aggie said, "Goddamned tourists drivin' around here like we was Boston. Least they're killin' their own."

My look stopped her short.

"Sorry, Poppy. Joe would understand. And you bein' his guest and all, I figured . . ."

Joe would understand? Block Islanders felt a big affection for him. Joe goes to the island in winter too. Spends long weekends whenever he can. When island kids get sick, he flies them to the nearest mainland hospital, even through blizzards. Well, they may have accepted him, but they were sure wrong to think he'd concur that it was better for a kid from the mainland to die of an overdose than a local kid to die from appendicitis.

Aggie said, "A couple of those girls have been here, partyin' with my guests. I had to call the camp to come get them. Drunk. Young. Say, Poppy, would a cup of tea settle you some?"

I tried to muster a reassuring smile. "No, thanks, Aggie. Another time."

She tilted her head a little and started for the door. "I hear Tommy's truck."

I stepped in front of her. "I'll go. That way, if your guests do wake up, you can try to keep them from going down Coonymus. For now."

"Well, you and Tommy come in then, have some tea. After."

I went out the door. The constable's pickup appeared over the rise, the old red variety. Not a native, I supposed. No land to sell. He stopped just short of the crossroads, rolled slowly forward, and parked, damaging any sort of tire tracks or debris left by whoever dropped the body. He wasn't used to this kind of thing. In one of Joe's many riffs about the glory of Block Island, he'd told me there was no crime. "No skunks, no snakes, no fences, no banks, no lawyers, and, best of all, no crime." The elderly constable had volunteered to enforce town statutes, that's all.

Tommy got out of the truck and stood next to the body. I walked toward him. He put his hands on his knees and bent down to have a closer look. Then he became aware of me. He stood straight again. He said, "You the one found her, miss?"

"Yes."

He squatted all the way down. It wasn't easy for him. He stared at the dead girl. He pushed a strand of hair off her face. Her mouth was open as far as human jaws allowed. She'd died screaming. What drug could do that?

The constable pulled himself back up to his feet. "Thought I should confirm the death. By the look of her, no need bothering to feel for a pulse. She's gone."

"I think you should call the state trooper."

He was staring into my face intently. He knew he should, too. He sighed. "I'll have to stay with the body. I don't have one of those car phones. You drive a standard?"

I could, but more damage to the scene wouldn't help.

"Tommy, why don't I have Aggie call him?"

He squinted. "Trooper don't answer his phone much before noon anyway."

"Isn't there another trooper with him?"

"Officer Fitzgerald takes the phone off the hook."

"I'll go. I'll ride my bike."

"All right, then. Best you do that. And miss?"

"Yes?"

"Notice anything strange around here? Seen anything before Aggie called me?"

"No."

He looked up at the gulls and then back at me. "Been dead long enough to put off the birds, I'd say."

I didn't tell him I agreed. Since I arrived, I'd kept mum about what I do for a living. I don't enjoy being a conversation piece. Now Tommy had nothing more to do or say. He was not a policeman, he was the equivalent of a meter maid. He knew he had to wash his hands of whatever had happened to the girl and leave things to the police, even if the police consisted of a man, the likes of Officer Fitzgerald. Francis X. Fitzgerald of the Rhode Island State Police. Fitzy, Joe had called him. Plus there was a rookie supposedly learning the ropes.

The constable lived at the intersection down where Center crossed Old Town Road, halfway to the harbor. I reached it in minutes and slowed at his house, which had a little addition attached to its left side. Literally attached—a shack was nailed up against the house that seemed as though it were pulling away. Jake lived in the tacked-on shack. He was standing on the sandy untrimmed lawn, which was littered with electrical equipment, fiddling with a pair of BX cables. Jake was a savant. Joe told me at Christmastime he wired the whole island. Tourists returned over a period of a month to see his decorated tree at the harborside made entirely of piled-up driftwood and so bright with lighting you could make out the glow from the mainland, his display of singing angels strung above the town hall, and Santa and his sleigh plus all the reindeer led by Rudolph arched across the nearest rise of cliff.

Jake watched me, his eyes directed at the front bike tire. I called out to him. "Everything will be all right. Tommy will be back soon."

I got a response. "Would not take . . ." and he touched his chest. Jake didn't use names or pronouns, according to Joe. Then he turned away and looked down at his cables, twisting them again.

"He'll be back soon."

I raced down Old Town Road to the harbor and turned into a little side street Joe had taken the day before. A sign in front of a small cottage read RHODE ISLAND STATE POLICE SEASONAL. It was not a conventional police station, just a temporary trooper's residence, a ramshackle wood-frame house that served as an office too. It looked deserted. If it was deserted, I'd try the clinic at New Harbor. Maybe I could get the doctor to look at the body. Hopefully, he'd know what to do as far as getting someone official out to the island. Joe had picked one hell of a day to go dashing off to the mainland.

I threw down the bike and ran up onto the trooper's porch, opened the ripped screen door and knocked, waited, and knocked a little harder. I thought I saw movement over at the window. I let the screen slam shut, stepped off the little porch, and went to it. Trooper Fitzgerald's haggard, scowling face was up against the glass. I jumped. He gaped at me. The man was not wearing a shirt. I banged directly on the windowpane, hoping it wouldn't break. Maybe hoping it would. He grimaced. Then he shouted at me, "Hold on, goddamn it."

He disappeared and I went back to the door. After a

few minutes I pretty much started bashing on it again, a vicarious bashing of the idiotic man himself. Finally, he threw the door open and stood there on the other side of the screen. His eyes were red and watery. He had a shirt on now; he was buttoning it. His fly was open. He ran his fingers through his dirty hair.

Finally he said, "This better be good." He narrowed his eyes. "You're that ATF guy's latest, aren't you?"

I decided to act as though I'd never seen him before. "Are you the trooper?"

He smiled. "No. I'm Blackbeard the pirate."

I smiled back. "Oh. Well, there's a dead girl lying on Coonymus Road, twenty yards down from the B and B. But she needs a police officer, not a pirate." I turned toward the porch steps. The hell with him. I'd have to take over myself. I knew I wasn't meant for vacations.

"Don't move." I turned back. "What dead girl?"

"I wouldn't *know* what dead girl. She's quite overweight. I'd guess she must be from the camp."

"What the hell was she doing?"

"Doing? You don't understand. She's dead. She—"

"I mean, what *did* she do? Step in a pothole and break her neck?"

I said, "She was naked."

"Naked?" He started ripping through his hair again. "Shit."

"Tommy's with her. He's the constable."

"I *know* who Tommy is. Listen, she wasn't just spaced out, was she? That so-called constable sure as hell wouldn't know the difference between croaked and high."

"I would."

"Would you? Your boyfriend teach you a few things like that?"

Two tourists, running along the road, looked over. I
said, "Officer, the area needs to be cordoned off before
some jogger heads up toward Coonymus."

"Yeah." He zipped his fly and shoved the screen
door open. I stepped back in time not to get hit with it.
He looked toward the joggers. "Goddamn show-offs.
Want everyone to notice their tight little asses. Sight of
some dead girl might get a few of these nutcases off
the highways."

Highways.

Then he mumbled something about his rookie gone
patrolling and how he would have to find him. He said
to me, "Go in my office and call that slob that runs the
B and B. Tell her I'll be there in five minutes and not to
go near the body. Not to let any of those derelicts who
stay with her near the body either. Then call Doc
Brisbane at the clinic and tell him to get the hell up to
Coonymus Road with his van and not waste any time
about it."

He stomped down the porch and went to his car. It
was unmarked. He got in, started it, and shot off down
the road.

I did what he'd asked me to do, went inside and found
his phone. First, Aggie. She told me the guests were all
on the porch, didn't want to miss anything. "Too scared
to go near the body, though," she said. "Not to worry.
Tommy covered her with a blanket, so it's really all right,
Poppy."

No, that wasn't all right. Extraneous fibers now in
place.

I dialed the operator and told her I needed Dr.
Brisbane and to put me through right away; it was an
emergency. Block Island had a local operator, and the
call would go faster through her than if I dialed my way

through information. It didn't occur to me that my speaking with her meant the entire island population would know about the dead girl in a few short minutes.

When she got me connected, I told Brisbane's nurse who I was and said I needed to speak to the doctor. She said, "Is Joe all right?" I didn't think I'd met her but she knew my connections. I said no, and she cut me off before I could say anything else. "Sorry, the doc is seeing a patient." Whether *I* was all right or not didn't seem to matter.

"Listen, it's the state trooper who needs the doctor. And he needs him now."

She said, "Fitzy? What's he got, the DTs again?"

I told her about the dead girl and where her body was located. The nurse said, "Omigod. I'll get Doc up there now."

I went out, climbed on my bike, and headed back toward Aggie's B&B. Uphill. Took me a bit longer than it had to come down.

The maddened gulls were still circling and squawking. I stood my bike up next to Tommy's pickup, near the body. If Trooper Fitzgerald had half a brain, was even a marginally competent police officer, he'd have a fit over the blanket.

Tommy was between the body and Aggie's front porch, making sure none of her guests got adventurous. A couple of them were taking pictures.

We heard a roar. The car Fitzy had gotten into was now flying up Center Street. It screeched to a stop behind the pickup. The screech made the gulls even more crazed. The noise they made sounded like human screaming. The B&B's guests put their hands over their ears. Fitzy wasn't driving, the rookie was. He looked about twelve. I'm getting old, I guess. My stepfather used to say things to motivate himself, like, "You're as young as you feel." I was thirty-five. Last few days I'd felt eighteen. Right now I was a hundred and two.

Fitzy dragged himself out of the car, turned, and gave the rookie a dirty look. The rookie quickly emerged and slammed the door smartly shut. He stood by the car, stiff and tall. His uniform was immaculate, the trousers creased, the hat starched into perfect shape. He was also very nervous. His eyelid was twitching. He put on his sunglasses.

The constable walked toward us.

The state trooper said to him, "Okay, fella, what's the story here?"

The gulls were still screaming. Banshees rather than humans. Tommy said, "What?" Fitzy looked up at them, and I swear just his look alone sent the whole flock a little higher into the air. Tommy nodded toward me. "Lady here had Aggie call me. Found this body."

Fitzy was still looking up into the sky. "Can we do anything about the freakin' birds?"

Tommy said, "No."

The trooper shook his head. Then his eyes took in the blanket. He scanned the scene. "What's with the broken cup?"

"Figured the lady dropped it."

He raised his voice. "Figured? Well, you should've gotten me instead of coming out here to figure things. Why the hell'd ya cover the body? Jesus."

Fitzy grabbed a corner of the blanket. Tommy reached out, but there was nothing he could do to stop him. Fitzy threw the blanket off the dead girl. He went white. Now his voice wasn't so loud, though he let out a string of curse words. "Holy goddamn fucking shit." He turned to the rookie. "Johnny, get me—"

Johnny, staring at the body, was sagging. He turned his head and vomited his breakfast.

Fitzgerald said. "Wonderful." Then he looked at me. "How the hell come *you're* not throwing up? Don't tell me you're with the ATF, too."

"FBI."

"Oh. FBI. Well, that's good. That's real good. Maybe I can just get my commissioner to turn over whatever the hell happened to this girl to the FBI and leave me be."

The trooper went to his car and came back with two cellophane envelopes. He squatted down on his haunches and placed one over the dead girl's right hand. Then he taped it closed. He tried to move her other arm. It was rigid. He stood back up. He would leave it to the coroner. The trooper stuffed the second envelope in his pocket.

As he laid the blanket carefully back over the body so that every inch of her was covered, he said, "Damage is done." My instinct was to tell him not to do that, but he had a point about the damage having been done. Not unusual anyway. When someone comes across a dead body with no clothes on, that person will often throw a coat or jacket over the victim or run to the nearest house, not only to call the police but to get a blanket. The Rhode Island coroner would have to cope. Suspicious death; he'd have to pick out the blanket fibers. Tommy and I watched as, very gently, the cop bent over and went about straightening the edges.

With Tommy distracted, the guests from Aggie's had been creeping closer.

Trooper Fitzgerald stood, put his hands on his hips, and yelled at them. "What the hell are you people starin' at? Get back up on that porch or I'll arrest every goddamn one of you." Then he said to Tommy, "You too, old man. You disturbed any evidence we're gonna be wishin' like hell we had. And the road is covered with your tracks. Plus now we have my own tire tracks and we got the FBI's . . . bicycle."

Tommy said to him, "I saved any evidence. The birds might have started pecking at the body if I didn't cover it." Now the trooper's face showed frustration in addition to anger. He took a big breath, about to hurl another insult, when the distant sound of a siren filtered in through the gulls' screaming.

Fitzgerald said, "What the hell is that, the CIA?"

Tommy said, "It's the doc."

"Good. Hope he's got some Maalox."

Then he squatted down again. He lifted one end of the blanket, exposing just the dead girl's horrifically contorted face. He looked closely at her and said, "Poor kid. Someone sold her some real bad stuff." Not too terrible a man after all, perhaps. I went over and squatted down too, right beside him. He turned his head to face me. "You an investigator or a pencil pusher?"

"Investigator."

"Okay then, Agent. She was killed somewhere else and dumped here, wasn't she? Killed sometime last night, wouldn't you say?"

"I'd agree entirely with that assessment."

"Good."

"What would you like me to do?"

He looked into my eyes. "Just knowin' you're here is enough for now."

I have a friend. He's a shrink, a good one. He'd translate Fitzy's words to me—in addition to the expression on his face—as *reaching out*.

Reach out, Fitzy, you've got me.

2

Back in Joe's cottage, I switched from strong coffee to milky tea. I stretched out in a very comfortable chaise on the slate terrace out back and gazed across the ocean toward what I guessed was the direction of the FBI building on Pennsylvania Avenue. Spike had sensed something was amiss and jumped into my lap, tucked his big tail around his body, and made himself comfortable. First time he'd done that. I stroked his fur and closed my eyes. He began to purr. The placid ocean produced soft waves splashing in rhythm on the cobbles far below at the base of the bluff. Slowly, I calmed. To be calm is the reason for drinking milky tea, owning an affectionate cat, and finding a corner of the world with a vista of the wide blue sea.

An instant replay of the three days I'd spent in this once-charmed place scrolled across my brain. I stopped the screen at yesterday morning around ten-thirty, Joe and me hopping out of his jeep at the harborside, strolling along the pier.

Joe had said, "Sloppy chop."

This is the way people who are around boats talk. I was learning. When a swift and temperate breeze plays across the surface of the water, creating a nonuniform series of waves popping up unpredictably here and there, it's a sloppy chop.

A little fishing boat was tying up—the *Debbie*—a dilapidated wooden tub named after several generations of beagles, all called Debbie. There had never been several generations of the *Debbie*, no *Debbie II* or *III*. It was one very old boat, and the gents who owned her were older still. The latest Debbie beagle bounded onto the pier and threw herself into Joe's arms, licked his face, jumped back down, and ran around in circles. Joe wiped the doggy saliva off his three-day growth of beard with his bare arm. After that especially uncouth gesture, I had to say his stubble remained as sexy as ever. He knew the stubble was sexy, too. Back in DC he warned me he didn't shave on Block Island. I'd said, "Maybe I shouldn't shave either." He'd looked stricken. I laughed at him, so he laughed at himself, no longer stricken. Rather, relieved.

Billy, one of the *Debbie*'s grizzled owners, threw me a line. A line is a rope. Mick, the other owner, hoisted himself onto the dock and tied a second line around a post. He waited. I tied my line too. To *tie* means to loop the line around the post and then bring the end of the line through the loop, a half-hitch. Easy. The post has a nautical name just like the rope does, but I couldn't remember it. That's because nautical names are made up by men, so there is no rhyme or reason to them. I'd needled Joe. "Why is the bathroom the head? Why not the butt?" He'd said, "Poppy, you've just got to let it go."

Joe helped Billy and Mick's clients onto the dock.

Two couples, seasick, which is what a sloppy chop will do to you. Billy held up a neat string of, I think, porgies. He said to the couples, "Don't forget your catch now."

The greener and more wobbly of the male clients said, "Keep 'em."

The less green friend said, "I need a few stiff drinks, not dead fish."

The couples staggered off while Billy happily put the fish in an ice chest. He winked at Mick. Then he said to me, "You enjoyin' yourself, Poppy?"

"I am."

It was true. After three days on Block Island I'd woken up that morning and my first thought was not how many days were left before Joe would fly us back to Washington. Instead it was: I wonder what we'll get up to today. Each thing Joe planned for us—whether it was fishing or kayaking, biking or hiking, bodysurfing or just plain swimming—was more fun than the last. I even liked building sand castles.

Billy rummaged around in the chest. He came up with two very large lobsters and held them aloft. They waved their claws wildly but ineffectually in the air. He said, "Hey, Joe, how about these babies? Both girls and they're packed full of eggs. Delicious."

Joe said, "All right!" and then to me, out of the corner of his mouth, "we'll be eating an illegal catch tonight."

Billy held the lobsters out in my direction. The claw-waving now seemed more discriminate. "What d'ya think, Poppy?"

"All right!" I said.

He put them into a burlap sack, which became animated, and handed it to me. I took it, never flinched. Mick nudged Joe. I'd passed a test.

Joe said, "These lobsters are special. Let me give you a little something."

Mick said, "Nope," and he and Billy both tipped their battered, stained Red Sox caps to us.

We got in Joe's jeep, about as old as the *Debbie*. Joe calls it his ragtop. I'd said, "My stepfather referred to sporty convertibles as ragtops."

He said, "I call it that because it's in rags," and he pulled at one of the ribbons of canvas hanging down on our heads. "Let's just hope we don't get any rain."

"And if we do?"

"I drilled holes in the floor."

Joe's care of his car did not take in the possibility of ruining his hairdo.

We drove across the sandy parking lot, avoiding a boy known as Jim Lane's kid who sold postcards and bait right in the path of tourists getting off the ferries. We waved as we passed Tommy the Constable, who was making sure no one underage was renting mopeds. Jake stood behind him, playing with a box of batteries. We stopped in front of a liquor store. FRED'S LIQUOR STORE AND FINE WINES. The FINE WINES segment of the sign had been added on with yellow paint, and the word STORE had been crossed off with the same paint. Joe pulled himself up and out—the ragtop's driver-side door is forever stuck—and went in to buy beer. With boiled lobster you drink beer. Do something foolish to a lobster, like stuff it, you drink wine.

He came back waving two six-packs wildly in the air. Native habits are contagious on Block Island. Joe climbed back in. The ferry from Point Judith was pulling in. I'd forgotten if there was a term for the action that precedes *tying up*, so I said to Joe, "What do you do before you tie up? Cut your engines?"

He said, "No. That's a given. You dock."

I see. The ferry was docking, not pulling in. We sat there in the jeep, motionless, mesmerized by the smooth hypnotic operation just like everyone else at the harborside. Lines were tossed and fenders crushed as the ferry came to a stop. Fenders are nothing to do with the four corners of a car; they are oblong fiberglass cushions hanging over the side of a boat that prevent the boat itself from getting scraped during docking. I said to Joe, "Why aren't they called bumpers?" He said, "Bumpers are those old truck tires tied to the dock." Can't very well tie old rubber tires to your beautiful new yacht. But though the word may be *docking*, essentially, the enormous ferry slid smoothly and gracefully to a stop. I decided right then that the real reason everyone watched the operation so intently was a secret desire to see the boat crash, smashing the dock into a million pieces. Like when you watch a wrecking ball with such delight. Everyone at the harbor had that anticipatory, slightly mad look about them—including me, I was sure.

The cars and pickups came off first and then the stream of passengers, a few of the latter carrying suitcases, but most of them—day-trippers—lugging beach chairs, floats, and canvas bags brimming with towels, paperback books, food, and beer. There were two varieties of day-trippers: those who wouldn't spend a dime on the island because they were equipped with everything they'd need, and those who also didn't spend a dime because they'd come to shop. There are no shops. Just stores outfitted to meet your basic needs—FRED'S LIQUOR AND FINE WINES, WILLA'S GROCERY, the pharmacy, and a couple of enterprises that offer cheap souvenirs and even cheaper tank tops. So this second class of day-trippers would ask, "Where's the antique shops? Where's the Gap?" only to discover there weren't any such things.

They'd become disdainful. So the kid selling post-cards from his stand would say, "Try Martha's Vineyard." Then they'd ask their second question: "When's the next ferry out?"

Among the stragglers I'd watched yesterday making their way down the ferry ramp—surely it wasn't called a gangplank—were four teenage girls. Very hefty girls. Campers. Camp Guinevere. The locals referred to it as the fat farm, naturally.

Right there, at that memory, I stopped my brain from scrolling and fast-forwarded to this morning. A few hours ago. I didn't think the dead girl had been one of the four, and now I was sure she wasn't.

I returned to scrolling. Yesterday I'd said to Joe, while we watched the overweight girls with their burdens of backpacks and suitcases, "Poor kids. Can't be overweight in America, can you?"

"Nope."

"One of them looks a little young." She wasn't nearly as tall as the other girls. They all had on athletic shirts but her—one read GREENWICH HIGH RUGBY. The smallest girl wore a T-shirt with a Barbie face smiling out from it.

"Yeah, she does. Is that a doll under her arm?"

It was a vintage Cabbage Patch Kid. My assistant at the FBI has three small daughters, so I've picked up some data along those lines. "Definitely a doll."

Joe said, "The camp is supposed to be limited to teen-agers."

The day-trippers, who were standing around debating about which beach to go to or wondering aloud as to how speedily they could make their way to a more refined tourist site, stopped to stare at the girls. Jim Lane's kid had been joined by a few friends, and they were snickering as well as staring. The constable stared too. Only Jake, studying one of the batteries in his box with intense concentration, was not. When Joe had introduced me to Jake—who never looked up at me—he'd said, "Jake is Tommy's ward." Then, when we were out of Jake's earshot—though it's not unusual for people to treat a mentally handicapped person as if he were deaf—I said, "What do you mean, he's a ward? The guy must be forty years old."

Joe didn't know the exact circumstances. He only knew Tommy took care of Jake. He said, "You just accept things on the island the way they are, Poppy."

"You do?"

"Yes."

Okay. "What is a ward, anyway?"

"It's a term no longer in use except on Block Island."

"Sort of like, say, *constable*."

He smiled. "Sort of."

After picking up the beer, Joe was about to turn the key in the ignition when something banged the side of the jeep. A big red-faced man had smacked it. He had on a rumpled and dirty police uniform—sloppy chop, I'd thought. Now my scrolling through yesterday halted again: the trooper was as disheveled then as he had been this morning when he stepped out onto the police station porch and zipped his pants.

After banging Joe's ragtop, he said, "Man, those girls are an eyeful. How the hell are ya, Joe?"

The smile Joe gave him translated to distaste. He said, "Hey, Fitzy, back again?"

"I am. Assigned to the Block once more, lucky me."

Joe turned to me. "This is Francis X. Fitzgerald, Rhode Island state trooper, and how he got this cushy job only he knows. Fitzy, this is my friend Penelope Rice. Poppy."

The cop looked me up and down. "Damned sight better-lookin' than the previous one."

Nice. So I said, "Been working all night?"

Without a pause: "Slept in my uniform. Had a little party, went on longer than I expected."

Joe started the engine. "Gotta run, Fitzy. See ya around," and the jeep skidded away from the curb. Joe's nose was wrinkled like he was smelling something bad. He said, "Guy's an alcoholic. Loves to jar me. Me and everyone else. The Rhode Island State Police put him out here last couple of summers to keep him the hell out of everyone's way. I guess they hope he'll dry out."

"Why doesn't the Rhode Island State Police fire him? I would."

"That's because you're from Washington, not Rhode Island."

Joe detoured via a little side street to point out Fitzy's office. "The reason he's never in the office is because he'd have to deal with the rookie cop they assign to him. New rookie every year. Fitzy considers it the only fly in his ointment."

Back on the harbor road, we passed the camp van stopped on the side of the road. One of the four overweight girls stood by the open passenger door arguing with another girl, a skinny one, the driver. The skinny girl was yelling and waving her arms. "You're supposed to come right to camp, so you *can't* take a cab. You have to come with us!"

"I'll find my way to that camp when I'm good and ready."

"But I'll get in trouble."

The camper said, "Tough shit."

"I don't like your attitude much."

"Oh, fuck off." And the camper stalked past us, back toward the harbor, where there were two cars with the word TAXI hand-painted on their doors.

The Cabbage Patch Kid looked out at us through the rear window of the van. He was hideous. The camper holding him—she couldn't have been more than ten or eleven—shook his arm up and down. I looked at Joe. "Trying to make friends." We both waved back. Joe maneuvered the ragtop around the van. He said, "Wonder what started that altercation."

"Maybe the camper couldn't deal with sharing a ride with that satanic doll."

We drove up the hill and along the cliff edge and then across the middle hump of the island until we came to Joe's cottage on the southwest shore—isolated, beautiful, and a great place to unwind is what Joe kept insisting. At the time, he'd been right about that. I'd agreed to one week, not the two weeks—at least ten days—he'd originally tried to talk me into. His argument: "Poppy, don't look upon it as a vacation. You are recuperating from a concussion and ripped tendons in your ankle. Recuperating from injuries suffered on the job is not vacationing, even if you choose to do it on a spectacularly attractive island." My argument: "I already have recuperated. And since I'm not looking upon it as a vacation—I do not *take* vacations—I am calling it a forced leave."

Actually, I planned to jump ship whenever the hell I felt like leaving. Therefore, I sympathized with the overweight camper, the one who had gone for the taxi. Sometimes I get tired of butting heads with Joe, who is just as stubborn as I am. Once my assistant said, "What, are you both Leos?" I'd said, "Maybe he is. I'm a cynic."

After our morning encounter with the overweight camp girls plus both ends of the Block Island law enforcement spectrum—a constable always accompanied by his autistic ward and a wrecked state trooper—I'd been quite content to spend the rest of the day hiking the cliff edge with Joe, followed by an afternoon of lolling around on lawn chairs: reading, snoozing, drinking Grey Goose and tonic with lots of lemon and lots of ice, and then watching the sun drop into the sea. Once it was dark, we killed the lobsters, ate them, made love, and slept like rocks in the moonlight coming through Joe's windows. Reminded me of home. I've never gotten around to putting up blinds in my apartment in the five years, almost six, I've lived in DC, so I was used to streetlights instead of a dark bedroom. Maybe that did it, a reminder of home. Suddenly ten days away—maybe even two weeks—was beginning to sound very doable.

And then, early this morning, the first thing Joe said before he left for the airstrip was, "It'll be a warm one. Muggy now, but the humidity'll lift and a little wind will come up." He'd stood at the window, which was fitted with murk instead of moonlight. I'd thought, I am now thinking in boat terms. Then he said, "Yet another pretty day, rest assured." And I'd believed him. "Just more day-trippers than usual, Poppy, escaping the mainland heat. We'll have to go to the farthest reaches of the Crescent. Day-trippers never get out that far."

We'd planned on a day at the beach. Swimming *and* kayaking *and* picnicking. But first Joe had to gas up his Cessna, fly to the mainland, and pick up a cello. I'd said, "A cello?" and he explained that one of his fellow summer residents played with the Boston Symphony. The cello had been overhauled, and Joe volunteered to get it for him. "You'd like this guy a lot, Poppy, but you won't meet him. He'll be too busy practicing."

I said, "There are quite a few weird people around here, aren't there? Even the transients."

"The guy is a dedicated musician."

"I was talking about the guy who flies around fetching cellos."

"I'll be back with a filled picnic hamper."

The plan was that I would bike into town during the cello flight to buy presents to take home. There was a place just past the edge of town that sold framed maps, charts, various nautical records, and clippings from yellowed newspapers marking historical events. Joe had one on his wall. The headline read: KITTY HAWK, MAN'S FIRST SUCCESSFUL FLIGHT. It wasn't a shop, it was a woman's home. The woman framed the charts and clippings. The frames had style. "They aren't plastic molds with starfish embossed in the corners like the cheap prints for sale at the souvenir store. Like you get in Nantucket," said Joe, always defending his territory. He warned me it would be a little difficult finding the house. "Esther doesn't really like customers." I'd met Esther, an artist, forced to find a way to stay off welfare so she could devote herself to her painting. She didn't sell her paintings, though. She preferred to keep them, Joe said, or throw them away if she wasn't happy with them. She was a misanthrope. Only a few tourists managed to find her house. Joe had written out the directions.

So he drove off and I had slept another hour, fixed breakfast, and taken a shower. It was nine-thirty. Sleeping late was not necessarily a bad thing. In DC I didn't sleep, I worked.

Then I'd gotten the bike and left on my ill-fated shopping jaunt.

Now, sitting on the chaise with Spike, I just wanted to get back to Washington and chat up my director before filing a request to open an investigation into what killed that girl. Get to the topflight men and women at our crime lab and tell them to give Officer Fitzgerald of the Rhode Island State Police whatever he needed. Once I described to them the condition of the body I'd come across, they wouldn't hesitate for a minute. They'd be raring to go.

3

I have seen plenty of dead bodies since the day I finished law school. I first saw corpses in my initial job as an assistant DA in the Bronx. I went on to examining crime scenes, where I looked upon more dead bodies as a prosecutor in Florida. I have witnessed executions. When I was director of the FBI crime lab, before my present job there as a special investigator, I'd attended autopsies and watched my technicians observe remains and then comment on those observations before conducting their dissections. I watched them while they closely examined both entire organs and cross sections of tissue samples under their microscopes, and then we'd study images of all pertinent body parts projected onto wall-sized screens, where they'd zoom in until the skin looked like a crocheted doily. But I have never discovered a body. People chance upon bodies under terrible circumstances; a surveyor traipsing through a stand of oak trees comes upon a sex-crime victim under a pile of leaves and debris; a parent finds her child motionless in a crib, dead of SIDS; a husband discovers his wife in the garage, seated calmly behind the wheel of the car, the ignition still turned on but the car out of gas. So many instances which, suddenly, I could clearly identify with.

As I slowed my bike on Coonymus Road, registering what was right there before my eyes, not believing it for several moments, I'd been horrified. Now, hours later, my stomach was still in knots. Every bit of me was unsettled. On my lap, Spike did what he could, purring more soothingly, blinking up at me, commiserating. I stroked him and stroked him, enjoyed feeling his utterly relaxed muscles under the sleek smoothness of his kitty fur. Then his ears pricked up. He tensed and I heard what he had heard first with his big sensitive ears—the sound of the Cessna's engine as, overhead, Joe brought the plane into Block Island air space. Joe had pointed out the plane's unique little sputters to me when we'd taken short jaunts. So I waited—that was all I could do—though Spike leaped to the ground and dashed around the cottage. In ten minutes I heard the squash of the ragtop's wheels rolling down the sandy path and, a short time later, the squeal of its brakes on the graveled area at the foot of the rutted track.

Joe ran from around the corner, Spike right behind, and they stood in front of me.

"My god, Poppy, I am so sorry."

"You already heard?"

"On my radio."

He sat right down on the slate next to the chaise and took my hand. He said again, "I'm sorry."

Spike nudged him and Joe scratched the back of the cat's neck.

I said, "I swear to God, I've spent my entire adult life looking for trouble. Actually, I spent my childhood the same way. Now I get paid to look for trouble. But for the few days that I was determined *not* to look for trouble—here on Joe Barnow's island paradise—trouble has found me. Maybe that's why I have an irrational fear of vacations. Trouble finding me means I'm not in control."

Joe said, "We'll go home."

"Thank you." He kept patting me and scratching Spike. I said, "Joe, she was all twisted up. Like some kind of human corkscrew."

"I know. I heard that part too."

"Ecstasy—or whatever designer drugs kids are taking—which one does that?"

"When I get back, I'm going to find out."

"Unless my lab beats you to it."

"The race is on, then." He took my hand in both of his. "Poppy?"

"What?"

"First let's have the day we'd planned. We'll go to the beach, break out our picnic . . . We'll talk about it. Tomorrow morning we wake up, fly back. Start some serious research."

After you speak with people who have found bodies, you suggest they just go home, be with their loved ones, try to take it easy, and they always say, *Okay*. Dazed. And I found myself saying, "Okay." I wasn't dazed, though. I'd said it to temporarily brush him off. I was conflicted. I told Fitzy, the cop, I'd be here. But nothing concrete. I could be with him from my office, be of assistance by telephone.

So Joe and I did try to enjoy ourselves. For each other's sake we faked it, grabbed our gear, and were off. Our brains were in overdrive, though, back from mush state to normal. Halfway through our picnic we finally stopped commenting on the delicious sandwiches, the sweet breezes, the picturesque whitecaps and got down to talking business. Joe asked me a slew of questions: Were her eyes dilated? Did I see any tire tracks? Had I heard anything before finding her? Was she warm?

No, to them all.

He asked, "How was the doc?"

"What do you mean, How was the doc?"

"Well, he had a breakdown a couple of years ago. I think he's addicted to Demerol. Carol takes care of him, though. I was worried that he—"

"Excuse me. Come again?"

"Carol is his nurse."

"I wasn't talking about his nurse. You condone a practicing physician's addiction to *Demerol*? What do you call Demerol?"

"An analgesic. Sedative."

"Derived from?"

A little pause. "Opium. But I can't prove he's an addict. He just has that look about him—slides in and out."

Joe's paradise, it turned out, was protected by a chronic alcoholic, the people in paradise were attended by a lotus-eater, and it had an inn that looked out over the dump. I thought back to Coonymus Road. The doc had rubbed his forehead with his fingertips and taken a lot of deep breaths before he finally examined the body. I figured he was getting his own mushy brain cells into gear. But he'd been trying to drive his drug-induced tranquillity away.

I guess I got a little glum, because Joe suggested it was probably time to leave.

We drove back to the cottage, and while we packed our suitcases I went over and over with Joe what I'd seen and he began to get me spurred again, asking yet more questions. One of them was, "Did she die there? Or did she stagger along until—"

"No."

"No?"

"Someone dumped her there. Stopped and pushed her out of a car, I'd say."

"I don't understand."

"Which part?"

"I mean, I'd imagined she was off to the side of the road. In the shrubs or something. Where she'd fallen walking back to camp."

"No. She was out in the open. The perpetrator didn't have time to hide the body. Or else his plan to hide her was interrupted. She died somewhere else."

"What are you talking about?"

"I'm answering your question."

"We've been going under the notion that she'd died of a drug overdose."

"Well, I think she did die of a drug overdose. But her clothes had been ripped off. So we have to consider—"

"*What?*"

"You didn't know that?"

"No, I didn't know that. Damn. These people go out of their way to shield me."

"From what? You're an ATF officer. And why, even if you weren't?"

"Long story. She was raped, then?"

"I assume she was raped. And then her body was dumped in the middle of the road—"

"Poppy, if the body was moved, how in God's name is it that you're controlling the urge to go and find the actual crime scene? Jesus."

Crime scene. If a rape was shown to have happened,

there was a crime scene. If someone moves a dead body, it's a crime, and that makes for another crime scene. When a person dies of a drug overdose, the person who sold the drug committed a crime—and in some states they call it third-degree homicide, not negligent homicide. And another crime scene where the transaction took place. I surely did know all that. I said, "Because, Joe, I've been learning to follow the rules, that's how. Learning from you. Let Fitzy and his force find the scene of the crime. Maybe she wasn't raped. Maybe the Rhode Island State Police lab will explain what drug killed her and why her reaction to that drug was fatal. Then I won't have to help out that cop after all. I let him think I would. But it's supposed to be up to someone else, not me. I'm on *vacation*."

Joe scratched Spike a little more vigorously. Joe had spent the last six months sympathizing with me for what had happened in my last active case, where I'd come very close to getting myself killed. At the same time he lectured me oh so benevolently as to why we can't ever ride over the regulations that direct our activities. Riding over regulations was the reason I was almost killed. He had felt paternal, full of advice. I'd let him go on and on with his gentle lectures. That's because I did need a rest, why I really gave in to the idea of a vacation. I needed to put everything on hold, regain my physical and psychic strength. I asked, "So how are *you* controlling the urge?"

"By trying to set an example." Then he looked up from his cat, his face reflecting what he knew to be his utter foolishness. He said, "The problem is, I have obviously not been thinking straight. My advice was patronizing, not realistic. That's because I was so worried about you. Because, goddamn it, I love you, Poppy."

I patted Joe's wrist. "Oh, you do not. You're only

feeling crummy about what happened. And guilty because you believed you had all the facts when you had just a few of them. Guilty because the downside of this job is that we get too big for our britches. Those were the words my stepfather always used to warn me with—what's now called arrogance. So when you feel crummy and guilty, you need to offer love. But all the same, I appreciate the sentiment."

He said, "Do you love me?"

I said, "Of course I do."

"More than you love . . . say . . . your assistant, Delby? Or her three kids?"

"No."

Joe has learned to steel himself to a lot of what I say concerning our relationship, what with having come to the accurate conclusion that I never mean to be hurtful—it's just that the truth hurts but the truth is not my fault.

He got up, Spike in the crook of his arm, and pulled over the other chaise. He stretched out on it and put Spike down on his stomach, and then Spike stretched out on him. Joe folded his arms behind his head and leaned back. He gazed out to sea. Sea-gazing and cat-petting. Besides serenity, those things also make you realize you're far too insignificant to get hung up over life's annoying little details. Like falling in love with someone who doesn't quite feel the same way you do. There are too many big things out there that need to be taken care of so you can't slop around in self-pity for very long. In Joe's case, *very long* meant ten seconds. I admired his distaste for dwelling on the unpleasant. Probably why I love him just as much as I love Delby. She doesn't dwell either.

He looked over at me. He smiled. "I love you when I'm not feeling crummy or guilty. Just please don't ever let my love for you spoil whatever the hell it is you and I have going."

"Why would I do that?"

Then I got up, lifted the cat out of my way, set him down on the slate, and sprawled stomach down on top of my buddy, Joe Barnow. I said, "I don't purr, but I kiss better than he does."

I kissed his chin, his cheeks, his nose, his forehead, his ears, his hair, and his beard, and when I got to his lips he was ready to kiss back.

When we were finished, we talked, becoming very serious, stuck in each other's arms and covered with each other's sweat. We agreed it was maybe best, maybe more realistic, to let the Rhode Island police take care of things. After all, would I get involved in the situation if I hadn't discovered the body? If I'd simply heard about it? Heard that some kid had OD'd? Joe and I decided Rhode Island could go through the appropriate channels if they needed the FBI to help. I said I would tell Fitzy I'd cut the red tape if his superiors felt they required assistance from the FBI. That's what I could do for him. Then Joe and I disentangled, got up, and debated which to do next— take a shower or polish off the rest of the food in the picnic hamper. We decided to eat, a mistake. Spike returned to the scene and came begging, rubbing against me, leaving a layer of cat hair in his wake.

The next morning, we were heading out the door for breakfast at a little coffee shop behind Willa's Grocery that Willa and her husband Ernie ran. We'd eat and then we'd stop and see Fitzy on the way to the airstrip, let him know we were going home early. But there was Fitzy's car just coming down the track.

He'd cleaned himself up.

Joe shook his hand. So did I, but he didn't look at me. Joe said to him, "Tough, Fitzy."

"Tough is right. And I am fucking pissed off, I'll tell you that right now."

"What's the matter?"

"Commissioner says we're going to treat this crime as an accidental drug overdose because the girl brought the drugs with her from Connecticut—girl was from Connecticut. Dana Ganzi. Seventeen years old. We'll let the Connecticut force worry about where she might have gotten her supply. I says to the Commish, Who decided she brought it with her? and he says, I did. Then he tells me the coroner determined right away she wasn't raped. I says, Then who the hell ripped her clothes off? He says, Probably she was in a hurry to go skinny-dippin' with a gang of riffraff and took 'em off herself. Jesus. So as far as lookin' around here for the shithead who sold her whatever it was killed her, he tells me I'm on my own. I says okay. So after I hung up with him I traced the girl's final movements. She hitchhiked from the camp. Last people to see her were at the Club Soda. She didn't know how to get back to camp because it was late and she was afraid to hitchhike at that hour, but no one offered her a ride. Told her to walk down to the harbor and see if there was a taxi still around. None of them saw her after she left the bar, and the taxi drivers didn't see her either. Somebody picked her up, though, obviously."

Then he looked me directly in the eye. "How you feelin', FBI?"

I said, "I'm okay. Between Joe and me, once we get back to DC we'll find out what she took, and when we do we'll let you know."

"I appreciate that. When're you leavin'?"

"Right after breakfast."

He pressed his lips together. "Was hoping you'd be around awhile. Few things I'd like to—"

"I'll be more help to you in my office."

"That so? Well, I'll be by my phone when I'm not questioning some more of the riffraff. Meanwhile, you might want to go back with me to the Pleasant View Inn. Someone told me a few of the camp girls went there for entertainment."

I thought back. "Aggie mentioned that to me."

"What do you say?"

Joe said it. "I think this is something you have to take care of, Fitzy. Poppy and I—"

But I had changed my mind. "Joe, I think I *would* like to go with Fitzy. Maybe this is an opportunity to clear things up right now. Get the whole thing over with. When we're finished, we can go have breakfast."

Fitzy said, "There ya go, Joe. And if you want some extra company, I'll be ready for breakfast myself."

Joe said, "Okay, you two go, then. I've got things to do here. I'll meet you in town."

I said, "You don't want to go to the inn first?"

"I still have some flight stuff to fix so we can get going today. Let me work on that. Good luck." He gave me a peck on the cheek and went back in the cottage.

Fitzy said, "I was really hoping he'd come. He knows everybody. That woman at the inn is going to be nervous around me."

"Well, I had a cup of tea with her when I first got here. She'll be okay."

But Fitzy was right. When he told Aggie why we were there, her response was, "Where's Joe?"

I said, "He wanted me to tell you he had some things to do."

"He knows you're here, then?"

"Yes."

"Well, come on in. I don't like this, though. Don't want my place to get a bad name."

Behind her counter, just inside the door, there was a curtain. She led us through to her kitchen. We sat down at the kitchen table, and this time she didn't offer any tea.

Fitzy said, "I understand a couple of the girls from the camp came to visit guests here."

"One guest. And one girl, matter of fact."

"Was that same guest staying here yesterday? Day before?"

"He's here all week. Now, listen, this fellow is one of my regular customers. He's my only regular customer, if you want to know. Been comin' here for years. He's a loner. I'm always tellin' him he needs a girlfriend, but he tells me the girls won't look at him. 'Fraid he's right. He's one ugly fella. But he invited a camp girl here a couple of times. Figured she'd come because who else could he ask for a date? But it wasn't the dead girl who was layin' out there on the road yesterday. It was a different girl."

Fitzy said, "I'd like to talk to him."

Aggie looked to me. "Poppy, this guy stays here wouldn't hurt a fly."

I said, "Aggie, maybe the person who sold or shared drugs with the dead girl wouldn't hurt a fly either. Officially, her death was accidental. But still, Fitzy has to make sure whoever has the drugs doesn't give them to anyone else. He just needs information. Maybe your guest knows something the police don't, even though he's an innocent bystander."

She looked at her watch. "He should be wanderin' down any time. He fishes all day till around four. He takes a siesta; then he goes into town. Gets drunk. Comes back. He's got nothing to do with drugs."

Fitzy said, "I'll bet he doesn't. I just want to talk to him."

"Okay, then. Why don't I put on a fresh pot of tea?"

I said, "I could use a cup of tea. How about it, Fitzy?"

Fitzy said, "I've never tasted tea. Time I tried."

Aggie plugged in a kettle. She took a tin down from a cupboard and spooned tea leaves into a silver ball on a chain that she put in an old ceramic teapot, after first warming the pot with hot water from the tap. We watched the entire ritual until she brought the pot to the table and set out cups and saucers. Then she got a quart of milk out of the refrigerator. She said, "Do you like it milky?"

Fitzy looked at me. "This isn't how I usually operate."

We had our tea.

There were footsteps coming down a staircase on the other side of the kitchen wall. Aggie got up and went through the curtain. We listened to her explain to the guest what he had to do. She apologized. He pretty much grunted in response and came back with her. He was classically unattractive: beady eyes, huge nose, no chin, and his ears stuck straight out at right angles to his head. He was recently showered and shaved, his sparse hair parted on the side and combed straight down to his ears. He had on a clean T-shirt and shorts, both wrinkled and shrunken.

Aggie said, "Martin, this is the law."

The beady eyes shifted from me to Fitzy. "Recognize you both."

Aggie said, "Tea, Martin?"

"Wouldn't mind."

Martin sat down with us.

"Tell me," Fitzy said, "about the girl you dated from the camp."

He answered in about as straightforward a way as possible. "I picked her up. She was hitchhiking. A lot of them do that. I would too if I were trapped in the middle of a swamp."

Aggie explained, "Camp is smack between the two biggest swamps we got."

"I bought her a clam roll. She was starving. There was a party here that night. I invited her. She came, but not because of me. She didn't give a hoot about me. She came for the food and the beer. She had no money. Her parents—she said her parents were mad because she wouldn't lose weight, so they sent her to the camp. She said . . . let's see . . . she said she was incarcerated against her will without due process."

Fitzy asked, "Her name?"

"Rachel."

"Last name?"

"Never told me."

"What about the dead girl?"

"What about her?"

"Did you invite her here too?"

"Nope. I gave up on it. Girls don't much like me."

Fitzy said, "They don't much like me either. The important thing is this: Did Rachel take drugs? And did she tell you where she got them? Beyond pot, let's say."

"No."

I asked him how he could be so sure.

"This is a blue-collar place, ya know? Beer is what people take on Block Island, not cocaine. I've never understood why anyone would need to do anything beyond drinking beer to be happy."

Aggie piped up. "Go fishing, I'd say. Martin caught me a big striper yesterday. We had a swell dinner last night, didn't we?"

Martin said, "Thanks to your cookin', Aggie. I'm

supposed to meet some friends now at the harbor. The idea is to catch more stripers today."

"These friends stay here?"

"Day-trippers."

"Do these friends date the campers?"

He shook his head. "No way."

Fitzy told Martin to go fishing. We heard him go off on a moped. Fitzy said, "Maybe she did bring drugs from home."

"Why don't we go talk to the camper? Rachel."

Aggie said, "I'd give those girls a little time, Poppy. They're probably mighty upset."

Fitzy stood up. "We won't see them before breakfast, I'm starved."

Our breakfast place was called Richard's Patio. Joe and I had breakfast there our first two mornings but had skipped yesterday because Joe went to get the cello. It was how Joe said we'd start most of our days. The clique of regulars who had breakfast at Richard's Patio were Joe's island friends. No one else, Joe explained, knew or cared that the little breakfast joint existed, not even most other islanders. The year-round population of Block Island was around seven hundred, and all but a dozen of those were landowners. The landowners had sold off bits and pieces of their holdings to people who used to go to Martha's Vineyard or Nantucket only to disapprove of the ever-growing crowds spoiling their enchantment. So they'd island-hopped to the Block instead, where whalers had never lived, never built gorgeous mansions with widow's walks, and never left behind scrimshaw—since, at the time, Block Island didn't have a harbor. Now there was an artificial one plus a once landlocked pond that engineers had opened. The yachts had poured in and the sailors bought up the farmland hastily offered for sale and built new vacation homes, over a thousand of them in the last twenty-five years. Now, according to Joe, there were 688 Block Islanders with a lot of money in their pockets, plus the dozen others who'd never owned land—Billy and Mick, for example, who kept the 688 in lobsters; or Willa, who sold them milk and bread; Esther, who painted and lived on handouts; a few others. As for the new seasonal home-owners, if they wanted white asparagus, they packed it in their suitcases or they revved up their 58-footers and made a quick trip to the mainland.

Tourists who actually did notice Richard's Patio were turned back by Pal, Willa and Ernie's dog, a fierce-looking Doberman-shepherd mix who loved to let fly with a wicked growl. But Joe told me to look close and I would see he was too old to do any harm. He had no teeth. The regulars meant to have a respite from the people they waited on all day long, one way or another. On this day, Joe thought we should be sure to have breakfast there before we left because the regulars would want to know what happened. He said, "Why not let them know the death of the girl was as terrible as the rumors they've heard or whatever it is they're imagin-ing? They'll want to do their duty as good citizens. Someone is selling drugs on the island, so they'll want to find him. Then we'll say our goodbyes."

I agreed, and then I asked about the nouveau-riche 688. "Wouldn't they want to do their duty too?"

Joe explained how the 688 escaped the tourist-infested Block Island summers. "They're in the Dordogne."

Richard's Patio hadn't been Willa and Ernie's idea. The real Richard was an entrepreneur who'd rented Willa and Ernie's empty cottage behind the store. He converted it into a tiny restaurant with a pretty patio outside, paved it with bricks, set out a couple of white wrought-iron tables, and put tubs of flowers all around. But no one came. Richard hung on for two seasons, the second only because Willa and Ernie refused to charge him rent. The million-dollar-vacation-home owners, his intended market, seldom managed actually to fit in a trip to Block Island, what with their own summers in the Dordogne. There was nothing he could do to change the Budweiser-and-burger taste of Block Island's blue-collar day-trippers. It cost eight dollars and took one hour to get to Block Island from the mainland on the ferry. A ferry to the more chi-chi Massachusetts spots cost twenty-five and meant a serious battle through the heavy traffic making its way up the Cape. So Richard finally called it quits and moved on to Nantucket.

Willa and Ernie sold the wrought iron tables, threw out the planter tubs, and put back their garbage cans and Pal's doghouse. But they left Richard's restaurant untouched, except for the addition of a counter and four stools. Richard hadn't taken his Josef Albers prints with him, so blocks of bright colors decorated the walls, except in one corner where Ernie had thumbtacked a curling photo of the 1967 American League champions, the Red Sox, a yellowed pennant that read YAZ—400 HOME RUNS—3000 HITS, and a handmade sign, big letters: YANKEES SUCK.

The coffee shop was open from six to ten in the morning. Willa and Ernie thought of it as a kitchen where friends could feel free to stop by to eat—friends and any guests these friends might bring along was what Joe told me, but I believe he was the only one who ever brought a guest.

Fitzy and I passed the doghouse and Pal, snoozing in the sun. Fitzy said, "Hey, mangeball," and Pal lifted his head just long enough to bare his gums and growl.

I said, "That wasn't nice."

Fitzy said, "I'm not nice. They hate me in this place."

"Joe says they're going to want to know what happened yesterday."

"So tell them."

Joe was already there at our table, the regulars at their usual places. Billy and Mick were on their stools at the counter eating bacon and eggs. If when they'd finished breakfast they didn't find customers waiting for them out on the pier by the *Debbie*, they'd go shoot pool, a dollar a point. There was a sign at the pier that read FISHING EXCURSIONS LEAVE AT 10 AM. ADULTS $25, KIDS $25. Billy and Mick were dependent on the same market that Richard had been, but they also attracted fishermen who stayed at the three big inns, which made their enterprise profitable. Joe sometimes played pool with them. He said they'd been exchanging the same money back and forth for years, taking turns bragging about skunking each other.

Jim Lane's kid was at a table surrounded by his paraphernalia. He was the boy I'd seen each day selling postcards at a card table in the harborside parking lot— postage included. Since not having a stamp was the main reason tourists didn't buy postcards, he had a good thing going. Each night, he carted his stuff home so as not to interfere with the town ordinance requiring him to pay a kiosk fee for a permanent stand. This annoyed the off-island merchants who sold postcards in their summer-only souvenir shops, but their protests fell on deaf ears. Jim Lane *père* was the mayor. Mayor Lane— presently in the Dordogne—bragged that his son was saving his postcard money for college.

I'd asked Joe, "Where can you go to college on postcard money?"

"University of Rhode Island."

Jake was at his usual table, without the constable though. Tommy dropped him there, made his rounds, and then came back to help Jake with his breakfast. Jake wouldn't eat unless Tommy was there to help him. Now Jake was fiddling with some copper wires and a circuit box while he waited. Willa didn't care if Jake sat there all day, as long as he didn't start any fires with her electrical equipment. The story of Jake, according to Joe, was that someone found a baby forty years ago on one of the boats in the dead of winter, and Tommy took him in. By the time the authorities from Providence got wind of it, Jake was already a toddler, and when the social worker arrived and saw the child had an awful lot wrong with him and she would have no chance of finding adoptive parents, he became a foster child in Tommy's care. What was then called a ward.

Another thing I'd asked Joe was, "Did anybody bother to try and find the child's parents?"

He said, "Who knows? This being Block Island, Poppy, no one asks. People respect one another's desire to keep private matters private."

I said respect wouldn't have stopped me. Then I asked him about something I'd found curious: "Joe, how come none of the Richard's Patio folks are landowners? Speaking of boats, how'd they miss the boat?"

"Well, they're landowners now. Aggie bought the farmhouse. Willa and Ernie bought the store. Billy and Mick bought the *Debbie* after all these years. And Esther—"

"The *Debbie* isn't land."

"It's a long story. There are always going to be the haves and the have-nots."

"Like there's always a wrong side of the tracks."

"Yes."

He expected me to respect his desire to keep their private matters private, so I saved it. I'd be disrespectful another time when his heels weren't quite so dug in.

Now, Joe stood up and held a chair for me. Fitzy and I sat down. "How'd it go?"

Fitzy said, "It didn't."

Ernie called out from behind the counter, "Three coffees comin' up."

Fred Prentiss from the liquor store was always the first one there before he opened up. He didn't like to eat breakfast at home: too many kids. He was not a native, even though he'd married a Block Islander and had lived on High Street for over twenty years. His wife was descended from original settlers, and she'd made it clear to Willa and Ernie that Fred was to be welcomed at the coffee shop. His Red Sox cap, an attempt to be one of the boys, didn't cut it. He also wore new brightly colored polo shirts with the Sears lizard on the pocket. The shirts fit tight across his chest. He lifted weights. The regulars couldn't stand him. He was at the counter, an empty stool separating him from Billy and Mick. It would remain empty.

When Joe told me the history of Fred, I'd said, "Why didn't they tell Fred's wife to take a flyer?"

"Poppy, there's a certain hierarchy here. She's blueblood. One of the haves. This is really small-town America. You know how it is."

"No. I don't."

"Then count your blessings."

The town's two taxi drivers would be in from seven-thirty until quarter to nine. First they'd take tourists from the seven o'clock ferry to the inns and then get back to the harbor and be ready for the next ferry at nine. They were brothers. Joe said they worked from

April 1 to November 1 and then they took the money they'd made and went to Florida. I said, "What if someone needs a taxi after that?"

"No one does. No tourists off-season. The restaurants don't have heat."

"What do the taxi brothers do in Florida?"

Joe thought about that. "I have no idea."

"Aren't you curious?"

"Not really."

Because of our timing this morning, we were missing the taxi brothers.

The other customer was Esther, who sold the framed maps and articles I'd been on my way to look at when I found the body. As always, she sat alone in the far corner reading, today an old book with a broken spine. I had the feeling she listened to everyone's conversation even if she didn't join in. FBI agents recognize that ability in others since they have to train at it so hard themselves. Esther was a fixture, along the lines of an unlit, unfussy lamp.

Fitzy turned toward her. "Hey, Esther, come join us."

Esther looked at him as if he were a gnat and then went back to her book.

Fitzy laughed. "She won't take me up on my offers of dinner and dancing either."

Joe said, "Fitzy, for Christ's sake."

Fitzy didn't know about respecting privacy.

Willa was reading the paper at the end of the counter when we'd come in, ready to help Ernie if he needed it before she opened the grocery store. But as soon as she saw us, she jumped off her stool. Willa was always in a jumping-up-and-down state, at the ready, waiting for some signal to set her into action.

Except for Jake, they continued to stare, even Esther over the top of her book. Ernie hurried over with a pot of coffee and three cups, filled them, and stood in front of the table. "Get you anything else?"

Joe said, "We haven't decided. Just the coffee for now."

Ernie didn't move. He was waiting. They all were.

Joe said, "I suppose you guys want the gory details."

Immediately, Willa in the lead, they all pulled chairs up around us, again with the exception of Jake, who remained engrossed in his wires, and Esther, pretending to be equally engrossed in her book. Ernie leaned over, one elbow on our table. He pushed his Sox cap back. He said, "So was the gal really stark naked?"

I said, "Not quite. Almost. Her clothes were ripped off except for a few shreds."

They edged closer.

Mick said, "I bet that Aggie musta peed her pants."

Billy elbowed him. "We got ladies here, Mick."

"Sorry."

They waited. Fitzy said, "None of it is any of your goddamned business, Billy, old man. You know that, right?"

Joe stopped stirring his black coffee. "Fitzy, this island is their home. Something unpleasant has happened in their neighborhood. They deserve to hear it."

Unpleasant, I thought. Who was protecting who?

Willa said, "Poppy, drink your coffee, honey. Then tell us everything, right from the beginning. And Fitzy, I don't have to serve you if I don't want to."

"Okay, I'll shut up. Only because I'm real hungry."

I drank the coffee and then described my bike ride and the gulls and seeing the girl's body. And that she was almost naked. And overweight, so I'd assumed she'd come from the camp.

Mick said, "Confirmed. From the fat farm."

Billy elbowed him again, this time for interrupting.

I said, "I went into the B and B for help."

"What B and B?" Fred Prentiss asked me.

Willa rolled her eyes. "Aggie's old farmhouse up on Coonymus."

"Oh, that one."

Willa said, "What happened then?"

"I had Aggie call the constable. When he got there, he declared her dead."

Fred said, "Smart piece of work, our Tommy."

They all peeked over at Jake. He was concentrating so hard on his wires his eyes were crossed.

Ernie turned on Fred and hissed, "What else could Tommy have done? That's what he's supposed to do if someone's dead. You declare it. Ain't that right, Joe?"

Joe said, "That's right." Fitzy rolled his eyes.

Fred hung his head. He'd overstepped the bounds he was so grudgingly allowed.

I continued on. "I went for one of the troopers. He had me call Dr. Brisbane. Then I went back to see if I could be of help."

They all squinted at me. Willa said, "You a nurse?"

Joe said, "Poppy is an FBI agent."

They pulled back as if he'd told them I was a Martian.

Mick said, "You are not."

Joe confirmed. They looked at Fitzy.

He said, "That's what the lady claims."

They closed their mouths, which had been hanging open, and smiled at one another. Willa patted her hair and the fellows adjusted their Red Sox caps. I had gained a new respect; Mick confirmed it. "I told you people she wasn't just another bimbo."

I said to Joe, "Who do you usually bring here, chorus girls?"

Billy said to his friend, "Now see? You went and started a to-do."

Ernie said, "Never mind those fellas, Poppy. So when you went for the cops, which trooper did you talk to? The drunk here or the rookie?"

Fitzy choked on his coffee.

"Officer Fitzgerald," I said.

"He told you to call the doc?"

"Yes. While he went to find his rookie."

Willa said, "This morning, Carol came in to pick up egg sandwiches for her and the doc. Just before Joe got here. She said—"

"I'm sorry. Carol?" Sounded familiar.

Joe said, "Doc's assistant." Oh, yes. *That* Carol. The one who takes care of her boss when he shoots himself up with Demerol.

"She ain't a nurse either, but never mind that. She told us the doc told her the rookie cop barfed. Did he really?"

"I'm afraid he did."

"Can't blame him none there."

"And besides that," Fitzy told them, "he upped and quit. Boy thought he'd have an exciting career here, wearing those jazzy sunglasses, chasing speeders. Disillusioned."

Mick said, "Well, it must have been a very bad sight."

I said, "Confirmed."

Joe asked them, "Did Carol say what the doc thought?"

Billy told him she did. "The doc said he couldn't figure out what the hell happened to that girl, but if you ask me, I'd have to say it sounds like your basic rape case. Raped and strangled. Carol said there wasn't a drop of blood on her, either. That she was twisted up like some kind of whirling dervish, whatever that means. What does that mean, Poppy?"

"All her muscles had contracted."

"Oh. Well, raped and strangled is my bet. Thanks to these damned perverted day-trippers."

Mick said, "A strangled person would be purple with her tongue stickin' out." He demonstrated.

Billy gave him yet another elbow. "How the hell would you know what a strangled person looks like?"

"I seen strangled people in the war. While you were sittin' around here with your so-called high blood pressure. I seen 'em in *Itlee*. In France too. If we took prisoners? Then . . . well, say, some guy lost a buddy that day? He'd maybe take it out on one of the Jerry prisoners."

Fitzy said, "She hadn't been strangled. Or raped either."

Joe took over. "According to the coroner over in Providence, she wasn't raped. Maybe a party got out of hand, who knows? But if there's a rumor that a girl was raped and strangled on Block Island, all the overnight tourists will cancel their reservations and the ferries will come in empty."

Willa got the point. "Okay, forget what I said."

Ernie leaned in and rested his forearms on the table. "Then it had to be drugs that killed her."

Mick nodded firmly. "Had to be."

Willa dissented. "Nobody's got any drugs on this island or our Tommy would sniff 'em out."

Ernie would have his say. "I heard she brought a suitcase full of drugs from home, so Tommy never had a chance to sniff 'em out when you think about it. She could've maybe been so doped up she was hit by a car trying to get back to camp. All spacey, ya know? Car hit her, snapped her backbone. Damaged the nerves so's her muscles spasmed up."

Mick said, "That don't explain the naked part."

"Sure it does. She goes to this party, goes skinny-dippin' and, ya know, gets drunk and drugged up—couldn't find her clothes. No sex crime. Just kids havin' the wrong kind of fun." He turned to Jim Lane's kid. "Ain't that right?"

Jim Lane's kid had a faraway look on his face. He said, "I saw a fox get hit by a car once. He had a fit. He got all twisted up tryin' to bite off his broke back leg. Maybe Ernie's right."

While they took in the teenager's words, I couldn't help thinking that the image he conjured up for us was not all that farfetched. She did look like she'd tried to bite off her own leg. And her arms too.

I said, "I think I feel like taking a walk. I'm not really hungry, guys."

They were appalled at that. Willa jumped up. "Hey, honey, we're sorry you're upset. None of us got any appetite this morning. Billy and Mick just picked at their eggs, and they're a couple of bottomless pits. How about a nice little bowl of oatmeal? Warm your insides. Look at it like a way to feel better, not just eating breakfast."

Joe said, "Well, we're planning to leave shortly. We have to—"

Together they said, "*Leave?*"

Consternation was followed by all of them talking at once.

"Joe, now you listen here. Tommy's going to need your help."

Fitzy said, "What am I, chopped liver?"

They ignored him. "He's going to have to find out who that day-tripper is out there, sellin' dangerous drugs to those girls. Because I don't believe for a minute she brought the drugs from home, not drugs that dangerous."

"And Tommy'll sure need you too, miss. FBI! Whoa, mama."

"Invisible chopped liver," Fitzy said.

"Just stay maybe the week and have a look around. Whatever that girl took, who knows? What if there's more of it up at the camp? Who's going to find that out?"

Even Esther made her opinion known. We all turned to her when she spoke, answered that final question. "Joe," she said. "That's his job."

Outside, Pal barked, and the constable came in the door.

Tommy ignored everyone. He went directly to Jake and sat next to him. Then he spoke. "Boy's ready for his pancakes."

Willa dashed to the table and started resetting it. Jake had cleared his napkin and silverware to one edge so he'd have room for his wires. Ernie went back behind the counter. "Comin' right up, Tommy. Nice and hot."

Under the shadow of their island's authority figure, Billy and Mick went back to their counter stools, Fred to his, Jim Lane's kid to his table. Willa returned to us. "I'm going to go mix up that oatmeal. I got a box of brown sugar somewhere, plenty of half-and-half—my oatmeal is nice 'n' creamy because of the half-and-half—and I'll run into the store, get some raisins."

I had to smile at her. "Sounds like cookie dough, not oatmeal."

"Only way to eat oatmeal, unless you're one of those health nuts."

"I really don't need the raisins."

" 'Course you do. What about you boys?"

Joe said, "Sounds good."

Fitzy said, "Sounds like something that would make

me gag. Ernie can make up another order of pancakes for me, plus some bacon."

She dashed off, wiping her hands on her apron as she went out the door.

Ernie took a stack of pancakes over to Jake. Tommy had to pry the circuit box out of Jake's hands. He said, "Sit up now, boy. Here's your pancakes. What do you say to Ernie?"

Jake worked hard to leave his own world and enter ours. He whispered, without looking up, "Fanks."

"Hey, ya welcome, Jake." Jake winced. Ernie's voice naturally boomed.

Tommy spread butter on the pancakes and poured the syrup. Then he cut the pancakes into bite-sized pieces. He squeezed a fork into Jake's hand. He said, "Eat."

Jake put the fork to his lips then back to the plate three times. He did this with each bite. Joe had explained Jake's habits at breakfast our first morning. "He ritualizes everything except whatever it is he does with electricity and all those gadgets he plays with. Fooling with wires and batteries is his only escape from his obsessive compulsions."

Each morning I watched Jake eat—three bites, three chews, three swallows, three gulps of orange juice, three swipes at his mouth with his napkin, which he picked up and put down three times. It was difficult not to watch him in the same way you can't not watch a Zamboni machine. Or a boat docking. Or a wrecking ball.

The oatmeal was all that Willa had promised, and not a little bowl but a big one—two of them. "That looks terrific, Willa," Joe said to her.

"Little bit of molasses too, just the way you like it, Joe."

Fitzy said, "Can this get more disgusting?" He was drenching his pancakes and bacon with syrup.

After several spoonfuls Joe finally looked up. He said to me, "I hate to admit it, but I am beginning to feel fortified. You?"

I hated to admit it too. "Yes." Then I said, "Joe?"

"What, sweetheart?"

"Let's stay."

How could I leave when I was feeling such an irresistible urge to poke around? I wanted to ask some questions. I wanted to find out what killed that girl, caused her to die so violently. I wanted to know if someone sold drugs to her or if she brought the drugs from Connecticut. I wanted to know who did the selling, whether it was here or in Connecticut. I wanted to know who dumped her nearly naked body out on the road with no thought of helping her. And I wanted to know where her clothes were. I wanted to look for the place where death had occurred. I wanted to consult with my people in Washington between those questions—by phone. Nothing new there, they were used to me sticking it out in the field. And at the moment, I also wanted to eat every spoonful of my fortifying oatmeal. I would do all that.

When we'd finished scraping our bowls, Joe said to Ernie, "Poppy and I are going to take our walk. Poppy thinks we should stay after all. The two of us need to talk."

I said, "Your wife's oatmeal made me see reason."

Ernie grinned. "Willa's oatmeal'll do that."

Willa jumped off her stool. "Thanks. Aim to please."

Ernie folded his arms across his chest. "We've got to go out of our way to be extra nice to those fat girls when they come into town. Once word gets out, our campers are gonna be the second biggest attraction on the Block, after the South Light."

Fitzy said, "Enjoy your walk. Hope you like heat. And don't sweat too hard. Ernie, get me another stack."

I said to him, "Fitzy, we'll see about talking to the camper . . . Rachel. Okay?"

He said, "Give it a day."

We left. Joe didn't pay Ernie. That was because Ernie wouldn't take money from him, just like Billy and Mick wouldn't. One night a few years ago, Willa had woken up in a lot of pain. The doc said it was gallstones and her gallbladder was inflamed. Joe flew her to Providence.

We headed toward the door. The little bell up above had been wrapped in duct tape. I knew something was amiss but I hadn't been able to put my finger on it till just then—the little bell hadn't tinkled when we'd walked in. Willa saw me looking up at it. "Bell was bothering Jake."

We went outside into the hot sun. Out around the store, the sidewalk was giving off a glare in the white light. Joe said, "Fitzy has a point. It's hot. How about a swim instead of a walk?"

Sounded good to me.

We went to the bathhouse at Crescent Beach, changed into bathing suits, and stepped over the strand of cobblestones, smooth almost circular granite disks, pastelcolored, once harvested by islanders in the nineteenth century. They were shipped across the narrow band of sea to the mainland and then sent north to Boston, south to New York and Philadelphia, all the way down to Washington and beyond—Charleston and Savannah—

where they were used to pave the city streets along the eastern seaboard. Our first time on the beach, Joe told me it was good luck to find one as close to a perfect circle as possible and take it home. I found a dozen in about two minutes. He'd laughed.

Now we walked across the just-warming sand. Joe said there used to be more sand and a lot fewer cobbles, but the island had lost most of the sand to the perfect storm, which exposed the cobbles beneath.

"Really? *The* perfect storm?"

"The very one."

We had the long curving expanse of beach to ourselves. We swam about a yard before the oatmeal dragged us to a stop. We put off swimming. Instead, we lay on the beach blanket Joe had dug out of the back of the ragtop and watched as the Point Judith ferry showed its great hulk, bearing down from around the cliffs at the end of the beach. We would soon be inundated with merry day-trippers. We agreed we wanted more beach time but without the volleyball games, so we got back in the jeep and drove to the northern tip of the island, Sandy Point. Leading out to the point was a two-mile sand spit. I hadn't been there yet. We found a few mopeds parked where the road ended, overnight tourists from one of the inns. We stopped the jeep beside the mopeds and walked along the spit past four vacationers, who nodded at us from their blankets. We didn't stop until we were twenty yards from the point, the whole stretch deserted. Joe spread his blanket.

He said, "Beautiful."

"Yes." But my enthusiasm had diminished to its former state.

"Look, Poppy, the very end of the spit is a gull rookery. See that thing sticking up?"

I did. It looked like a wide dead tree trunk, all its branches eaten away.

"The remains of an old lighthouse. It's completely covered with guano. They nest in there."

"I don't see many gulls."

"Hatching season is almost over. Not many young left in the nests. Except for the last of the new parents, they're all out doing what gulls do: scavenging."

I didn't say that I'd seen some very frustrated gulls disappointed in their scavenging routine twenty-four hours earlier.

Joe was lying on his back, propped up on his elbows. So was I. "Poppy . . ."

"What?"

"You've left something out, haven't you?"

ATF. Alcohol, Tobacco and Firearms. His job was detecting secretive behavior. For example, why was David Koresh secretive? That was an easy one. Because he had an arsenal so extensive it could have equipped an army division.

I closed my eyes, let the sun sink into my pores, and officially allowed myself to think, to observe more closely what I'd seen, if only from memory. Scrolling. Immediately, a frame of the film came to me. The girl's hands. She'd torn her clothes off herself. It was why the trooper had made sure to wrap one of her hands at least, even if he couldn't get to the other one. There were fine shreds of fabric between her fingers. Her T-shirt had been dark blue. The band around her neck matched the shreds in her hands.

"Joe, it wasn't rape I saw. A sex crime, maybe." And I told him what detail had just come back to me.

"She ripped her *own* clothes off? And you're only remembering that now?"

"Yes. Because of your rules training. Because I wanted to be a normal person having a real vacation. I've been having such a good time, Joe. I resisted my usual habits. Selfish of me, wasn't it?"

He looked at me. "Not selfish. Self-protecting. You've been through an awful lot this year." He smiled. "But I didn't think I'd be creating a monster."

I wanted to smile too. But I couldn't. I couldn't rid my consciousness of the image of the dead girl. "She was just a kid, Joe."

He rolled toward me onto his side and brushed my hair off my forehead. Wound a frizzy tendril around his finger. "I understand." He unwound it and took up another one. "But why would she tear her clothes off?"

"I don't know that yet, but I will. Or maybe Ernie is right—crazy party, she was stoned and wanted to swim, had trouble with her shirt, so she just ripped it off." I squinted at the dazzling dark blue sea. "Tell me about this camp of theirs."

He sighed. "There's not much to say about it. They opened last year. It's a miserable excuse for a camp, though. The buildings are left over from World War Two, when there was a training program here for the Air Corps. A metal Quonset hut and a few wood barracks. It was all left intact—deserted by the guy who owns the land. It's swampy and too far inland for any ocean views. Guy grabbed at the chance to rent it. Heard he got a couple thousand dollars for the summer."

"Who would send their children to such a place?"

"I suppose parents desperate for their overweight daughters to be skinny. Can't be fat in America, remember? Or maybe the girls wanted to go there themselves. Desperate too. Agreed with their parents to give it a try."

"And one bored miserable girl went out looking for drugs."

"Yeah. Unfortunately, she found some."

He'd finished playing with my hair. He laid his warm hand on my shoulder. Kind of gave me a spot massage.

"You've been there?" I asked him.

"Where?"

"The camp."

"I was around there before it was a camp. Used to go snoop when I was a kid—pretend I was in the Airborne."

"You came to Block Island as a child?"

"Yes. Couple of times. With my parents."

"And you dreamed of having a place of your own here?"

"Exactly."

A small brownish gull followed by two very large ones—snow-white, the way gulls are supposed to be—flew over us. The brown one seemed to be having trouble. He landed clumsily in the water. The two white gulls dove at him.

I sat up. "Look, they're trying to rescue him."

Joe looked. "Speaking of the Airborne . . . they're dive-bombing him, actually." He looked at me. "Poppy . . ."

Several times the two white gulls flew up and then zoomed back down, knocking the brown one under water. He came up squawking each time.

Joe said, "He's young. He must be sick. Or injured, maybe. They're killing him."

"They're what?"

"Euthanasia."

I pulled myself up to my feet. "Then we should rescue him."

The two white gulls landed next to the brown one, floated along, one on either side, and started pecking him. I turned away.

Joe stood next to me, put his arm over my shoulders. "Mother Nature. I'm sorry. It's that or he starves to death. Probably can't get food on his own."

"Joe?"

"Yes?"

"Can we go see it?"

"See what?"

"The camp."

"When?"

"Right now."

"I don't see why not."

We reorganized ourselves and threw on T-shirts and shorts over our bathing suits. Before we headed back to the ragtop, I looked out on the water. The little brown gull was gone and the two big white ones were soaring back to the rookery.

4

By deciding to visit the camp, I'd begun an unofficial investigation. Shortly, I'd have to file a report and then it would be official. That's what my director required of his independent investigators. I could enter or begin any investigation, and my first filing, in addition to describing the physical aspects of the crime, was mainly to explain why I believed the FBI should be involved. Sometimes it was for the usual reasons—wire fraud, a crossing of state lines—and sometimes outside the usual reasons, through a loophole, as in: She was from Connecticut, and she came to Rhode Island with contraband. Then my director and I would talk. He would play devil's advocate. Once he'd said, "Poppy, the devil is not much of a match for you." He hadn't denied me thus far. And of course he owed me for getting the disastrous crime lab in order, the reason I was first hired. The rest of his departments . . . well, he was an extremely busy man. Which worked to my advantage, as did his trust.

We got on well, my boss and I: got on well during my stint running the lab, got on well since I'd first told him I wasn't happy being a desk jockey. After all, once I had the lab up and cracking, what was left for me to do? He granted my request to return to the field, one of a handful of independent operators. The only time I'd gotten annoyed with him was when he'd backed Joe and insisted I take a leave after last year. He said, "We've reached a point where I ask little of you. I do not interfere when you deem a case important to investigate or reopen. All I expect is that you will do your job, and that's what you do. Superbly. Allow me this one exception." The two of them wore me down—not too difficult, considering the state I was in. And considering Delby, who said, "Do it, boss."

Forced leave.

The entrance to the camp was a track through a dripping wet web of vegetation that looked like a mangrove swamp. I asked Joe what the growth was. He said, "Bracken."

There was a large professionally constructed sign by the track, brand new, poodle pink and white. Superimposed on a large heart were the words, CAMP GUINEVERE and, in smaller print beneath, *For Young Ladies Whose Hearts Are Set on a Trimmer Figure*.

We drove through. Within yards we came to a clearing. Joe braked the ragtop. The sight was miserable. Two dozen teenage girls were slumped on the ground in groups, leaning on—or sprawled upon—their backpacks. Some girls were really big, though by no means morbidly obese. And there were a few who were just a little bit pudgy. All the rest fell somewhere in between. Two thin girls were trying to get them moving.

We listened to the protests.

"It's too *far*."

"I hate and detest that beach."

"No. N-O! I am totally not going."

One of the counselors said, "Listen up. If we go to the beach today, we'll have pizzas from town tonight. For dinner. I promise. I'll go pick them up myself."

The promise worked. The campers pulled themselves to their feet, helped one another with their backpacks, and followed the counselors to a path beyond the clearing, more a dank green tunnel than a path. Amid their chatter, one of them called to the leader, "There better be extra pepperoni on mine." The counselor, though, was already attempting to redirect the focus. She was singing "Be Kind to Your Web-Footed Friends." The campers chose not to join in. We watched as the tunnel swallowed them up.

Joe said, "The weight-loss counselors bribe them with pizza?"

I redirected my focus too—on the shocking condition of the camp. The metal Quonset hut was rusted and all four barracks were tilted, their windows dirty and cracked. A couple of panes were gone, the openings covered with newspaper. The only thing new in the entire place were the signs, one on each of the buildings: on the Quonset hut, BLAIR IRWIN, DIRECTOR; the four barracks, MERLIN HOUSE, LANCELOT HOUSE, KING ARTHUR HOUSE, and ROUND TABLE DINING HALL.

I said to Joe, "How about first we see this Irwin?"

He wanted to do that too. We got out of the ragtop and walked across the clearing.

"Joe, do you see any facilities at all?"

"Yeah. There are four Porta-Potties behind the so-called dining hall. I hope they have running water. I'm not seeing electric wires, are you?"

He was right. I couldn't believe it was possible. If you wanted to lose weight, was living in a variation on a homeless shelter the answer?

We knocked on the director's door. A pretty girl opened it, a thin girl, college age. She smiled. "Yes?"

I said, "Is Mr. Irwin here?"

She said, "May I tell Dr. Irwin who's calling?"

Joe was fast. "Mr. and Mrs. Everett. We just happened to be spending a few days on the island and thought we'd inquire about a camp stay for our daughter."

"Hold on."

A man appeared behind her, middle-aged, wearing a Palm Beach suit and a tie. His thin hair was sprayed into position across the top of his head. He smiled at us and said to the girl, "You may go along on the beach hike with the others, Liz." He spoke as if he had a mouth full of marbles. He thought sounding like William Buckley was impressive.

The girl's own smile left her face. "But you promised I could—"

"Run along now." He nudged her out the door as he held it wide for us. "Please come in."

I heard the girl mumble *Fuck*, under her breath.

We went in. He took in our attire: beach bum. My hair was still wet. Someday I would cut it and liberate myself.

He said, "We have no empty slots here at Guinevere for the moment, but one could come up if any of our August girls decide to cancel. I would doubt that though, alas." He gave us a look of huge sympathy.

He led us into a room sectioned out of the hut. It was his office; his name was engraved on a length of chrome at the front of his desk: BLAIR M. IRWIN, PHD. Behind the nameplate was a dinosaur of a computer from Radio Shack. He had a file cabinet, some furniture upholstered in yellow vinyl, and a generator. Irwin had electricity. He also had an air conditioner in his window, which was on, humming loudly and vibrating, giving it an added loud knocking. Air-conditioning is almost unnecessary on Block Island, the constant sea breeze is always refreshing. But sea breezes couldn't reach the swamp where the camp with its decaying buildings was located.

"Please have a seat."

He looked us over, his eyes lingering a moment on my wet T-shirt.

"Been swimming, Mrs. Everett?"

"Yes."

He put on half-glasses and turned on his computer. "Now let us speak about . . ." He hit a few keys. "Your daughter's name?"

Joe said, "Suzie. But before we start filling anything out, we'd like to know—"

"Susan?"

"Suzanne."

I looked at Joe. Always full of surprises, one of the many reasons for my liking him as much as I do. Dr. Irwin keyed in our daughter's name.

I said, "This is a very spartan camp."

He glanced over his glasses at me. "Yes, it is. No frills. Exercise, diet, and excursions throughout the island—both hiking and biking."

"You have a gym, then? For exercise when you're not biking and hiking?"

He was back to his computer. "No, we don't. We follow the program used by the United States Army with new recruits. Modified, of course, although teaching through discipline, as with the Army, is our main drive."

"Is swimming part of the program?"

"Of course."

"Where is the pool?"

He smiled. "Our pool is the Atlantic Ocean, right down below the cliffs."

I said, "You mentioned discipline. What sort of discipline?"

"Discipline that replaces sloth with self-esteem. Discipline that includes orders to be followed rather than benevolent advice. Tough love, as some would call the method. Since teenagers are impervious to advice, after all."

Joe cleared his throat. That meant, *Poppy, if you're thinking of arresting this character for child neglect, get some substantial proof first.* He said to Irwin, "How much cash are we talking here, Blair?"

The camp director rolled his eyes ever so subtly, he clicked a few more keys and he said, "The season is ten thousand. A discount of course for siblings. One month, August, would be six thousand."

"You're talking dollars, I take it."

Irwin smiled again. "Yes. We're quite exclusive, unlike most camping facilities."

"How many girls here?" I asked.

"We try to stay at around two dozen. Twenty-six at most."

Exclusive to the tune of pocketing around $250,000 for the summer. His overhead was negligible.

"People pay that much?"

"I assure you, it's a bargain when you consider the fact that a girl who is overweight will come home to you after a summer with us in a weight range suitable to her height and frame."

Was a parent supposed to believe something so patently absurd? I said, "The condition of the girls we just saw leaving for their hike didn't seem to reflect any weight loss."

He held his hands out, palms up. "Mrs. Everett, the camp has been in operation just half a month. Ten *weeks* will show the effects of our efforts. Of course, the girls who are only here for a month—as would be the case with your . . ."

I drew a blank. Joe said, "Suzie."

"Yes. Suzie. Your Suzie would be started on a routine that she and the other one-month girls will be expected to follow for the rest of their lives, reinforced by attending camp each summer during their high school years. We make an exception for a few college girls; the parents often beg us. They don't want them to lose the ground gained. The ground lost, actually."

He smiled, pleased with his clever pun, and studied his screen.

"We do have a cancellation, as it turns out. I will be happy to take down information on your daughter, and then you can fill out an application form and mail it to me with a deposit."

I said, "Do many of the parents come to see your camp before they register their daughters?"

Another smile, entirely condescending. A man with a large repertoire of smiles, like all con artists. I wondered how many kinds of frowns he'd be able to muster once I crossed him.

"Block Island is a bit off the beaten path. Registration normally takes place on-line or by mail after the parents see our advertisements. And, naturally, many of the girls are sent here through recommendations that come to their parents via word of mouth."

Joe said, "From last year's camp?"

"Yes."

"What is the return rate?"

"Excuse me?"

"How many campers are here who were here last year?"

"I don't have those figures immediately available."

"And you've run other such camps?"

"Certainly."

"Where?"

"My credentials are in the application packet, which I will be happy to send to you once we receive a fifteen percent deposit to hold Suzanne's place." A new smile. Victory grin. "I'm sure you would like to discuss privately the possibility of your daughter's becoming part of our regimen. Do that, then feel free to get back to me."

He began to rustle a stack of papers. He didn't bother to stand or put his hand out, but we were dismissed.

Joe and I got up. I said, "I heard a rumor. I heard that a camper died here."

His face darted upward to mine. Now he did stand. He puffed out his chest. "I work very hard to maintain high standards regarding our admissions policy. Unfortunately, two days ago a girl who was on a trip with her house to town—to the library—managed to sneak off. The counselor in charge of the trip was, of course, sent packing. As it turned out, the camper had brought an illegal substance with her from home and apparently ingested too much of it. I'm sorry to say she overdosed. All of us here at Guinevere—the staff and the campers—are understandably distraught. None of us really had gotten to *know* the girl—she was a loner, as is so often the case with that element—but I take full responsibility for not recognizing her weakness during the application and acceptance process. She was from a family with an impeccable portfolio, sad to say." He pressed his fingertips together as if in prayer.

We left. Blair Irwin knew we wouldn't send a dog to his camp.

As the ragtop bumped along out of there, the first

thing Joe said was, "Haven't ever seen a tie before on this island. Ever." The second thing: "The son of a bitch."

"He's perpetrated a fraud. People like that can zero in on the weakest-willed with incredible success."

"This has to be an illegal operation."

"I doubt it. It's for children, after all. Anyone who wants to open a camp probably has to meet a requirement that says you should be able to sign your name on a dotted line. And then, if no inspector appears, you can do whatever you like."

I told Joe about my assistant, Delby. "When Delby went looking for child care, she found out you could be a hooker with a sixth-grade education and a history of schizophrenia and still get a license to run a day-care center."

We drove back toward the road that had led us to the camp and soon after we turned on to it we came upon two of the campers hitchhiking. Escapees. One of them wore a hat. The other one had a towel over her head. The sun was high in the sky. It was hot. Joe stopped.

"Where're you girls heading?"

The one in the hat said, "Anywhere. Town."

Her friend filled us in. "We, like, just escaped a forced march."

I'd had that right. Joe said, "Hop in." He looked at me. I had to get out and flip up my seat.

They climbed in, squeezing past the flipped-back seat with great difficulty. The ragtop sank noticeably. The girl in the hat said to me, "I guess *your* diet works." She was smiling, though, making a joke.

I introduced myself. "My name is Poppy Rice and this is Joe Barnow."

The hat said, "I'm Christen. This is my friend Samantha."

Samantha tried to say hello but couldn't because she burst into tears. Her friend put her arm around her. "It's okay, Sam. We'll go buy a couple of Cokes and have a burger." Then to us, "She's never been away from home before. We don't even have phones. Cell phones are against the rules. So we all chipped in and bought one, but the girl that's in charge of hiding it is on the hike. We're going into town mostly so we can call our parents."

I said, "How old are you two?"

"I'm sixteen. Sam's fifteen. A *young* fifteen to boot." She looked at her friend. "Please don't cry, Sam." Then she said, "Another reason we're going to town is because we had a bowl of gross white water that was supposed to be Cream of Wheat for breakfast, and we've both run out of supplemental rations."

Joe said, "What are supplemental rations?"

"Food our friends mail to us from home. We sent out an alert the day we got here."

Joe and I had brought some oranges. I took them out of my bag. "Would you like a couple of oranges until we get to town?"

Samantha's tears stopped. I peeled the oranges for them, broke them into sections, and passed them back. That's what Delby would do for her girls even though, unlike the campers, they were under six years old. It seemed like a good idea. Christen and Samantha were both big and tall; the oranges wouldn't make much of a dent. But the purpose of snacks, according to Delby, is to distract from whining and/or tears. After I'd passed a few sections back, I wanted to tell them to take the time to chew the oranges, not just swallow the pieces whole. But they'd no doubt heard that kind of thing before. And who was I to tell someone how to eat an orange?

Oranges devoured, Samantha's tears started again. She said, plaintively, "They're all going to be staring at us in town. Laughing at us. Besides their . . . their verbal abuse. I mean, *really* staring at us because of Dana."

Joe said, "Who's Dana?"

They didn't answer. And then he remembered, bit his lip when Christen said, "The girl from camp who died."

Joe said, "I'm sorry."

Christen—the hat—said, "She wasn't in our house. We're Lancelot, she was King Arthur. So we didn't really know her too well. We still feel, like, rotten, though."

I shifted away from Dana Ganzi. "Who exactly is going to be laughing at you?"

"Everyone. Tourists. The kids that hang out at the postcard stand."

Joe said, "Then come use my phone. I'll be happy to make you some hamburgers."

The girls put their heads together and whispered. Then Christen said, "Are you sure you don't mind, miss?"

I turned. "No, we'd like the company."

We had a barbecue lunch. While Joe got the grill going, the two girls called home. Christen wailed to her mother about having to go to the bathroom outside, and lumpy mattresses, and how the food was horrible and not nutritious. She said, "Ma, I *have* stuck it out. Like, for two weeks. I've had it." Then she told her father that she'd just had her first piece of fruit besides bananas since she'd left home. There was a long pause. In a quiet voice she said, "I know bananas are good for you, Dad." She'd lost any hope of getting bailed but she played her trump card. "Irwin called you about Dana

Ganzi, right?" Christen listened for quite a while. Then she told her father she had to go and hung up. She looked at us. "Irwin basically slandered Dana. She never took any drugs, right, Sam?"

"No. The girls in King Arthur said she just wanted to find a place that had live music."

Christen handed her the phone and Samantha had a try. The ray of hope in her eyes dimmed as soon as the phone was answered at the other end. She said, "Hello, Myrna. It's Sam." She put her hand over the mouthpiece and whispered to us, "Our housekeeper." She told Myrna to tell her mother when she came home that the camper who died didn't die of a drug overdose. "She left camp because the counselors don't watch out for us so Dana went into town alone. Nobody really knows what happened to her, Myrna. Tell my mom that her body was found in the middle of the road." A pause. "I'm not exaggerating. I know he told her. . . ." She waited and then gave up just as her friend had. She said goodbye.

But Samantha didn't have a chance for another round of tears because I made an announcement. "Joe, those burgers sure smell *good*."

It worked. Anticipating the taste of grilled beef distracted them. Delby, I'm learning. I had a cheeseburger, Joe had two, and so did the girls. It pained them to say no to yet another, but they said no. They were hungry but they weren't about to go on a binge. And they didn't say much else, at least not to us. Instead, they chatted with Spike, who knocked off a cheeseburger of his own. They told him how much they missed their own pets and they scratched his chin. Homesick. Punished. Because they didn't wear size eight jeans. I watched them. So much trouble to be a teenager to begin with. Both girls had on expensive sneakers, the kind you can only get in places like Neiman-Marcus. Special editions. They were from families with money, as Joe and I had assumed when Irwin quoted his rates with such panache. Families who would try anything to get their fat girls skinny.

I said, "Are you kids okay? I can see you're unhappy. But I mean healthwise."

Christen said, "We don't have rickets, if that's what you mean. But we're a lot worse than unhappy. I can deal with unhappy. We're miserable. We're pitiful, too, in case you hadn't noticed, but I guess not as pitiful as Dana." She made eye contact with Samantha. "Should we tell?"

"Yes."

Christen petted Spike a little bit more and then she stopped. "We lied. Dana did buy stuff in town once in a while, but only pot. From that kid who sells the postcards. But she wasn't any kind of addict. She'd bribe a counselor to take her in to the harbor. Then she'd hang out at the Club Soda—she really did like listening to bands. I think she handed her pot around there. I mean, nobody at camp ever saw her smoke. She bought it so she'd have some friends. A lot of kids'll do that, right, Sam?"

"A lot. People don't mind your being fat if you have something to offer."

"So after she went to town, she'd spend a few hours and then hitch a ride back. She was one of the oldest girls. Nobody worried about her."

"Was the counselor the last to see her?"

"Yeah, the last from camp. But she'll never admit it. She left Dana with some kids just off the ferry. After taking Dana's twenty bucks, the counselor returned to camp to see if there were any more fares. Everyone knows it."

"Irwin ended up firing her?"

Samantha said, "Yeah, right."

"She's his favorite. She has very large breasts."

Samantha agreed with her friend's assessment. "It's all true, everything we told you. We don't know what happened to Dana. We only know she wasn't a druggie. But the thing is, someone's been spying on us. We had to hang a blanket over our window. Even though it's really hot in our house. I mean, we're nervous, you know?"

"Who would spy on you?"

Christen said, "I guess any one of the dorks who lives in this stupid place. I mean, Block Island is *nowhere*." She looked at Joe. "No offense."

"How do you know someone spied on you?"

"Because there are these beach roses in front of the window, those things with the humongous prickers. There's this little space where someone pushed them apart, and underneath on the ground are all the petals."

Samantha said, "Christen has this uncle who's a lawyer in upstate New York. So she knows a lot about cop stuff."

Christen said, "He's fat too."

Joe got up and went in the house. He came out with a box of Dove Bars from his freezer. There are four Dove Bars in a box. Joe and I were still trying to get the wrappers off ours when the girls were holding bare sticks. We offered them ours. I said, "It's okay. We all overeat when we're stressed." They took the Dove Bars. Then I said, "I'd like to see where this spying went on, if you don't mind."

They didn't. It meant they'd have a ride back. They'd been too polite to ask.

Samantha said, "Thank you. I sure was afraid of hitchhiking. Even if there are two of us. I've never hitchhiked before."

Her friend said, "This camp, I tell you, is entirely full of wimps."

They would hang in their house—Lancelot—till the rest of the campers returned. They weren't worried that the counselors would have missed them, and so what if they did. Their friends would not betray them. "Even if the counselors gave a damn," Christen said, "which they definitely don't."

We parked along the road and took a path behind the camp through the swampy growth to the back of Lancelot House. Christen and Sam bunked with six other girls and one counselor.

They showed us the window where they had definitely been spied upon. Neither Joe nor I touched anything. But we noted the threads on the thorns and the faint footprints in the soggy dirt beneath. The threads were thick and coarse. Grey. Someone knew he'd need heavy work gloves to part the rose canes. Joe said to me, "We'll tell Fitzy to come have a look."

Christen said, "Who's Fitzy?"

"A police officer."

She smiled. "Well, that makes me feel better. I didn't know we had any of those on the Block. I mean, besides that lame constable."

Samantha said, "Christen, at least he checks on us once in a while."

"I wasn't talking about his personality, Sam. Then there's that weirdo he's always dragging along behind him. Jesus."

I felt uneasy leaving them. A voyeur is more than meets the eye. I asked what they'd do until the other campers returned. Christen told me they had their laptops and they'd keep barraging family and friends with e-mails until someone came and got them or sent a plane ticket. I asked her how they charged the batteries.

She said they had a generator that powered a light from eight until ten at night. Two hours. She pointed to the center of the ceiling at the bare bulb hanging by a wire. "That's the light. We take turns charging our laptops, and when Irwin leaves the camp we bribe the counselors and use his phone jack."

The girls thanked us for the use of the phone and lunch.

Back in the ragtop Joe said, "Good kids, aren't they? They shouldn't be living this way."

"Great kids. And, no, they shouldn't."

We stopped at Fitzy's on the way home and told him all that the girls had revealed to us. Fitzy said, "That's it, time for me to head on up to that camp, cut to the chase, and have a look around. Take a few pictures of the footprints, extract a couple of threads from the thorns." He said to me, "You come too. We'll look up Martin's friend Rachel."

"Okay."

"Joe?"

"One visit per season to Camp Guinevere. You two go. I'll plan my afternoon. It's my vacation, something I can't seem to impress upon people."

I said, "Pick me up, Fitzy. The girls are all on a hike so give me an hour. I need to take a shower and change." To Joe, "We shouldn't be long."

"Sure. No problem."

When Irwin let Fitzy and me into his Quonset hut, he looked me up and down once more. "You're from the state, aren't you, Mrs. Everett?"

Fitzy said, "The only thing you need to know is that she's with me. I need to talk to a camper named Rachel."

Irwin looked past us through the window. "They're all coming back from their hike now."

The campers were a sweltering mass, breaking up, dragging themselves back to their houses. He went to the door and called to a counselor. She came trudging in.

"Do we have a Rachel?"

"We have two."

"Run out and grab them before they head to the showers."

He brought a couple of plastic chairs in off his porch. A minute later, the two Rachels stood in the doorway. One was the girl Joe and I'd seen coming off the ferry with three others, the one who argued with a counselor, refusing to get in the van. She looked just as furious now as she did then. Irwin told them to come in and sit down. The other Rachel did and the furious Rachel said, "I need a shower."

Fitzy told them who he was. He crooked his finger at the reluctant Rachel, and she came in too. He got right to it. "I know you're tired out, but this won't take long. I need to ask you a couple of things. Did either of you kids go to a party at the Pleasant View Inn?"

The belligerent Rachel folded her arms across her chest and didn't answer. The other one said, "Hey, are we, like, material witnesses?"

"I'm here to see if I'll be needing any of those."

She said, "This is so, like, *Whoa*!"

"Just answer the question."

"I'd love to go to a party, let me tell you."

Fitzy looked at the other girl. "What about you?"

"Yeah, I did. So what."

"Did Dana Ganzi go too?"

"No."

"Were there drugs at the party?"

"There was a case of Saint Pauli Girl. Tasted like rotgut."

I asked, "So what happened to Dana?"

She said, "Who cares?"

The other Rachel looked at her. "You're such a shit, you know that, don't you?" Her fellow camper ignored her. So she said to me, "We don't know what happened to Dana. She was a nice girl. She shared a Twinkie with me when we first got here." She gazed at Irwin for just a moment. "We were just beginning to realize the meals here wouldn't be enough to fill a mouse. Dana only had one Twinkie and she broke it in half."

The other Rachel said, "She never shared anything with me."

"I wouldn't share anything with you if you paid me."

The other Rachel uncrossed her arms, gave the girl the finger, and walked out the door. Irwin got up and went after her, hurling a few threats.

The Rachel with us said, "Not to worry. She's all bark and no bite. Pathetic. Anyway, I'm leaving tomorrow morning. I got a check from my parents in the mail today. I'm going into town, cash it, and get home. I'd wanted to come here. I wanted to spend the summer losing forty pounds. But this place hasn't exactly measured up to the brochure."

Fitzy said, "How tall are you?"

"Five-ten."

"Keep the forty pounds. You look good."

"No, I don't. I've got shoulders like my brother. He's a linebacker. I'd be real popular if girls played football."

Fitzy said, "What about hockey?"

She laughed. "I live in Tucson."

"Go to a hockey camp for the rest of the summer. In Minneapolis."

"Well. . . . Who knows? Maybe I will."

We shook her hand and she was gone. Bounded out the door.

I said to Fitzy, "You're a cop because you want what's right, don't you?"

"That's what you want, ain't it?"

"I do."

"Good. Let's get out of this rat hole."

But before we left the rat hole, Fitzy got a camera out of his car and took a few pictures of the footprints under Lancelot's window. He took some of the threads hanging from the rose canes too.

The next morning, Fitzy was at Joe's door first thing. "Thought I'd catch you before you went to the Patio. I just had another visit to the camp, talked to a few campers, to Irwin. Yesterday I couldn't trust myself to deal with the guy. I might have strangled him with my bare hands. Figured Poppy would want to hear about how things went."

We invited him in. Joe had just made coffee. We took our cups and went out back and sat in Joe's comfortable wicker chairs. Fitzy took in the view.

"Not too shabby."

Joe thanked him.

He said, "Someone who likes overweight girls has been watching them through that window. So basically I threatened Irwin. I told the bastard to get a security guard up there and then open an account at Willa's Grocery, and I would check personally on the camp's tab. Prick is giving those girls powdered milk to drink, and he's got this huge closet full of big cans of beef stew. I read the label. First ingredient: water. I told him I'd arrest him if he didn't get some fresh food in every day. Christ almighty."

"Can you force Irwin to hire a security guard?"

"Of course not." I hadn't thought so. "He won't, either. But I tried. So here's the other reason I came calling."

He leaned back in his chair and put his feet on Joe's table, which was an old sea chest that liked having feet on it. "Commissioner called me. Gave me the general drift of the preliminary autopsy report. You interested?"

I just raised an eyebrow.

"The girl died about two hours before you nearly ran your bike into her, FBI. The body showed no needle marks, and no drugs were found in her system. Apparently, she'd given all her pot away at the Club Soda, hadn't saved any for herself, just like the campers told you and then told me. What the bartender told me too. Also, she was intact. No sign of sexual abuse. But drugs weren't ruled out altogether—something about the degeneration of the central nervous system and internal damage to hollow organs, and to her heart. So some quiet drug that affects your spinal cord, your lungs, your heart, and then vaporizes can't be precluded. Never heard of a drug like that before, though, have you?"

We both said no.

"So I says to my commissioner, who's reading all this to me, Since when do seventeen-year-old girls have weak hearts? And what's a weak heart have to do with the central nervous system degenerating? And he says, Well, she was carrying a lot of weight. I says, so am I. Then I ask him—just between the two of us, I says— what he thinks caused damage to her hollow organs, et cetera, and he says it all might be connected to bulimia. I says, What bulimia? She was five foot two and weighed a hundred and seventy pounds. He says they don't know her past history. Fuck."

I asked, "Do you know the number offhand?"

"What number?"

"The Commissioner's phone."

He held his coffee aloft. "Here's to you, FBI," he said and then gave me the number.

I identified myself to the Commissioner's secretary, told her who I was, and where I was calling from. Within a minute I was talking to the Commissioner of the Rhode Island State Police. I explained to him that I was vacationing on Block Island, and I was the one who had come upon the body of the dead camper, Dana Ganzi, and that I'd like to speak with him about her.

He said, "Fitzy told me there was an agent on the island. I thought he was bluffing, trying to influence me in the way he is especially good at."

"He wasn't. But I'm not official yet, so perhaps it was part bluff."

He said, "Fitzy is a great manipulator."

"Listen, I need a favor."

"I figured that."

I asked if he would fax everything he had to my office, including the preliminary autopsy report, plus the results of the toxicological and microbiological tests as they came in. There was a long silence. Then he said, "Agent, after Fitzy questioned the results of the report, I looked at them a little more closely. Personally. I made a point to have a look at photos of the body. To tell you the truth, I'm curious myself. Already asked to have more than the usual tests performed on the girl. So I'll be glad to accommodate you."

After I hung up, I reported to Joe and Fitzy. Then I

called Delby. I dialed while Joe explained to Fitzy who Delby was. Delby Jones, formerly a girl singer with every light jazz band coming through DC, presently my assistant and single mother of three—little girls who spend most of their time in our day-care center, where Delby has lunch with them every day, twelve to one, no matter what. At her job interview, when I'd listed my requirements, she'd listed hers. They were all connected to the needs of her daughters. They came first. But the FBI would be a very close second, she'd promised, in deference to her own priorities. Her references all raved about her organizational skills, her loyalty to her various managers, her intelligence and practical wisdom. I'd said I was impressed and then I'd said, "You've had a lot of different employers."

"When there's nothing left for me to learn, I lose interest and move on. I need a job where there's a whole lot to learn because I really do want to hang in."

That had been my attitude exactly as I'd followed my own career path. I hired her.

Delby Jones told me shortly afterward that just keeping track of me was an endless learning curve. And she has become as loyal to me and to the FBI as she is to her girls. Everyone—including my director—wishes Delby were theirs. Recently she told me that on Saturday nights she'd started singing again. I've been shaking in my boots ever since. I told her that if she ever leaves, I'll need a ten-year notice. She thanked me for the compliment. She said, "I'm not leaving till Bunny Rabbit is in college." Bunny Rabbit is how she refers to her youngest.

I'd said, "What if you become a singing star?"

She'd smiled. "I'm not a contender. It's just something I like to do. Sing. Jacks me up. Here's where I want to be a star. Right in your office, doin' some good."

I told her if Bono ever wanted a girl singer, I would

understand the enticement of U2. She went from smiling to laughing out loud as she went out the door shaking her head, mumbling, "U-Two. Hah!"

The FBI invented Caller ID. Delby picked up on the first ring. "Hey, boss."

"Hey, Delby. Things still smooth?"

" 'Course. I'd have called you if I so much as sensed a bump. That's what you people pay me for. How're things over there in the ocean with Prince Charming?"

"I had a bump."

"Uh-oh."

"A girl died a little over twenty-four hours ago. Seventeen years old. We guessed she'd OD'd on some nasty drug but the local . . . force . . . just got the preliminary autopsy report and there was no residue in the body. Looked like a sex crime, but no evidence of penetration or abuse. No typical sex stuff. So, Delby, I wasn't about to just forget about it and go fishing."

"I'll bet."

"I'm having the Rhode Island State Police send you the PA report. Get it directly to the lab. Tell Auerbach to stop in his tracks and look at it. Then call me if his guys find anything particularly awry." Auerbach, lead technician at the FBI crime lab, is the expert extrapolator. He puts jigsaw puzzles together for us, ones that are missing half the pieces at least. He and his computer. Constructs what's missing and fits it in.

"Count on it. But . . . uh . . . boss?"

"What?"

"I take it you saw the body?"

"I *found* the body."

"Oh, man. Oh, *man!*"

"I can't believe it either."

"I'll get back to you as soon as Auerbach sees to pushing your orders through."

"Thanks, Delby."

"Welcome. Sorry, boss."

I hung up. Fitzy said, "Wish I could press buttons like that. You're a pretty big cheese, aren't you?"

"Yes."

Then Joe said, "How about we all go for a bike ride before breakfast. Pick the steepest roads on the island."

Fitzy drained his cup, slurping the last dregs of cold coffee down. "I get the picture, tough guy. But I've got plenty to do, plenty of buttons to press, even though I'll come up empty. Keep people on their toes, at least." He stood up. "So enjoy your ride."

When he left, I said to Joe, "You knew he wouldn't take us up on that one, didn't you?"

"That's right."

"I don't think I would have minded going to breakfast with him. Get a chance to talk to him some more, maybe hear a little more of what the Club Soda clientele had to say."

Joe said *he* would have minded.

"You really don't like him, do you?"

"No. He's a waste. He didn't used to be. No excuse, as far as I can see."

"Maybe there's an excuse you can't see."

"I wonder if we'll need to pump up the tires a little."

We didn't bike Coonymus Road, we took the long route along the western shore of the island, the Western Road. Joe said the road had never been named because it was hardly ever used except by cows traveling their pastures. Eventually, the road was paved and the nickname stuck. According to Joe, it passed a series of tracks, the first to his cottage, and the others mostly to beaches that didn't stand up to the ones along the rest of the shoreline. While I rode, I planned what I'd say to my director.

At breakfast, Fitzy didn't show. When Joe and I got

home again, I took a shower and then I was ready to make my all-important phone call.

First, the big boss asked me how I was enjoying my vacation. I told him. I dwelt especially on my discovering the body of Dana Ganzi and its shocking condition. Then I said, "I've already asked the Rhode Island State Police Commissioner to send some stuff to Auerbach to look at. Depending on what I get back from Delby, I'd like to begin investigating this crime."

He sighed. Then he said, "It's too soon, Poppy. You're personally involved or you'd accept that it's too soon. I believe the Rhode Island police can solve this without us. Why not give them a chance?"

"All I'm doing is involving Auerbach. If he sees more than Rhode Island did, the stuff he offers them might help them figure out what's going on sooner than later, and they won't need us after all."

"Your offering help from us was also premature. How has this incident met the criteria—"

"It hasn't. But we're not official until you give me the okay. I'm simply taking a little poetic license." I described the loophole that had come right to mind. "And if that doesn't cut it, then under the terms Congress gave us when they said we could do some preliminary findings before evidence of wire tapping—"

"Poppy." His voice was now several decibels lower.

"Yes, sir."

"This will be the extent of the preliminary findings until the crime meets the criteria as set forth by law."

"Fair enough."

"Several members of Congress have told me you should be a lobbyist when you get tired of the FBI."

"I'm flattered."

"You're not getting tired of it, are you?"

"No."

"Whatever Auerbach gets will go back to Rhode Island, and then you wait for further instructions. From me."

"Sir, it's just that I'd hoped to avoid what so often happens during a wait."

He knew what I meant—any criminal involvement and the criminals had time to cut out. "Still, for the protection of us all, caution must prevail, mustn't it?"

"Yes."

"Sit on it awhile, Poppy. Then come back to me if you feel you need to go further, and we will reconsider our role."

I agreed. Because he was right.

The next afternoon I got my call back from Delby. She said, "Boss, Auerbach's finished and he is one nerved-up dude. Twitching the way he does when he's got a brand-new trail. He says that girl died from shock. Blood pressure crashed, basically. She was traumatized in a very fierce way. But Auerbach says nobody can explain how. Could only determine that the structural changes in her tissues were not caused by disease but by extraneous violence. The spasmed muscles were cadaveric contractions. That means she'd been in such physical torment *before* she died that *after* she died the rigor was extreme. He had me ask the coroner's office in Providence to do a few specific tests on a selection of tissues. I requested that they do them today."

"Good."

"You're not havin' much fun, are you, Poppy? I mean, recreation-wise."

"I had been. It's a great place as long as you can do without Starbucks."

"I hate Starbucks."

"Then maybe you should consider coming for a visit."

"Any black folk on Block Island?"

"None that I've seen."

"I'm stickin' here in DC, then, with my own kind."

We both laughed.

That night, Joe and I were at Fitzy's office, picking the cop up to go to dinner at an inn at the harborside. The chef there had temporarily left a well-known restaurant in Boston to help out his sister, who'd renovated the defunct hotel. Joe had called Fitzy and invited him along. Guilt. Joe told me that guilt was something he'd never experienced till he met me. He didn't think his job description allowed for it. For a long while, instead of guilt he drank, just like Fitzy, only in binges. He'd cut back earlier this year—no more binges—right about the time I took a brick to the head. Now, he was enjoying a fairly calm period at the ATF, a chance to become familiar with such things as guilt so he could handle his work with less self-destruction. My stepfather once said to me, "Why don't you find a man who plays the violin for a living?" I asked him where to look. "The Charles River on the Fourth of July." There was a reason I'd loved him so.

At about eight o'clock, we were standing on the police station porch, Fitzy just opening the door, when a taxi pulled up. One of the taxi brothers waved to us. I still didn't know which was which. Irwin got out and told the brother to wait right there. He turned and saw us. He noted immediately I was wearing a little black dress instead of a T-shirt and that my hair was up instead of in a wet and straggly state. "Mr. and Mrs. Everett— we meet again." Very sarcastic tone.

Joe said, "Yes."

He also noted the change in Joe. You don't need to

see the label on a blazer to know it reads Armani. Then, choosing not to worry that we were not who we had pretended to be, he said to Fitzy, "I am feeling pressured by the campers to tell you that one of the girls made her way into town tonight and has not come back. They tell me she hitchhiked, even though I gave very specific directions to the campers not to do that. Now I'm sure—"

Fitzy said, "Get in my office here, Jack."

He gestured to Joe and me to join him, though it would probably have been about as impossible to keep us from following as it would have been to keep the rats from hustling after the Pied Piper.

Fitzy's office was at the end of a hall leading from the front door. The two interior doors, one on each side of the hall, were open: the one on the right gave an up-front view of Fitzy's unmade bed and a bureau with all the drawers pulled out, their contents spilling forth; opposite, the door to the now-departed rookie's room revealed a stripped bed and a bureau, its top as bare as the top of Fitzy's. No mementos for our trooper, no pictures of someone keeping the home fires burning. In the office, there was a desk with a chair behind it and another chair off to the side.

Fitzy barked, "Sit down," to Irwin. Joe and I melded into the corner.

Irwin sat while Fitzy booted up his computer.

"Okay, then, who's missing?"

"No one, really. A few of the girls do this sort of thing. Go into town and hook up with kids off the ferry. They party. She'll be back tonight. She only took off an hour or two ago. This is actually ridiculous. The counselor informed me that the girl is not a druggie, like the girl who killed herself with an overdose of God-only-knows-what. And according to my counselors, she has managed to do this before—sneak off for a few hours."

Fitzy looked up at him. "I want the name of the girl who's missing."

"I *told* you. . . . Never mind. The girl who went into town without permission is Rachel Shaw. You and Mrs. Everett met her in my office yesterday. Her and our other Rachel."

"One Rachel said she was leaving for home today."

"She did leave. It's the other one who went to town."

"Address."

Irwin handed him a three-by-five card. Fitzy copied what was on it and handed it back.

"Last time you saw her?"

"I have two dozen girls in my charge. I suppose the last time I was even aware of her was when you insisted on talking to her."

"Three days ago one of your campers turned up dead. If I were you, I'd start to be aware."

Irwin was not moved. "I had punished her for the attitude she showed during your interview with her. She was housebound. But the counselors say a taxi picked her up. She was not hitchhiking like that girl who died. I told you, this is not the first time she's done this."

Fitzy stood up. "Hold on," and he went outside to talk to the taxi brother. He came right back. "She took the same taxi you've got waiting for you out in the street. He saw her, as you say, hook up with some kids off the ferry. All the same, have you notified her parents?"

"I don't see why, at this point. It's only just dark, for God's sake. However, I will look for her myself. And she'd better—"

Fitzy had picked up the receiver of his phone. He

handed it to Irwin. "Notify them." Then he read the phone number off the card.

"This will cause unnecessary—"

"Dial, Jack."

Irwin got an answering machine. He left a message that Rachel had gone into town which was in violation of camp rules. Even though he hated to upset them for no reason as he expected her to be back shortly, his personal policy was to inform the parents when their daughters broke a camp rule. "You know how teenage girls can be," he explained to the machine. "At any rate, permit me to apologize for my counselor's lapse. She has been put on notice, rest assured." He would call them again when Rachel returned. He added, "I have my two most experienced counselors in town, and we'll no doubt find her at one of the teen hangouts. As I say, I'm sure she'll be back shortly. I know that because we're showing a movie tonight and"—he glanced at the card—"Rachel won't want to miss it. Naturally, I am considering not allowing her to attend as a disciplinary measure. I will call you back within the hour. Actually, I will have Rachel call you from my office." Then he hung up. He said to Fitzy, "Satisfied?"

Fitzy said, "You're a scam artist, Jack, and I am doing everything in my power to get someone out here to close up your camp. Those girls might as well be in prison; they'd be better off."

Irwin rose. "Tough love, I admit, is dreadful. But it has proven effective for managing children out of control. A teenager out of control must be coerced—her will broken whether she likes it or not. At any rate, my understanding, officer, is that you *have* no power. And if you insist on using my first name, it isn't Jack. It's Blair."

Fitzy said, "I know what it is. Blair is not a name."

Blair left.

Fitzy said to us, "He's right. I *have* no power." We watched the taxi drive off. "Camp van must have broken down. No surprise there."

We went outside. We would walk to the restaurant. It was a beautiful night. The moon had just risen above the horizon, a waning moon at three-quarters. Joe had timed our vacation so it was full the night we arrived. At three-quarters, still spectacular. We decided that after we ate we'd go up to the camp and make sure the girl was back. "Maybe have another chat with her."

We left the jeep in front of the station.

As we walked along, we found that the camp van had not broken down after all. It was hurtling along the road, bearing down on us. We leaped into the grass as it screeched to a stop. Christen and her friend Samantha clambered out and opened the back door for the girl we'd seen get off the ferry three days earlier—in the group with Rachel Shaw—the young girl with the Cabbage Patch Kid. A lifetime earlier, it surely seemed. The doll was wearing a different outfit, a Seattle Mariners uniform. His owner was not so much overweight as she was roly-poly. She was less than five feet tall. She needed adolescence, a growth spurt. She hung back behind the older campers.

Christen, out of breath, said, "We stole the van."

I introduced her and Samantha to Fitzy. He said, "You want to come in and give me a stolen vehicle report?"

They weren't sure what to make of him. Samantha, in fact, had sunk back alongside her younger friend. I said, "He's joking. What's the matter?"

Christen grabbed the arm of the girl with the doll. "C'mon, Stupid, don't be shy. We already know these people. Tell this cop what you told us." The girl's head was down and she clutched the doll for dear life. Christen said, "It's about Rachel Shaw. Stupid was spying on her this afternoon."

Rachel Shaw. Yet again.

Stupid was not as retiring as she seemed. She lifted her head. High. She said, "I was *not* spying. I do not *spy* on people."

I asked, "When was that? I mean, when—"

Christen said, "She was following her during our swim time. We were at the beach from two until five."

The girl with the doll bristled some more. "I *said* I was not *spying*, and I was not *following* her either. Elijah Leonard just wanted to see where Rachel was going." She looked down at the doll. "Right?" She nodded his head for him. Elijah Leonard confirmed.

Fitzy said, "How old are you, kiddo?"

"I'll be eleven day before school starts."

He muttered something under his breath; then he said to Joe and me, "Camp's supposed to be limited to girls thirteen to eighteen. Maybe I got that crook after all."

The girl and her doll took a step forward. "He made an exception for me. My mother begged him to."

Joe said, "Christen, does your friend here have a name?"

"Yes. Stupid."

Samantha explained. "That's her nickname because she doesn't know anything." She looked at the girl. "You don't mind though, do you, Stupid?"

The girl shook her head.

"See, if she minded, we wouldn't call her that," Christen said, "I have a younger brother. You should hear what I call *him*. We're used to names a lot worse than Stupid."

And the girl with the doll said, "Yeah, like Meat.

That's what they call me at school." Then she said to Christen, "Is your little brother fat?"

"He's a damn toothpick."

I said, "We'd like to know your real name, all the same."

Christen shrugged. "I don't know her real name, do you, Sam?"

"Nope. What's your real name, Stupid?"

"Kate."

I said, "Kate what?"

"Kate Bailey."

"Kate, we're on our way to dinner with Officer Fitzgerald. Would you girls like to join us? That way we can all relax and Kate can tell us about Rachel."

Kate's eyes slid from me to the other girls. Samantha said, "Say yes, Stupid."

She said, "Yes."

Fitzy draped his arms around Christen and Samantha's shoulders and pulled them in to him. "How about you kids first get the stolen vehicle out of the middle of the road."

Christen had been the driver. Now she climbed back in, started the van, shifted into reverse, and stalled. She stalled two more times as she bumped and ground the van into a position half on the road and half on the sidewalk. Then she climbed out again. On the sidewalk she was sheepish. "I don't have my license yet. I haven't even finished drivers' ed."

Fitzy said, "Consider taking the course over again, from the beginning."

"They don't teach you shifting, you know."

"Forget it. You did fine. So now Irwin's got three more missing girls. Plus a stolen van. Good. Let's go. I could eat a horse."

Kate Bailey walked in step with him. She said, "Elijah Leonard could eat a moose!"

The woman at the inn put two tables together for us. Kate, eyes about as big as big gets, lashes so long they touched her cheeks when she blinked, asked if Elijah Leonard could have a chair too. The innkeeper looked around. I said, "I think she means her doll."

The woman smiled. "Sure."

Fitzy asked her, "You a Seattle fan?"

She gazed at him with those eyes. "How did you know?"

Samantha said, "We told you she was stupid."

Fitzy poked a finger into the doll's chest. "Well, I guessed he was a ballplayer. Seattle. Him being in full uni and all."

She looked down at the doll and giggled. "Oh."

Christen said, "Stupid, try to get with the program. Sheesh."

Kate giggled again. She didn't see the name they'd given her as insulting but rather a term of endearment, since the girls who used it had taken her under their wing. She said to Fitzy, "My grandpa gave him the uniform. He gave me a Seattle shirt, too. For me to wear to match with Elijah Leonard's uniform. Like, not the whole uniform, just the shirt. It's back at the camp. I don't wear it because I don't want to get it dirty. We have to wash our clothes in a *sink*."

We were handed menus. The three girls opened them as though they were Christmas presents.

Joe said, "Whatever you like, kids."

Kate turned the menu over, checking out the desserts. Her eyes sparkled. "Omigod. Elijah Leonard's favorite! Would it be all right if he has some rice pudding?"

Christen said, "For Christ's sake, Stupid, you are

such a pain in the butt. Just order something and give him a bite from your plate."

Fitzy said, "Watch the language, sister."

"Sorry."

The girls ordered drinks. Cokes. They sucked their glasses dry in one swoop. Joe waved to our waiter and pointed at the empty glasses. And to the bread basket, also emptied. The glasses and basket were refilled and we all ordered. Then, over dinner, Kate Bailey told us what she saw Rachel Shaw doing during their swim time.

"They make us hike this really steep trail down to the beach. It's the beach nearest to our camp. It's not a real beach. It's the pits. You can't actually swim because the water is about up to your ankles. Even at *high tide*."

Samantha said, "It's some kind of mud flat."

Kate continued, giving us a pout. "Christen and Sam didn't even go today. They hid out. And they didn't take me with them."

Samantha said, "We would have, Stupid, but we get so sick of Elijah Leonard sometimes."

Kate pouted harder. "He just wants to be our friend."

"Then tell him to find some boys," Christen said. "What is he, queer?"

Fitzy leveled his fork at her.

Kate Bailey said, "So do you want me to tell you what Rachel did or not?"

Fitzy aimed the fork at her. "Go."

First she filled her baked potato with a large chunk of butter and a great spoonful of sour cream. Then she took a bite from Elijah Leonard's rice pudding. Then back to the baked potato, scooping it into her mouth while she told us her tale.

"That Rachel was really *really* hungry. I'm not too hungry usually. My grandpa put a lot of cookies in my suitcase. Like, bags of them."

Christen said, "Pepperidge Farm."

"Elijah Leonard says it's all right to share with Christen and Sam, right, Elijah Leonard?" She bobbled the doll's head again, up and down. "He's a good sharer too." Another taste of rice pudding.

Samantha leaned over to Fitzy. "See what I'm talking about?" She twirled her finger next to her temple.

He sighed. "Go ahead, Kate."

"Anyway, Rachel starts walking away from us toward the point at the end of the beach. I asked her where she was going and she said to me, 'I'm going to the point, idiot.' So I asked her if me and Elijah Leonard could come too but she said—" Kate slapped another dollop of sour cream into her potato—"she said no." Kate picked up the doll and looked into his big blank eyes. "But you wanted to follow her, didn't you?" She gave him a good bounce. His head went up and down vigorously.

Fitzy said to Samantha, "Maybe I do see what you mean."

All three girls looked at each other and laughed.

I said, "Fitzy, you have children, don't you?"

He said, "My wife has them." Then, "Okay, Kate, you followed her. What next?"

"*Elijah Leonard* followed her. So I had to go too."

"Fine."

Christen asked her, "Are you in middle school, Stupid?"

"We have K through eight at my school."

"Well, that's a damn good thing, let me tell you. You'd be laughed out of middle school."

Fitzy tried to pick up the story, "Okay, Elijah, let's hear it."

"Elijah *Leonard*. We stayed way back but we could see what Rachel was doing. She really was going out to the point. See, there are a billion mussels at the point. Big ones. But it's real rocky over there, hard to walk. Rachel didn't care. She was going to, like, *eat* the mussels. Some of the kids do. Yucko."

My fork was poised over the bouillabaisse in front of me. It was, like, littered with mussels. Christen noticed too. She said to Kate, "Mussels are very good, Stupid."

"Yeah, if you *cook* them. Christen, may I taste your pasta?"

Christen lifted her plate and scraped a pile of penne next to Kate's steak. Kate shoved a forkful of them into her mouth. "Mmm. Yummo."

Fitzy told her to keep talking.

She chewed, she swallowed, and then she had another forkful, talking the whole time. "Rachel starts pulling mussels off the rocks, and she lines them up, and then she picks up one of those round rocks, a big one, and she smashes all the mussels. Smash, smash, smash, smash-o. Then she, like, eats them. Then she keeps walking, picking mussels and picking more mussels, smashing mussels, smashing mussels. A billion of them. She keeps eating them, too. Gross."

Samantha said to her, "They wouldn't be so gross if you were starving, Stupid." To us: "Stupid's grandfather shipped her a crate of Drake's Cakes. That's besides the suitcase he filled with Pepperidge Farm."

Kate said, "My grandpa told me Drake's Cakes don't add weight because there's no chocolate in them, so I should eat however many I want."

Christen said, "Your grandpa is a moron, Stupid."

"No, he's *not*."

Samantha tried to soften the criticism. "He's an enabler."

"He's a grandpa," Fitzy said. "That's what they do. But let's forget the Drake's Cakes. And forget the mussels too."

Christen sighed. "Yeah, we've got that part down."

I reached over and patted Kate's hand. "Honey, just tell us what else you saw."

She carried on, carving away at her steak. "Rachel goes around the point, *past* the point. That's when Elijah Leonard wanted to stop following her because he didn't want to walk *that* far. So we stopped at the end of the point where he could still see her without having to, like, keep walking. Elijah Leonard gets tired real easy." The doll slumped for effect. "So I'm standing on the point and I could see her on the next beach. Christen, how come they don't take us to *that* beach instead of ours? It's got *sand* on it."

"I wouldn't know."

Fitzy said to Christen, "Is this going anywhere?"

"Yes."

"Rachel, then. Go."

Kate mopped up the tomato sauce from Christen's penne with her bread and began eating that. "There was this man there—over on the nice beach—and he had a blanket spread out on the sand. He was having a picnic. He had a ton of food. He had fried chicken."

"You saw fried chicken?"

"No. I already said he was far away. But I could *smell* fried chicken. So then Rachel sits down with him and starts eating all his stuff. He didn't eat anything, I don't think. He just, like, watched Rachel. Then Rachel lay down on the blanket."

Kate stopped. Her eyes went down. She'd been diverted. Her eyes had shifted to my plate and she pointed at a large scallop. "What's that?"

Christen said, "It's a scallop, Stupid. And it's *cooked*."

Kate's eyes traveled from the scallop to my eyes.

"Would you like to try it?"

"Yes, please." I spooned it over to her plate; she speared it with her fork and popped it in her mouth. "Yummo." Then she picked up another roll and started buttering it. The other girls did the same, all three taking a good long time about it. We waited.

Finally, it was Christen who broke the ice. "See, we've already asked Stupid if Rachel had sex with the guy."

Kate looked up from her roll. Butter now glistened on her chin. "I go to Christian school, but I still know about sex and all that stuff even though we don't have sex ed. That's because my family has horses. We have a man who breeds them. They actually *tie* the stud to the mare, and then—"

"Skip the horses, kid. Back to—"

"I know. To Rachel. Okay. Rachel and the man didn't, like, do it. After Rachel lay down she got right back up again. Then she stood there for a few minutes talking to the man, and then she walked back toward the point. Toward me. So me and Elijah Leonard ran back to our camp beach. The *skank* beach."

Fitzy was chewing his own steak. "Kate, who was the man?"

"What man?"

"The man having the picnic."

"I don't know."

I said, "Had you ever seen him before?"

"I don't know. He was too far away to really see his face or anything."

"What can you remember about him?"

"He had on a baseball cap. I think it was a baseball cap. I couldn't tell the team."

"Was he young or old?"

"I couldn't see him good."

We all chewed. Then Samantha said, "Stupid, tell them what Rachel said to you later."

Kate put on an especially emphatic pout. "She came up to me on our beach. She said she'd seen me, and if I ever followed her again she'd rip Elijah Leonard inside out and throw him off a cliff into the ocean."

Christen said, "That's what *I'd* like to do with him."

"No, you wouldn't!"

"I was only kidding, Stupid."

I said, "Kate, what else did Rachel say to you?"

"She said, *He's all mine.* And then she, like, walked away from me. I asked Samantha what she meant. Sam said she meant the *man* was all hers and I shouldn't get any ideas about going over to that beach in case he was there again having another picnic. But, jeez, he must be a nice man to—"

Christen said, "No, he's not a nice man. He bribed Rachel with food. So obviously, Rachel made plans to see the guy again. Obviously, tonight. And they probably *will* have sex this time around."

Kate said, "Blech."

Samantha continued. "She gave her bunkmate ten dollars to keep quiet. She either hitched into town or took a taxi, I don't know. But since she probably used up what money she had for the counselor, I think the picnic guy came to get her. I don't know that either, but she hasn't come back. Just like when Dana took off that night after dinner and never came back. I mean, Rachel's done this before, but still. . . . Because of Dana we wanted to tell the cop. That's why we stole the van. We couldn't call a taxi. The counselors were watching our phone girl. They know she has it so she has to be careful before she can pass it on." She swallowed. Then, with a quaver in her voice, she said, "What if Rachel—" She looked down at her plate.

I asked, "Did you tell Dr. Irwin what you told us, Kate?"

"No."

"Why not?"

She looked at Christen. Christen had taken a couple of deep breaths. Her voice was haughty once again. "Frankly, we were going to. We went to his office but he was a little busy, fucking his favorite counselor. Another reason we stole the van."

Kate said, "Gross-out."

"It took us an hour to get to the police station, because I went the long way around so no one would see us."

Kate knew better. "It took us an hour because she, like, stalled the van a billion times. Some of the times, we had to wait for someone to drive by and start it up again."

Christen said, "I told you. I haven't learned stick yet."

Fitzy said, "Well, somebody eventually interrupted Irwin's activities with the counselor. While you girls were stalling the van all over the island, he came in and reported Rachel Shaw missing."

Samantha said, "He did?" And she and Christen exchanged glances. Worried glances.

I said, "So why are we sitting here?"

"Because we're eating," Kate told us all. "Real food."

We told the waiter we had an emergency and to put all our dinners in doggie bags. I told the girls, "We'll eat the rest at the camp. It's time to see if Rachel is back, isn't it?"

5

Fitzy didn't drive to the camp with us. He'd catch up. Something alcoholics say a lot. Had to brace himself. "Leave a message on my machine if she's at the camp. I'll stay in town and have a look around in case she's still hanging out."

I volunteered to drive the van back to the camp, with Joe following in the jeep. Samantha and Kate were much relieved. Christen said, "Just when I was getting the hang of it."

Joe and I didn't worry about whether Irwin might be bothered by visitors. "After all," I said to Joe as we left the restaurant, "the Everetts should be expected to get some feedback from the campers before making a decision about Suzie." And then I whispered, "Besides, he's probably gone back to fucking counselors and won't even notice us."

Samantha said, "I heard that."

Joe said, "Maybe it's not what you think. Maybe the counselor is his girlfriend."

Christen corrected him. "She's not a girlfriend. He pays her. She's a ho'."

"We know what that means, don't we, Elijah Leonard?"

I found myself glancing at the doll as if he were going to answer. His eyes remained blank. I found him menacing. Or maybe it was the situation we were in that gave the doll his discomforting expression.

At the camp, the girls made sure everyone in Lancelot House was decent, calling out, "Man on the premises." We heard a bit of a scramble, and then Joe and I were escorted inside. I was immediately struck by the riot of color from the junk food wrappers and Snapple bottles littering the beds and the tops of trunks. The girls had arrived at camp prepared. They were gathered at one end of the bunkhouse sitting together on the floor, noshing. It was past the hours of allotted electricity, so they had surrounded themselves with candles.

Christen said to them, "Did Rachel get back?"

"No. But Irwin broke down. He's out looking for her. In a *cab*. You should have *seen* him running around. 'Where's my van, where's my goddamn van?' So what took you guys so long? Did you find the cop?"

"Yes. He's looking too. But first we went to dinner with him. And with these people. We told you about them before." She introduced us. They loved my dress. They wished they could fit into a DKNY dress. And then Christen distracted them by describing what she and Samantha and Kate had ordered for dinner, eliciting moans and groans of greater envy. She mentioned Elijah Leonard's rice pudding. Then the three girls broke out their doggie bags and Joe and I offered up ours. All of Lancelot House dug in.

I observed them, sitting there in their T-shirts and shorts. The amount of bare skin seemed like a sea.

They all had great hair—a girl doesn't have to be skinny to take care of her hair and then flaunt the results. There was a mane of chestnut brown highlighted with perfect streaks, scrunchies holding back two flowing blond ponytails, a cloud of red curls spilling down the back of a fourth girl, and a black girl with short hair like Halle Berry's. They talked about the food they were eating, comparing flavors, wondering what ingredients went into my bouillabaisse . . . guessing. Besides the contents of the doggie bags, they munched away on chips and Tostitos, cookies and crackers, and those orange things, Cheese Doodles. They held the big cellophane bags under their arms like footballs.

Christen was reading my expression. She said, "We tend to binge. My psychological counselor at home that my dad sends me to says that when you eat a ton of carbohydrates, there's this natural opiate in your body that builds up, just keeps building up, and then you get dependent on the carbs. This guy says it goes beyond craving. He told me I was an addict. He recommended a camp."

The redhead said, "Oh, the guy's full of shit. I just like to eat. Am I bored? Am I stressed? Am I worried? No. I just like food. I'm interested in food. I'm very strong. I lift weights at home. I never catch colds." She held out a bag of Doritos to me and Joe. "Have some carbs."

Joe declined, explaining that we'd really been able to eat most of our dinner, and Samantha's eyes lowered, embarrassed. So I said, "But we didn't have a chance to order dessert, Joe," and then thrust upon us were a large assortment of goodies: Milky Ways and M&Ms, any number of candy bars, plus Twinkies, Hostess cupcakes, Devil Dogs, and Kate's Drake's Cakes. Samantha said, "Wait," dashed to her trunk, and came back with a box of Turtles. "These are for special guests."

Kate said, "Like, you guys are our only special guests so far."

Someone else: "Elijah Leonard is our special guest."

Kate blushed.

Samantha said, "Here, Kate, take a turtle for Elijah Leonard. We don't want him to feel deprived."

I tried not to look at him but I couldn't help it. He didn't look menacing any more, he looked grateful.

The teenage girls had new-millennium names reaching back throughout the history of English literature: Amanda, Emily, Lucy, Charlotte, Tessa. I asked where they were from. California, Michigan, then a twang—a girl from *San Antone*.

The black girl said, "Jamaica."

Christen said, "We all thought she meant the island. She was talking about Queens: New York."

Kate said, "I'm not the only stupid one."

Food had brought us into their circle. Once they trusted us, their conversation became spigots turned on full. Like Delby's daughters. When I'd first met them, they watched me. When they were assured their mother was right—that I was a friend—I could count on hearing the plots of their new books and their favorite television shows. When Delby took them on a trip to visit grandparents, they were allowed two stuffed animals and two dolls each. While they were gone, I had to baby-sit for the rest of the shortlist—a purple thing from the youngest, Barney, a red item for the middle kid, Elmo, and seven Barbie dolls belonging to the eldest, lined up in a row on the floor.

Now I brought the girls around to why we were there. "Would Rachel have stayed out this late?"

"She stays out this late whenever she can. She doesn't have much money so she doesn't get in to town a lot. Mostly, she hitches."

Joe said, "Maybe the picnic man gave her money."

Christen said, "Omigod, I bet he did."

I asked, "Does she do drugs?"

"Yes. Sometimes. Not Dana, though. The girls in Dana's house were really worried that night. The night she didn't come back. She never stayed in town very late. Not like Rachel."

Christen said, "We already told them Dana didn't want trouble."

"But Rachel, the one who's in town right now, she smoked pot all the time. And she'd snort cocaine if the opportunity arose. She'd trade stuff to the counselors for it."

"Trade stuff?"

"Yeah. Her watch. Stuff like that."

"She sounds tragic."

Christen said, "It's hard to feel sorry for her. She's really never liked the rest of us."

Kate said, "She, like, hates us."

"The thing is, it's not so much drugs. That isn't her big problem. The big problem is that Rachel will do anything for a meal. She had these earrings. They were diamond studs. I know she sold them in town. Because she'd stopped wearing them and then she had a whole bunch of food around. I did feel sorry for her when that happened."

"So did I."

"Dana had plenty of money. Rachel doesn't have any."

Samantha said, "Most of us don't want to go to those clubs in town. Older people go there. We go into town to stock up, or we go to the library and study stuff for the fall, things like that. Or we hang out on Crescent Beach, watch the skinny kids play volleyball. Sometimes we play. I'm pretty good."

The black girl said, "Me too. I have a mean serve."

Another: "None of us can spike a ball, though."

Kate explained. "Like, I can't get high enough off the ground."

Christen said, "You couldn't get *two inches* off the ground. Nobody can play volleyball holding a Cabbage Patch Kid."

"Well, I can't just leave him sitting there."

"So someone must have grabbed Dana. Because she wouldn't hitchhike."

Joe said, "Grabbed her?"

"Well, I hate to say it," Samantha said, "but if no one just grabbed Dana, maybe one of those cab drivers murdered her."

Unanimous affirmation.

"Let's not get melodramatic, here. There is nothing—"

Joe was interrupted. The girls were all anxious to spill what they'd been deliberating. I touched his wrist. They had a right to express what was on their minds. I discovered very early on that listening is a strong investigative tool.

"From what we heard . . . I mean, everybody's talking about it . . . we think Dana was kidnapped and *tortured* to death."

Joe said, "Now hold on. It's dangerous to start—"

But they ignored him. "Maybe that Chinese water torture where someone puts this metal helmet on you and then they keep dropping these little drips of water down on your head until you confess or else it kills you."

"Chinese water torture kills you by driving you mad and then you strangle, I think. Choke to death on your own vomit."

"Yes. On your own vomit."

Joe jumped in. "One of my jobs is to stop drugs from entering this country. There are drugs that can do terrible things to you. Just what you're describing, as a matter of fact. So—"

"Which drug would that be?" Christen asked.

"A lot of them. I'm looking into it."

Kate said to Joe, "Do you work for the President or something?"

"Sort of."

She was holding on to Elijah Leonard a little more firmly. "I sure don't want to get tortured to death."

Christen said to Samantha, "Give Elijah Leonard another one of those Turtles."

I asked them if anyone knew specifically where Rachel might have gone.

"Wherever she could find any action. She looks for parties and crashes them."

"But where in particular?"

"Tonight, obviously, to wherever she thought she could hook up with the guy who was having the picnic on the beach. Must have promised her more of the same. In exchange for sex, I think." Christen looked at Joe and me. "Some men *like* fat women, believe it or not."

Kate said, "But I *told* you. They didn't do anything when I saw them."

"Stupid, maybe he didn't like doing it to her on the beach in broad daylight. Especially if he saw you watching them. He probably did. He took Rachel to his hotel, where else? He might be torturing her right now."

Joe rolled his eyes. He said, "Kate, was there anything else you saw at the beach? Was a vehicle parked there?"

"Yeah. But I could only make out part of it."

"What color?"

She was chewing on Elijah Leonard's Turtle. Took her a minute to get it down. "I don't remember. I didn't really look that good at it. The sun was shining so bright. I lost my sunglasses. My grandpa gave them to me. And they were the kind *ballplayers* wear. They flip up and down. Christen told me they were dorky."

"I was trying to make you feel better when you couldn't find them."

I said, "Kate. The man was definitely alone?"

"I bet I left them in the library."

"*Kate.* Try to forget about the sunglasses for now. Think about what you saw when Rachel was with the man having a picnic."

"Okay. I think maybe there could have been another guy in the truck."

"Truck?"

"Yeah. Or an SUV. I thought I saw something inside it. Maybe it was a dog."

I said, "And you're sure it was a truck or an SUV? Not a car?"

"I'm not *real* sure."

Christen said, "And you aren't sure of the color?"

"The color of what?"

"Jesus, Mary, and Joseph."

Kate said, "Well, I *am* sure of one thing. The picnic man had on a baseball cap. The thing is, I was mostly looking at Rachel." She sucked the chocolate from her fingers. "Don't you guys wish we had a *television*?"

I said, "Listen, girls. The main thing here is this. You don't go wandering off alone. Whatever reason you might have for getting yourself into town without permission from Irwin, go in a group, okay?"

I knew I was in trouble the minute the words came out of my mouth. Christen looked at me with disdain. "I think we've figured that one out by now. It's what my mother's been telling me since I was twelve—always go out in a group. Like some cute guy's going to ask me to the movies, right? It's true that some men like fat girls. Older men, though, not high school guys. High school guys wouldn't admit it even if they did. We tend to go out in groups because we haven't got much choice. But now we have a clue about who the picnic man might be, don't we? The guy having a picnic was definitely not a high school junior."

"Listen, I'm sorry," I said, "but Rachel went out alone."

"Rachel was starving."

"And we're not."

Then one of the girls said to me, "You're the one who found Dana's body, aren't you?"

"Yes."

"I knew it was you, because someone said the lady who found Dana was an FBI agent. You look like an FBI agent. You know how all firemen are hunks? Well, all women FBI agents are sassy. And skinny. I hate skinny girls. I mean, I really, really hate them."

They all laughed.

Christen said, "You're an *FBI agent*?"

"Yes."

"Hey, cool." And then, "Awesome," followed by, "Sweet," followed by "Crazy!"

Kate said, "Omigod," and then, all excited, "Do they take fat people? I mean, the FBI?"

I had to tell her no. "But they don't fire you if you gain weight."

Christen said, "Forget about it, Stupid. They sure as hell aren't going to take that butt-ugly doll of yours." Elijah Leonard slumped. Then Christen gave me a grin. "Wait till I tell everyone at home I had dinner with the feds."

Kate gave us all a big yawn. I looked at my watch.

Just after eleven. I told them they should get to bed. That the State Police officer would find Rachel. And Joe warned them to be sure to blow out all the candles. "This place'll go up in thirty seconds if one spark hits these walls."

Christen said, "Hey, that's what we should do. Torch Camp Guinevere."

As Joe stood, one of them whispered, "He is a *specimen*." More whispering: "Looks like the guy who plays with that band. What's that band?"

"I think I know what band you mean. Wait . . . The Pac-Men! Guy with the Mohawk. Who plays bass. He looks *exactly* like that guy."

Outside, I told Joe he should shave the sides of his head and reveal his true identity. We got in the jeep and took off. I looked back. The girls were at the windows, watching us.

On the way to Joe's, we passed someone walking in the deep shadows alongside the road. Joe said, "Jake."

"What's he doing?"

"He's taking a walk. He likes to go out walking at night when no one will bother him, touch him. Or talk to him, expect an answer."

"Maybe he's the one who watches the girls through the windows."

"He's curious about circuit breakers, not people."

Back at Joe's, both of us headed for the answering machine. We could only hope what I'd told the girls was true. That Fitzy had found Rachel Shaw. The red light was blinking; there was a message from him. But it was difficult to understand what he was saying. "Don't know what the hell time it is. My watch is blurred." So was his speech. "No sign of the girl anywhere in town. I hit the clubs, knocked on a lot of doors—people having parties—a few knew who I meant, told me she was looking for someone. I gave up, came home, was about to call Irwin—call the two of you—see if she'd come back. If she hadn't, I was going to rouse my commish, tell him to muster the troops. Then I saw I had a message on my machine. It was your basic anonymous call. Believe it's the horse's ass who runs the liquor store. Fred something. Recognized his voice because I do a lot of business there. So can you people get over here? You'll want to hear this message, trust me. Right now, I can't think straight till I drink a few gallons of coffee. I'll wait for you. Give you half an hour."

Joe said to me, "What would Fred have to do with anything?"

"One way to find out."

We changed to jeans, got back in the ragtop for the third time that evening, and drove over to Fitzy's. He was one wired drunk, working on walking a straight line across the office floor. He offered us some of his coffee. It looked like mud. We declined. Then he said, "Okay, listen to this."

It took him several tries to press the PLAY button on the answering machine. A near-hysterical high-pitched male voice came on: "There's one of those fat girls from the camp at the bottom of Rodman's Hollow. And she's dead."

Whoever it was—Fred from the liquor store if Fitzy was correct—hung up the phone with a bang.

Fitzy asked Joe, "Sound like Fred to you?"

"Play it again."

Fitzy did.

Joe said, "I'm not sure if it's him. Could be."

"What the hell is Rodman's Hollow?" Fitzy said. "I go by the sign a hundred times a day."

Joe told him. "A protected piece of land with nature trails. But you don't want to go traipsing around in there after dark. The trail off the road is half gravel, half slime from the dampness. Slippery. It's dark enough during the day, but it's pitch black at night. We'll have to wait until morning."

I thought that was fairly wimpy. "Joe, we can go back for our boots. And there's a mighty big flashlight in the jeep."

"It would be foolish to try to go down there at night, and we can't go pounding on Fred Prentiss's door at this hour."

We can't? Normally, Joe is not a dismissive sort of guy. Maybe he was tired. There's a first for everything. I said, "So who can we get who knows the trail? Someone to lead us if it's all that dangerous."

"Bird-watchers. But they only come during migration, in the fall."

Fitzy said, "No local birdbrains around?"

Joe made a little sigh. "Esther knows the trails, all of them. We could try her. I hate to involve these people, though."

I said, "Joe. What's the matter with you? Rachel Shaw never came back tonight. And some character called Fitzy to tell him he found a body. You wanted to involve them after I found Dana Ganzi's body. And it seems to me they wanted to be involved."

"Then it was one victim of an overdose. Now—if it's Fred and if he found another girl from the camp, dead— Jesus, I can't believe this. This is Block Island, not Washington."

I said, "Maybe the call was a hoax."

"That's what I want to think. But why would some-one like Fred Prentiss perpetrate a hoax?"

"I thought you said you couldn't tell it was him."

"I couldn't."

"Then I'll bet Esther could tell whose voice is on Fitzy's tape. She sits in the coffee shop all morning listening to everyone. What do you think?"

"I think she probably could."

"Then let's go."

Fitzy had one more thing to say. "Hold on a minute. Are we talking about the dyke who sells junk out of her house?"

I couldn't believe him. "Fitzy, how can you talk like that?"

"Because she told me that's what she was when I made a move on her last year."

"She told you she was a lesbian?"

"No, she told me she was a dyke. I've been blown off with more colorful lines than that, though."

"Let's take the tape to her, whatever she is."

Then we waited while Fitzy tried unsuccessfully to open his answering machine.

He said, "How the fuck do you get the tape out of this contraption?"

Joe said, "Bring the whole machine, Fitzy. Esther won't have one of her own." Then he said, "I don't know about this."

"You don't know what about what?"

Fitzy stood up. "Nothing says you have to go with us, Joe. If it is Fred from the liquor store who called me, he isn't in your jurisdiction. Doesn't smuggle in his bottles of Absolut, far as I know. *And* as far as I know, he isn't smuggling tobacco or firearms either."

Joe said, "I'll come."

I'd have to get to the bottom of whatever his problem was.

Joe drove. Fitzy did not protest.

Esther lived on the eastern side of the island just up from town at the end of a long dirt driveway on Spring Street. She was sitting on her screened porch, drinking wine and chain-smoking. Her cloud of wiry gray-streaked hair reminded me of mattress stuffing. But her face was not unattractive. Her skin was dark, her eyes blue, and her lips full and chiseled. Exotic. Plus, she was tall and strong. Esther had a presence. She watched us pile out of the ragtop but didn't bother to move. Fitzy whispered, a little more loudly than his normal speaking range, "If she'd told me she was a witch instead of a dyke, it would have been a more believable excuse."

At Esther's door, Joe apologized for disturbing her and explained that we needed her help. She said, "Then what are you doing outside?"

We went onto the porch. She didn't say anything else, still didn't get up, didn't offer to share her wine, just looked at us and waited. A little oil lamp sitting next to her bottle on the table in front of her glowed faintly. Abutting it was an overflowing ashtray.

Fitzy told her about getting a message and needing somebody to identify the caller. "If it won't kill you," he said. He looked around the porch. "Hopefully, you've got electricity."

She snorted and stood up, gesturing with her cigarette for us to follow. Ashes fell on the floor. We went inside, into her dark, musty living room and shop where the floor was slanted, the furniture looking as though it had been scavenged from a dump, her paintings leaning against the wall, all of it in deep shadow.

She turned on a lamp and pointed to an outlet behind it. Fitzy plugged in his machine, took awhile fiddling with it. I looked around. The lamp threw so little light, I couldn't make out the subject of her pictures. Fitzy said, "You got another lamp, Esther?"

"No. I'm never inside at night."

Fitzy looked up at her.

"I'm either on the porch or in my bedroom."

"Sounds real exciting. I don't know what's the matter with you. You could be spending your nights with me painting the town red. Seeing as how you're a painter."

She said, "What will you use for a brush?"

Fitzy laughed. "You're a pisser, Esther. Why I like you."

The tape played and we all listened to the overwrought message.

Esther said, "It's Fred Prentiss. Drunk, obviously."

Fitzy rewound and played it again. "You sure?"

"Yes. I was sure the first time."

"Guy who runs the liquor store, right?"

"That's right. He must have been hallucinating. He drinks most of his profits."

"I sure as hell hope so. All the same, refresh my memory. Where is this Roadman Hollow?"

"Rodman's Hollow. Do you have a map?"

"Sure, but I couldn't put my finger on it at the moment."

"I have a boxful." She disappeared into the blackness of the next room. It didn't take long for Esther to come back with her map. She held the one-inch stub of her cigarette clamped between her lips and spread the map out under the lamp. It was hand-drawn. Pen and ink. She must have drawn it herself. She said, "Block Island is shaped like a pork chop. The rib end runs due north." She ran her finger from the loin, on up the rib and then back down again. "Right in the middle"—she poked her finger mid-loin—"there's a wide deep bowl, dense with brush. Rodman's Hollow. Some insist it's bottomless. It isn't, but it sort of is."

Fitzy crossed his arms over his chest, a man beginning to feel a bad headache coming on.

I said, "Esther, we're trying to follow you. We need you to be specific."

She took the remains of the cigarette and put it out in a clamshell on her windowsill. Then she lit up again, took a few drags, and started her attempt at specific. "Twelve thousand years ago, a mile-high glacier cut a rift through the island. The contours of the rift are visible across the landscape. Long time ago, the rift was called the Devil's Causeway. They say Dutchy Kitten named it that."

Fitzy said, "Who?"

"Someone who died three hundred years ago," Joe told him.

"Can we not get into her story now, Esther?"

Esther took a very long drag on the cigarette, blew out a heavy stream of smoke, and went back to the glacier. "At the center of the rift a bowl was reamed out, three hundred yards across. This hollow is actually below sea level, even though its rim is ninety feet above. Marcus Rodman acquired the land. He renamed the rift after himself."

"Does he still own it?"

"Dead two hundred years," Joe said.

"Okay, Esther. What say we get this show on the road? Forget the goddamn history of the place. Just tell me what it is I'm lookin' at here."

"All right, then." Esther had no intention of forgetting the goddamn history of the place. "There is no water table in the depths of the Hollow, so that's where the legend came from—about its being bottomless.

But there used to be twenty feet of peat bog down there. Got cleaned out in the eighteenth century. The only source of heat we had then. Anyway, the peat was broken down spruce. Twelve thousand years ago—"

Fitzy held up his palm. Must have done some duty as a traffic cop at one point. "Listen, Esther, we're not interested in three hundred years ago or two hundred years ago, and we're especially not interested in twelve *thousand* years ago. Can you move on to the present?"

Not yet, she couldn't. "—a glacier denuded the island of an extensive spruce forest, just like the first colonists did who came much later and denuded it of a hardwood forest. Which is why there was no wood for heat."

Now I understood the dearth of trees.

Fitzy said, "Okay, so correct me if I'm wrong. What you're fucking trying to tell us is that, bottom line, this hole in the ground is a good place to hide a body."

Another big drag, more smoke. "Yes. Because if someone put a body down there it would decompose in no time. A month. Wouldn't leave a trace. The present layer of peat at the base is two or three feet thick. A body would sink right in and be covered. It would be hard to drag a body down the trail to the bottom, but a body could probably be rolled down from the road. It's steep where the road skims a small section of the Hollow. We had to set up a metal barrier, matter of fact. Mopeds can't make the curve at high speed."

I said, "But Fred . . . Prentiss, did you say?"

"Yes."

"If he wasn't hallucinating, he saw a body that obviously hadn't sunk in."

She didn't say anything. Joe did. "I don't want to think there's a body in the Hollow. But if there is, maybe it didn't roll all the way down. Got snagged on something. Shrubs have branches thick as my arm."

I said, "And if there is a body down there, perhaps Fred saw the person who pushed it. Witnesses make anonymous phone calls all the time."

Fitzy said, "Or maybe he's the one who rolled her down and then got to feeling proud of himself. Another motivation for all the goddamn anonymous phone calls people make."

Sad, but true enough.

Esther said, "There can't be a body. I refuse to believe it. And there is absolutely no reason for Fred Prentiss to kill anyone. Isn't that what we're saying here, that Fred might be a killer?"

I said, "No. We're not saying that. We're only saying we have to check out an anonymous phone call that might be a hoax." And I knew Joe and Fitzy were thinking what I was thinking. If we didn't have a hoax then, yes, we had a killer. If someone gave Rachel Shaw what Dana Ganzi had been given, he knew she would die. That's what Joe hadn't wanted to face up to.

"Well," Esther said, taking one more drag, "if there *is* a body and Fred *is* a killer"—she stabbed out the cigarette—"then the body is his wife's. I could kill her myself."

Time to end that conversation trend. "How far is this place from the spot where I found Dana's body?"

Joe said, "The trail into the Hollow is off Coonymus Road. Coonymus borders its steepest rim right where Esther's talking about. It happens to be very close to where you found Dana Ganzi's body."

"So it could well be the place where Dana's body was meant to end up. But the plan was interrupted."

None of us spoke. It was Fitzy who put the thought

in words, not me. "If that's the case—if there's a second dead girl—we've got more than a drug dealer here. We have a killer. He knew what happened to his earlier client."

Joe said, "I—"

"Yeah, we know. You don't want to believe it. Me neither. Ditto my boss, for sure." Fitzy turned to Esther. "You able to lead us down the trail?"

She had taken her cigarette pack out of her shirt pocket. She shook it. Nothing. "There is no choice that I can see. Let me change my shoes. We'll be walking through sludge. And I need some more smokes."

Fitzy said, "Where's your john? I got to get this cheap scotch out of my system."

"Out back."

"Out back of what?"

"Of the house."

"Jesus. Then first you can lead me there. I ain't about to fall into some dyke's cesspool. Then we'll go have a look at this Roadman Hollow."

No one corrected him.

While Joe and I waited, I whispered, "How can she not have a bathroom?"

"I've already explained that."

"Another with no land to sell?"

"That's right."

I asked, "How sludgy is the sludge going to be?"

"Not bad. We've had a great summer. No rain."

"We're all right with sneakers?"

He was distracted. "Sure."

Outside, the night was overcast, dank and dark. We all got into the ragtop. Joe and Fitzy had flashlights and Esther had brought two more, powerful ones. As we headed toward Coonymus Road, Fitzy asked her why she felt the need to light up the whole planet. The whole *goddamn* planet. She said Block Island was subject to power outages all the time. Storms tended to appear out of nowhere and thunderstorms could be fairly wild. But Fitzy hadn't been looking for an answer. He'd only meant to be sarcastic. "Esther, I don't want a meteorological report. I've got a headache. If it wasn't so damn humid around here, breathing fresh air might do me some good."

No one responded. He tried again. "This jeep makes you feel like a real he-man, right, Joe?"

Now Joe gave Fitzy what he was looking for, a little fight. Joe said, "I'd rather be a he-man than a lush."

I like my testosterone in a different format. "Listen, fellas, we're going to see if there's a dead body in Rodman's Hollow tonight. I believe a little decorum is in order."

Fitzy and Joe clammed up. Then Fitzy said, "You're right, Joe, I gotta get off the sauce."

Esther said, "I'll drink to that."

I glanced back and saw Fitzy's head turn toward her. "I'm beginning to appreciate you more and more, Esther. You sure you're a dyke?"

She blew smoke in his face. She liked him.

Joe drove the southeast rim of the island from Esther's house, up Spring Street, along the edge of the Mohegan Trail bluff, past the South Light. He turned toward the interior and in a few minutes reached Coonymus Road where it ended at Center Street by the Indian cemetery— the spot where I'd come upon Dana Ganzi's body.

Esther leaned forward between the two front seats. "This is all protected nature land."

Fitzy snorted. "Well, then, maybe we'll find a few nature lovers, in addition to Fred, who maybe saw something out of the ordinary."

Joe parked by a hand-carved sign. The local Boy

Scouts had placed it at the start of the nature trail that led, according to Esther, around the perimeter of the Hollow before it made its descent downward. The name RODMAN'S HOLLOW had been covered with extra carvings—graffiti—the usual scatological suggestions prevailing. Fitzy said, "You know what I'd like to do with these graffiti punks?" We knew he wouldn't need us to make a few suggestions. "Toss 'em down this hole."

We got out of the jeep. Esther bent down to touch the large round buds hanging off a few leafy plants at the base of the sign. She said, "I planted turk's cap lilies around the posts. Wildflowers, but they took. I knew they would. They're pretty during the day. They close at night."

When laypeople must accompany law officers to a crime scene, they tend to find a reason for hesitation. Knowing this, Fitzy showed patience and restraint. Finally, Esther stood. Flashlights switched on, we followed her between a tangle of bushes beyond the sign to the trail.

"These are chokecherries," she said. "Very fast-growing. Need to be trimmed back. We don't have to worry about briars, though. Not yet."

Fitzy said, "Tell me when to start worrying."

We'd only walked about ten yards when I told them to stop so I could shine my light on fresh footprints, two pair. "They were made tonight. Step around them where you can, Esther."

Fitzy pulled a rag out of his pocket, bent down, and covered a few of them. I said, "Fitzy, they're not the same as the ones under the girls' window."

"I know."

"You'll still have to . . ."

"I know. I will."

Esther said, "Someone was looking through . . . ?"

Fitzy turned toward her. "Not your problem, Esther." Then he said, "What the hell was that fool Fred doin' down here? I mean, if he wasn't the one who dumped this body he claims he saw."

Esther flinched. Joe said, "We can only hope he was drunk."

Esther said, "Yes. And came here to hide out. I hate to think what Doris will do to him when she finds out."

I said, "Women who are married to alcoholics tend to be fairly impatient with their husbands' behavior. Why they stayed married to them I'll never know."

"Don't get her started, Esther." Joe appreciates my easily triggered annoyance but often prefers it to lie dormant.

Once the trail had circled around the Hollow, it descended very steeply via a series of short hairpin turns. We followed it down. Sludge was the perfect word for the gravel below our feet, mixed with decaying foliage and peat. Slippery was not an exaggeration. Fitzy and I pretty much skidded along. After about ten minutes, we came to a level area ahead of us, where the trail seemed to take a straight drop, no more hairpins. The beam of Esther's flashlight disappeared down a dark green tunnel. About thirty feet below we could see another level area dotted with more shrubs. My light scanned that ledge, once, twice, and then on a third pass it touched over a white patch nearly hidden by the growth. I held the beam steady.

All of us knew the white patch was skin, even Esther. She said, "Dear God." And again she did what laypeople do. She closed her eyes and her chest heaved, but she controlled herself. She recited the Lord's Prayer. We didn't interrupt her. Then she took out her pack of cigarettes. It was going to take Esther longer to light up than to say her prayer. Her hands shook. Fitzy had to take the match-book from her hand and light the cigarette for her.

Joe looked up. "As the crow flies, the closest part of the road is right up there. That's where he pushed her down into the Hollow. But that lower ledge stopped her. Because she was so . . . so big." He knew it had to be Rachel Shaw. We all did. Then he said, "Fitzy, you've got some serious trouble."

"Yeah, I do. Esther, you want to stay here while we go down the rest of the way?"

"Yes. But listen to me. The drop to the ledge is dangerous. The trail is less than a foot wide below us. Be careful."

We made our way, kept having to grab at branches to remain on our feet. Esther called out, "Watch the briars!" Too late. Thorns stuck in the skin of our palms and ripped at our clothes. I pointed out threads that hung from them already, none from heavy canvas gloves, though. Fitzy said, "We'll let the forensics people gather those."

And then we were standing next to her. It was Rachel Shaw. I said, "This is exactly what the other girl looked like, Fitzy."

He didn't answer, only nodded.

The girl's limbs were spasmed, her head thrown back, the face contorted in a death scream. Joe's face reflected the shock I'd seen on Fitzy's just a few days earlier in front of Aggie's B&B. Same picture of shock Aggie had seen on mine when I'd stumbled through her front door. Aggie said I looked like I'd seen a ghost. Worse than a ghost, Aggie, much worse.

Rachel Shaw wasn't as naked as Dana. All the same, what clothes were left on her were in tatters. She had ripped them off, though not as completely as Dana had. Shreds of shirt were in her hands. Fitzy was looking at a sex crime even if it turned out no one had engaged in a sexual attack upon her that left evidence of such. Gave her something that so tormented her she tried to pull her clothes off. And he watched. He watched until she was dead and then he dumped her.

Joe moved his beam of light in an arc around the body and proceeded to retrace the path it had taken from up above to where we stood. We could see, clearly, the line of disturbed growth. And we could see Esther's shadow against the moonlit sky. The clouds had cleared. The end of her cigarette burned red. She was sitting on an outcrop of rock, her head in her hands. She had switched off her own flashlight.

Joe moved the beam out a few inches and formed a new arc, down the trail, around the body, and back up. He repeated his search, each time a few more inches outward.

Fitzy said, "Hold on. Go back."

The light retraced its path and stopped a few feet from the girl's head. A pair of men's sunglasses were lying there.

Fitzy started toward them.

I said, "You shouldn't disturb anything, Fitzy."

"Can't be helped."

"Let the forensic people get them."

"I know who they belong to. I'll pass them on to forensics once I've finished with them."

"Fitzy—"

His eyes met mine. "Let me do what needs doing, FBI." His eyes read, *Trust my instincts*. Okay.

He went and got the glasses and came back to us, never bothering to use a cloth to keep from smearing any prints. Instincts or otherwise, it was a good thing he didn't work for me.

Joe's light traversed the ledge and trail again. Nothing was obvious. Far below, perhaps at the very bottom of the Hollow, we all thought we could make something out. Something different from black-green nothingness. Fitzy and I aimed our flashlights too. It was pieces of cloth, what was left of Rachel's clothes. Whoever had disposed of her body had rolled up her clothes and thrown those down too.

Fitzy said, "That's a sneaker down there." We aimed all three lights. It was the toe of a sneaker. It had sunk in to the peat, almost completely swallowed up as its mate must have been. "Let's head over to Fred's house. These are his glasses. First, though, we drop off Esther; then we stop at my office and I call the Commissioner and tell him to get forensics out here pronto. And while we wait for them, Fred'll get to answer a few questions. Let's go." He started back up.

Just as Fitzy had a few moments ago, Joe looked into my eyes. He regretted ever agreeing to come to the Hollow with us. I knew that because an FBI agent worth her salt has to read minds as well as eyes. It had taken me a little longer than it normally does. Joe's mind is not easy to read.

6

While Fitzy talked to his commissioner inside, Joe and I talked too, in the ragtop parked outside the station. About what I'd seen in his expression. Joe said to me, "Here is what you're reading in my face. If we accompany Fitzy while he questions Fred, we are in on this."

"We're in on this already."

He put his hands on the steering wheel and gripped it as if he wanted to press the gas pedal to the floor and escape. He spoke to me but aimed his voice at the wheel. "Poppy, these people are family to me. I am feeling emotions here that aren't appropriate to the situation."

"Joe, it's not a conflict of interest as far as I can see, if that's what you're thinking."

After a little pause he looked at me. "Fitzy is about to go in and accuse a neighbor of mine of murder. Someone I've known a long time. If that's not a conflict of interest, what is?"

I have to watch myself when it comes to skipping

over the obvious. "I'm sorry, Joe. I guess my mind is calculating in its self-absorbed way."

"Besides that, Poppy, sometimes you forget that I don't investigate murders. It's what *you* do. What *he* does." His eyes went to Fitzy's door. "Like the man said, Fred isn't smuggling alcohol, tobacco, or firearms. I'm pretty much not interested the way you are. Besides, I don't want to believe this could be happening. I think I said that, didn't I? If that seems selfish, I don't mean it to be. And Poppy?"

"What?"

"I have a tough time understanding how you've got the stomach for it, sometimes. That's selfish, too, I know."

"Joe, you've been in gun battles."

"Not of my choosing. I never fire first. Here, I have a choice. I'm not going to be part of this."

I rested my hand ever so gently on his hard forearm, even though what I really wanted to do was reach over and shake him. And yell, too. As in: *A horrific crime has been committed. What about that dead girl? What about the other girls who aren't dead? Christen and Sam and Kate. They're in danger!*

But I didn't shake him. Fitzy and I needed him. So I lied. I said, "Listen, Joe, I understand. I do. But it won't hurt for you to come along with Fitzy tonight. You don't have to say anything, take any active part. Maybe just your being there will give Fred some reassurance. Since, as you say, you've known him a long time. He'll be more apt to be truthful if you're there. Unless, of course, he did it."

"He didn't."

Fitzy came back out.

Joe said to me, "Okay. I'll go." Good.

We drove to Fred's house.

Fred Prentiss and his family lived on High Street, the prettiest street on the island, a hilly lane of Victorian homes—steep peaked roofs trimmed with gingerbread and wide porches shaded by young sycamores. The trees were making a comeback. The houses were all neat and trim and had been converted to bed-and-breakfasts or small inns, updated, gentrified, freshly painted. All but Fred's. Joe and I had walked on this street, stopping for lunch at an inn. The yellow paint on Fred's house—same paint he'd used to expand his liquor store sign—was peeling away from a gray layer beneath, which was peeling away from a brown one. The shrubs were overgrown and the porch sagged. There were children's toys strewn across the porch as well as over the scrubby lawn, plus a few barbells. No one had bothered to put them away at the end of the day—or at the end of many days. There was a sled among them.

On the sidewalk in front of the house, Fitzy said, "Guess I don't have to tell you, Joe, the guy only makes money Memorial Day to Labor Day. And he's got a slew of kids. Maybe one of the older ones sells a mystery drug—got his hands on something really lethal that the FDA hasn't come across yet and enjoys killing people with it. Maybe Fred decided to help the kid get rid of the bodies. Who knows?"

Joe said, "I don't see it."

"Me neither. I have a real tough time imagining an imbecile like Fred turning out to be a serial killer."

Serial killer. I'm always glad when someone else says it first. What is inevitably set in motion by using that term requires a lot of personnel, a lot of time, a big chunk out of the budget. You don't want to be wrong about it because there's no going back, though at the same time you don't want to be right, the term so rings of dread. Jack the Ripper and all the rest of them to follow. They just never seem to stop coming.

I said it aloud. "Serial killer." I had to believe it in my bones. Joe remained silent. He didn't want it in his bones, and he was a man of the law. What was his problem?

It was now long after midnight, as dark on Fred's street as it had been in the Hollow. The moon and stars were covered by clouds. There are no streetlights on Block Island except at the harborside parking lot, so cars driving onto the ferry at night won't plunge into the Atlantic. We went up the porch steps, and Fitzy pulled open the screen door. The bottom was torn to shreds. Pets of the undisciplined variety. From somewhere the scent of cat urine came, an odor I'd almost come to terms with when visiting Joe in his DC apartment. Fitzy knocked on the front door. He knocked again, harder. The curtains in the living room window parted. We all saw it. But whoever parted them to get a better look at us chose not to respond to the knock. After maybe five seconds, Fitzy shouted very loudly, "Fred! You hear me? Answer the goddamned door, or I'll close down your store for selling beer to minors."

Fitzy turned to Joe and me. "Does it all the time. He sells booze on Sunday too. To me. Illegal in Rhode Island."

A light came on just inside the door. A woman opened it. Her hair was in pink plastic curlers from a forty-year-old home perm box. She had on a chenille bathrobe—the bottom edge unhemmed and ratty—short black socks, and leather slippers. She lifted her chin high and said, "State your business and get out." Doris.

Fitzy took hold of the handle on the screen door. But she'd already taken hold of the handle on her side. Fitzy

said, "My business is with your old man. Get him." Then
he yanked the screen door out of her grip and barreled
past her. Joe and I were right behind him. The woman
gaped at me—an alien entering her home—and said to
Joe, "I'm surprised at your being a part of this, Joseph."

Joe said, "Doris, I'm afraid it's pretty serious."

She humphed.

To the right was the living room. No, the parlor. The
slipcovers on the lumpy overstuffed furniture were
stretched and faded. By the window, Fred was sitting in
a chair in the dark. He'd been the one to part the curtains. His eyes glistened. Fitzy said, "You want to turn
on a light for us, Fred?"

Fred pulled the chain on the floor lamp next to him,
and a low light came on. The lampshade was pink with
yellow stains. Around the bottom of the shade, the last
remains of a fringe hung as unevenly as the hem of
Doris's robe. Fred stood up. He wore striped pajamas.
He was bent over a little so he could hold on to the arm
of the chair for support. He smiled a very weak smile,
about as weak as the lightbulb in his lamp, and asked,
"What can I do for you, Officer?" followed immediately by, "Hello, Joe." And then he smiled a little more
pathetically. At me. "Nice to see you, Patty."

Fitzy said, "Got your call earlier, Fred. Thought you
might like to elaborate on it just a touch."

Fred's wife came past us, turned, and stood as solid
as an oak tree next to her husband. "What call? Fred
has been asleep for the last several hours."

Fitzy said, "Fred, you want to ask your wife to remove herself so we can have a little talk here?"

"Doris? Honey?"

But Doris was planted firmly. Through the door at
the end of the corridor I could see the stairs to the second floor. Many children, all in pajamas, lined the ban-

ister. When they saw I'd noticed them, they scrambled up the stairs without making a sound.

Doris enjoyed giving orders. "Like I told you people before: State your business and get out."

Fitzy waved a hand, brushing her off as though she were a gnat. "Lady, go make yourself some coffee, and get your kids to bed."

"I don't want coffee. And my children *are* in bed."

"Well, I could use some. And as for your kids, they're all eavesdropping at the top of the stairs."

She stormed past him, yelling to the children that she would whip them all within an inch of their lives if they weren't in their rooms. Running footsteps pounded above us.

Fitzy held out the sunglasses for Fred to see. "These are yours, right, Fred? Seen you wearin' them."

Fred looked at the glasses in the palm of Fitzy's big hand. His gaze remained riveted for several seconds until his wife reappeared. He looked at her and then back to the glasses. He let go of the chair and stood straight, taking strength from his wife's presence. He said, "Doris, glasses like those there are a dime a dozen, aren't they?"

She said, "What in God's name are you talking about? What glasses?"

"See, Fitzy," he said. "That's what I mean. What glasses?" His voice became more firm. "I don't recognize those glasses."

Fitzy said, "I do. They're yours. I traced them to make sure. I can tell you where you bought them and when. I took prints off them, needless to say."

Fitzy could lie through his teeth without missing a beat. I was coming to admire him more and more. I watched Fred, waiting to see his reaction. Fitzy was watching him just as intently. He waited for what he knew would happen. And it did.

Fred's forehead wrinkled up like an accordion and then, slowly, his face collapsed. He put his hands to his cheeks and pressed hard. But control was lost. He burst into tears. Doris's eyes widened. Now she looked at her husband as though *he* were the alien. She said, "Fred Prentiss, what do you think you're doing?"

Fitzy said, "He's crying. Fred, sit back down and pull yourself together. Then tell me the entire story and don't leave out one single detail, understand? All I want to do is straighten this out, and then we're out of here."

Fred's body collapsed too. He pretty much fell into the chair. Fitzy gestured to Joe and me to join him on the sofa, which we did. Doris took hold of the arm of Fred's chair, steadying herself as he had while she stood guard. It was several moments before Fred gained enough composure to get any words out. Finally, when he did, he looked at his wife and came up with an explanation for the chaos surrounding him.

"Honey, she threw herself at me. There was nothing I could do."

Fitzy said, "The camp girl threw herself at you?"

"Camp girl? What camp girl? She wasn't . . ." His chin quivered. "Oh, God, not *her*. I didn't have anything to do with the *fat* girl. The fat girl was just *there*. *Lying* there. All twisted up like some . . . Like some . . . I don't know . . ." He was sobbing again. "Like someone . . . oh, God, I don't know!"

Fitzy leaned back comfortably into the sofa. He'd been leaning forward like Joe and me, but now it was time to act the part of the person who'd won the upper hand. We followed his lead.

"Now, Fred, what say we start at the beginning. Which girl threw herself at you?"

Doris's back became straight again, ramrod straight.

She let go of the chair and crossed her arms over her chest. She looked down at her husband. "There'd better be some explanation for what is going on here. A *very good* explanation. I demand to know the same thing this so-called police officer wants to know. *Who* threw herself at you?"

Fred looked up at her. He had the face of a dog who's been smacked with a rolled-up newspaper. He said, "A schoolteacher. At least that's what she said she was. Honey, I'm just a normal guy." His gaze swiftly returned to the floor.

Fitzy held fast. "A schoolteacher threw herself at you?"

"Yes. She had on this little bikini . . . I couldn't help what happened. I told you, I'm just a normal guy."

The vast majority of lawbreakers follow a pattern. First, they act shocked and appalled at an accusation, and when it dawns on them that you've got them, their faces collapse. They cry, not out of any feeling of repentance or remorse, but rather self-pity. And then, when no sympathy is forthcoming, no hope to wriggle out of their predicament, the last step is, of course, to blame the victim. In this case, a hypersexual schoolteacher in a bikini. And we hadn't even gotten to the actual victim, a teenage girl named Rachel Shaw.

Next round, Fred had to formulate a credible story. He needed time. He turned back to his wife and smiled sheepishly. "Listen, honey, I think all of us are going to need some coffee after all. Why don't you—"

"Don't you honey me, Frederick Prentiss! I make coffee for invited guests only. I am about to call my lawyer and have Joe Barnow and the officer and"—she looked specifically at me—"whoever *you* are, tossed out of my home."

She picked up the receiver from the telephone on

the table under the lamp. Fred grabbed it from her and
whimpered, "Honey—Doris . . . see, me and the officer
need to clear up a misunderstanding." He hung up the
phone gently. "We don't want to go making a mountain
out of a molehill, do we?"

Doris's face turned red. Her cheeks puffed out. She
said to her husband, "Do not *dare* to talk to me as if
I'm one of your lowlife customers. Go right ahead and
do as you please. Clear up this *misunderstanding* on
your own. But you'll be digging your own grave, you
fool!"

She went and sat on a little rocking chair in the corner that started to creak as she rocked violently back
and forth.

"I only hope I don't hear what I think I'm going to
hear."

Fitzy said, "Lady, if you want to hear it, good. But
just keep quiet and let your old man talk or I'm going
to have to arrest him and hear what he has to say at my
office in the State Police station."

Fred gripped the ends of the chair arms again, this
time to pull himself up. "Hey, Fitzy, how about a little
belt first. I got some nice twelve-year-old Scotch in—"

Fitzy held up his hand, the traffic-cop gesture again.
We all have to get our start somewhere. "Fred, don't
move. Just tell me what you know about that dead girl
halfway down Roadman Hollow."

"Rodman's."

"Whatever."

Doris flew out of the rocking chair as if stung by a
bee. She shouted, "Dead girl? There's another dead
girl? Dear Lord!"

Fitzy said, "Try to calm yourself. Things are going
to get a lot worse before they get better, trust me."

But she just stood there, horrified.

Fred said, "I should have told you, Doris. I'm sorry. I was scared. I don't know anything at all about the dead girl. Like I told the officer, she was just lying there."

"And what were you doing?" Fitzy asked him.

Fred looked at Doris. Then he shored himself up. He wanted to avoid having to answer that particular question, no matter what. "Listen, Fitzy, the only thing I did tonight is perform my civic duty as a good citizen. I found a body, and I called the police to report it just as soon as I could get to a phone."

"Forgot to identify yourself, though, didn't you? That's part of a good citizen's civic duty. Could have saved yourself a headache. Lot of embarrassment, too, taking Doris over there into consideration. So tell me, what were you *doing* when you found the dead girl?"

Fred swallowed. "Fitzy, what say I just get a little drink for myself?"

"No. I have no intention of giving you time to use your imagination while you're having yourself a pop."

Doris said, "Fred has no imagination."

Fitzy turned to her. "Ya know, lady, you're a pip. I don't need any opinion on Fred's personality." He glanced at his watch. "Fred, I want the truth and I want it by the time the little black hand on my watch gets to the twelve. That's less than thirty seconds. Go."

Joe said quietly, "Are you going to read Fred his rights?"

First Fitzy said, "Hah!" Then: "I'm not arresting him. Not unless he forces me to take him to my headquarters, like I said. Fred and I are just havin' a friendly little chat, that's it." He made a show of bringing the watch up to his eyes again, squinting. "Ten seconds left, Freddy old boy."

Joe nudged my leg. He and Fitzy were on the same wavelength. Neither wanted Fred arrested. But Joe's words had brought a new look of panic to Fred's eyes. He said to Doris, "Listen, honey, I'm real sorry. I couldn't help it if—"

Fitzy shouted, "Goddamn it, Fred! You tell me what you saw and apologize to your wife later, or I will be readin' you your rights after all. Here in your freakin' living room!"

Fred cowered. He said, "Sorry, officer." Then he cleared his throat. "All right." He took a big breath. He took a second one. He surrendered. "See, Fitzy, this here school-teacher picked me up tonight when I was coming in from doing a little fishing. Went out just after dinner. Heard the sandbar was squirmin' with flounder."

"What time?"

"Around five-thirty."

"Five-thirty? What the hell time do you eat dinner?"

"Five."

"Jesus. Go ahead."

"I came in from fishing—this was around eight— and it was almost dark and she was out there swimming in her little bikini and she . . . she picked me up."

"Exactly where?"

"By the dock in the harbor."

"She was swimming."

"Yes."

"When it was almost dark? By the *dock*? Great. Now let me be sure I've got this straight. We've got a schoolteacher who likes to swim around docks—at *night*—bumping into boats and breathing gas fumes. Schoolteachers pretty dumb these days, I take it?"

"I mean she'd *been* swimming. She—"

"Okay, she'd *been* swimming. And now you're going to tell me she was walking *on* the dock as opposed to swimming *around* the dock, right? In a little bikini."

"Yes."

"Kind of chilly at that hour."

"Well, she wasn't exactly *wearing* the bikini, she was carrying it in a towel. Like I said, she'd been swimming and—"

"Fred?"

"What?"

"Tell me how this scenario grabs you. You were out lookin' for a little adventure, a little fun, and some horny schoolteacher with nothing better to do lets you pick her up."

Fred didn't say anything. The only sound was Doris's breathing.

"Okay, Fred, we got that. Now tell me the rest of the story, and if you change a single detail I'm going to take out my weapon and *blow your freakin' head off*."

Fred's face lost all its color. He said, "Okay, okay. This is what happened. This is the straight truth. This is it. The schoolteacher got in my truck and we went to have a little harmless . . . fun."

"You didn't take her to a hotel."

"No. I didn't want anyone to see us."

"You did it in the *truck*?"

"No, we drove to Rodman's Hollow."

"Fred, you're telling me this schoolteacher agreed to have sex in a swamp? Maybe schoolteachers *are* a lot dumber these days."

"The Hollow isn't a swamp. And I have a big sleeping bag. I carried it down into the Hollow. We spread it out on a ledge."

Doris made a small sound.

Fitzy said, "Don't stop now, Fred, whatever you do. Who saw the dead girl first?"

"What?"

"Who saw the body first, you or the schoolteacher?"

"Uh . . . the schoolteacher. She screamed."

"Then you saw the body?"

"Yes."

"What did you do?"

"Do? I ran. I got the hell out of there." He looked up at Doris. "See, honey? We didn't even get to . . . we never had the chance . . ."

Fitzy said, "Still counts, Fred. Tough. Work it out with Doris later. So didn't you first try to see if you could do something for the girl?"

"Do something? The girl was dead. Real dead. Never saw anyone so dead in my life. If she was alive, she could have been in a freak show. Don't know how she got to be so discombobulated."

"And what about the schoolteacher?"

"She ran too."

"Did you touch the body?"

"Are you kidding? At first, I wasn't even sure it *was* a body. At first I thought I was just seeing a head. Like a dummy's head. I was lying two or three feet away. Then I saw the rest of her. All I knew was, I wanted out of there."

"That's when you dropped the glasses."

"Yeah. Musta been."

"Okay, Fred, the name of the schoolteacher?"

"I never asked."

"Not a local woman, I take it."

Fred said to Doris, "That's something I'd never do to you, honey."

Doris's lips had been pressed together. She unpressed them. "*You will pay for this, Fred Prentiss.* You'll soon find out what's it's like to live out on the sidewalk in a *cardboard box*."

Fitzy said, "Fred, tell me where was this schoolteacher staying."

"I don't know."

Suddenly, Fitzy stood up. "Find out. Ask around. I ain't got the time to go checking every fleabag hotel on this blasted island. See me tomorrow by noon with the answer." Fitzy came up from around the table and stood in the middle of the living room floor. "Now, Fred. I believe you. But I'm going to need all the information I can get. Whoever did to that girl whatever it was that killed her, he knew it would kill her. He knew it because he'd done it already. He murdered the first girl, and he murdered this one too. So we've got to find him before another innocent kid ends up dead at the bottom of Rodman's Hollow. Maybe the killer's real skinny. Maybe he hates fat people. Whatever. I want you to do some real thinking about that while you're finding out which hotel the schoolteacher's staying in. Get it?"

"Yes."

"Good."

There was one question to be asked, and so I asked it. "Fred, did you see anyone on the road on your way to the Hollow? Or on the way back? A car you recognized? A truck?"

Doris answered me instead. "If he did see anyone, it wouldn't have been anyone he knew. People who live here are decent. We go to bed at a decent hour. Somebody from off the island is who you're looking for. Not one of us. Isn't that right, Joseph?"

Joe said, "I'm afraid I don't know, Doris."

"Well, then, I'm surprised you don't."

Fred looked at me. "Ma'am, there was nobody on the road to the Hollow. Not comin' or goin'."

We left to the sound of children's footsteps scurrying back to their beds again.

In the ragtop, I said to Fitzy, "Did you really know those sunglasses were Fred's?"

" 'Course not. Didn't you hear him? They're a dime a dozen."

From Fred's, Fitzy said to go directly to the airstrip. Joe attempted to beg off but Fitzy told him he wouldn't be able to fit everyone in his car. He needed Joe's jeep too. We'd have to go up in two cars. So Joe agreed. Our timing was perfect. A small plane with RHODE ISLAND STATE POLICE printed on its side was just landing.

The commissioner had accompanied the team. His name was Robbie Brown. Fitzy formally introduced us, and while he exchanged a few "How are ya's" with the others, Commissioner Brown whispered to me, "Thank God you people are here. Fitzy's a good man. *Was* a good man. He's a friend of mine, besides. But—" He stopped and shrugged.

A state police commissioner is seldom a former cop. It's a political patronage job. But Commissioner Brown had indeed been a cop. Fitzy told us that on the way to the airstrip. There had been so much corruption in Rhode Island, a study of the State Police organization determined that an experienced and upstanding law officer needed to be in charge, even if he was expected to answer to the governor first and foremost. So ever since Robbie Brown was appointed, whenever there'd been a suspicious death, he took it upon himself to be a physical part of the investigative team. Fitzy said there were only about eight or nine homicides a year in Rhode Island. "Used to be fifty. Then the Mafia lost its grip on New England and we didn't have any more ginzos from one family whacking ginzos from another family."

I had learned a new ethnic slur.

Robbie Brown talked about that same issue once

Fitzy finished catching up with the team. He was a big man, and he threw his arm across Fitzy's shoulders. "Fitzy here is the reason the Mafia got cleaned out of Rhode Island. He was our bulldog, and it's nothing short of a miracle he's alive. He'll always be my main man."

Fitzy said, "Yeah, right. Put me where I can't cause any trouble, and son-of-a-gun, now look what you've got."

Robbie Brown ignored him. "Now correct me if I'm wrong, Agent Rice, but I do believe you're the lady who cleaned up the crime lab in DC, aren't you?"

I'm not modest. "Yes."

Then he said to Fitzy, "We've got the best investigator in the country here with us, even if it is some kind of pro bono work."

Fitzy said, "And you've got the reluctant ATF. Imagine that."

Joe reiterated. "Homicide isn't my line of work. I'm just the chauffeur."

Robbie Brown said, "Who said anything about homicide?"

Fitzy: "Me."

"Fitzy, you're not a grand jury." He turned his attention to Joe and me. "You two are vacationing?"

"Yes."

Fitzy said, "Joe owns a house here. Comes every summer."

Robbie Brown said, "Too bad you're reluctant, then. Your take, reluctant or not, would be valuable."

"I'm not sure of my take."

The commissioner ignored that, introduced us to his detective, to a pathologist from the coroner's office, to a forensic photographer, and, finally, to two troopers.

We took the commissioner and the detective with

us; the others piled into Fitzy's car. Joe said, "Sorry about all the junk in the car, Commissioner. Like Fitzy said, I'm on vacation."

The commissioner said, "Call me Robbie."

But we noticed Robbie called the detective *Detective*, and so did we.

At the entrance to Rodman's Hollow, the troopers got out their yellow tape and closed off the trail at the road. Fitzy put a light on the roof of his car and the blue dome sent off its persistent flashing signal. Fitzy told them, "The problem is, this'll attract the entire island."

The commissioner said, "Good. I want a strong buzz going. I want this fully in my jurisdiction. If we've got some slimeball selling tainted stuff to the kids out here and it's killed two of them, I think the governor is going to forget the story about the drugs coming from Connecticut. But we wait before we make any judgment, got it? First we determine if it's manslaughter; then we go from there."

Fitzy caught my glance at him. His look was vindictive, I'd have to say.

Each member of the team had a powerful flashlight, and the pathologist carried a large portable spot. We weren't far into our slipping, gravelly skid down the trail when the photographer said, "How the hell are we going to get the deceased out of here? Can we squeeze a stretcher through all this growth?"

Fitzy said, "You're going to need a helicopter. Even if we could balance a stretcher, the deceased weighs too much to bring her up that trail."

Robbie said, "Why didn't you ask for a helicopter when you had me on the phone?"

"Figured you'd think I was exaggerating."

"I wouldn't have. I had a look at the pictures of the first victim before we left."

Fitzy said, "You've got a phone on you, sir. You can get the helicopter."

"Don't call me sir. You're my friend. Call me sir in front of the troopers, that's all. I'll see the body first and then I'll call. We'll have plenty to do while the copter makes its way over here."

He didn't trust Fitzy. He'd still wait to see for himself. And I caught Fitzy's eye again.

Robbie Brown flipped open his cell phone about two seconds after the detective's light passed over Rachel Shaw's body. While he ordered the helicopter, Fitzy helped the photographer set up the big light. Robbie said, "Anyone identify the body yet, Fitz?"

"No. But we're pretty sure we know who it is. You'll have to get a family member once you've got her in Providence. I've got her address and phone number in my office."

The pathologist bent over the body and pressed his fingertips to Rachel Shaw's thigh and then her shoulder. He said, "Rigor is fully set in. We'll never untangle her."

I told him her condition was cadaveric contractions. I said, "Time of death is so important, isn't it?"

He pressed other areas of the vast field of flesh, her knees, her shoulders, her ankles. "Joints are locked. Yes. Cadaveric contractions. First time I've seen such a phenomenon. I thank you, Agent."

The detective was gazing at the growth to our left, a mass of shrubs and saplings clinging to a rocky incline. The vegetation was crushed. "She was rolled down from up there. What's up there?"

Fitzy said, "The road."

"We're going to have to determine just where on the road and block it off, too."

Joe volunteered. "I'll go do that."

The commissioner looked at him. "Appreciate it. We're obviously shorthanded here."

The detective began putting markers around the body at spots where he felt something was present extraneous to the vegetation—mostly strands of Rachel's hair and pieces of snagged skin. And fibers from Rachel's clothes. Probably from Fred and his teacher friend's clothes, too. Rachel's skin was covered with scratches.

Fitzy knelt by the body. "Detective, I want you to look good at the face of the deceased. This girl died exactly like the last one did, experiencing some kind of terrible suffering. This is not the face of fright, is it? Seen plenty of those. You have too, haven't you, Doc?"

The pathologist said quietly, "Yes. Your words are my thoughts exactly. It's as if she died because her body could no longer bear the suffering it was subjected to. If she was having some kind of seizure when her eardrums ruptured—and her right eardrum is ruptured, can't get to the left but I suspect it's the same— all such an injury would elicit is a very serious earache. It certainly wouldn't kill her. So now we have two victims exhibiting similarities besides the nudity and the spasms, something very significant—broken eardrums. She and the other girl suffered some sort of intense trauma. We have all we need for a full-fledged investigation into wrongful death."

I said, "I didn't know the other girl's eardrums were ruptured."

"Probably didn't make it into the report. And besides that, both girls have shreds of cloth stuffed deep in their ears. Some kids stuff cotton in their ears when they're listening to loud music. But the music doesn't break their eardrums or no kid would have intact eardrums today."

Fitzy said, "Well, I'm glad to know that, since the

last place the other girl was seen was in one of the clubs, listening to music. Maybe she had her head up against the amplifier. Can't find a single person who saw her leave the place, though. Workin' on it. And I can't tell you, Poppy, how many things don't make their way into reports."

Robbie said, "Fitzy, you only saw the preliminary report. We're finishing up now. We're trying to clean up, too. You know we are. But we won't meet your standards"—he looked to me—"or this lady's, for a while. Listen, I'd made a decision with the last girl to begin a full-fledged homicide investigation—just so my friend Fitzy here knows—but I was overruled. And now this fine woman from the FBI knows that too. This time, believe me, I will not be overruled by some asshole politician, believe me."

Fitzy said, "You like your job, Commish. Don't go making any promises you can't keep."

"I keep all the promises I make."

The pathologist said, looking at me, "I can't imagine what the connection is here. A spastic body and broken eardrums. But I am relieved to know that we now have just about the best person around to find out what the connection is. To find out in a hurry. You'll do that favor for us, Agent Rice, you and that lab of yours. Cut some red tape?"

"I already told Fitzy I would. But my technicians will need to be in on the autopsy this time. So they'll have a report of their own with nothing left out."

Robbie said, "Have them send us whoever you want, then. I'll put in my formal request for FBI assistance. Even though we don't meet the criteria here."

He was talking the usual—mail fraud.

"Consider it met," I said to him. "You have sure-fire criteria. We've got a sociopath, one who officially fits the definition of a serial killer. All our psychological profilers will be involved. And they'll start tomorrow."

The detective's sigh was loud. "Serial killer."

"Damnation." The commissioner didn't want to hear it either.

I looked down at the remains of Rachel Shaw. What fury did the killer harbor that he would take a young girl's life? This was so far beyond a sex crime. He had perpetrated a cruel and inhumane brutality upon her. What motivated him? What made him choose these overweight teenagers?

I said it aloud, I couldn't help it. "What the hell did he do to them?"

None of the men answered. They had no idea.

The pathologist said, "The girls at the camp need to be taken off the island immediately. But when there aren't any more fat girls at his convenience, who is this maniac going to settle for?"

We all knew the answer to that. Fitzy gave it just the same. "He'll move on. He'll start killing overweight girls in Florida or California."

I remembered Joe's words about the nouveau riche of Block Island—where they went in cold weather.

Fitzy had more to say. "Man, isn't it a shame that psychopaths always look like your brother, or the guy next door, or the fella who owns the local liquor store?"

We all knew what made it so hard to find them. They don't look like ogres, they look like ordinary people— like Fred Prentiss. And besides that, they get better at it each time, enjoy it more, revel in the power of continually eluding the police. After five victims or so, they leave calling cards, taunting us: *Catch me if you can, you dumbbells*. There would be no calling cards under my watch. I would get him before five.

It was to be a long night. Guiding the helicopter required reinforcements from a special Coast Guard team, with the equipment and know-how necessary to lift a struggling, drowning victim from thirty-foot seas. Up on the road, the two guardsmen who emerged from their helicopter said, "We can handle this thing. Not a problem." None of us said, You might have a problem; we just thought it. Let them figure out how to do their job.

Once they were down in the Hollow, the young men were horrified. They could barely look at the body, let alone prepare it for the lift.

The basket they carried was piled with blankets. I said to the commissioner that we could cover her now that all the necessary samples had been taken, the camera put away. "I think that would make it simpler." He agreed and so did the man from the coroner's office. So they took one of the blankets from the basket and did just that. Then the Coast Guardsmen wrapped and bundled Rachel Shaw as if she had hypothermia and tied her into the basket. After the guardsman in command gave the signal to lift the body, after she had disappeared into the belly of the helicopter, he apologized to us before he had himself hoisted up.

Fitzy said, "For what?"

"For my lack of professionalism. When I first saw her." He didn't have to make any apology. We had all observed him in the final stages of securing the body. He was very gentle with Rachel Shaw, took care not to jostle her any more than was necessary. Just before she went up, he patted the basket. He wasn't that much older than she was. I wondered if she'd ever experienced a gentle pat when she was alive.

Later, at dawn, we gathered at the airport to see the police team off. It was then that Fitzy chose to confess.

"Commish, I found a piece of evidence when we first got to the body last night. I withheld it."

Robbie Brown shut his eyes for just a moment. Then, "Why am I not surprised? Fitzy, for Christ's sake. Tell me first what the evidence is and then why you saw fit to withhold it till now."

"Pair of glasses. Belonged to the guy who discovered the body. Dropped out of his pocket. They're in my office. I'll send 'em to you right away."

"You don't intend to file a report, do you? That's why you've decided to tell me this, isn't it?"

"Right."

"I take it you questioned the guy."

"Yes."

"Then at least tell me what he was doing there in the first place."

"He and an unidentified woman were about to have sex a few yards from the body when he made the discovery. All the threads you people found are probably from his clothes and his guest's. Clothes they grabbed when they ran back up the trail. That's probably when the glasses fell out, when he picked up his shirt."

"Jesus, Fitzy."

"You can arrest him. But he didn't do it. See that he has his lawyer present and just question him as a material witness. Meanwhile, I'm going to find that lady." He looked at his watch. "In about two hours, she'll be on the seven A.M. ferry, first ferry out. Last night, she decided to have a tumble with the guy who lost his glasses. So she'd missed the final ferry run, and that probably influenced her decision. The tumble was a good decision. For us. We might never have found the victim if she hadn't been the tumbling type. You can go after the woman too, as soon as I question her and let you know where she calls home."

The plane took off. Speaking of reports, I would file one on this night, an official request to my director with the term *serial killer* prominently displayed. Fitzy's superiors had given up on getting him to do anything he chose not to do; my director knew what to expect from me.

7

At a quarter to seven in the morning, Fitzy and I went down to the dock to board the first ferry. Joe begged off, said he had a flurry of messages from his office he had to see to; a big drug shipment had been confiscated from a container ship in the Gulf of Mexico off the Texas coast. Told me he'd meet us later at Richard's Patio. Okay.

Fitzy was in uniform. That, and my flashing my FBI badge under the harbormaster's nose brought the ferry captain hustling out onto the dock to see what the problem might be.

Fitzy said to him, "I'll be escorting a passenger from your boat shortly. So don't sail till we're off again. We shouldn't hold you up past your scheduled departure."

Boat people are laid back, even ferry captains responsible for moving three hundred passengers and a hold full of vehicles including, in this morning's voyage, a stretch limo. Newlyweds were honeymooning at one of the inns. "Not to worry, officer," the captain said. "I can make up time lost if I have to. No problem. But . . . uh . . . you going to have to draw a weapon?"

"Wouldn't think so."

"Last time I had a cop come aboard, that's what he did. He must've been undercover. Only problem came when a dozen passengers drew theirs. Thought the cop was going to pass out, had to explain to everyone the guy wasn't a terrorist."

Fitzy said to me, "That would be my predecessor. He never wore his uniform." To the captain, "I doubt my perp is going to put up any fuss."

"Glad to hear it."

We followed him on board. Fitzy said, "We'll start topside. Doubt she'd be in the closed deck. Be needing some wind in her face is my bet."

We climbed the stairway and went through the door onto the deck. We made a visual sweep across the faces of the passengers standing at the rail or sitting on four rows of long benches running port to bow. I'd say Fitzy and I saw her at the same time, since he nudged me the second I decided it had to be her. She was hunkered down on the far end of the back bench. She had on shorts and a tank top, a sweatshirt thrown over her shoulders— protection against the early offshore breeze. Not too different from the rest of her fellow tourists, but we couldn't miss the scratches on her arms and legs. Her eyes were red and she was puffing away on a cigarette behind a large floppy hat she'd held up to her face in deference to the NO SMOKING signs. Like us, she hadn't gotten any sleep.

Fitzy planted himself in front of her. She looked up. It took a moment for her to register that her imagined worst-case scenario was about to be played out. Fitzy let it sink in and then he said, "Frankly, ma'am, I'm going to have to ask you some questions, aren't I?"

She snuffed out the cigarette under her foot and stood up. "Frankly, I didn't think that pea brain would have had the guts to call you."

"And why didn't *you* call me?"

"I was going to. Once I was home. First I wanted to extricate myself from this nightmare."

"Would have made that call anonymously, I take it."

"Of course. Do I look like some kind of idiot?" Her gaze turned to me. "Don't tell me I'm going to be searched."

I said, "No."

A little smile came to Fitzy's face. But he didn't say what he was thinking. He would be a professional cop and stifle his personality. He said to the woman, "Just come along and you can talk with me in my office."

"And then I can go?"

"Then you can go. But a detective will meet you when the ferry docks at Point Judith."

She breathed in, her shoulders went up, and she said, "Fuck."

Fitzy said, "Fuck is right."

In Fitzy's office, she added nothing of substance, only confirmed everything Fred had claimed. She'd been bored, Fred had hit on her, and she figured, What the hell. Yes, she did see a few cars go by, two or three, leaving the harbor just at the time she and Fred had left. "The headlights anyway." But she saw none, not a single car, on Coonymus Road, not on the way to the Hollow and not on the way back either. She added, "We were going about ninety miles an hour afterward—on our way back into town—but I know I didn't see another car then because we'd probably have plowed into it. The guy was crazed. He may have great pecs, but let me tell you he was scared shitless." She added one more detail, which also wasn't much use. "When he spotted the body down there, this character just grabbed his stuff and took off. I didn't know what he was doing. I'm yelling at him, *What's the matter with you?* but he's gone, and then when I went to pick up my stuff I saw it too. The body."

"You made sure to gather up everything."

"Thought so. By the time I got out of there, reached the road, Fred—I think that's his name—was already in his truck. Basically, banging his head against the steering wheel. Son of a bitch was going to take off and leave me there, except he couldn't find his keys. They'd fallen out of his pocket. Then he actually asked me to go back down with him and help him find them. I told him to go fuck himself. So he left and came right back. They were on the trail. He didn't have to go all the way down there again." She shivered in the hot cramped office.

Fitzy said, "Too bad. Might have found his glasses."

"What?"

"Never mind. Have you still got the clothes you had on?" He looked down toward her overnight bag.

"Sure. And they're damned dirty."

"The detective who meets you will want them. To eliminate any fibers that weren't hers—or her killer's."

"Killer?"

"That's right."

"You're kidding. Isn't it more like her fault? For taking whatever it was that did that to her?"

"Maybe she didn't take anything."

"Jesus. Then what the hell happened to her?"

"We intend to find out. And of course, like I said, we also intend to find out the identity of her killer."

I asked her, just to cover another base, "Did Fred offer you any drugs?"

"Yeah, right. I'm the one offered *him* a joint. Looked

at me like I had two heads. Said he didn't smoke funny cigarettes. Asshole. Figured the guy might offer me dinner in return. I'm one of the poorest judges of character I know."

Fitzy said, "Are you aware it is illegal to possess marijuana?"

"Yeah, I am. But you've got bigger fish to fry, haven't you?"

"I sure do."

"Besides, I smoked it all last night anyway. You won't find any on me."

The last question he asked her was, "What do you teach?"

She said, "Second grade."

Fitzy held his forehead. "What hope is there, Poppy? Tell me."

I said, "I do wonder sometimes." Then I told him to meet me in half an hour for breakfast at Richard's Patio. In the meantime, I'd go up to the camp and tell Irwin and the girls about Rachel.

Fitzy went off to put the woman on the nine o'clock ferry.

The girls were already getting the news when I arrived. From Irwin. They were in the dining hall and had just finished their yogurt and bowls of canned peaches. They knew the worst already. They were still and quiet, a few in tears. I stood at the door, listening.

Irwin had added a safari hat to his Palm Beach suit outfit. He stood behind a table as if it were a podium, a hand grasping each side. "I know you girls are of the belief that the two deceased campers were not under the influence of drugs. That someone deliberately kidnapped and hurt them. But we must not be in denial.

They bought or were given an illegal substance that they took of their own free will, and their lives were ended. You will therefore be confined to the campground except for nature hikes together. There will be no more trips into town, and I have hired a guard, someone to see that no one leaves on her own. I will be calling all your parents shortly. Hopefully, once I explain the situation to them, they will not insist you return home. I will leave that decision to them. When they understand I've confirmed that the rest of you are not foolish enough to go out asking for trouble, I know they will—"

Protests rose. They tried to defend the two dead campers. But the girls were scared, their protests weak. Irwin became stern, hushed them up. "Enough of that. Face the truth. And face this. I will confiscate whatever phone you are managing to make calls from. If I find it, the owner will be confined to her house.

"Camp Guinevere will ride this out. You are all here for your own good. It is my job to make you understand, to make your parents understand, that you arrived here incapable of disciplining yourselves. Sloth and overindulgence can be conquered through discipline. I hope that by forcing discipline upon you, you will come to accept discipline as the only road to your recovery.

"Now, if the counselors will serve tea."

He went out the back door so I circled the building to meet him.

He got right in my face. "On your own today? I take it the cop is hung over."

I said, "Where's the guard? No one stopped me when I came in."

"He won't be on duty during the day. Hardly necessary. He'll be here tonight after dinner. It's at night when the girls tend to sneak into town. He'll see they don't."

I said, "Wait a minute. His job should be to protect *them*, not—"

"Exactly. To protect them. My staff and I will keep the girls under wraps during the day and he at night. Group activities every day with everyone participating, no exceptions."

"The parents didn't pay the full tuition in advance, did they?"

"Actually, I was surprised at the number who agreed to do just that. But no, a minority will have their final payment in by the first of August. I will keep this camp operating through then, rest assured. And I happen to know there is nothing you can do about it. I know the regulations for my enterprise as set forth by the State of Rhode Island."

He had me. He had Fitzy. He had almost all of the two dozen sets of parents who had already footed the bill. He had us all.

I said, with great conviction, "If I see one girl in town, you're closed down."

"You won't." Then he flashed a look of charm. "I understand your misgivings completely. It seems cruel, our method here. But if you've ever seen a dog trainer teach a dog to heel, you know the technique is to be commanding and to jerk the dog's leash suddenly and hard. A dog has limited intelligence and a choke chain is required to train him. These girls have a problem because they've been spoiled all their lives. No more coddling. Our treatment here will not hurt them, but a choke chain is in order."

And he walked off to his Quonset hut.

The campers were coming out of the dining hall. Christen and Samantha spotted me, and the girls from

Lancelot rushed over, Kate stumbling along, Elijah Leonard's face buried in her shoulder.

I told them I was sorry about Rachel. I couldn't say much more because Kate was wailing. "If only I'd ratted on her!"

I put my arm around her. "She still would have managed to find a way to leave."

She was crying hard, shaking. "Rachel was tortured to death."

"No, she wasn't. She took something that was very dangerous and she died from it."

I hugged her and Kate wept into my shoulder just as Elijah Leonard wept into hers. Kate wasn't the only one in tears. Even Christen seemed on the verge. She said, "You have to be the one to call our parents, Poppy."

The redhead Joe and I had met at the camp two nights ago stepped forward. "My parents sure as hell will listen to the FBI."

"I intend to. Christen, if you can get to Irwin's phone line, e-mail me a list of all your names, your parents' names, and your phone numbers. The rest of you girls help her put the list together."

They wiped their cheeks. They stood a little taller. They had something productive to do. Kate dried Elijah Leonard's face with the corner of her T-shirt. She said, "But why? How come Dr. Irwin hates us?"

"He doesn't hate you. He loves to acquire money by scheming. Instead of working for it."

Christen said, "The downside of capitalism. Sounds like my father. Except Dad is a lot more subtle."

The bravado was back again.

I stopped at Joe's cottage before I went on to town. He was on the phone behind a closed door. There was a fax from my director. It read GET THE BASTARD. He'd obviously heard from Auerbach.

I ran into Fitzy just as he was heading around behind the grocery toward the Patio. He said, "They don't like me in this place. They'll like me more now, though. That's because they like Fred Prentiss so much less. How are the girls?"

"They're shocked and they're upset. But Irwin means to see that they stay. He's determined. Most of the parents have already paid the balance of the tuitions. Christen's going to try to e-mail me the girls' phone numbers and addresses. I'm calling their parents."

"I should just go up there and shoot the motherfucker. That'd close down the camp."

Everyone was inside the Patio except Esther. She was usually the first one there, the first to leave. Aggie was at a table. She said, "Hey, Poppy, where's our Joe?"

"On his way. Had some catching up to do."

"Well, my place is cleared out. Rumors are flying now. Fred's kids told everyone what happened last night. Guests went to town, got money wired to them, jumped on the ferry. Just as glad for that, have to say. Gives me a little rest. Not that I have catching up to do. Not like Joe."

Billy said, "Wish I could've seen it. That nitwit Fred in handcuffs."

I said, "I don't think there were any handcuffs, Billy. He wasn't arrested."

Mick said, "Billy, I keep tellin' ya, Fred ain't no drug dealer. You know that."

"Still needs some comeuppance, that boy. Takin' some gal down into the Hollow like that. Man is nuts. Would still like to've seen it. Even without the handcuffs."

Willa said, "Fred gets plenty of comeuppance every minute he puts in with Doris. Now there'll be nothin' *but* comeuppance over there. He is about to become more miserable than he is already. Poppy's right. Doris says he was brought in as a material witness, that's all."

Fitzy and I sat down just as Joe arrived. "Find the schoolteacher?"

"Found her."

"Good."

Billy craned her neck toward us. "Was she a looker?"

Fitzy said, "Mind your business, old man."

The phone rang, and Willa jumped off her stool. Ernie said, "I got it," but she beat him there and picked it up.

The ringing agitated Jake. Tommy scolded, "Never mind about that, Jake," but Jake put his hands over his ears and wasn't about to bring them down again.

Joe bent his head to me. "Jake's overly sensitive to touch, to smell, but especially to noise. I don't remember the phone ever bothering him, though. Guy gets worse instead of better."

Willa said into the phone, "No kidding? Well, now we got some trouble, don't we?"

She hung up and made an announcement. "Someone from CBS is here, and a couple of local channels too. All kinds of cameras and stuff. Bad publicity."

Her husband said, "Any publicity is good publicity, is what people say."

The taxi brothers stood up. One had his keys out already. "If any TV people came in a boat, they're sure as hell goin' to need us. Maybe we got Dan Rather here."

Jim Lane's kid gathered together his paraphernalia. "They'll interview me. I'm local."

Billy said, "Sure. Me and Mick too. After all, we're Fred's friends."

Mick said, "We are not."

"But, see, that's what we'll tell 'em."

They left and Aggie went with them, smoothing her flowered polyester folds and flounces.

Fitzy said, "I'm the one they'll want to talk to. But they'll never find me back in this place, that's for sure."

Ernie asked Willa if she'd mind if he went down to the harbor.

"Go ahead. Tommy and Jake are all set. I got no one to feed now except Joe and company. Meet you in the store later. Tonight, I'll get to see all our stars on the TV." But she scolded Ernie as he was going out the door. "Ernie, I told you not to set that phone ringer so loud."

"It ain't that loud, Willa. Any lower and I can't hear the phone when the bacon is sizzling."

"Then clean your ears." She turned to Tommy and Jake. "Now, Jake, look at what Willa's doing. I'm turning down my phone ringer. Keep it real soft."

Jake didn't look up at her but he whispered, "Soft."

It turned out, the media—Dan Rather not among them, just a reporter and a camera guy from the CBS affiliate in Providence—were under the impression that Fred had been arrested for selling lethal drugs that killed two girls from out of state. When Ernie told them Fred was only invited to Providence for some questions because he was the one who found the second body, they headed out to see if there was someone they could interview at Fred's house. According to the taxi brothers, when the cameras arrived at Doris Prentiss's door, she threatened to throw a pot of boiling water at them if they didn't get off her porch. "They believed her, too. Might have been because she was holding a great big pot, steam comin' out the top."

Then the TV people returned to the harbor and found the coffee shop regulars standing around the dock. Mick told them Fred was not a native Block

Islander but rather a well-meaning damn fool. That he discovered a body, reported it, and was now in trouble because he forgot to identify himself when he made the phone call. The producer's face fell. Then Billy told them about the schoolteacher. That perked them up. They hastened to their boat so they could get back to the mainland and harass her.

I said, "Why didn't they go up to the camp? Expose it?"

"They didn't even know the girl was from the camp. Figured she was just another day-tripper. And her identity's not out yet either. Still haven't tracked down the parents. The TV folks only know a second teenager OD'd on the Block."

While the gang was out posing for the cameras, Willa made us French toast. Fitzy said, "Not bad. Only burned on the one side."

She was unfazed. "I try to remember to burn yours on both sides. You got lucky."

I said to Joe, "Did you get done what you had to get done?"

"Not quite. There were illegals on the freighter, couple dozen of them. Most were dead, some only half dead. Captain knew nothing about the two tons of cocaine or the smuggled aliens. What else is new?"

While we ate, I told them our first priority was to get the girls off the island, which is what I intended to do as soon as Christen e-mailed me.

Fitzy said, "I'm workin' on that myself. The only other way to get the girls off this island is to get the camp closed. Social welfare department will have to take charge then, tell the parents they've got no choice but to get their girls home. I intend to see that happens before the day is out. Soon as you have that list,

Poppy, I'll have a copy. We'll go at the parents from two very strong fronts."

The coffee-shop door opened; the bell gave a little muffled tinkle. Doris stood there. She scanned the room until her gaze fell on Joe. She said to him, "I need a favor."

"What can I do for you, Doris?" Joe's tone reflected some sort of devil-may-care attitude, as if there weren't a thing wrong.

"Fred has been released. I hope you don't mind flying over to Providence to get him. He's got five dollars in his pocket and I never let him have any credit cards."

Joe told her that would be fine. Fitzy said, "And I need to hitch a ride with you, Joe. I should speak to a few people in person. *Threaten* a few people in person. I'll call you from there, Poppy. You can fax me the numbers."

I told Joe I'd keep busy, bike down to Esther's, and finally buy the presents I wanted to take back home. Shopping instead of thinking even if my heart wouldn't be in it. Then see if the girls had sent me my e-mail. This time Joe wasn't concerned with how I'd entertain myself while he was flying to Providence. He was about as removed from me as he could get without being on the moon. I gave him the jeep keys.

Before Doris left the Patio she said to Tommy, "Constable, I've seen your boy wandering late at night. Get him on a curfew." With that she was gone without bothering to say thank you to Joe.

"I do my best," Tommy said, to no one in particular.

The bike was outside next to the doghouse. Fortunately, Pal wasn't guarding it very well, finding it sufficient just to growl at me a little more loudly than usual. I pedaled to Esther's. She had an easel set up on the porch. She was sketching something on a canvas with a pencil. She looked up. I got off the bike. "Hi, Esther. I'm disturbing you, right?"

"Right. What do you need this time?"

I pushed down the kickstand and set my bike up. I said, "Thought I could find something to hang on my walls back home. They've been empty ever since I moved to Washington. In the mood to show me what's for sale?"

She waved me to the screen door and I went in. "Go on into the living room. The bin is in the corner. There's maybe twenty-five things in it I'm selling. I'll be with you in a minute."

Once inside, I felt free to put on all lights available. Her house was entirely overhung with heavy, overgrown shrubs. The branches lay all across the roof. I'd noticed the condition of the roof shingles—dark with mold and gummy with sap. I had no idea how she could paint with so little light. She couldn't very well paint out on the porch in winter. Then I looked around at the paintings. She'd either done them from memory or maybe she did do her work in the half-dark.

Esther painted seascapes—bleak, mean seascapes— deep troughs of black ocean between climbing, menacing, swollen swells. All the paintings were of the sea before, during, and after storms. The skies were the same color as the water, and the two met in sprays of foam and rain and wind. She could paint wind; I could see it. The waves were roiling, sexual; they sprang out of the canvas. All were empty of any sign of life. And that last is what I said to her when I felt her behind me.

She said, "I wanted to show the death and destruction that lies beneath our waters while depicting just the sea's surface. I want people to look at the painting and imagine what's down there. See the ribs of crushed ships, the bones of the drowned sailors." She looked from the painting to me. "How nice that I'm obviously getting there."

"You're beyond getting there, Esther. I'm feeling just what you're saying. Was Joe right when he said you wouldn't sell your paintings?"

"He was. I'll sell them if I get there."

"I like them."

"They're better than my last batch. Still, I'm not there yet." She walked to the large bin in the corner. "Here's what keeps me off welfare. You're welcome to go through this stuff."

The bin was six feet long and ran against most of the wall. It was made of used plywood, as were the dividers jammed inside. She'd framed old maps and charts, ancient newspaper and magazine articles, bits and pieces of obscure historical events. The pieces were both large and small, and there was a collection of framed poems, or what looked like stanzas from poems, just three-by-four inches or so. Joe had described the frames she'd made as lovely. I told her they were just that.

"I have a trusty little router. I enjoy sanding the wood, staining it. Mindless work."

I flipped through the bin, but I was most taken with the poetry in the tiny frames that I could hold in the palm of my hand. I read one to myself:

> *Set at the mouth of the Sound to hold*
> *The coast lights up on its turret old,*
> *Yellow with moss and sea-fog mould.*
>
> *Dreary the land when gust and sleet*
> *At its doors and windows howl and beat,*
> *And Winter laughs at its fires of peat!*

She was watching me.

"Creepy, Esther."

"Wonderfully creepy. From *The Palatine*. John Greenleaf Whittier." She dug through the bin herself and came up with another one. "A few other stanzas. Much nicer." She read it aloud:

> *But in summer time, when pool and pond,*
> *Held in the laps of valleys fond,*
> *Are blue as the glimpses of sea beyond . . .*
>
> *Then is that lonely island fair;*
> *And the pale health-seeker findeth there*
> *The wine of life in its pleasant air.*

"Very pretty, Esther. What was the *Palatine*?"

"A wreck. Our most famous lost ship. There are hundreds of them under the sea by us. Those seas." She pointed toward her paintings.

"So what happened to it that was special? I mean, that made Whittier write a poem about it and not the others."

"The *Palatine* was a steamer from the Netherlands full of immigrants, bound for Philadelphia. Christmas week, 1744. Hit a shoal off Sandy Point. Almost everyone on board drowned or froze to death. Hundreds of people. For some reason, Whittier wanted to make villains of us all. He had a commercial bent as well as an artistic one, obviously. So he wrote an epic poem—the kind of poem some drunk could read aloud in a sailors' dive—about our setting out false lights and then waiting until a ship crashed into the offshore rocks. Waiting some more until the screaming stopped. Then once it was quiet, off we'd go to raid the ship." She acted as if the scenario she'd described had happened yesterday. And she'd used the pronoun *we*.

Esther dug around in the bin some more and read on:

> *The eager islanders one by one*
> *Counted the shots of her signal gun,*
> *and heard the crash when she drove right on!*
>
> *Into the teeth of death she sped:*
> *(May God forgive the hands that fed*
> *The false lights over the rocky Head!)*

She looked up at me. "None of it true. The *Palatine* did crash and go down, and there were wreckers here, but they were pirates who'd set up a camp, hiding from the militia. Our country's first declaration of war was against the Barbary pirates. Us—the islanders—we saved the handful of survivors from the *Palatine*. Buried the dozens that washed up. The cemetery is over by Trustrum's Tughole. Near where the camp is, actually."

"What's Trustrum's Tughole?"

"Trustrum Dodge owned the land. A swamp, really, with great depths of peat, far deeper than in Rodman's Hollow, much more extensive. A tughole is where peat is harvested. There are several of them. Block Islanders called peat *tug*, because you needed a team of horses to tug the clumps out. Tugholes were abandoned once we were able to heat with coal."

"The graves are there?"

"Unmarked. Coffins were sheets of sail. We had no wood, no trees. I think I told you that . . . the other night. The tug took care of the bodies. Told you about that too, didn't I? But we still save sailors at sea. Saved ten people off a great big yacht last fall during a nor'easter. Water was still warm, lucky for them." She shook a cigarette out of a pack. Lit it up. Held the pack out to me. She hadn't done that the other night.

"No, thanks."

"Anyway, my earliest Block Island ancestor was saved from the *Palatine*."

"You've traced your genealogy to him?"

"Her. Yes. A girl, twelve years old. She was one of four survivors. The other three didn't know who she was. Must have sailed in steerage. Couldn't speak English. Islanders took her in, revived her, nursed her—she was probably frozen solid—and adopted her. They called her Dutchy Kitten. I mentioned her to you, too. Her name was probably Katerina, I'd have to say. Islanders heard *Kitten*. She had many descendents, me included."

I said, "Now that's what tourists would like. A family tree with Dutchy Kitten at the top. Maybe you could do it in needlepoint." I smiled.

She laughed. I was surprised. I realized I didn't think she knew how to laugh until right then. But it wasn't a merry laugh, more a dutiful one.

I told her I wanted the six stanzas of poetry she had. Then I shuffled through the bin and came up with a framed posting of the Jim Crow laws.

"This is authentic?"

"It is." She turned it over. She'd glued a card on the back telling what newspaper it had come from and the date.

"I know someone who would appreciate this." Delby. "Do you have anything that has to do with law enforcement?"

She did. An article with a picture of Bruno Hauptmann, arrested by the FBI for the kidnapping of the Lindbergh baby. Two grim-faced agents stood on either side of him, holding his elbows. It would put my director in heaven.

"How about for children?"

"Nope."

I would get Delby's kids T-shirts.

Then Esther showed me a portrait she'd drawn of a man in the uniform of the British Admiralty, circa sixteen hundred-something. She said, "Admiral Adriaen Block. From my imagination. He discovered what is now the state of Rhode Island as well as our island, which he chose to name after himself. He never called the state *Root Island*. That's what it says in the history books—supposedly because roots sustained shipwrecked sailors who washed up there. But I believe a different legend—that Admiral Block became nostalgic for his own home when he first gazed upon our coastline. Named it after his birthplace. The Isle of Rhodes."

"A much better story, Esther. Is he for sale?"

"No."

I asked her the price of what I had in my hands. "Fifty dollars."

"For which?"

"For all you've got there."

"That's ridiculous."

"They're worthless."

"To you, maybe. Not to me."

"Then pay me whatever you want."

She turned and went back out to the porch. I followed her and put a hundred dollars on the table where, again, there stood a glass of wine.

"Esther, I'll have to come back for these. My bike doesn't have a basket."

She didn't answer. She gestured to the floor. She'd picked up her pencil and was staring at the canvas. I put my purchases at her feet and left.

* * *

Back at Joe's cottage there was no e-mail from the camp.
I headed up there. The girls were sitting in the shade of
Lancelot House. They were listless but appeared re-
solved—playing cards, reading, listening to their CD
and MP3 players, expensive ones.

Samantha and Kate and Elijah Leonard were sharing a big bag of potato chips. They saw me as I walked
toward them and waved.

"Hi, everyone. I didn't get my e-mail."

Kate said, "I told you he hated us."

Samantha explained. "He caught Christen. He went
out but came right back because he forgot something
just as she was setting up. Probably his stupid hat.
Confiscated all our laptops."

"What?"

"He said we were conspiring to break his rules."

The little sound I could hear inside myself was my
blood coming to a boil. "Where's Christen?"

"In her bunk. We're scheduled for a hike later. Resting
up for it, she says. But she's depressed. She feels really
bad about Rachel Shaw. She keeps saying we should
have tried to be nicer to her. She can't stop thinking
about her."

Kate said, "Me neither."

I went inside. Christen was lying on her side watching the door. She said, "I don't want to be warned one
more time about drugs. The rest of us aren't about to
go around experimenting."

She dragged herself off the cot, got down on her knees,
and pawed around underneath. She came up with a couple of pieces of paper. She held out the written list of
names and phone numbers and I took it. And then she
gasped.

Irwin stood behind me. He looked down at Christen's papers. He said, "I have called the girls' parents. I know you will be happy to hear that three have decided their daughters should return home. That is their choice entirely. If you'd like to call them yourself, Mrs. Everett— or whoever you are—go ahead. But I will cause a great deal of trouble for you, if you don't leave these premises immediately." He turned his attention to Christen. "I will deal with you shortly."

I reached into my pocket and came up with my little leather folder. I opened it and he looked down at my badge. I said, "This is who I am. And I do intend to call their parents."

He sneered. "I have a very clever lawyer. There is no reason for the FBI to ask me so much as one question. Rachel Shaw was eighteen. Dana Ganzi was seventeen, but she was from Georgia. Legally, I was not responsible for either of them, even if they did attend my camp. What happened to them happened off my site."

He walked out. He didn't sneak out the way he had snuck in. This time he let his heels bang against the floor.

Christen said, "Turd." She didn't say the word vehemently. I could understand. I can be vehement but only when it's productive. Squandered energy depletes reserves.

"Listen, you're all going to be okay, Christen. The trooper is in Rhode Island now. He's going to do everything he can to get you home."

"Or maybe we'll get ourselves home. We're working on a plan to get a boat."

"Christen, it would have to be a boat big enough to handle at least twenty of you."

"I know."

I felt a tad incredulous, but she was sixteen years old. I humored her. "Can you handle a boat that size?"

"Poppy, I'm talking about *chartering* a boat—a boat with a *crew*."

Forgot. These were rich kids.

8

I called my director when I got back to the cottage. He was in Yemen. I spoke to our top-dog legal consultant instead. I asked his advice about calling the girls' parents. He asked me what other options were in play. I said Irwin had already called them and that a Rhode Island state trooper was focused on getting the camp closed. He told me someone else would have to make the calls; I would be interfering with the camp director's first amendment rights. "Whereas, if someone unofficial does the calling, an informal conversation would not be considered as such. Not so with calls from you."

I said, "I'll call anonymously. Tell them I visited the camp as a mom with—"

"Poppy. You must remain above it. An officer of the law cannot play with the law."

"I know."

I would wait to hear from Fitzy before I played with the law. Maybe phone calls wouldn't even be necessary.

* * *

Fitzy and Joe returned that night with Fred, dropped him off, and arrived at the cottage. Joe was feeling more social. He broke out a couple of six-packs. "Fred didn't want to come back," Joe said. "We had to make him understand he had nowhere else to go."

"Poor slob of a guy," Fitzy said.

"Poor slob of a wife, married to him," I said. "Shall we drink to both sides of the story?"

The two of them looked at each other and decided to join me. We hoisted our dripping cans.

In Providence, Fitzy had discovered that Irwin wasn't Blair Irwin, he was originally Lester Boren. Between his christening and his present ID, he'd been several people, each transformation offering him new insight into loopholes that kept him just ahead of an indictment while he scammed people. He had broken no laws—didn't have so much as a parking ticket that anyone could come up with—and as of now he'd not breached a single statute, or even a rule, to give cause to close his camp.

Fitzy said, "Kids are at the mercy of their insolvency. They can't vote, they can't make contributions to political parties, they hold no power. In other words, we're stymied. I went to Social Welfare. Woman said the girls' parents have the right to remove them from the camp if they are dissatisfied with the service they are receiving. Quote, unquote. So I said to this bozo who I'm quoting, 'Usually when there's a suspicious death, the state checks on the service the dead person was or was not receiving.' But, quote, unquote, these deaths happened away from the camp. Would have been a different story if the girls had died in the dining hall. Shit. So I told her to consider a day trip to

Block Island, just have a look. Told her I'd give her two to one she'd come up with a reason to close the camp within one minute of laying eyes on it. So finally she said she'd try to send someone next weekend. Best I could do. I'll have another beer, Joe." He leaned back and closed his eyes.

I told them about my conversation with the FBI lawyer. Fitzy said, "I'll ask Esther to make the calls."

Joe said, "I think it's a lot to expect of her."

"Yeah, it is. Doesn't mean I shouldn't ask. She's pretty upset about what's happening. Maybe she'll go along. Give me the list, Poppy."

I went and got it for him. I said, "I think we're all right for now. Irwin's got a guard at night and the girls are scared. They're sticking together."

Fitzy's eyes opened; he gazed at the ceiling. "Scared is good."

None of us spoke for a while. We let ourselves enjoy our cold beer out of the icy cans. Fitzy was far away. I said, "Fitzy, what happened to you?"

"When?"

"Where did you start the downward spiral? What are you doing here on rest and recreation when you should be on top of the heap?"

He came back. "Who asked you to nose into my spirals?"

Joe started to make an excuse for me but I didn't give him a chance. "Sorry, Fitzy. I'm used to being in charge. When one of my guys gets—"

"I'm not one of your guys."

"No. But you're my friend."

"Who says?"

Joe looked at his watch. "Drink up. We're going to church."

Rather an extreme statement. Fitzy said, "Well, Poppy, I guess you heard what I heard. Hey, Joe, when did you lose your marbles? Was it something I said?"

Joe stood up. "I haven't quite lost them. There are six or seven left. We need to do something, and this is something no one should miss. Poppy can't leave Block Island without experiencing one of our most satisfying tourist attractions. It'll get our mind off things here."

Joe never wanted to get his mind off work. But this wasn't his work. It was mine and Fitzy's.

Fitzy said, "You did say church, right, Joe? Well, my stomach's growling so I think I'll take a pass and head for—"

"We'll eat right after. First we're attending the Star of the Sea's Sunday Evensong service. Church is Episcopal liberal, doesn't stand for anything except offering an enjoyable hour of entertainment. There's always a full house and we don't want to be late." He paused. "Hear that?"

We did. Ferry horn.

"All the ferry services put on an extra boat—from Point Judith, New London, from Sag Harbor—to take the tourists back home again. The choir's made a name for itself. The whole island will be there. Maybe the nutcase himself will show up."

I guess I raised an eyebrow.

"I want to be helpful, Poppy, even if I choose not to be involved."

I insisted on changing my clothes. "I don't go to church in shorts."

Fitzy said, "I don't go to church, period."

"Tonight we're all going," Joe said. "Poppy, we should leave in ten minutes."

"Call the stylist, then, and cancel my appointment. I'll be ready."

While I dashed around the bedroom, the fax machine started shooting out pages. I glanced at them. They were for me, from Delby. I gathered them up. I'd have something to read during Evensong.

When I came out, Fitzy looked at the folder under my arm. "If she can bring office work along, I'm bringing some beer."

Joe drew the line.

Fitzy pulled himself out of his chair. "Well, FBI, let's look at it this way—if another kid meets up with the picnic man while we're in church, we'll be able to rule out the choir as suspects."

"Fitzy, shut up."

"It's a valid observation."

It was.

We drove across the island to the harbor and up the east side of the pork chop passing Esther's dirt driveway. Just before the curve leading to the South Light we turned left onto a track. I'd never seen the tiny church called the Star of the Sea Chapel. Perched on the edge of the bluff, it wasn't visible from the road. Joe said it had weathered wind and storm since 1938, when the hurricane of the century—the twentieth—demolished everything along the coastline. Star of the Sea had been rebuilt on the same spot then, just as it had been destroyed and then rebuilt following the hurricane of the preceding century—the nineteenth.

After Joe's historical presentation, I said, "Why didn't they move the church inland?"

"Because then it wouldn't be the Star of the Sea, it would be the Star of the Road, which means no one would come."

The church was already packed. We squeezed into one of the last rows. The tourists chitchatted noisily, as if they were at the movies, and they were dressed for the movies, in shorts and jeans. To think I wasted a good thirty seconds deciding what to wear. Then the organ rang out, a heavy loud chord, and the congregation, like a class of kindergarteners, was stilled.

Billy and Mick led the procession down the aisle, Billy carrying a Bible, Mick holding something that looked like a divining rod aimed at the floor. The minister followed and then the choristers, eighteen of them, in white robes and red collars, half the faces very familiar. They sat in two facing rows on either side of the altar. The organist hit a chord.

The chorus may have had only eighteen voices, but they created a strong, breathtaking sound that rang through the space yet was softened by the acoustics of the old wood building, unlike the usual tone of a church choir's songs reverberating off stone walls. I whispered, "Joe, I can't believe this! Sounds like a hundred people are singing."

"You should hear them in spring and fall when they're all home. Chorus is doubled in size. Sounds like a thousand."

Willa sang, Ernie sang, Doris Prentiss sang, her miserable-looking husband was made to sing, the taxi brothers sang, and Tommy too. Jim Lane's kid was a soloist. He would have been head chorister at St. Paul's if he'd been born in London.

Fitzy leaned into me. "Now we know which guys are bald and which ones have hair."

The men did look odd without their Red Sox caps.

Esther was in the choir too, unrecognizable, chin up, singing her heart out. Fitzy whispered some more. "Where's that woman coming from anyway?"

"My guess, the throes of depression, same as you."

"Why do you want to get personal with me?"

"Because I like you."

"Well, anyway, now it's obvious what attracted me to Esther: we're both depressed. What's the attraction between you and the ATF? Just sex?"

All right, I would stop getting personal with him.

When the chorus was in the middle of "Joyful, Joyful," the doors were thrown open, sent banging against the walls. The next organ chord was discordant and the voices of the chorus petered out. Jake had burst through the doors and was running down the aisle. He ran in a manner not unlike a centipede that had just had a rock removed from its back, and he was babbling something incomprehensible. The minister came down from the pulpit, met Jake just shy of the altar, and led him up the altar steps to a chair. But he wouldn't sit down. Tommy extricated himself from the row of choristers and joined them. Jake started babbling more fervently, a string of words all running together. The minister spoke softly to Jake, asking him to slow down. He patted his hands, but Jake wrenched himself away.

Joe whispered to me. "Never touch an autistic. Besides that, they're atheists."

"Who says?"

He spoke even lower. "I looked into it because Tommy could never get Jake to church. Jake doesn't identify with morality. If an autistic wants something, he takes it."

"Maybe an autistic just doesn't understand the concept of ownership."

Fitzy leaned over. "Maybe autistics are heathen communists."

I said, "Churches are noisy, that's all. Music and bells—to say nothing of the odor of incense."

Joe: "All I know is, Tommy felt better, knowing it wasn't Jake's fault."

The minister stepped aside. Tommy talked to Jake.

And then Jake spoke again, the way he normally did, haltingly. One word, then the next, in a monotone. Tommy nodded to him and then led Jake back down the aisle and outside. The tourists stared.

The minister returned to his pulpit. He said, "Gentle-men. Ladies. I must make a troublesome announcement. Jake came to us tonight with a message. The girls at Camp Guinevere visited the South Light this afternoon under the auspices of the Coast Guard in residence. Then they hiked down the Mohegan Bluffs and walked back to the campground via the beach trail. I am afraid one girl has not been accounted for." He spread his arms. "We must find her."

Except for Fitzy whispering to me, "Scratch the chorus," the silence to follow was the kind found only in a church full of people waiting for the next thing to happen—for the priest to put away the wine, the bride to come down the aisle, or the coffin to arrive. Then the organist banged out another one of her loud chords and the choir went into action, pulling off their robes, dash-ing off the altar, down the aisle and out onto the street. Many of the members were part of the rescue brigade. Willa had sworn, "Next time we hear about a girl miss-ing, we're going to find her." She'd meant it. She'd seen to volunteers patrolling the camp at night, too. "Can't trust that Irwin," she'd told me.

But they didn't find the missing girl. She'd already been rescued while we were all still inside the chapel, just about the time Jake was delivering his mayday. When we arrived at Fitzy's they were on his front porch, knocking on his door. The rescuers were an at-tractive couple wearing top drawer sailing clothes and boat shoes that cost as much as plane tickets from New York to LA. No socks. The woman had her arm around the girl, who had the hiccups.

Fitzy got them inside, the girl into a chair. He scrounged around the bedrooms for two more chairs for the couple. Joe and I took up our spot in the corner again.

Fitzy said to the girl, "Are you all right?"

"No. I am totally not all right."

"What's your name?"

"Catherine Powers. Everyone calls me Cass, like Mama Cass. Just as fat, but I don't intend to choke to death on a ham sandwich. I will never forgive my parents for this. Never."

He asked her if she wanted something to drink. She said, "Yeah, I'll have a Bud."

"You'll have a glass of water."

He filled a glass and handed it to her. "Drink this, and try to calm yourself. I need to know what happened. Start at the beginning."

Cass guzzled the water, then banged the glass down on Fitzy's desk. He filled it again for her. She stared at the glass for a moment and then she began. "That bastard Irwin made us hike all the way to the lighthouse today—no exceptions. Seeing that we stay together the way everyone wants so we don't all turn up totally dead. There was no bribing the counselors to get out of it. And there won't be. Not anymore. They're real nervous, too.

"So we get to this frogging lighthouse—we must have hiked an hour in the burning sun—and they actually expected us to climb the goddamn thing. Like, all the way to the top. Hel-*lo?*"

She downed another glass of water. "We're talking about a thousand steps, minimum. *Winding* steps. I thought I was going to blow lunch just looking at them. Bedsides that, we'd just climbed the platforms up the side of Mohegan Bluffs, and there were about a million of those. We refused to do it. So can you *believe* one of those fart-sack Coast Guard guys told us we would be able to see Massachusetts from the top of the lighthouse. Oooh, *exsqueeze* me! What are those guys, totally clueless? We're supposed to get all hot and bothered over *Massachusetts*? I told him, Who the hell *cares* about Massachusetts? I told him to *fuck* Massachusetts. But the shithead made us go up anyway. He got us in single file, one at a time, because the stairs are narrow and we're fat. *Mis*-take! I ducked out of line. I hid in the Coast Guard quarters on the first floor."

She pointed to her glass. Fitzy filled it again. He said, "Thank you."

She said, "Whatever."

With her third glass of water finished, she banged the glass on the desk again. Fitzy refilled it. He said, "You're gonna be peein' all night, kid."

I said, "Where was the Coast Guard when you were in their quarters?"

"With the counselors." Her hiccups were gone. "It was a conspiracy. They sent us all up those *crummy* stairs while they went *swimming*. The lighthouse station has a *pool*. So they go for a swim while we're supposed to sweat our brains out climbing up *twenty million stairs*. Motherfuckers."

Fitzy told her to stay calm. She said, "I'll never be fucking calm again."

I asked her, "But Cass, why didn't you go back when the rest of the girls did?"

"Because I fell asleep. First thing I did was raid the Coast Guard's refrigerator. They had a ton of bologna. Oscar Mayer. And a whole shelf of Wonder Bread. I had a few sandwiches, then I ate their jar of mayonnaise. Hellmann's, my all-time favorite food. Wait till they go to make one of their bologna sandwiches. Sur-

prise! Then I fell asleep on their couch. Like, we're up all night talking about picnic man, the guy Stupid saw, trying to figure out who he is, since obviously *you* can't." She looked from Fitzy to me. "And neither can you."

Fitzy said, "Just keep to the story."

"You got a candy bar or anything?"

"No."

"Shit."

"What happened after you woke up."

"I didn't wake up till it was starting to get dark. The place was empty. Everybody was gone. So I called a taxi to come and get me. The driver told me to walk out to the road and he'd meet me there because there's a gate across the drive. I took a big knife with me just in case the taxi driver invited me on a picnic. I went out to the road, waited around, and then I saw this guy hiding under some bushes. He looked like the psycho murderer in *Halloween III*. He comes crawling out of the bushes straight toward me, so I started screaming my freakin' head off. I totally forgot I had the knife. I must have dropped it. I ran back to the lighthouse, but the door had automatically locked behind me and I couldn't get back in. So then I ran around behind the lighthouse where the platforms go down the cliffs and I could hear this guy clumping after me. The thing is, I'm screaming and he's screaming too. I mean, he's chasing me and *he's* screaming. But I didn't look back, I just ran down. I could've broken my neck but at least I wouldn't have had my clothes pulled off—nobody was going to turn me into a human pretzel." She looked from Fitzy to the couple sitting next to her. "And then these people saved me."

Fitzy turned to them. "Want to give me your take?"

The gentleman sailor was ready with his perspective. "Well, where Cass left off, that's where we came in, like she said. Me and . . . my wife. I'd anchored the boat just off the cliffs. We heard this god-awful scream-ing. Sounded like banshees. Shit. We nearly jumped out of our skin."

Fitzy said, "Why weren't you at the marina?"

"I don't know."

"You don't know?"

The woman said, "We wanted some privacy."

Fitzy's eyebrow went up. He couldn't help it.

I said, "How did you get to her?"

The skipper said, "First I put my spot on the stairs and then I saw her coming down. I was worried she was going to kill herself. We're talking a very steep cliff. I got in the dinghy and reached the beach just as she got down there, and she was pretty much hysterical and falling down and told me the guy who killed the campers was after her. I figured she was delirious. Whoever was chas-ing her must have taken off when he saw my light, be-cause there was no one behind her."

He glanced at Cass. "I mean, I believe what she said. *Somebody* must have been chasing her, but he probably gave up when he saw us. So I got her into the dinghy and zipped back to my boat, and we brought her around to the harbor, where everybody and their brother was looking for her. They're looking for her under *parked cars*, for Christ's sake. Geniuses. I asked for the police station and they sent us here."

Cass said, "Listen, can we get back to normal? I've got to see my friends at camp. They must think I'm dead somewhere in a swamp. Plus, I want to brag about the food I scarfed up, courtesy of the Coast Guard."

Fitzy said, "Getting back to normal. Sounds great to me."

He called Irwin, who arrived ten minutes later in the

van. Irwin had two campers from Merlin House, where
Cass bunked. When she saw them she said, "Am I, like,
totally gonzo to see you guys." They were gonzo to see
her too, because they both started crying and then Cass
was crying too, and a lot of hugging went on before
Irwin could get them out the door. Before he did, he
turned to us. "I'm not the ogre you've made me out to
be."

Once they were all in the van, the yachtsman leaned
back in to his chair, stretched his legs straight out in front
of him, and said, "Well, that was fun." Then he con-
fided in us. "I'll tell you, folks, when we had the light on
her and we could see her coming down the platforms—
I mean, she scared the shit out of us she was making
such a racket—I said to my . . . uh, friend here—I
mean, my wife—'Christ, the circus must be in town.'
And how she didn't capsize the dinghy, believe me, I'll
never know. So what's the story? Some guy is going
around selling lethal drugs to girls at a fat farm?"

Fitzy said, "Yes."

The yachtsman faced his friend/wife. "Where were
we heading next, Orient Point?"

The woman stood up. "Yes. And I say full speed
ahead, captain. Roger and out." She saluted.

Fitzy took their names and they made their escape.
He said, "We all know who was chasing her, right?"

I said, "Jake. He was probably taking one of his walks."

Fitzy picked up the phone and dialed Tommy. "Gotta
tell him to keep a rein on that guy. I'll be out, middle of
the night, can't sleep, and I'll see the locals drivin' all
over the island real slow. Used to stop them but I always
got the same answer: looking for Jake. Usually find him
in some bog taking a radio apart. Then they go tell
Tommy where he is. Tommy comes out and gets him."

Esther was at Tommy's. Jake was home and she was

helping out. She told Fitzy that Jake liked to go to the lighthouse and watch for the beam to come on. Jake told her he'd scared a girl who was in the lighthouse, but she'd gotten on a boat. Jake never meant to scare anyone. Jake wouldn't hurt a soul. And right now, Jake was still shaking like a leaf. Tommy was trying to get him into bed.

Fitzy hung up. He said to Joe and me, "Thing is, do we figure the retarded guy's the serial killer?"

Joe said, "He's not retarded, he's autistic. An autistic pushed to his limit will try to kill anyone persistent about breaking into the isolation chamber he's built for himself in order to cope. Notice I said *try*. Well, they don't succeed. They'll do something like hurl a pair of scissors at you from a hundred yards. Their throwing range is maybe two feet and not necessarily in the intended direction. They're impotent when it comes to the violence they wish they could perpetrate, so they can survive without tremendous anguish. Unless we're talking a crying newborn. That's easy. They'll throw a crying baby out the window. Documented, by the way. The sound of crying is impossible for them to handle. Autism can be true madness."

I said, "You found all this out for Tommy?"

"Yes. If he was to care for him, he had to know."

"Maybe, Joe, those girls were annoying Jake somehow. And maybe his aim with the scissors was better than you want to give him credit for. Maybe—"

Joe's voice rose. "Jake is not the one. That's it."

"You don't have to jump down my throat."

Fitzy said, "Poppy, Jake doesn't drive. He couldn't have dragged the girls' bodies to where we found them. So what say we not get off the track. We'll just—"

I said, "Who says he doesn't drive?"

Fitzy again. "Listen, Poppy, we can have a talk with Jake. Why not? But he won't answer us, will he?"

Joe said, "No."

"Poppy, we'll make a plan for talking to Jake. Okay?"

Joe said, "I know a plan. Throw a net over him."

"I'm talking a consult with the psycho people in Providence. We'll ask for advice. Being more objective than you, Joe, they probably won't suggest the net idea. Meanwhile, let's put our feet up here and go over what little we've got."

I said, "I still haven't read the faxes from my assistant. They're out in the jeep. Maybe something more came in from the lab."

Joe stood up. "You know, I don't fit in here. I've got plenty of stuff that's come in from my own assistant. Something's going down at headquarters. I'm heading back to the cottage. Listen to my own messages, check the fax machine. I've got to see that all's quiet on the home front."

Then he asked me what I wanted to do. "I'm on the home front right where I am, Joe."

"Okay, then."

I asked Fitzy if he'd drive me back later.

"Sure."

Joe said to him, "Then maybe only one drink for tonight, old friend," and he walked out.

Fitzy said, "What's with him?"

"He has a very big job."

I dashed to the jeep to get my faxes before he drove off. Joe had just turned on the ignition. I pointed. He looked down at the seat where they lay and handed them to me. I said, "See you later."

"Right."

The jeep zipped away. He didn't even wave.

I went back up the porch steps and into Fitzy's station, reading as I walked, squinting in the dark. I finished reading sitting in the chair where Cass had told her story. Then I read out loud to Fitzy the eight separate conclusions reached by my lab man, Auerbach, and his cohorts. Fitzy was leaning forward, eager for something, anything. He got it.

"One, there were no needle marks anywhere on either of the bodies. Two, no residue of drugs present in any organs. Three, their stomachs were empty; both victims had vomited shortly before death. Four, no semen in any apertures; no evidence of sexual tampering. Five, hearts were strong and sound. Six, slight head injuries, as if both victims had banged their heads against something hard. Seven, spasms occurred after death—cadaveric convulsions."

Fitzy said, "If we knew what they'd eaten, we might have had something to follow."

"True. Too bad, I know. Now, about the eardrums, which Auerbach saved till the end. Number eight. Not only were the tympanic membranes ruptured, there was hemorrhage just behind them. And the sensory cells—little microscopic hairs that sway with the sound waves that reach them—had disintegrated."

"Disintegrated?"

"My man points out that with loud noise they lie flat. Like when kids listen to blasting music all night. But then they come back up again not too long after the music stops. He says if the music doesn't stop, and it's above eighty decibels, some of the cells begin to disintegrate. They'll never stand back up because they're gone. A very slight hearing loss ensues, the loss exponential to the extent of disintegration.

"The sensory cells in the girls' ears had completely disintegrated. All of them. He said they'd tried to protect themselves from the music, or whatever it was; the victims' own clothing was stuffed in their ears. They hadn't gone to wherever they went with earplugs at the ready. He said most kids know enough to do that; how he found that out, I don't know. Says they put lumps of beeswax in their ears. The girls didn't have beeswax, they had pieces of their own clothes stuffed as far back into the ear canals as they could get them.

"Fitzy, here's my guy's conclusions. He says whatever they were listening to exceeded eighty-five decibels, which causes injury to the cochlea, which in turn leads to vertigo, disorientation, and emesis—throwing up. Then he says"—I looked up from the fax pages at Fitzy—" 'Everyone on that island would have heard the explosions. Because explosions are the usual cause of this particular lineup of physical trauma, not rock 'n' roll.'

"Fitzy, do any of the clubs at the harbor play rock music as loud as a five-thousand-pound bomb going off?"

"Nope."

"Didn't think so. Bottom line"—I looked down again "—according to this fax I've got here," and I read verbatim, *"Cause of death: unknown."*

Fitzy sighed. "I love fascinating information that's entirely unhelpful."

"Not entirely. Now we know why the girls ripped off their clothing. So they could stuff pieces of their T-shirts into their ears. How loud can music get, for God's sake?"

"Not that loud. Unless they have some kind of powerful amplifiers I'm not aware of."

"So maybe it wasn't a sex crime after all."

Fitzy said, "Could still be a sex crime. He watched them rip their clothes off."

"Yes. But what in God's name did he do to them to

bring about such a thing? Put their heads between two steel drums?"

"Seems like it, doesn't it? Of course, I don't know about *your* superiors, but if I suggest a steel drum theory, mine will tell me to take two aspirin and jump off the nearest dock."

"There'll be more tests, Fitzy. I'll tell the lab I want scenarios, other cases where people died the way the two girls did. Meanwhile, the campers' parents are going to hear what's in this report. If it's scaring the shit out of me, what'll it do to them? Nobody is going to kill any more of those kids."

"If they were my kids, I'd have sent them plane tickets after we found the first girl, gotten them the hell out."

"The parents believe Irwin. He's convinced them that the two girls who died were troublemakers who got what they asked for. The parents want to believe him. Him and all he promises."

"Parenting ain't what it used to be."

"How about a can of beer, Fitzy?"

"Sure." He got up and brought me one.

"Where's yours?"

"I think I just quit."

I cracked the can. "Fitzy?"

"What?"

"How'd you get control of the gangsters in Rhode Island?"

He sat down again and leaned way back, into his musing position, hands and arms cradling his head, rear legs of his chair all that held him. "Set rat traps. I was undercover. I took a few foolhardy chances. Chances I was told not to take."

"Like what?"

"Like tapping wires without authorization from the Justice Department."

"I do that."

"Figures. How else you gonna have any success? Anyway, there's a million-dollar contract out on my head. Organized crime is still organized. They're just a little less ethnic, that's all. After you convict these Mafia people, there's a period of disruption, new guys all jockeying to be on top. But until you've got a new head honcho you're stuck with a lot of violence. So the job wasn't over and my wife knew it. Couldn't blame her for what she had to do. But me go into hiding? Fuck that, I told the Commish. They find guys in hiding. They find their families too, unless the guys aren't hiding with them. I had no choice."

"I'm sorry."

"She's got a new name and a new identity, her and the kids. I don't know where they are."

"I'm sorry."

"You already said that."

"What will you do?"

"I'm doin' it."

"I mean, really. What will you do now? Seeing as how you've quit drinking."

A corner of his mouth went up a little. "Apply for a job with the FBI. Now that I've got connections. Now that I'm off the sauce."

I finished my beer. I said I'd walk back to Joe's cottage. He told me it was on the other side of the island.

"I know."

We said good night.

I'd only walked five minutes when the jeep pulled up alongside me. Fitzy had called Joe.

Joe and I didn't talk until we got back to the cottage. He didn't want to. He didn't want to hear about the faxes. He wanted to chitchat as if nothing were amiss. He said, "Who'd have thought this? Turns out I'm going back to DC while you get to stay here."

"You're going back?"

"Yes. Something serious."

"What?"

"Can't tell you."

"Okay. Can you tell me what's wrong with you then? Why you won't talk to me?"

"I need to think, that's all."

"Thinking means shutting me out?"

"Yes."

The truth does hurt. I supposed a shouting match was in order. But it would have only been for effect. So I said, "You know the phone number. Since it's your phone."

"I do."

In the cottage, I noticed his suitcase on a chair. Packed and closed. "It's our last night here, isn't it? Together."

"Yeah, it is. So what do you want to do?"

"Joe?"

"What?"

"What the hell do you *think* I want to do?"

And that's what we did. Joe and I communicate best through sex, not shouting matches. Fitzy's glib retort in church held some truth. I figured we'd do what we do after sex, lie around naked, entwined, nothing to hide so why not bare our souls too? How else had we gotten to be soulmates? But he wasn't quite as capable as usual, and afterward he got up and went and stood outside the cottage for a long time. Preoccupied.

* * *

Joe stayed preoccupied right up until I drove him to the airstrip the next morning. The night before he'd been preoccupied because our island idyll had been spoiled and he was feeling sorry for himself, I guess. Damned selfish of him. And in the morning he was preoccupied over Spike. We couldn't find him.

Joe kept looking at his watch while we searched the cliff top. He said, "Spike just wants to stay. Poppy, I can't hang around anymore. Do you mind seeing to him?"

I didn't mind. It wasn't like I'd have to muck out a litter box. On Block Island, Spike was an outdoor cat.

Joe said, "Around his dinnertime, stand at the door and shake his box of dry cat food. He'll come to that sound."

"Okay. I only hope no one is watching while I'm outside shaking boxes."

He took me in his arms. "You're showing a lot of patience with me, Poppy. I can only hope you know how much I appreciate it. I need to work things out."

"What things?"

"I'll tell you what things when I get back. I promise."

"After you've worked things out."

"Yes."

"I wish you'd let me—"

He hugged me tight. He told me he'd miss me and he'd be back Friday night. We'd have the weekend together and then we'd fly home on Sunday. He said, "You'll have things wrapped up by then, Poppy Rice. I'll bet on it."

Imagine that. Joe being patronizing.

9

The next morning, on the way to breakfast, I went to Esther's to pick up the things I'd bought and to wonder aloud about whether Fitzy had asked any favors of her. I didn't have to wonder. She invited me to have a Bloody Mary with her. "My breakfast when I skip the Patio."

"Why'd you skip the Patio?"

"I lost my appetite. Fitzy asked me to call all the girls' parents. Of the ones I could reach, a few were coming to get their kids, but the rest were convinced that Irwin had things under control. I didn't know there were so many rationalizations for negligent child care in my life."

"I've found people believe what they want to believe. Denial, we call it."

"Or as my grandma used to say, positive thinking. I really hate positive thinking. All lies."

I told her I was glad she tried and that a Bloody Mary was a capital idea. She apologized for her barware. I hadn't drunk anything from a jelly jar since I was seven years old. I told her not to worry, I liked the feel. I did.

And I said, "Esther, you sure you don't want to change your mind about some scrambled eggs? They go really well after a Bloody Mary."

"Not in the mood."

She looked preoccupied. I was damn sick and tired of preoccupied. "There's something else, isn't there? Besides failing to convince those parents."

"Yes."

"What?"

"There are a couple of things." She looked over my head, out into the pine branches hanging in front of her porch. Then she said, "I'm worried about Jake."

"I think everyone is worried about Jake."

"Tommy can't control him anymore. And it seems to me he's lost weight lately."

"Go to Tommy. Talk to him about it."

She smiled a little.

"What?"

"On Block Island, we don't talk. We beat around the bush."

I'd just learned that firsthand from Joe. But Joe had talked to Tommy about Jake. I told Esther that.

She picked up her jar and sipped her Bloody Mary. "Joe may be one of us, but he's got another life."

"You have another life. You're an artist."

"I throw away my work. But never mind that. I did try with Tommy, not too long ago. I approached from the angle of maybe Jake needing a doctor. Told Tommy that with the weight loss, Jake might have diabetes or something. Told him to take Jake to Doc Brisbane. He wouldn't."

"Why not?"

"Said Jake's afraid of doctors. I told him everyone's

afraid of doctors. I couldn't change his mind, though. Looks like we'll have to wait for an accident to happen, or for Jake to collapse, and then Tommy will have to deal with Jake's fear of doctors, like it or not. I've mentioned around that maybe we should call the Department of Mental Health. That went over like a lead balloon." She put the jelly jar down. "Listen, Poppy, I'm beating around the bush. I found something."

"Found what?"

"Something you have to see. But you're going to think I'm crazy."

I already thought she was somewhat crazy. I humored her. "Nothing you want me to see will top some of the things I've seen many times over since I first began enforcing the law. I see things in my line of work that make me think *I'm* crazy. All the time."

Esther got up, went out of her living room, and came back with a cardboard box that served as a file drawer. She took out a folder and handed it to me. She said, "There are three newspaper articles in here. No dates, and the name of the newspaper is cut off. But all the clippings must be fifty years old. Someone besides me needs to look at them, preferably an FBI agent who won't think I'm crazy."

As I opened the folder, she lit up. And she came within a centimeter of touching the match to the filter end of the cigarette before she turned it right way around.

The first clipping was an article describing the misery of a young child who had become mute for no reason. His parents described his horrible nightmares and hallucinations to the reporter. The only time he spoke, they said, was during the nightmares and hallucinatory events, when he screamed and begged, "Stop, stop!" A priest practiced the rite of exorcism over him, to no avail. Then he was treated by a doctor who had studied the art of psychiatry. *Art* of psychiatry, not *science*. The doctor, a woman, felt he had been subject to beatings—beatings that had left no mark upon him. She was quick, however, to agree with the authorities that his family was kind and loving. They were not the boy's tormenters. His parents were poor, the father, an Italian immigrant, was a groundskeeper on an estate in Newport. The boy had nine brothers and sisters. The psychiatrist asked the parents if he could be placed in her protection. The desperate parents agreed to the arrangement. The article ended: *The boy will not be identified so as to shield him from the curious.*

The second article was in the police log. The Rhode Island State Police log. Based on medical findings, it was determined that the boy who had lost his sanity a year earlier had been tortured. Although the police had observed no marks on him initially, upon examination by several doctors they'd reported minor injuries to his head, which had healed, as had his eardrums, which had perforated and then scarred over. Next to the police log was an article telling how the woman doctor had officially adopted the child and moved from the area, *with the hope the boy will take comfort in new surroundings*.

I looked up at Esther. "If what you've found reveals the cause of this child's injuries—if he'd gotten into something toxic—we'll finally have something."

She looked away, concentrated on exhaling a stream of smoke.

"You're aware the dead girls had ruptured eardrums."

"Everyone knows that."

The last article was long, accompanied by a photo. I couldn't bring myself to study the photo carefully since my heart skipped a beat after one glance. I would get to the photo after I read the article. The words were blurred, though. I had to blink a few times before I could read them.

Three sisters, children of the estate owner where the Italian groundskeeper worked, had been charged with torturing the boy. They'd put him into a well, into which they'd also lowered large heavy brass cowbells on ropes and then rang them. They enjoyed watching the boy as the bells clanged loudly and incessantly, the echoes resounding off the stone walls of the well sending him into agonies. *This, readers, is how the sisters spent their summer in Newport, Rhode Island, on their vacation estate.* The reporter declined to offer more facts because *such vile details would give great offense to this newspaper's family readership.*

Now I looked back to the photograph, a picture of the guilty girls, a formal portrait: sixteen-year-old twins and their fifteen-year-old sister. They wore velvet coats, fluffy white fur at the collars and cuffs, and matching brimmed hats also trimmed with fur. I could see the fur was not bunny, sticking out in all directions as though touched with static electricity; it was ermine. The brim of each hat had the shape of a heart. The girls' hands were hidden in white fur muffs. But the coats and the hats and the muffs could not hide their obesity. Their faces were hugely round, their cheeks and chins enormous, their narrow eyes sunken into the flesh of their eyelids, nearly hidden.

The sisters were identified by the reporter. The article was an exposé. The newspaper had exposed them because they hadn't been arrested; warrants had not gone out. They had not been remanded for trial, had not been incarcerated, had not even been sent to a juvenile facility. Instead, they'd been sent home to be disciplined by their parents.

The newspaper had taken advantage of a loophole. The law states that juveniles charged with felonies, or on trial for a felony, cannot be identified. These girls, however, had never been charged and therefore would never be tried, never held accountable for the brutal crime they'd committed. The story simply related the psychiatrist's version of the events. She named the family the boy's father worked for. In addition to the portrait of the sisters, there was a photograph of the well, so there was no mistaking the premises where the family summered, leaving no doubt as to who exactly that family was.

The reporter and the psychiatrist were people after my own heart.

There was another article describing the boy's journey on the road to recovery. The psychiatrist had hypnotized him. He no longer had any memory of his summer-long ordeal; his adopted mother had erased it just as she had erased for him the environment where he'd been attacked.

There was one page left, behind the one I'd finished. I didn't know what else there could be. I turned the page over and found another photograph: the boy's tiny face, compelling and pale, his eyes downcast. He may not have had a memory of his ordeal, but he hadn't been able to smile for the camera either, the way his tormenters had smiled for their portrait.

I looked up. Esther was watching me, waiting for the first and most obvious question. I said, "Does the child look like anyone?"

"No."

"So some tourist arrives on Block Island, sees our overweight campers, and his suppressed memory is triggered. He goes nuts, puts a couple of the girls down a well, and rings cowbells till they die. How simple."

She took her perennially crushed pack of cigarettes from her pocket. She struck yet another match and said, "I suppose sarcasm is understandable given the circumstances. But we've never needed wells here. We have three hundred and sixty-five freshwater ponds, one for every day of the year. Besides that, this is a very small island. We'd hear cowbells. Cowbells are loud, meant for places where cows have free range. That never was the case here, and now there are no cows to boot. And, of course, Jake would have gone nuts at the sound of clanging bells and we'd have heard him as well as the bells. But you're the expert. Could such a thing happen at all? Could noise be intense enough to break an eardrum?"

As to the second question, I didn't know. Probably yes to the first. Anything can happen, is what I've come to find out. But I would share those answers with Fitzy and my crime lab, not Esther. "Can I have these articles, Esther?"

"That was the idea."

"Where did you find them?"

"People give me stuff they dig up in their attics. Don't know who gave me the bag I found these clippings in. But I'll do some research, and if I figure it out I'll tell you. While you're doing your own research. Will you tell me what you find out?"

"Yes. I'll tell you within the limits of the investigational parameters."

She said, "All right, then. I suppose you'll have to tell Fitzy."

"He's not such a bad guy."

"Actually, I can't help but like him. All the same—"

"All the same what?"

"Nothing."

"Sure you don't want to come to breakfast?"

"I'm sure. They're a little annoyed with me."

"How come?"

"Because I had the nerve to suggest that the person who did whatever he did to the girls might not be a tourist. They want to believe what they want to believe, as we just said. A drug dealer who comes in and out on the ferry."

"That's what Joe wants to think too."

She said, "Yeah."

"But what if . . . I mean . . ."

"There is no drug dealer, is there? We all just jumped to that conclusion."

"I'm not paid to jump to conclusions."

"You're human. You believed what you wanted to believe."

"No. Don't let me off so easy, Esther. You know what happened here? Profiling. A dead teenager? She must have taken an illegal substance."

"But what else would a healthy teenager die from? If you found a forty-year-old man in the same condition, what would you assume?"

I thought. Then I said, "Drugs."

"Poppy, when do you eliminate drugs from the assumption?"

"When you stop believing what you want to believe. My God, what am I looking for here?"

She didn't know.

I left, hoping to find Fitzy at Richard's Patio. But first I'd dash back to the cottage and ask Delby to make a few calls.

I pulled up in front of Willa's Grocery, got out, and went around to the Patio. I walked past Pal, sprawled on his side, sleeping so peacefully, and opened the door.

No muted tinkle. I looked up. The bell was gone. Not a cowbell, Poppy. Willa saw me and jumped off her stool. She pointed over to Jake to explain the bell's disappearance and shrugged. This morning Jake was slumped at his table, his head on his arm, asleep.

She said, "He's knocked out, poor thing."

I looked over at him. I wondered if his face was the little boy's in the newspaper.

"Where's Tommy?"

"Making his rounds. He leaves Jake with me till he's done."

"Has Fitzy been in yet?"

"No."

"May I use your phone? I want to have a little business meeting with him. Maybe we can sort a few things out."

"I think he's gone, Poppy."

"Fitzy's gone?"

"No. I think the killer's gone. That last girl turned up alive, thank God. He had enough of his business so he left. Good riddance."

"I hope you're right."

The Patio door opened. Fitzy came in.

Willa said, "I'll see the gang steers clear of your table, Poppy."

"Great."

Fitzy had on an ironed shirt. He hadn't had anything to drink after I'd left him. Maybe Fitzy could make his way back.

"Hey, Poppy." He plopped down next to me.

"I need to talk to you."

"Your FBI scenarios came in this fast?"

"Not quite. You ready to eat?"

"I'm always ready to eat."

We gave our orders to Willa, and she went back behind the counter. "I've got something you have to see." Exactly Esther's words to me. I took out the folder. I told him Esther had given it to me ten minutes ago. "Fitzy, read what's in here. Take your time. And before you do, I have to tell you that Esther was a little hesitant at first, before she gave it to me. Because what's in here is so . . . It's . . . I don't know what it is. I just need you to—"

He said, "I'll read it, Poppy."

He took the folder, opened it, glanced down, and then looked back to me. "Am I going to need coffee before I get into this?"

"Probably."

Willa brought coffee and two plates, loaded with scrambled eggs, toast, bacon, and home fries. I watched Fitzy drink half the coffee down in one gulp and take a couple of bites of his breakfast. Then he stopped eating and concentrated on the articles. When he started reading he was holding a piece of toast, about to put it down onto his plate. He had to turn a page before he noticed the toast in midair and carefully set it down. Then he looked over at me.

I said, "Read it all before you say anything, okay?"

He didn't take my order. "I want this to be a review of a horror movie."

"I know. Read it twice. Let it sink in."

"I will. It sure as hell hasn't sunk in so far. I only hope tabloids have a long history. How old are these?"

"Esther thought fifty years or so, give or take."

"Where'd Esther get them?"

"She's trying to figure that out."

"Kid would maybe be dead by now."

"Maybe."

He finished reading the clippings and then he read them again. He drank the rest of the coffee in his cup. He said, "Mother of God."

Willa came over with a coffeepot and refilled our cups. Fitzy showed her the picture of the boy. "Look like anyone?" he asked.

Willa looked down, cocked her head. "Nope." She went to pour, sloshed a little into the saucer.

"Sorry, Fitzy."

"Not to worry." He put a napkin under the cup. Willa went back to her stool.

Now Fitzy looked down at the boy's photo again and then at me. "Kid looks like Joe."

"Shut up."

"Let's eat, Poppy, we'll take a walk. The walls in this place have ears."

We headed out along the harborside and around to Corn Neck Road, skimming Crescent Beach. Our eyes were focused straight ahead and we put one foot in front of the other. We weren't having a nice stroll. Nice strolls were what I associated with Corn Neck Road. Whenever I'd turned onto Corn Neck with Joe, I couldn't take my eyes off the sweep of white sand, the deep blue water, the hedge of beach roses, and the rise of the cliffs at the end of the crescent. Spectacular. Today I saw none of it.

We started with the givens. First, the comprehensible aspects of the crime against the little boy. I didn't have to tell Fitzy the cases I knew of where some mild-mannered fellow who seems to overcome abuse suffered as a child only to have the long ago trauma triggered, whereupon he turns into a psychopath. Fitzy had been involved in cases like that himself. He said, "Honest to God, Poppy, there was a kid whose father was a golfer. Used to beat him with a club. Kid grew up, beat people to death with a nine iron."

"But he didn't kill tennis players."

"No. Only male prostitutes, prostitution being a victimless crime and all that horseshit. Then there was another guy went around killing dogs. He'd follow some guy home who was walking a dog, stalk them for a few days, and then kill the dog when he was tied up in the yard. We found a pattern. Dogs belonged to middle-aged men. Turns out the father killed *his* dog when he was a kid, and so he snapped one day and started getting even."

"Always goes back to child abuse, doesn't it?"

"Always. Kids who are hurt, they're not only psychologically damaged; that's the minor part. They've been repeatedly concussed. Their actual brains are damaged. Seriously. The dog man's father killed the boy's dog— beat him the same way he'd beat the kid up. The kid survived the beatings even if the dog didn't, but then look what happened."

We walked on.

Even law enforcers can't discuss injured children for long. And lawyers who defend people who maim and kill children usually do it once and swear to God they'll never do it again. And they keep their promises.

"Thing is, Poppy, have you ever documented death by some infernal racket?"

"Not me. Maybe someone else. Called my assistant after I left Esther's this morning. She'll find out."

"So if it turns out to be possible, what do you think happened?"

"If it's possible, someone re-created the well."

He sighed. "I don't know of a sound studio here on the Block, that's for damn sure."

"Maybe the guy is gone. That's what Willa said to me. She thinks he's gone."

"What's that got to do with the price of rice? Someone's still going to have to find him."

"I know."

"Feet getting cold, Poppy?"

"I don't know."

"Ever been close to a crime? Someone you knew?"

"No."

"It gives you cold feet. The way it did your friend Joe. He's close to all this because this is his home."

"So that's the problem I'm having here, Fitzy?"

"Yes. It'll pass."

We headed back. I kept walking after he left me. We'd said all we could to each other. Now, we both needed to be by ourselves to think. I took one of the greenways, extensive trails like in England, maintained by volunteers, carved out of the bayberry bushes blanketing everything. Joe had said to me my first day, as we drove from the airstrip to his cottage, "At one time, the island didn't need all these trails you're seeing. You could just walk through the meadow grasses wherever you wanted to. But once the islanders stopped raising grazing animals, we became completely covered over with these bushes. Can't really see the contours of the land anymore."

"It's still beautiful."

"Yeah."

Grazing animals. Maybe cows did have bells around their necks at one time, in case they got past their fences. Or Esther could just have been wrong about that. I kept walking, heading in the general direction of Joe's cottage. Perhaps I'd come upon a vegetable cellar in a hillside. Joe had showed me the remains of one not far away. But I didn't find anything. All I found were more trails, plus one fabulous view after the other—

blue sky, bluer sea, soft gray-green bayberry. And as Esther said, even coming from a cellar, people would hear cowbells from one end of the island to the other.

I wandered most of the morning. Wanted to be sure Delby had the time she'd need. I'd told her on the phone, "Delby, I need some information on a case that happened around fifty years ago, give or take ten. Twenty, I'm not sure. It happened in Rhode Island, in Newport. I don't think it's on any official books because the perps were juveniles and they never went to trial. But I have their names. They summered in Newport, but that doesn't mean they lived year-round in Rhode Island. Doubtful, actually."

I gave her the name of the family.

"What did they do?"

"They tortured a little boy. Three teenage girls."

"I'll send you what I find."

Usually, she'd ask for a little more information. But where children came in, she didn't tend to ask, but rather suggested what someone should do to the perps. As she'd done this morning before she hung up.

"Find them, Poppy. Then put those three girls in the back of one of those trucks where they compact garbage."

"They'd be little old ladies by now."

"Same punishment holds."

For the moment, I let her think I was considering solving a fifty-year-old crime. She didn't blink; it's something I'd done before. Recently, I threatened a governor—if he didn't grant a condemned killer a reprieve so I could reopen the investigation, I'd reopen it anyway, even after he signed the death warrant, after the state had executed her, didn't matter.

After speaking to Delby, I'd called this shrink friend of mine who is the best psychological profiler in the business. He's an academic. He won't work for us. He's also a high roller. The FBI would not approve. I met him in England at a conference a few years ago. We had this thing going for a while. He took me to meet his mother. The family homestead was not unlike Buckingham Palace, only with more land. Half of England, it seemed to me. His mother told me I was the only woman her son had ever brought home. "You must be quite special in addition to being beautiful," she'd said. I thanked her. She also told me her son was the last of the male line. "The very last," she'd said sadly. Then she took me to a room with a safe. She opened it and took out "a bit of the family jewelry" and laid it out on a desk. It was a large desk, and the jewelry display covered it. The rest was in London, in a vault. It would all be mine if I married her son.

"I'm not being obtuse, Miss Rice," she said. "I just want you to know what such a marriage would mean for you."

And then we left the room and joined her son, who had spent a half hour making sure to inquire after each of the servants and staff, since he hadn't been home in five years.

There was this emerald ring. . . .

My rich ennobled shrink picked up the phone. Good. He wasn't in Vegas. When he was in Vegas, he turned off his voice mail. He said he could hear the messages as they came in. In his head. He couldn't have this happen while he was sitting at a hundred-dollar blackjack table counting cards; he would lose track of how many kings, queens, and jacks were out. I told him he needed a shrink. He said that if he didn't live to excess, what would be the point to living at all? I thought back on his mother's excessive jewelry collection.

Now I said, "I'm so glad you're in."

He laughed. "As soon as I heard the first note of your voice, Poppy, I was glad I was in too. Tell me, dear angel, how is your lovely head and your perfect ankle?"

"All healed, thanks."

"Come and have a tryst with me then, seeing as how charmed you are that I'm in."

"It'll have to wait. Listen, I need you."

"And I need you."

Best to ignore him a lot of the time. "Listen, this is a case you're going to identify with—you can connect it to the dreadful visceral assault created in a cavern packed with slot machines all paying off at the same time."

Incredibly, he said, "I'm all ears."

First I spoke of events that trigger a person to do something terrible. A person who has never been known to look at anyone cross-eyed and then turns around and kills in cold blood. He said, "We both know, of course, the commonality here and that its source lies in trauma to that person as a child."

"Yes." He and I knew that, as did Fitzy.

"We are making enormous strides in this area, I am relieved and happy to say. We used to think that a deliberate injury to a child created a tiny cancerlike cell—this is metaphor, Poppy—that remained benign until some set of circumstances occurred, causing it to grow and split and wildly multiply, pushing the cells of rationality out of its way. We no longer speak metaphorically. Now we know that when a part of the brain receives physical damage during the time the victim is a young child—irreparable damage when it comes to the brain—that child will behave abnormally. Sometimes in small ways—hyperactivity—and sometimes in serious ways—a child who is unable to learn to read or to play with other children, say. When that child reaches adulthood, the injury can manifest itself in many new ways, also abnormal, but not terribly unusual—reclusive living, alcoholism, various destructive phobias. But once in a great while, we do see the development of psychopathy. We see the serial killer."

"We know all that *now*?"

"Of course, we've known it a long while. We're only just now beginning to say it aloud. Not so politically incorrect a notion today as, perhaps, ten years ago. And we do need money from the government, after all. We must go slowly."

"We execute people whose brains have been damaged when they were children. Damaged by parents who get off scot-free. We *can't* go slowly."

"Not *we*, you. I'm a British citizen. We don't execute anyone."

"Forgot. You know, you're losing your accent."

He laughed. Then he said, "When do we get to the part about how this conversation is connected to slot machines?"

I described the connection, telling him the story of the three sisters and what they'd done to the little boy. Even though I couldn't see him, I could tell he never batted an eyelash. The more farfetched a crime, the more intrigued he'd be. So when I was finished, he immediately mused. "Overweight girls coming together, walking together, near this man damaged as a child. . . . Maybe one of them taunted him. Or maybe none of them did anything at all. He could still have been triggered, just by their mere physical presence in his life. In his ongoing daily life, I'd have to say."

I came right out with what I'd wondered, what I'd so tentatively suggested to Esther. "The thing is, would he take it upon himself to re-create what was done to him and do it to these girls?"

"Obviously, he has."

Good. This shrink never had the need to censor discussion of possibilities, no matter how farfetched, no worry as to a supervisor thinking he'd gone off the deep end.

I said, "Not in a well, though. There are no wells here."

"It needn't be a well. It could be a basement, no?"

"But ringing bells?"

"No. Not from your description of the corpses. Torture through sound. But it would take more than bells to create what must have been a horrible death. A noise far worse. Something more high tech, diabolical as that sounds. But, of course, that's outside my line of expertise. Once I know exactly what went on—what measures the killer took—then I can tell you who to look for. Who that child grew up to be."

There was no evidence of anything high tech on Block Island that I'd seen. "So you have never heard of a death caused by relentless, overwhelming sound?"

"No, I haven't. You must ask your friends in Washington if they have."

"I am."

"I detect a tentative note in your voice."

"What if they say no?"

"Then your work is that much harder, isn't it? I have never known you to shirk hard work, my darling. But if you're not feeling up to the challenge, go back to your neurologist, make sure that head of yours is all right. After all, you were coshed twice in a very short space of time. An adult's skull can take much more than a child's. All the same, I do wish—"

I interrupted and told my shrink friend how much I appreciated him, always taking me so seriously, his unquestioning respect, his comfort, his advice.

"Your reputation precedes you. Everyone takes you seriously, Poppy."

I had to admit to myself that if I told Joe this story, he would have choked on it.

Then I said, "I really like these girls. They're wonderful."

"Of course they are. Why wouldn't they be?"

"I just don't understand why they're here. Why they came to begin with. You can lose weight at your neighborhood gym."

"Your neighborhood gym would require that you wear minimal clothing. Why should you expect that these girls would put themselves in such a humiliating position? No one is interested in making fools of themselves."

Oh. "I like to think I'm sensitive. I guess I'm not."

"You are, darling, you are. Sometimes we just can't see the forest for the trees. Overweight teenage girls are outcasts. But at such a camp as you describe, they're not. Simple. Comfort in numbers and all that, so off they went."

I said to him. "You're never skeptical, are you? I do appreciate that."

"Ah, if you only appreciated my romantic side as much as you do my professional one."

"I do appreciate it."

"But not enough, Poppy, not enough."

True.

"Poppy?"

"What?"

"How long between the deaths of the two girls?"

"Three days."

I had to wait a moment for him to respond. Very unusual for him to have to take any time to think. He never needed to. Fear is what gave him pause. He said,

"That is treacherous, then. A serial killer will leave quite a length of time between the initial victims. He'll actually feel a kind of remorse after the first, though the remorse is mostly in the form of self-pity, as in *Why me, God?* Months might go by while he re-creates the killing in his mind, and only then does he begin to understand that he did it because he received so much pleasure. And only then and under the right circumstances will he do it again. After the second victim, he's hooked. The space diminishes with each subsequent murder thereafter. A serial killer may eventually come to kill more than one victim in a single day, but that only happens—if he remains unhampered—after two or three years.

"But, Poppy, this serial killer—the little boy in your newspaper articles—is unorthodox, because he is on a *mission*. He is not receiving pleasure, only eliminating the danger to him that he perceives. I would wager this is not a sexually motivated crime although there is a sexuality inherent in most of the work of those who torture. He has not raped the girls, so he is acting on something far outside of rage. He has an overpowering need simply to wipe out the enemy before the enemy wipes him out. He only has the summer to kill them all. Most serial killers might be psychotic, but they're never delusional or they'd be caught far more easily. They're never reckless, either. Serial killers take great pains to be sure to hide their victims so they're never found. They destroy them if necessary. Cut them into small pieces and see that the pieces are properly disposed. Or eat them, if they really want to be sure. At the same time, serial killers, though aggressive with their victims, will not fight back once you corner them. They elude, but they don't go after those who seek them. They have no interest in revenge. When confronted, they become quite meek. They're intelligent, they know when the jig is up, they don't fight it. Your man, though, *is* reckless. He is in a hurry. He would like to hide the bodies efficiently, but he's in too much of a hurry to take the time. He is suffering from a severe psychotic paranoia. Your man is entirely unpredictable here.

"Poppy, my dear girl, please—" He stopped. Fear again.

"What?"

"Be ever so vigilant."

I continued my way from one trail to the other, all across the island, eventually skimming the south bluffs, until I came to Joe's cottage. I found a message from Delby to call her. Good. I dialed.

She said, "Auerbach just talked to the histologist. He's getting up a report for you. Him being Pokey Pete, I thought I'd pass along what he's been saying."

I could always count on Delby. Our histologist was a little gun-shy and therefore overly officious. That's good, though. I'd made clear that a verbal overview coming from him was necessary to prepare me for the coming more thorough written report. Face-saving is always key with some people. Like everyone else, he'd come to see that he could trust Delby as my telegrapher.

"Pokey Pete says even though none of the structural changes in the body tissues could have been caused by disease, many of the samples looked as though they'd *been* diseased all the same. They'd been drained of oxygen, like what happens when blood cells stop working. He says the only thing that could cause that phenomenon other than disease would be strong and relentless physical exertion, like you find in a lab animal forced to run around a wheel till it dies. Such a phenomenon has shown up in victims of a death march. Told me he'd dug up some World War Two studies. He said such exertion, combined with a starvation diet, especially in a victim who was used to an abundant diet previously, could kill the victim and leave behind that particular trail he's found. Then he had some studies of torture, which he said needed to be analyzed."

I nearly fell over at the next thing Delby reported.

"He said Chinese water torture, turns out, is no myth. Brass helmet covers the head and water's dripped onto it, bigger and bigger drops. What's created is somewhere between a chime and a gong. A chime is sharp and clear like a hammer hitting an anvil, but the brass helmet also has the properties of a gong, which is complex because it has overtones that die away at different rates. So the victim of this torture is getting quite a cacophany, sounds that seem louder and louder to the victim until the water drops start feeling like sledgehammer blows. Bottom line, it becomes so unbearable you'll confess to anything. In the absence of confession, however, even though there are no signs of visible injury, you die because of internal damage to hollow organs, which we already knew something about. But what we have now is the actual cause of death. There is immense pressure to the chest, which ruptures lung tissue, lungs also being hollow organs. When lung tissues rupture, air bubbles are admitted into the arteries that lead to the heart and brain. Air bubbles stop the blood flow, and you get sudden death. Histologist says documented cases show death comes rapidly. Body can't withstand more than a few hours of the torture before it folds up.

"Poppy, he gave me a second scenario that would be

easier for him to document. What would take place on the battlefield—we're talking World War One, now, not Two. Continuous guns discharging and explosives going off do all of the above. It was not uncommon. Guys didn't usually reach the point of ruptured lungs, but some did. The cause was mostly the soldiers' own weapons, which they were firing themselves. After World War One, soldiers had to wear sound protectors.

"The rest of the stuff we've got comes directly from Auerbach. You won't believe what he has to tell you, boss, just thought I'd give warning. But I'll say this: You'll sure be wanting a stiff one after you hear it. I know I am."

"I am already, Delby."

I usually talk to the back of Auerbach's head while his eyes remain riveted to whatever's on his screen. So I was on speakerphone now. That way he didn't have to unrivet.

"Auerbach, you've got the histology stuff that I just heard from Delby, right?"

"Right. And what you need to know is if we have documented cases of sound killing people so we don't have to wait for histology to do their double-documenting. Well, we do. Weaponized sound."

"Weaponized sound."

"Yes. *Weaponized* is not a new adjective like everyone thinks, Poppy. When I came across it, the term roused my curiosity big-time. First I decided to find out if a victim who dies under the Chinese water torture is dying purely as a result of the nonstop sound he's hearing."

Purely. "And have you been satisfied?"

"Yes. But I had to start with the walls of Jericho."

Here we go.

"They came tumbling down with the blasts of Joshua's

trumpet. So here's what is proven: When the frequency of the matter of rock is known, a correct frequency that is loud enough will cause the rock to disintegrate in the same way a singer's voice can shatter a wineglass. Once the frequency of sound matches that of mass, it causes the atoms to dissociate at the weakest bonds of the whole mass. The weakest bonds in the human body are the heart, brain, and lungs. Ergo, that is what happened to those two girls. Instead of a wall collapsing, their hearts stopped beating. And if they'd been revived, they'd have been brain-dead."

"This is theory, right?"

"Until half an hour ago."

"How's that?"

"We've turned up a case. South America. Rio. Woman cheated on her husband, so he says. He'd beaten her many times, injured her badly. But what with the macho culture—honor and all—he never paid. No penalty for defending your honor. So the woman's father threatened the husband, told him he would kill him if he ever laid a hand on his daughter again. The father was a cop. Cops in certain cultures mete out justice. So next time the husband was in the mood to vent, he put the woman in a barrel. Heavy steel. He bashed it with a crowbar for hours on end over the course of the day. Neighbors heard. Saw him. Woman was dead when he took her out. Cause of death determined to be asphyxiation. Father had an autopsy performed. Woman's eardrums were ruptured. Cadaveric contractions. That's all they found. Not much more than what Rhode Island found."

"And who concluded it was sound that killed her?"

"A professor at Harvard Medical School. He was on vacation in Rio when it happened. In on the autopsy. Noted several other phenomena not unlike what histology is telling us. Professor wrote an article published in *JAMA*. He theorized on four other cases that he documented in his article. Three were similar to what I just told you. The fourth was a case in—speaking of Rhode Island—Rhode Island. And you know all about that one."

"Auerbach. My God. But—"

"I'm talking to the professor. We're back and forth. So Poppy, give me more as soon as you've got it, okay?"

"Yes. Of course. Auerbach, what happened to the husband?"

"What husband?"

"The one in Rio."

"Oh, yeah. When I talked to Delby she said you'd probably want to know even if the time required for me to find out would—"

"Live with it, Auerbach."

"Sure. The father—the cop—strangled the guy. The husband's the one who died of asphyxiation, not the wife. The cop got a commendation for subduing a perp dangerous to himself and others. The culture—"

"Good. That's all I need. Thanks."

"That's what Delby said. *Good.*"

I said it because now I wouldn't have to worry about Delby heading for Rio and strangling the guy herself.

10

That evening it was difficult to be alone with my thoughts. Spike had not shown up, even when I shook his box of kibbles. I was no longer used to being on my own. So many evenings in a row with Joe and the sound of the surf. Even when I spent the night at Joe's apartment in DC, or he at mine, one of us would often wake to the commotion of the other rushing off to answer some call. And besides that, in the evenings in DC, whenever I get home at a normal hour instead of 2 A.M., I bring work home. Or, rather, work set up to do at home via a computer hooked into the FBI's system. I don't really sit thinking, I sit in front of my screen computing. Auerbach has taught me a lot.

So I ate. The leftovers in Joe's refrigerator contained a great variety of temptations as he likes cooking, he likes serving food, and he likes eating. He'd made shrimp salad from the extra he bought when he did shrimp and pasta; he'd let the remains of barbecued steaks get cold, whereupon he sliced what was left of them paper thin with a machine you only see behind deli counters and made his own horseradish sauce to go with the slices; and there was a bowl of curried vegetables that was so delicious I had to control my urge to take the whole bowl plus fork out onto the slate terrace and eat the entire contents. Instead, I treated the refrigerator like a buffet table and put a little of this and a little of that on my plate.

Like Esther, I plunked a bottle of wine next to my glass on the table by the chaise.

It was a hot night, hot because there wasn't a breeze, a Block Island rarity. Joe said it happened once per summer. Nothing to be done about it but sit on the terrace and star-gaze. This morning at the coffee shop before Fitzy had arrived, Billy and Mick said we could expect a short spell of heat and then we'd all be rewarded afterward when a twelve-hour front of clouds and showers passing through brought crisp dry air in their wake. "Air clear as a bell, the sky blue as Rebekah's eyes, ocean purple as ink."

I'd asked, "Who is Rebekah?"

"Statue at the corner of Old Town and Center."

"Isn't there a stone horse trough at the corner of Old Town and Center?"

"Rebekah used to stand on top of it."

Mick said, "Rebekah's bein' restored."

Billy added, by way of explanation: "He means dried out. Some idiot filled the statue with cement after some kids knocked her head off. Figured no kid could knock her over if she weighed two tons. But cement draws water. Rebekah started crumbling from the inside out. Trouble is, the bill for fixin' her up is forty-thousand and something. That was in 1972. Nobody wanted to pay up. Lord only knows what they'd want to fix her now. So Rebekah gets to stay in storage in Jim Lane's garage, right, kid?"

Jim Lane's kid said, "Wrapped in a tarp."

I asked, "What's the statue made of?"

Billy said, "Whatever statues are made of."

The kid said, "Cast kettle iron."

Not all statues.

"So how are her eyes blue, Mick, if she's made of iron?"

"Well, if you want to see Rebekah today, you have to close your eyes and imagine her. If you do, you'll see her eyes are blue."

I said, "That's very romantic."

Billy hooted and Mick pulled his cap down over his eyes.

I was really beginning to get a kick out of Joe's Block Island coterie. There was definitely a hidden charm.

Now, tonight, I watched a half-moon, all that was left of it, rise out of the eastern horizon. I could smell the salt of the sea hanging in the air. Suddenly, I was grateful to be alone, though at that moment I actually missed Spike. I didn't miss Joe. Joe would have been talking where Spike would only purr. Sometimes Joe helped me think, but tonight I realized I needed to muse uninterrupted.

It was not meant to be.

I listened to my thoughts, to the waves and the cicadas and then, after the night had drawn on and the moon hung suspended right above me, I listened to something else that didn't belong. Soft footsteps. It wasn't Spike, who would have crept in on little cat feet, i.e., soundless. I sat up straight. I couldn't tell if they were behind me, next to me, or what. A half-moon doesn't give much light. I listened some more but could only hear the pounding of my heart because the footsteps had stopped. I looked over my shoulder. No night creature was standing there. I scanned the cliff top. The bayberry was a murky green carpet, covering all. Beyond the line of growth that ended just a few feet from the cliff edge, I saw someone sitting—a night-loving tourist who didn't realize the danger he was in—his legs dangling over the side.

The drop was eighty feet. Not to mention the fact that, on Block Island, the bluffs are gradually crumbling into the sea. One doesn't sit on cliff edges. Joe told me that in one hundred years his cottage would also crumble into the sea.

The fellow was kind of bobbing. I'd seen the motion before. It was Jake.

I got up, walked across the terrace, and took the path to the bluff edge. I tried to make enough noise for Jake to hear me but not enough to startle him. I was ten yards away when he saw me. He didn't startle. He was calmed by the quiet of the night.

"Hello, Jake."

He looked over my head. "Hello." Autistics, Joe said, don't make eye contact. Too intense. It would hurt Jake to look anyone in the eye.

"It's a very beautiful night, isn't it?"

"Beautiful night."

"Would you like to come and sit with me? Have something to drink? Maybe a snack? Over there at Joe's house."

"No."

Okay. "Well, if you change your mind, I'll be sitting outside on the terrace."

He looked away and I turned back, reached the terrace, sat down again, and poured another glass of wine. I watched Jake swaying a little, bobbing a little, and then he got up. I closed my eyes and waited a minute. If he was going to fall over the edge, I didn't want to see it. I opened my eyes again. He was heading down the path that paralleled Joe's drive, on his way to the road. Then he looked my way. He stopped, turned, and walked toward me. When he reached the perimeter of the terrace, he stood in front of me staring at his shoes and said, "Like chocolate milk."

"Let me go and see if Joe has syrup."

"Has it."

"All right then." I got up. He didn't move. "Please sit down, Jake."

He did. Right where he'd been standing. I meant for him to pull up another chaise. He got up and sat down again two more times.

I went in the kitchen. Joe had everything so Jake was probably right—just a matter of locating what you wanted. There was a bottle of chocolate syrup on a shelf on the refrigerator door. The bottle was glass. It wasn't Nestlé's Quik. The syrup was imported from Switzerland.

I was still stirring when I brought the chocolate milk to Jake, sitting there on the hard slate. I took the spoon out and handed the glass to him. He handed it back. We made three exchanges. Then he said, "Spoon." I gave him the spoon. Another three exchanges. He licked it clean, three licks. I said, "Would you rather sit in a chair?"

"No."

I sat down in mine. He took three slow spoonfuls of chocolate milk and then drank the rest in three gulps, knocking the glass back as if he were drinking shots of whiskey. He banged the glass down on the slate, picked it up, banged it down again, picked it up, banged it down. Joe has serious glasses. They don't break easily.

Now Jake sported a chocolate-milk mustache. I studied his face. He could have been the boy in the newspaper, I thought, but that was because his face was so childlike.

"Jake, does Tommy know you're out?"

"Don't know."

Couldn't care. Amoral but always truthful. No reason to deceive. Joe had told me another time that Jake did not anticipate.

"Will he worry about you?"

"Don't know."

Jake didn't comprehend caring that someone might be worried about him. That was not his problem. He had enough problems keeping chaos out of his head by doing everything three times.

He stood up. "Going now."

Joe said he didn't use pronouns or names. Too intense.

"All right. I could give you a ride."

He cringed. "No."

He walked around the cottage to the drive instead of going back to the path. He'd walked around the cottage before. Probably many times, a place where no one would talk to him, try to get him to say a pronoun. Joe told me he'd see Jake around the cottage once in a while, walking the paths once it was dark. "Until I started bringing Spike. The noises animals make are difficult for him." Joe had felt bad about it.

Now Jake stopped and looked over his shoulder at me. Not at my face, but at a spot just above my head. "Fanks." He pointed a finger at me. My guess, a replacement for not being able to say my name. And he couldn't pronounce *th*, couldn't say *thanks*. Neither could Delby's youngest. Immaturity, not autism. But Jake wasn't three years old.

"You're welcome, Jake. Jake?"

He looked at his shoes.

"Jake, have you seen anything strange? Do you know what happened to the girls from the camp?"

He didn't answer.

"Do you watch the girls through their window sometimes?"

"Yes."

Then he bobbed up and down, turned, and galloped away, arms akimbo.

Had a camp girl said something, done something, that Jake couldn't tolerate? Could he have killed those girls in some mad-genius way? No. No reason to deceive.

Could he have grabbed Spike and thrown him over the cliff? I should have asked him.

Fitzy, the next morning, over yet another breakfast, knew all the particulars on the sisters who had tortured the little boy. First of all, the whole thing was true. The case was sealed, though. There was no identifying the boy. The reporter hadn't wanted to do that. Fitzy said, "But I'm starting the tape unrolling so the homicide department may be able to get the information for us. The guy who runs the dead files room is in his seventies now. Maybe he'll remember some old fisherman who's been coming to Block Island every year during striper season who may have been that kid."

"This is striper season, I take it?"

"Yes."

"How long to unroll the tape?"

"That's the problem. Unless we find another dead girl, I'll have to steal the tape. The number three is important when it comes to investigating a serial killer of-

ficially. Our number is two. I can only hope the killer is
so old he'll just kick the bucket and our troubles will
be over. Then all that would be left would be to prove
that what we know to be true is true, and then we can
give the parents of the dead girls the answer they're
sorely needing. Part of it anyway. That they were murdered. We won't have to say how."

Somewhere behind the facade, Fitzy was one sensitive man. Unrealistic, too. They go together. That was
probably what had led to his downfall. Taking to drink
didn't help.

"The footprints at Rodman's Hollow were Fred's.
The one's under the camp window are generic. Rubber
fishing boots."

I lowered my voice. "They were Jake's."

Fitzy didn't lower his. "What?"

"I ran into him and asked."

I told Fitzy about Jake's visit with me.

"He didn't answer when you asked him what happened to the girls?"

"No. He must know something. But as to what happened to them, Jake doesn't know or he'd have told me.
Joe was right. Not a thread of compunction. I think he's
like Esther. He watches, but he doesn't delve. In his
case, delving would disrupt his compulsions."

"She delved inadvertently."

"True."

He scanned the breakfast regulars. "Where is Esther
anyway?"

They were all there but her.

We wondered about Esther out loud to Ernie when
he trundled our coffee over to us. He said, "Thinkin'
about that myself. Maybe she's workin' on some picture and can't tear herself away. Or caught a cold, who
knows? Or she's still upset after seein' that body." He

turned to his wife. "Hey, Willa, how about we make a little something for Esther. Poppy wouldn't mind taking it over." Back to me. "Right, Poppy?"

"I wouldn't mind at all."

Willa jumped off her stool. "Esther would call if she wanted something. I'm going to the store."

She took off her apron, hung it on a hook, and left. Ernie said, "She's got a lot of produce comin' in today. As if Esther'd call. I'll make a little something for her. My wife gets nervy when she's under pressure. And Esther—ya know, she's startin' to—never mind."

Fitzy said, "I'll take the breakfast over to her. See if she'll give me the time of day." Poor Fitzy. As if the only sort of person he might have a chance with was a depressed misanthrope. "But you come too, Poppy, otherwise she might not let me in the door, breakfast or otherwise."

"Okay. Maybe we can push her on figuring out where she came up with those clippings."

"Yeah, we'll do that."

As we were finishing our own breakfasts, Ernie gave us a Styrofoam box of French toast and sausage.

Fitzy said, "This smells good. Tomorrow, instead of bacon, I'll have sausage. Don't let me forget, Ernie."

"Gotcha."

Fitzy patted his beer gut. Then he said to me, "Where the hell do you put all the food you gorge, FBI?"

"Eating is only my second priority. Give me a choice between a doughnut and a bike ride, I get on the bike."

"I'd take the doughnut in a minute."

I shrugged.

"Goody Two-Shoes, aren't you?"

"You asked."

"So let's give Esther her breakfast before I open this box and sneak out the sausages."

Esther was not on the porch. We knocked, waited, and then went in. Maybe she did have a cold. Summer cold. The worst kind.

The door off her porch into the living room was opened. I stepped across the threshold and stopped. Fitzy walked into me. But instantly, he saw over my shoulder what had stopped me. Esther's body was sprawled across the floor, twisted and contorted, arms wrapped around her torso, her legs bent up. Her clothes, though, hadn't been ripped away. Her face was mottled, and copious amounts of saliva had dried on her chin and cheek and on the floor beneath her face too.

Fitzy and I reacted in the same way. We turned toward each other, face-to-face. We said nothing. We breathed each other's air. And then we both went to Esther and knelt on either side of her. Fitzy was the first to speak. He said, "Jesus Christ."

He laid the Styrofoam tray with Esther's breakfast on the floor. He said, "Poison." Then he bent her left arm and moved it down to her side. No cadaveric contractions. "Copy cat."

"Yes. Except the killer didn't know about the bells."

"That's right."

"Esther found out other things too, didn't she? Not just the story of the boy."

"I'd say so. Not inadvertently either."

"I'm sorry, Fitzy."

"Yeah."

Fitzy looked more carefully into Esther's face, gazing down at her intently without speaking. He was not studying her face for forensic information; he had the crux of that at a glance. He was mourning her death.

"Fitzy, did you ever discover a body before? I mean, without a dispatcher first reporting a homicide? Without benefit of an anonymous call?"

"No." He looked up at me again.

"That's what happened to me. A few days ago."

"But you didn't know her."

"So it's much worse for you. Take a minute."

I stood and stepped away, looked around. The sale bin had been emptied, the framed souvenirs scattered over the floor. The papers from Esther's stack of folders were strewn everywhere. The folders had names on them. All our names. Esther collected information. Great hobby, a lot cheaper than most. Dangerous, though.

"Fitzy, whoever did this probably found what he was looking for."

"Probably. I'll have to go through all the stuff anyway."

He stood too. We went through the house, room by room. Esther was not a neat housekeeper. You can't vacuum and dust if you're a painter or there'd be no time to paint, or to think about what you're painting. And she certainly didn't have the money to hire someone to clean for her. Several Styrofoam boxes were still on the kitchen table from her other meals. She was sloppy, but it was clear her killer hadn't needed to tear the rest of Esther's house apart to find what he was looking for. She held the spirit of organization. Everything he might have been interested in was in that plywood bin or in the box of folders.

I started going through the scattered clippings on the floor, positive that what we needed to find was already gone. But Fitzy was right, he'd have to pore over all of it. Sometimes what is left in a robbery leaves an investigator able to guess at what was taken.

I opened a file with my name in it. There was one page. She'd written my name, that I was an FBI agent, and that Joe Barnow was in love with me. I showed it to Fitzy. "Why would she want to do this?"

"Maybe she didn't like crossword puzzles . . . television . . . who knows?"

I picked up Fitzy's file and handed it to him. He opened it, read his paper, and did that smile, one corner of his mouth tilted up. He chose not to share with me what Esther had written about him.

He took a handkerchief out of his pocket and picked up the phone. Fitzy described to his commissioner what we'd found. He talked to several different people after that, assuring a few that the body was accessible, it was not down in a swamp. It wouldn't be long before the state police helicopter was making its way back to Block Island. I listened to all he was saying in bits and pieces while I looked through Esther's papers. I didn't read the file with Joe's name. I didn't want to intrude. The Rhode Island investigators would do that. It would take many days and a lot of shoe leather before any of it might lead to whoever wanted to shut her up forever.

I spotted a genealogy. The title on the file was DUTCHY KITTEN. Esther had already done what I'd suggested, only not in needlepoint. With pen and ink she'd drawn a fine and many-branched family tree, tall and wide. A majestic tree, the kind that won't be found on Block Island for a lot of years, however long it takes a young sycamore to reach forty feet. In the file with the drawing of the tree, on several sheets of paper, she'd written a narrative, putting a story behind the names sprinkled amid the tree's branches. I read the first line and was sucked in.

Four years after Dutchy Kitten was rescued from the wreck of the *Palatine*, she'd given birth to a baby girl named Cradle. Esther noted that the islanders probably could not say the baby's real name just as they didn't understand her mother as a child when she'd tried to tell them her name was Katerina. Esther guessed the child's actual name could have been African.

African? I read on. On the tree, Cradle had no last name. Her father's name was next to Dutchy Kitten, though there was no marriage date. His name was Orange; he was the same age as Dutchy; both estimated to be sixteen at the time of Cradle's birth. The date of Orange's death was just a few days after Cradle was born. I flipped to the narrative and found an explanation of his suicide. Orange had been a slave leased to Captain Ezra Dodge. He'd killed himself because the lease was about to expire. He wanted to avoid being sent back to Virginia. He was buried in the Indian cemetery where Dutchy later built a shack for herself and Cradle just a few feet away from where he lay. Dutchy's grave was dug next to his sixty-seven years later.

Cradle married the grandson of Orange's temporary owner, Captain Dodge, an original settler. They'd had twelve children; three survived.

I went back to the tree. From Cradle and Hiram Dodge came a line of descendents through to the present day. All the names on the tree were the names of settlers and their descendents—Dodges and Littlefields, Howes and Motts, names engraved on plaques all over the island. Some of the living descendents had asterisks next to their names. I went to the bottom of the page; those were the people presently living on the island. The list included all the Richard's Patio regulars: Ernie and Willa, Billy and Mick, Tommy and the taxi brothers, Jim Lane, Esther herself, and Aggie from the Pleasant View. Even Jake. But Jake's parents had blanks where their names should have gone. Esther had chosen to make Jake part of the lineage. Next to his birth date: *Adopted*. Also listed, with a tiny sword next to the name, was Joseph Barnow. The sword reference at the bottom of the page noted that he was a seasonal resident. Joe had been visiting Block Island all his life because he was connected to it by blood.

Next time I talked to Delby, I'd have to tell her there were plenty of black folk on Block Island, one of whom she knew fairly well.

I showed it to Fitzy when he got off the phone. He said, "There's a name for this."

"What?"

"Incest."

"That's a bit harsh."

"Inbreeding, then."

I didn't comment further.

"But so what," he said. And his eyes went from hard to compassionate. "Esther found out something she wasn't meant to." He looked into my eyes. "So did you, maybe."

Back at the cottage, I called Joe and broke the news. First, about Esther's death. I let the jolt set in and when he emerged a few seconds later he said, "What in God's name was I thinking?" Then, he went back to being stunned. I waited. The next thing he said was, "I've got a couple of days ahead of me here, things I have to take care of. Then I'll be back, Poppy. Because if Esther's habit of keeping a history of that place has evolved into her finding secrets that were meant to remain secrets— at least in the eyes of someone who would murder her—Jesus. I could have prevented this."

"I don't think so."

"Esther said I should find out what the girl took. That day in the Patio."

The girl hadn't taken anything. But for now I would let sleeping dogs lie.

I proceeded to break the other news—what I'd learned from the genealogy Esther had drawn and narrated, the story of his ancestors, Dutchy and Orange. I said to Joe, "At least we know no one would murder anyone to keep the history of your family from being known. The killer didn't take the genealogy."

"The history of my family has never been a secret, it just wasn't . . . parlor talk. But, Poppy, shame and humiliation were thrust upon Cradle's descendents, and their descendents, and theirs, in order to keep an underclass alive. Orange and Dutchy were courageous people. So was their daughter and her husband. But the children of Cradle and Hiram Dodge and those children's children—right on down—they were the underclass. There was a statute that said the descendents of slaves could not own property, a statute passed by the brothers of Hiram Dodge. This island used to be as segregated as any town in Mississippi. Until 1961, we had a Negro school. Esther's mother was the last teacher. It was where my grandparents were educated, Willa and Ernie, Billy and Mick. Everybody went to school there. And there was no opportunity after finishing school. They couldn't buy land, couldn't even own a car, for God's sake. Most got out. My grandparents got out. When I came back I found the ownership law my father told me about was true. My father wasn't joking. It was still on the books. Which is what happens when everyone is mute.

"Keeping that group impoverished, Poppy, allowed the economy of the island to function. Someone had to clean the fish."

"So what changed the law?"

"Me. When I found out it really did exist. From

Esther. I pointed it out to the state legislator who represents Block Island. First he laughed. Thought I was joking just the way I'd thought my father was. When he realized I wasn't, he had the statute removed. So I bought a cliff top and built my house. I set everyone free by doing that, didn't I? I'm sorry, I'm not being caustic. It just came out that way."

"I cannot believe what you are saying."

"I know. But Poppy, Willa's family has worked in the grocery since the middle of the nineteenth century. She bought it. When Billy and Mick went to the owner of the *Debbie* about purchasing it, he gave it to them. They used to pay rent on it in catch. They still give the former owner a couple of lobsters every week. Because they feel like it. And Aggie bought the guesthouse where her mother and her grandmother used to do the laundry.

"There has been no shame in our history. Not the history. The shame was in the impotency it rendered. Children should be seen and not heard. The way it is. Because, in a way, they'd all remained children—powerless. But what we have to focus on now is that Esther found out something grievous to one individual having nothing to do with genealogy. And we've got to find out what it was so we'll know who killed her. That poor woman. This crime—"

I waited. "You okay, Joe?"

"Yes. I'm in, Poppy. I'm in now. I'm getting back there as soon as I can. The first thing I intend to do is— no. The first thing I'll do is apologize to you."

I said, "No need. You don't know my life secrets either, Joe."

"I'm not talking about what we choose to keep from each other. We'll stop doing that as soon as you trust me enough to marry me. Though how I can expect you to trust me. . . . I need to apologize for deserting you."

Good Lord, was he proposing? He picked a swell time for that. Then he said, "Any sign of Spike?"

"No."

11

The next time I heard from Fitzy, he was smashed. He called me late that night, the night I talked to Joe, many hours after Esther's body had been removed to the coroner's office in Providence, after the Rhode Island State Police had swept through her house with their fine-tooth combs and vacuum cleaners. He was ranting, demanding I come to his office. I looked at my watch. Little after midnight. I said, "Fitzy, listen, I feel bad too. She didn't deserve this."

He said, "It's not about Esther. It *was* about Esther, so I opened a bottle of scotch. Finished it. About to open another but not now. I got this . . . fax." He hadn't been able to come up with the word right away. "I need you to come tell me I'm hallucinating." He hung up.

I got in the ragtop. Before I left, I ran back into the cottage and grabbed the box of dry cat food. I stood out on the front porch and shook it. Spike's tail did not rise up from the grass. Damned cat had better be back before Joe got here, give him some comfort. He wasn't going to get much from me.

I found Fitzy behind his desk. He had on the same clothes he'd been wearing that morning. Hadn't gone to bed. There was an empty bottle of Johnnie Walker Red on the desk. I stood there looking at it and then at him.

He said, "I can't get up yet, Poppy. I'm not being rude. I'm afraid my head will break open if I move." He looked at the bottle too. "Fred left a case on my doorstep. Grateful because I didn't arrest him. So, thank you, Fred." He ran his fingers through his hair, something he did when he knew he had to sober up. "Jesus fucking Christ, our miserable governor is a piece of work, Poppy."

"Is he?"

"Sit. You're going to give me a headache making me look up. I can only look down or it hurts."

"Too late. You already have a headache. But I'll sit."

He pulled open a desk drawer and took out a second bottle unopened. "Want some?"

"No, thanks."

"Me neither." He put it back. He slammed the desk drawer, his usual habit—slamming—and it forced him to grit his teeth. "Damn my head. So hear this. Governor spoke to Atlanta today. Disease control people. After we found Esther. Would you believe some asshole down there has decided that the problem we've got on the Block is some fatal disease like Legionnaires' carried by—who knows? The wind. Or a fish. A fucking fish. A disease-carrying fucking fish that will turn you into a corkscrew before it kills you.

"The governor of Rhode Island decided he's got two choices: One, does he want to admit we have a serial killer and end tourism to this little gold mine for the rest of the season, maybe a lot of seasons, depending on whether the psycho gets caught; or, two, does he want the island closed down for, say, three days and then show everybody the place is just as normal as can be and that the girls who died were doing some bulimia thing and ended up having heart attacks like that singer. What's her name?"

"Karen Carpenter. She weighed seventy-eight pounds when she died, not a *hundred* and seventy-eight."

"Yeah. Tell me about it. As for Esther, the word has gone out—committed suicide. Clinically depressed, rumored to be recently jilted. *Their* rumor, the bastards. They know the autopsy will show something mixed with the wine. Drink cheap wine, someone can put cyanide in it and you won't notice.

"Governor made his decision. He chose number two. And now we've got—Poppy, are you ready to freak out?"

"Not really."

"A travel ban. Implemented by the Coast Guard, who have presently barricaded the island."

"You're hallucinating."

"I wish."

"They can't do that, Fitzy. We won't be able to get the girls off the island."

"That's right."

"And we can't get any kind of help in."

"That's right too."

"Joe's coming out."

"Not any more he isn't."

"Shit."

"Miss him that much?"

"No. Fuck."

What came to my mind was my shrink friend's warning: Be vigilant. Vigilance had just flown right out the window. Some corrupt governor had taken care of that.

"Fitzy, this is ludicrous."

"No. It's politics. And want to know what I think? That things around here would have been goddamn different if that fat farm were a gymnastics camp. One skinny little dead gymnast, and the governor would have called in the National Guard, turned this place upside down, and taken all the little girls out himself."

Fitzy opened his drawer again and this time took out the bottle. I picked up his phone.

I didn't have any trouble reaching the director of the Centers for Disease Control right then, at home in Atlanta. I have everyone's emergency number, including his. His name is Harry. He is a man I have consulted many times over the last ten years, during the time I was a lawyer in the Bronx and a DA in Florida, and especially while I've been with the FBI in Washington.

Harry said, "Poppy Rice, how the hell are ya? Not too good, I'll bet, considering it's, let's see . . . getting on one A.M."

"I'm calling from Block Island, so that probably gives you an indication of why I happen to be disturbing you in the middle of the night."

"Oh, Jesus. Shit. What are you doing there, for Christ's sake?"

"I'm on vacation."

"You are? Damn, Poppy. If I'd known I'd have tipped you off. I'd have—"

"Harry, we have no plague here. There is no mystery germ, no little unheard-of bacterium attacking anyone. The only thing you can get on this island is Lyme disease, just like everywhere else. Instead of bugs we've got a serial killer who is on the loose. He is killing—"

He interrupted me because of the magic words and probably, too, because my voice was rising fairly uncontrollably. "Whoa, Nellie. You said serial killer, right? Nobody mentioned anything about murder, serial or otherwise. Just that three people had died, although the woman—"

"No, Harry. Three people have been *killed*. The woman was the victim of a copycat. The serial killer murdered two teenage girls."

"Two girls dead, yes. I know about them. The woman, suicide. But maybe illness made her suicidal. That's what I'm to find out. Let me explain to you what came down, Poppy, before you yank my head off. A doctor on Block Island went screaming to the governor that two girls who were assumed to have died of an illegal drug overdose did not die of any drug overdose. He said they must have picked something up, some bacterium. So the governor consulted with his coroner's office and concluded that the victims may have succumbed to a contagious disease. An infection that causes the tympanic membranes to perforate while it's killing you. Often, we've seen—"

"Harry, the doctor in question is addicted to Demerol, and most of the time he's asleep on his feet. He must have reached the governor during his strung-out stage."

"What did you just say?"

"I'm sorry. You heard right."

"You've got a doctor there addicted to Demerol? Call the AMA. Turn him in to the authorities. Because, from my end, the wheels have been set in motion. I mean, they are *heavily* in motion. We don't fool around, you know that. We move fast and we—"

"Harry, there is a camp on Block Island for overweight teenage girls. The place is a travesty, take my word for it. The police officer in charge of this island cannot get it closed, but that's another story. I'll be glad to tell you about it over a beer someday. But meanwhile, there's some nut running around who has decided to torture and—"

"Torture?"

"Yes. He tortures these girls until he's killed them. He's giving them something that kills them in such a way that is none too pretty. Maybe an extra-large dose of Demerol, for all I know. Call my man Auerbach, and have him copy the autopsy reports for you and the documentation he's dredging up. Meanwhile, here's what I've concluded. Your decision not to let these girls out or allow investigators in has placed them all in grave jeopardy."

He said, "Shit." *Shit* was turning out to be a big word today. Then he said, "Poppy, listen, we're taking air samples now. Okay, then, if they check out negative, our team'll go out tomorrow and have a look around. You can tell them what's what. They come back, I'll push the lab to wrap things up in twenty-four hours. Island will be opened up again in two days. I can do that for you. Unless, of course, we actually find a bacterium. Then, like I said—"

"*There is no bacterium!* The FBI would have found it; they were in on the second autopsy. Ever since we learned that the Atlanta Centers for Disease Control don't know a goddamn thing about anthrax, we depend on ourselves, not your idiots."

He took a breath. I could hear it go in and out. "The *crime lab* has checked this out?"

"Yes."

"I thought you said you were on vacation."

"I was supposed to be."

He sighed. "I am so between a rock, you know? If those girls—if that woman had been strangled, shot, stabbed, whatever—things would be different. But I was told there was no evidence of homicide. I was told the three corpses exhibited unusual changes in various tissues. On top of that, I've got the governor of the state involved, a governor who belongs to the same political party the President does. Protocol demands we see if there is bacteria harbored out there in a stagnant pond. I'm holding up my end: looking for evidence of bacteria. You hold up yours: find evidence to the contrary that says—"

"Harry, the girls died in one place and were dumped in another."

"No. I was told they were hitchhiking. If you pick someone up and she dies, you might get real nervous and dump the body."

"Not me. I'd get her medical assistance before she died."

"I'm sorry, Poppy. All I can suggest is that you get the police to guard the girls."

"Get the police? I don't think you quite understand. We have one state trooper here. There is no one else and we can't *get* anyone. Travel here has been banned, remember?"

"What about the local force?"

"The local force consists of a man, a *constable*, who upholds the town statutes—which, as far as I can see, are few and far between."

"Okay, then keep the girls sequestered."

"When I was a teenager, no one could sequester me."

"I'll bet."

Speaking with Harry was no longer productive. I slammed the phone down. Fitzy and I had that quirk in common. We knew who you could effectively hang up on and who you couldn't.

I said, "Fitzy, can you rouse that detective from your force who went down into Rodman's Hollow with us?"

"Sure."

Fitzy dialed and handed the phone back to me. The detective didn't like my waking him up. Tough. The first thing I learned from him was that he knew all about the ban. He said to me, "I agree with you, of course. Plague, schmague. But I've thought long and hard. Let's face it. It was drugs. There was not a mark on either body. The girl I saw—her heart gave out. Just like the first girl. Drugs can do that to you. That movie star, the kid in LA? Goes to a nightclub, takes I-don't-know-what, walks outside, and drops dead on the sidewalk. You're waking me up over something that happens every day of the week. Kids who—"

I tried not to burst. "Listen to me. One of the girls didn't do drugs at all and the other one smoked a joint once in a while. If pot did whatever it did to those girls, the country would be littered with contorted dead bodies."

Fitzy was watching me. I knew what he was thinking. That I could not say to anyone that perhaps noise killed the girls. If I said it to this detective, he'd think we were *all* using Demerol. I tried a new tack.

"Maybe they were poisoned. Esther was. The woman who—"

"No. She *took* poison. That's what we have to assume now, considering the information we have on her."

"From who?"

"From the doctor out there. Brisbane."

Shit. "Please, Harry. Someone is enticing these girls with food. And then he puts something *in* the food—"

"If he put poison in their food it would have shown up."

"Not in the stomach contents, it wouldn't. The girls vomited. The FBI is looking at tissue samples. There are poisons that don't show up in the usual places."

"Since when?"

"Since I told you. These campers are not drug addicts and they have families. Some of those families are finally beginning to understand that their daughters are in danger, but now these same daughters can't get out. We have over twenty girls left. *And we have no security for them.*"

"Then handle it like this. Those people out on the Block take care of each other. They have a rescue squad. Have them get up some volunteers to patrol the streets and keep the girls in the camp till the ban ends."

"The citizens here rescue people from capsized *boats*. In nor'easters. They are not the police. And what if a *volunteer* is the killer? Or what if a volunteer gets *killed* trying to protect a girl?"

He didn't say anything at first. Then he did. "If there's a killer, it's just the woman who was the victim. Probably the boyfriend. Isn't it always the boyfriend who's the killer?"

"It is. But there is no boyfriend in the picture, and boyfriends don't use poison. Boyfriends go out and get a gun. Fun to point a gun and say, 'You want to leave me, honey? Good. You're gone.' Bang. Except O.J. He got a great big knife. Even more fun that way. Listen—"

He interrupted me. "You can't know that. This boyfriend used poison because he saw an opportunity. He could copy. Boyfriends don't want to get caught, and this one probably didn't have the wherewithal to jump on a plane to Chicago. But the two girls? I'm sure it was drugs. There are studies being done on substances that give you a high, and they're not categorized as drugs. There are drugs that don't show up in your body after a few hours. Unlike poison, that you and I both know doesn't go anywhere. The dealer who sold this stuff to the dead girls isn't a killer, he just doesn't care if things don't go smoothly. Pretty common type of personality trait demonstrated by drug dealers everywhere. You must know that."

"You're wrong, and you're especially wrong about this killer's personality. This one does care. He *takes* care to see that these girls die at his hand. He knows exactly what he's doing. He's murdering innocent teenage girls and because you don't know how he does it you're in denial. Or maybe the governor is pulling your strings, since you're not putting the lid on the phony leak that the woman who was poisoned committed suicide. Two girls were killed. It has happened twice. Twice. Doesn't *twice* do anything for you?"

"Twice? No. Three times, yes. Get the girls together in a group and explain carefully why they just have to say no, and then there'll be no number three."

Idiot.

I hung up on him too.

Fitzy sat there, still gazing at me. He said, "I couldn't bring myself to tell the commish about the boy in Esther's newspaper either. How do you tell someone the weapon used in a murder was probably a goddamned bell?"

It was true about the island wanting to help. In the morning at Richard's Patio, Willa was coaxing Jake to eat his breakfast while Tommy was out organizing a team to guard the camp and patrol the roads. Apparently he was used to organizing rescues at sea. Tommy, Ernie told me, would go out into the teeth of a January blizzard and come back with frozen fishermen who he'd thaw out, fill with brandy, and see on their way. So when he asked for help from his fellow islanders, everyone available came running, including those recently back from the Dordogne and those who had intended to leave but now couldn't. In fact, Tommy was already out there, checking all the docked boats, flashing his badge, looking for drugs. Fitzy and I watched the militia form at the Patio: Billy and Mick would take the eight to midnight shift, camp guards. They were making their plans. Billy said, "I got to see my rifle is all ready."

Fitzy just shook his head.

The taxi brothers would patrol the roads during those same late hours. Jim Lane's kid, plus his buddies, would be out on their bikes taking spins around the campgrounds during the day. Everyone had an assignment.

It had taken Esther's death for people to get serious. It had taken one of their own. Ernie had been storming around ever since it happened. "We can't get her body back here for burial! A travel ban!" He spit the words out. "Who can believe it?"

Now he was picking up dishes and cups and glasses, crowding them onto a tray, piled high, ranting about such insanity. And then he dropped the tray. The tray was metal. We all jumped. Willa leaped. Jake clamped his hands over his ears and started to keen, the sound of the wind, I thought, a powerful terrible wind. Willa rushed over and put her arms around him. He screamed and yanked himself from her. She started to cry. Ernie rushed over to the table. He grabbed Willa and held on tight while he tried, at the same time, to calm Jake.

"Jake, I broke some dishes. Some glasses too. See them there on the floor? I don't care about some old dishes. But now everything is okay. Look, we're all here, nice and quiet again. I'm going to sweep up the mess. Willa is going to throw all of it away and we'll get new dishes, right, Willa?"

She whispered, "Yes."

"And Jim Lane's kid will help you finish your breakfast."

The kid got right up and went over to the table. Ernie and Willa started their work. Fitzy and I had already picked up the biggest pieces of crockery and glasses and put them on the tray. Jim Lane's kid stabbed at the cut-up pancake with a fork. He said, "Hey, Jake, look. I got three at a time here."

Willa wiped her eyes with her apron when she got the tray from us. She said, "I'm sorry. You folks eat your breakfast."

We went back to our table. Except for Jake's whimpering, Richard's Patio was back to normal but I'd lost my appetite. Fitzy ate my breakfast too. I said to him, "Listen, this morning before I left, I called the camp. I reached a counselor and then I talked to Christen. Apparently our friend Irwin remains unfazed." I told him what Christen had said—that Irwin was busy fielding phone calls, assuring parents that camp activities had resumed, that the infection control center did this sort of quarantine thing all the time—we should be grateful they took such matters seriously. But not to worry. There was no such illness, as they would find out in just a few days. At the end of the short quarantine everyone could feel secure once again. As to the girls who died, they were an element he had tried diligently to screen out. Unfortunately, he'd failed in these two instances, so he apologized and promised the parents that the rest of the girls were not of that ilk. He continued to assure them that not only was the Rhode Island State Police—meaning Fitzy—seeing to it that their daughters were protected, though he knew that was hardly necessary, but a volunteer force was doing the same. He described the friendliness and concern of the locals. He assured them there was even an FBI agent and a top gun from the ATF on hand who happened to be vacationing on Block Island and who had taken charge of the whole situation.

Christen said she got most of her information from her mother, who'd talked to Irwin and then insisted on talking to her. Christen told me her mother said Irwin reminded her camp tuition was nonrefundable. Her mom said she didn't care about the money—he could keep it—she just wanted Christen home as soon as the travel ban was over. She was wiring money through the post office. Then she was going to call all the other girls' parents.

"Fitzy, finally."

Turned out Fitzy had called the camp this morning too. He'd reached Irwin. "I instructed him to hold a meeting. I'm going to talk to the girls." Fitzy looked at his watch. "Due there in fifteen minutes. Coming?"

"Yes. I want to see them."

Before we left, Willa said to me, "Poppy, when the ban's called off and the campers leave, you should too. This was supposed to be your vacation, yours and Joe's. Let Fitzy and the state take care of this. Come back next year, start again." Her eyes were full. I gave her a hug. But only a few days ago she and everyone else said I shouldn't leave. They needed me.

Fitzy and I went up to the camp. The girls were there, sitting together on the ground, just like the first time I'd seen them—no backpacks, though, no hike in the offing. And instead of sprawling on the grass, they were huddled together. Kate was in the middle, Samantha's arm around her shoulders. I counted. Eighteen. Some parents had seen to getting their daughters out after all, before the ban went into effect.

Irwin came out onto his porch when he saw Fitzy's car pull up and watched us get out of the car. As we approached, he smiled down at his campers and said, "Are we all here, girls?" "Almost all," Christen called out. "Some have left and two are dead." I detected a sag to Irwin's shoulders. He introduced Fitzy, telling them the police officer was setting things to rights and they should all listen carefully to what he had to say. As usual, he looked right through me.

Fitzy climbed onto the porch and sat down on the top step, facing the girls. He said, "Okay, kids, this is the story. One, there is no germ that is going to kill you. Instead, you've got two things to look out for. Drugs, for sure. On general principle, don't take any. Don't smoke a joint. Don't swallow a Tylenol unless you brought it from home yourself. Mainly—far more important—don't go off with anyone who offers to make you a chocolate cake." The girls smiled a little. Then he lied to them, based on the rumors following Esther's death. "Maybe what's going on here is some kind of poison somebody went and slipped to the two deceased girls. Maybe did it as a joke, who knows? Maybe gave them date-rape stuff, too much of it. I'm here to make a promise to you. We're going to find him, arrest him, and see that he never has the opportunity to do to anyone else what he did to your friends.

"And here's the most important part: In two or three days, the infection control people will announce that this disease business is a crock. And then you will all go home if I have to take you myself."

I watched Irwin. He didn't move, didn't even twitch. He knew his scam had folded.

A camper raised her hand.

"What?"

The girl said, "My dad's a doctor. He told me there's no such thing as plague. And, trust me, he reminded me to just say no, too, until I'm out of here. So I don't appreciate having to hear it from you. We're not complete idiots, you know."

A lot of nodding heads agreed. The campers had found themselves in the same position for too long—on the receiving end of lectures instead of help.

Fitzy said, "First, girls, I'm sorry to condescend. That's what people do once they pass thirty, and all of you will do it someday. The way it is. In any case, no matter what your parents have decided, I am going to see to it that an inspector from the state comes out here and looks around, closes the camp, and orders you home. In a couple of days, the minute the ban ends." He turned to Irwin. "I'm done."

The girls applauded.

Fitzy came down the steps and over to me. He said, "Soon as I can get out of here, I'm heading over to the *Providence Journal*, where I plan to dump a jar of canned beef stew on the newsroom desk. That stew will contain highly visible mouse droppings, bat droppings, and dog shit besides. I'll tell them it's food from the camp on Block Island." Then he calmed himself. "Seriously—" he gestured toward Irwin—"our boy knows the party's over."

"I'd say so. Small consolation."

"Yeah."

At nine o'clock that night, I was out back on Joe's slate terrace once again, sitting on the chaise, contemplating the black sky dotted with stars, the moon gone, the swath of the Milky Way visible. The air was clear, but we hadn't gotten the line of showers Mick figured we would. So I could see Orion distinctly, the Three Sisters and the Big Dipper and the little one too. I was lulled by the cicadas again, but not so lulled I wasn't also aware of crickets chirping, frogs peeping, and owls whooing. The gulls are calm at night, thank God. And there were no footsteps in the dark, no Jake coming to sit on the edge of the cliff.

I closed my eyes, and the second I did someone started pounding on the front door, hard and furiously, using both hands, I was sure. I got up. What had brought Fitzy out; why hadn't he called me first this time; why was he in such a panic? Drunk, is what I thought because I would not believe someone had gotten to one of those girls. Not now. A shiver ran up my spine.

I went through the cottage and could see Jim Lane's kid—not Fitzy—outside the window. I opened the door. He was completely out of breath, standing there huffing and puffing. His bike lay on the grass where he'd let it drop. I got him inside and sat him in a chair, and he tried to tell me why he'd pedaled ninety miles an hour across the island to summon me. But he couldn't get any words out. His eyes were dilated. He was shocked but he wasn't *in* shock; his skin wasn't dry. He was, in fact, sweating bullets. I said, "Take a couple of really good deep breaths," and went for a Coke.

The boy emptied the can in several gulps. Then he looked up at me, stricken, but making eye contact, which helped to steady his vocal cords. He said, "I had to go see the state cop, but he's asleep. I could hear him snoring from the road. I don't like him. Then I remembered about you, so I came here."

I said, "He's a good cop, he's just got a few problems. What's wrong?"

The boy didn't move. He said, "My dad says you can't judge a book by its cover."

"Your dad's right. Where is your dad?"

"Boston. Got caught up in the ban."

"You have to tell me why you wanted to see the police officer."

He swallowed. His Adam's apple went down and up. He said, "I saw a skeleton out on Sandy Point."

"A skeleton."

It wasn't a question; I was just making sure the words he'd spoken registered with me. I didn't even think I said *a skeleton* out loud. But I had, and he heard me and thought it was a question and he answered. "Yes. A skeleton. It's almost to the lighthouse just about where the rookery starts."

"It could have been animal bones."

"No, it couldn't. It was a person. We have the skeleton of a person at school in our bio lab. Those weren't animal bones."

I got the keys to the ragtop. I said, "Let's go." He didn't move. So then I said, "What's your name?"

He said, "I'm Jim Lane's kid."

"I know who you are. But you must have a name of your own."

"Jim."

He still wasn't moving. His hands gripped the arms of the chair.

"Jim, I know you're scared, who wouldn't be? But we have to go to the police station now. If the two of us have to sober the officer up, we'll sober him up. It shouldn't be too difficult once you tell him what you told me. Ready?"

He stood, but he wasn't steady on his feet. So I said, "Joe's cat is lost. Have you seen a big furry orange cat around?"

"Joe's cat? Spike?"

"Yes."

"Nope."

"Will you help me look for him? Tomorrow, maybe?"

He was sufficiently distracted. His legs worked. "I can come tomorrow, sure. Got no customers because of the ban. What time?"

"In the morning. Before breakfast or right after. Whichever you'd rather."

"Before."

We went out to the ragtop and when we pulled up in front of Fitzy's, I told Jim to sit tight. When I needed him, I'd call him. I went up the porch steps. I didn't knock on Fitzy's door; it was unlocked. The barracks for the girls at camp didn't have locks until last night, when Ernie went out and put dead bolts on their doors.

I didn't know what condition I'd find Fitzy in. I went inside and peeked in the bedroom. He was in bed in his clothes. He even had his shoes on. I stepped away from the door and called out, "Fitzy," a couple of times. I heard him roll over. He came out of his bedroom as disheveled as the first time I'd had to rouse him, the morning I'd discovered the body of Dana Ganzi. He looked at me and he said, "Shit." And then, "I'm afraid to ask. Now what?"

"Fitzy, we've got to check on something. Something Jim Lane needs to see you about. He's outside in the jeep."

Fitzy said, "The mayor's in your jeep?"

"No. His kid. The boy's name is Jim, too."

"If that wimp of a kid admits to killing anybody, I'm going to quit this job for sure."

We heard a shuffle. Jim was standing on the porch just outside the screen. He said, "I got scared out there. I am a wimp."

I said, "You're not a wimp. The officer has something nasty to say about everyone."

Jim said, "I'm a wimp."

Fitzy said, "Get in here, kid. I don't much like talking through a screen door."

First Fitzy had to use the bathroom and Jim and I got to listen while Fitzy peed a gallon.

When he came out, he said, "Okay, Lane, you got something to tell us that you don't want your old man to find out about, isn't that right?"

"He's going to kill me."

Fitzy looked at me. "Poppy, those are the words of a good kid. Bad kids don't give a damn whether their father might kill them." He turned back to Jim. "Okay, so now that we've established you're a good kid instead of a delinquent, what's the problem?"

"My dad says people should mind their own business. Well, I was minding my own business. Maybe when he gets back you could tell him that."

"His dad's stuck in Boston." I didn't know if Fitzy was quite with us. I said, "Fitzy, it's worse than whatever you're thinking. But Jim needs to be the one to tell you. He needs to say it again. A couple of times." With maybe a few more details than he was able to give me. There was no hurry. Not with a skeleton.

Fitzy said, "I already know it's bad. I can tell it has to be bad by the hour and, to tell you the truth, your face. Both of you come on in my office and let's sit down." We did. He said to Jim, "So what business of yours were you minding and what happened while you were minding it? Start right at the beginning."

Jim Lane's kid chose to look at the ceiling while he described what happened. That way he was able to keep the images his words conjured up out of his field of vision. "I was digging for night crawlers out on Sandy Point. Me and Rusty."

"Who's Rusty and where's he at?"

Jim stopped staring at the ceiling and his gaze went to Fitzy. "My dog. I told him to stay there till I got back. He's waiting for me."

Fitzy ran his hand through his hair. I'd wondered when he would. "Okay, you're out digging for night crawlers. Planning to fish at midnight?"

"No. I sell night crawlers. Thought I'd stock up for when the ban gets lifted." He began rubbing his pant leg. "If it gets lifted."

"Thought you sold postcards."

"I do. But sometimes day-trippers want to fish, so they come to my stand and ask where they can buy some bait and—"

"You sell drugs?"

"No. I told you, I'm a wimp. My father would kill me if I got caught selling pot. The guy who rents the kayaks is the one who sells pot. Don't tell him who told you."

"I won't. And Poppy here is right. You're not a wimp, you're an entrepreneur. Go back to what happened with you and the dog."

"Rusty got bored, so he took to walking in the sea grass, sniffing around the rookery, and—"

"The who?"

"Gull rookery. When the gulls took over the old lighthouse, the state made it an official rookery so they could raise their young."

"You mean that old shack out there covered with bird shit is some kind of state park?"

I said, "It's a preserve. I've been there."

"This country's nuts. You're still on, Lane."

Jim said, very quietly, "Officer, there's a skeleton in the grass."

Fitzy mumbled something. He'd chosen not to curse aloud in front of the kid. I said, "I already asked him if it could have been an animal."

"I'll bet you asked him that. Well, look, it's not one of the girls. There isn't another one missing. This skeleton might have been there for years for all we know."

Jim said, "If it was, Rusty would have found it. One of the places we go regular for crawlers. When we went just before the season started, toward the end of June, it wasn't there. I think it's one of the girls. It wasn't laying straight out. I mean, the arms were all—" And with that, the image appeared before him and he started to shake.

Fitzy stood up. "Your mom here?"

"She's with my dad."

"Who's watching you?"

"I'm watching me."

"Okay, then. You and Poppy go out and get some fresh air while I wash my face."

Jim stood up and I put my arm around his shoulder. I realized how big he was when I did. Wide shoulders, muscled. I led him out onto the porch. "Jim, when this is over you can call a friend. Stay at a friend's house."

"It's okay. My two brothers are around."

Fitzy came out with wet hair. "We can take my car."

Jim said, "We'll need that jeep unless you want to walk halfway up the spit."

"Jeep it is."

But Fitzy went first to his own car and came back with a roll of yellow tape. As we drove Jim gave us more details, said he was putting the worms in a plastic bag when Rusty started to growl a few feet in front of him. "Then, like, all of a sudden, he went crazy. I mean, totally crazy, barking louder than anything. I shined my flashlight over where he was and saw it. I ran. Rusty ran too. But I told Rusty he had to stay. To guard her." Jim looked down at his hands. "I left the worms, I guess."

The tide was out and the sea was calm. A fine, invisible mist had settled in, wetting the cobbles that lined the high tide mark. Gulls were circling the old North Light. There were hundreds of them. A cawing set in as six or seven birds rose higher than the rest and headed toward us. A foghorn on the nearby shoal moaned across the water, fifty yards from where the point of the spit disappeared into the sea. The sandbar that took out the *Palatine*.

Jim told me to stop. I braked. "It was right around here." We got out and he hollered, "Rusty!"

A short-legged mutt came running out of the grass.

The dog ran around us, sniffing. Then he looked back toward the grass and growled. The arriving gulls reacted, their low cries turning to sharp squawks. More of them were joining the first wave. A few began diving just in front of us, maybe the ones I'd watched kill their offspring one bright and beautiful morning just a week ago. It seemed like years.

Fitzy said, "These goddamn birds gonna attack us?"

Jim said, "Not in the summer."

"They got nicer personalities in the summer?"

"In the spring, when the eggs hatch, they'll dive right into your head. But not now." He looked up. "They're afraid of dogs besides."

Fitzy switched on his searchlight. "Okay, kid. Where?"

Jim said, "Go, Rusty!"

The dog made a beeline toward the grass, ran through it for several yards. Only his tail showed, the way Spike's would have. When the tail stopped, the dog lifted his head and growled again, a much deeper growl than the first one. This time, the gulls backed off. Jim said, "They're *really* afraid of dogs."

Fitzy mumbled, "Saves me from having to take a few shots at them."

We walked into the grass. Jim told us the skeleton was a few feet ahead. The dog looked over his shoulder and bared his teeth. Big teeth, not anything like the sight of Pal trying to bare his.

Jim said, "He's guarding it just like I told him to." Then, to his dog, "It's all right now, Rusty. Good boy. C'mere."

Fitzy said, "Thought I was going to have to shoot Rusty too."

Jim bent to the dog and put both hands around his muzzle.

Fitzy only half believed Jim. He didn't want to believe him. Neither did I. The beam of the flash swung through the grass just the way it had when we were halfway down into Rodman's Hollow. But this time, it didn't pass over a wide patch of flesh, it passed over a white stick, slid past, stopped, and glided back. The stick was a shinbone. The skeleton's arms and legs were twisted around its ribs, the skull thrown back, the jaw wide. The bones were so white they looked as though they must have lain there since the *Palatine* rammed into the shoal. The gulls had picked the body immaculately clean of any and all flesh. Remnants of clothes had been pulled away and dropped. Gulls are finicky—they separate out what they don't want.

Fitzy put his yellow tape around the perimeter of where the bones lay. Then we brought Jim and his dog home to his brothers. I told him I'd bring his bike to him the next day. He said he'd come back for it in the morning; his brother could give him a ride. "Then I can help you." I didn't know what he was talking about. He said, "You know, look for Joe's cat." Good kid, indeed. Back at the police station, Fitzy dialed his commissioner and waited for staff to wake him. Didn't take long.

"Hey, Commish, if I'm bothering you, sorry about that. It's because I've got no choice. We have another body." He paused. "No. A skeleton. Now as far as I know we don't have another girl missing, but considering how—" Pause. "Well, sure, it could be anyone. But the bones were twisted around themselves. I don't think anyone arranged them either. Not the way whoever it was rearranged the body of the woman who was poisoned. My feeling, paranoid though I usually am, is that—"

Fitzy paused again. He stood up. He said, "What?" Then he paced back and forth. His next message to the commissioner was a very loud, "Fuck," and he slammed the receiver down.

"Poppy, we're dealing with assholes."

"I know."

"The body stays right where it is, until the travel ban gets lifted. Told me bodies have been washing up on Block Island since the Pilgrims. Suggested I appoint a deputy to guard the body. Yeah, right. Think I'll appoint Jim Lane's kid's dog."

"Seemed like the commissioner was on our side. What happened?"

"Ex-cop or not, he's appointed by the governor and his job is to be on the governor's side. He jumped at what I'd said—that no girls were missing."

"Call Tommy. He'll guard the body or get someone to do it. But you should call him right now. Jim Lane's friends will all know what he found by now. Teenagers have a morbid curiosity about them. They're probably on their way to Sandy Point already."

"Yeah, you're right. Isn't Tommy guarding the camp?"

"No, he has other people doing that. He's got his hands full keeping Jake home."

"Okay, I'll get him out there. He can bring Jake, leave him in the truck or something. What do you think, Poppy? Is Jake capable of behavior so rational he could connive to kill the campers?"

"I can't imagine it."

"Me neither. But it wouldn't be the first time I was wrong."

"Fitzy, I'm going to check in with that doctor. He should go have a look at the skeleton."

"Goddamn quack. Could *he* come down far enough so that both his feet are on the ground and kill the girls? Kill Esther?"

"Same answer as before." I started to leave, but then I didn't. Fitzy looked defeated. The wind was out of his sails. I said, "Fitzy, there are always mistakes. Always. And a slew of them have been made here, left and right. But mistakes can be overcome. You know that."

"This is worse than a mistake."

"But it doesn't change anything. The case is not hopeless. That's what's important for us to remember."

"Should have been a piece of cake."

"No. There are no pieces of cake in our business. It seems like it should be a piece of cake because we're on this little tiny island, not in a big city where bad guys can hide out in twenty million different places. This island doesn't even have a decent tree to hide behind. Now we're frustrated because we can't find our killer under the nearest bush. We have to be even more patient than the killer, who is biding his time, watching for his opportunity. Solving a crime is painstaking, Fitzy, tedious, even on little tiny islands."

"I have no patience. That's my problem."

"My problem too. But as long as you recognize your problems and deal with them, it's okay. Fitzy, the Unabomber milled his own screws for the bombs he made. He knew we wouldn't be able to trace the manufacturer if *he* was the manufacturer."

"No kidding."

"No kidding. You know what our best hope is, don't you? The only hope for impatient people like us. You must."

"Yeah. We need another Fred. Only one who saw more than Fred did. We need a tip."

He was coming around. He was with me. "We sure do." We needed a tip from someone close to the perpetrator, close either through a relationship or just plain physical proximity.

"Poppy, what you're forgetting is that we had a tipster. Esther. We blew it."

"Esther blew it. She kept the tip to herself."

"Yeah. What if our copycat was the actual perp and he meant to have Esther's death look like a copycat killing?"

"We always dread that but it's rarely true, isn't it? Let's not get distracted. We still can't tell if Esther knew who killed her or if some tourist wanted to steal an old map."

"We do know that, Poppy."

"I was grasping at straws. Is that what you want to do?"

"No."

"We don't depend on straws. We have no choice but to depend on what investigators always depend on."

"Luck."

"Exactly. Only luck *seems* about as reliable as straws. But luck is far more reliable, because it doesn't exist where there isn't perseverance. Which is why I'm a lucky investigator and I suspect why you have been lucky as well. Back when you were working. We persevere."

He smiled. "So we figure we'll just stumble on him—maybe a coincidence will lead us to him—as long as we stay a couple of diehards. That's your philosophy. The Stumble Philosophy."

"It's the only philosophy."

"Yeah, it is. The only one. It's just depressing to admit it." I left him dialing his phone and went back out to Joe's jeep.

The doctor came to his door. Carol was right behind him. They both wore ratty bathrobes. They had more than a professional relationship. Brisbane didn't wait for me to speak; he felt he had the right to be angry with me. "Atlanta called me today. Like to take my head off." He added a note of defense to his scold. "Listen, I know you're FBI and maybe I should have come to you first, but for all I knew you were a secretary or something. And you'd aligned yourself with that cop. Well, as far as—"

"Aligned myself with the cop? Who was I supposed to align myself with? You?"

"Never mind. The thing is, there might be some bacterial infection these girls are carrying, maybe spreading. Something highly contagious."

"But only overweight teenage girls can catch it?"

"It could have been a coincidental cluster. And if so . . ."

I let him babble. I didn't listen to anything else. When he was finished, I said, "Jim Lane's kid found a skeleton halfway down Sandy Point."

He reacted the way I had. He mumbled to himself, "A skeleton."

Not Carol. She said, "You're shittin' me."

"I'm not."

The arrogance slipped from Brisbane's voice. "When?"

"Tonight."

Carol said, "Probably washed up from God knows where."

"The limbs of the skeleton are wrapped around its torso."

The doctor shuddered. But then he lifted his chin and tried to be professional. "I hope you didn't touch it."

"I did. And I haven't washed my hands yet. I could go into a bacteria-induced spiral any minute."

Carol jumped to his protection. "What exactly is that supposed to mean? This isn't funny."

"No. It is definitely not funny. The good doctor is the only comedy show around." Then I pretty much let him have it. "You had some drug-induced panic attack, didn't you? Took more than you should have. And because of that, we cannot get a forensic team out here to examine the body that poor boy found. I'm here on your doorstep because I've made an executive decision, seeing as how there are no other executives around that I know of. Here it is: *You*, Doc, have to be the one to examine the body. And while you're doing that you can think about the girls up at that camp who are at the mercy of a lunatic. Go out to Sandy Point. After you have a look at the body, maybe you'll call Atlanta again and tell them what a reckless mistake you made."

Carol got a pack of cigarettes. She lit one up and

passed the pack to the doctor. He had trouble lighting his because he was hypered up. Demerol will do that to you. Keeps you groggy for long stretches and then, when it's time for more, you're a puppet jangling on a string.

Carol said to me, "I'll see he does what he has to do."

"Good. Fitzy's asking Tommy to guard the scene. Tommy will be glad for the company, I'm sure, trying to keep an eye on Jake and do this too." And then I stepped up into the doc's face to be sure he was in the real world. "There is no fucking plague on this island, Brisbane. There's a serial killer. And we've got to find him. Make Atlanta understand. Just the way you convinced them that we have a plague."

I stomped back to the jeep. I didn't ask the doc if he'd been adopted by a psychiatrist when he was a young child. He hadn't. I'd checked his genealogy on Esther's family tree.

12

By morning, stranded tourists learned of the skeleton and began offering huge bribes to people with boats to smuggle them off the island. Some boat owners at the marina took them up on it, but they were all turned back. Billy and Mick gave it a try and met the same fate. That was why they arrived at the coffee shop late. They'd taken a hundred dollars apiece from four tourists and then had to give it back. They couldn't wait to describe their adventure.

Mick said, "Coast Guard boat offshore carries a mean loudspeaker, let me tell you. Nearly blew my head off bellowing orders." Mick curved his hands and held them to his mouth, forming a megaphone. He shouted, "*Violating the ban means a fine, an arrest, and a quarantine on a private colony.* Hell with that."

"And the people we had on the boat—thought they were going to dump us overboard. Told us we were all crazy for living out here. Used to that, though."

Ernie said, "How far'd you get?"

"Right about the spot where the Coast Guard used to

catch up to us when we were runnin' rum. 'Course they only caught us fifty percent of the time. Now they got radar."

Fitzy said to me, "He's talking about Prohibition. As if it were yesterday. These Block Islanders live to a ripe old age, don't they? Buncha crooks."

Billy, who heard him along with everyone else, said, "Times were pretty rough."

"They're still so rough you want to gouge tourists?"

"Who asked ya, fuzzbucket?" Billy and Mick chuckled together.

The little bell over the door, back up, taped, made its muted ding. Ernie had insisted, telling Willa that it was dangerous to spoil the boy—meaning Jake. Tommy had left Jake in Willa's care again and he kept himself occupied taking an old radio apart. Now he let out a shriek. But it wasn't the bell that did it. The three girls standing in the doorway must have scared him. He knocked his chair over and charged past them, out into the low glare of the morning sun. Willa made a move toward the door, but Ernie grabbed her arm. "Let him go."

"Tommy will—"

"I'll handle Tommy."

Christen, Samantha, and Kate didn't know whether to come in or go back out again. Elijah Leonard's head was tucked under Kate's arm, his face turned away. They hadn't stolen the van this time. They were red and hot and sweating. Jim Lane called to them—"Hey"—no longer judging books by their covers, maybe.

Ernie said, "Never mind Jake, girls, he's a nervous boy. Now get on in here and tell me what I can get you."

Christen said, "We don't want anything. Water."

"Don't be silly. Willa, get something up for these kids."

The girls spotted Fitzy and me and hurried over to our table. Christen said, "We know who the skeleton is."

Chairs scraped across the floor, making a circle around us, and Ernie dragged three more over for the campers. Willa got a pitcher of juice and a plate of pastries. I said, "Sit down, girls," and Fitzy, "We're listening."

The campers drank the juice. Christen wiped her mouth with the back of her hand. "See, there was this one girl who got here a week early, a week before camp opened. Her parents made special arrangements with Irwin. The mother was going to be in Paris and the father—who was divorced from the mother—was traveling on business, so Irwin agreed to—"

Kate interrupted. "Like, *imagine* what Irwin *charged* them!"

Then they all started talking at once. "He took her early. And when the first of the real girls arrived—six of them—the day camp officially opened, they met her. They said all she did was sit on the floor in the corner."

"I mean, they tried to be nice, but she was completely stressed out. She was stressed out because she'd been on Irwin's so-called twelve-hundred-calorie-per-day diet for a week and couldn't get to extra food. She wasn't able to sneak any in her suitcase. The girls gave her chips and cookies and everything—shared what they had—but she was wrecked."

"When I got here I gave her a *million* Drake's Cakes."

"So then, all that week, there was a lot of commotion because the campers were coming in, and then at the end of the first week the six girls who were the first to get to camp realized that the *actual* first girl was gone. The girl who wouldn't move from the corner. So they went to Irwin, and he told them she was a runaway. That she was with her father."

"So this morning when we heard about the skeleton, we paid off the counselors to get the first girl's application. And we called her mother, and her mother said that right after camp started, Irwin called her to tell her the girl had run away. The mother told us she ran away all the time. To her father."

"So this time, the mother says, the father can handle her himself. The mother said, 'I've had enough. I try and try but my ex-husband just keeps giving in to her.' She kept saying stuff like that. Pissed. So we called *him*—the first girl's father. In Santa Barbara. Well, guess what? She's not there. She never was there either!"

"The first girl is nowhere!"

"She is, like, *nowhere*."

"We were so totally crazed we went to Irwin to tell him what we'd found out but, guess what else? He's *gone*. And the van's gone, and he has a boat in New Harbor, so we bet that's gone too."

"And we bet he's *on* it!"

"He's, like, *gone*." Kate's blue eyes blinked and blinked. "He *escaped!* And . . . and . . ."

Christen said to her, "Stupid, try one of these. It's really good," and handed her a pastry.

She took a big bite then looked at it. "What's in it?"

Ernie looked at it. "Prune."

"Prune? Omigod, I'm eating *prune*."

The two older girls were on a roller coaster. They were nearly hysterical, but they still were mothering Kate. I said, "Christen, did you do anything more, once you realized Irwin was gone?"

All three said at the same time, "Yes!"

Thought so.

"We looked through his office and we looked through his files and in his closets and everywhere. We found Erin's stuff. Erin Seldes, that was her name. The first girl. Her suitcases were there, her backpack, and all the books on her school's summer reading list were in a box with her name on it."

"He *hid* her stuff."

"So, see, Irwin must be the one doing it. He killed the first girl and then he killed Dana and Rachel, and now he finally figured he'd get caught because of the first girl's skeleton."

I said, "No. He just believed what he wanted to believe. That the first girl, Erin, had run away to her father's."

"Then why didn't he send her stuff to her?"

"He would wait for instructions. He wouldn't spend money shipping her things until he heard from the father. But he didn't throw them away. He would have if he'd—Listen, who's up there with the rest of the campers?"

"We've got two counselors left. They're all together in the dining hall."

Fitzy asked Ernie for his phone. He called the Coast Guard. The girls had been right about Irwin's departure. The guardsmen had spotted him and warned Irwin to turn his boat back. He wouldn't, so they were forced to fire across his bow. With that, he cut his engines. They detained him at sea, which is what the Coast Guard will do if it orders you to stop and you don't. Not an empty threat, as with Billy and Mick, which they try first. But Irwin decided to take his chances even with the gunshot. They chased his boat, got up some reinforcements, surrounded it, and trained several guns at him. They followed orders to guard him while awaiting further instructions. They floated food and water to him. They floated metal containers for him to store his wastes. They threatened to shoot him if he urinated overboard.

Our three campers all felt good about that because they were convinced Irwin killed the girls. Not me. Not Fitzy either, I could tell. Because Irwin didn't do it. It's rare that grifters kill. They simply want more money than they can earn selling used cars. What they don't want is trouble. But it was just as well to let the girls believe it was Irwin. They felt safer. They had simmered down.

Willa took the girls back to camp. She said she was going to call every one of the girls' parents, and those who still remained reluctant about getting their kids after the ban was lifted—those were the ones she'd tell about the skeleton. "And if they still don't agree to it, I'll tell them they'll be charged with endangerment to the welfare of a child by the Rhode Island State Police. You can do that, right, Fitzy?"

"You tell them that."

She said to the girls, "I was fat when I was a kid. Then, one day, I guess when I was about your age, Christen, or you, Sam, I decided I just had to stop eating so much food. I didn't lose weight, but I didn't gain any more either. I stayed the same. Later, when I teamed up with Ernie, we got so busy with the store, I liked spending time taking care of the store more than eating. So I lost weight. Not enough to put me on the cover of *Glamour*. You can see that, but so what. And I didn't even know I was losing weight till my clothes got too big. Someday, that'll happen to you. Then . . . no more camps, see? Meanwhile, for now? Today? You girls eat. We'll all eat. Or these pastries'll be stale before you know it."

She picked up a pastry. So did we. We would join in with the girls to support Willa's theory.

Before she left, Willa told us she intended to stay with them, get a couple of women up there to join her. Then Jim Lane went with me to look for Spike. No luck. I watched him pedal away. Just a boy, but big and strong. Maybe not a wimp at all. Maybe he just pretended to be a wimp. Maybe he did sell the girls terribly tainted drugs. Maybe the other boy who'd been tortured a long, long time ago did not arrive on the island and end up killing the campers. Maybe it was this boy who did it. Maybe he found the skeleton because he'd put it there in the first place. Happens all the time.

I got Delby on the phone. "I need to know how long would it take a colony of gulls to strip a body of every shred of flesh. I need to know right away and I need to know definitively."

"A colony of what?"

"Gulls. Seagulls." I wouldn't explain that "sea" was redundant.

She said, "I know just the place on Yahoo! to find out."

She'd find an answer to a question like that faster at her computer than she would if she checked with the lab. I had to wonder if labs would eventually be replaced by search engines.

She called back within fifteen minutes and first verified a few facts. "Are you talking a large colony of seagulls?"

"Yes."

"More than a hundred birds?"

"Yes."

"A hundred will pick the bones clean in an hour. But was the body alive before the seagulls got to it?"

"I hope not."

"Sorry, boss. Well, here's the thing: seagulls don't eat anything that's been dead more than half an hour. A dead something in the sun, that is. In the shade, hour and a half. That would be at sixty degrees Fahrenheit, give or take. And here's what I had the misfortune to find out without having to ask. Ninety-nine percent of all living creatures die by being eaten alive. How about that? Humans are the exception—they're only rarely eaten alive—alligators, sharks, starving pet dogs, or zoo animals being the guilty parties. Man."

Man, is right. Sometimes, while sitting on the chaise, I'd watch gulls carry crabs to the cliff edge, turn them onto their backs, and peck out their insides while their legs were flailing. And of course I thought of Spike, wherever he was, treating a small mouse like a soccer ball until he got bored and broke its neck.

I asked her, "You got all this on Yahoo!?"

"Yeah. Wonder what reference librarians are doing for work these days."

"Thanks, Delby."

"You want it, you got it, boss. Why I'm here. Listen, Auerbach's got some stuff too—probably not from Yahoo!—and he's really frantic so get ready. I'm putting him on."

He came on. When he began speaking, his voice was rattling with excitement. "Poppy, I can be an idiot. I'm looking into wackos hitting steel barrels with crowbars when here is what I should have been looking into instead: sound the human ear *can't* hear."

Here we go. "Starting with, If a tree falls in the forest, et cetera?"

"Well . . . no. There's no sound from the tree, period, if there are no sensory cells to—"

"Never mind, Auerbach. Just get back to where you were."

"I was getting to sound waves. They are very important when it comes to the transmission of sound. Frequencies above twenty-thousand Hertz, which we can't hear, will repel vermin and can dislodge the tartar right off your teeth. Too extravagant for your yearly trip to the dentist, though. And during the initial test trials of aircraft breaking the sound barrier wherein the crafts' engines created no sound, there was the same trauma to both pilots and crew that occurred with World War One gunnery soldiers: chest-wall vibrations, gagging, respiratory rhythm changes. Once again, the military had to break out the sound protection devices, but this time they accidentally fell into an altogether different scenario. The military looked into creating ultrasound *artificially*. To use as a weapon. But it didn't go anywhere, too costly. Just the research would have meant a significant budget increase. But here's what *did* go somewhere. Infrasound!"

"Never heard of it."

"It's sound waves with too *low* a Hertz measurement to be heard, waves that *bypass* the sensory cells. If the infrasound waves are directed at a victim with precision and intensity through a tube, the victim is very seriously injured. But if—"

"Auerbach, did you say a *tube*?"

"More a pipe, actually. Like an organ pipe. First thing that happens, the victim can't breathe; his head pounds like he's got a major migraine going; he has a panic attack and shakes like a leaf, he loses his ability to stand upright, he experiences extreme nausea and vomiting, and then he can't move. If the intensity is increased further, his vision becomes blurred, he has seizures, he convulses, and finally the hollow organs actually rupture, starting with the organs of the ear.

"And get this, Poppy. Infrasound weapons *have* been made and tested. Pentagon supports it because sound tubes cost less than Bunsen burners and would be capable of controlling crowds so much more effectively than tear gas—only the bad guys would be throwing up all over themselves. Cool."

His delirious voice reminded me of the campers. "Auerbach—"

"So, Poppy, these weapons are referred to as acoustic lasers and are patented under names like Consciousness-Altering Tubes and—here's my favorite—Nervous System Excitation Devices. That one combines strobe lights with the infrasound and induces complete sensory disorientation. We tried it in Somalia, and so did the Brits in Ireland in the seventies. Trouble is, the offense was equally affected, the guys at the offensive end of the tubes. The sound protection equivalent of gas masks hasn't been perfected."

"Auerbach, tell me you don't think we've got someone here with a Nervous System Excitation Device."

"I'm never surprised by anything."

I still am.

"Poppy, infrasound causes the organ of Corti—it's in the cochlea—to be torn apart. I went back to tissue samples. The organs of Corti in the girls' ears were torn into pieces so small you needed a microscope to see them."

His voice was closing in at twenty thousand Hertz, easy. "Stop and listen to me. Stop."

"Okay."

"Could real sound, if it were horrendous enough, do that?"

"Poppy, I *am* talking about real sound."

"And I'm talking about real sound to a *layman*."

"Oh. Sorry. I haven't got that information."

"Then go back to the autopsy in Brazil."

"Brazil?"

"The cop's daughter who was killed in a steel barrel."

"Oh. Okay."

"In the meantime, Auerbach, what's your guess? Was the Harvard doctor right?"

"You mean, can you kill someone by bashing a steel barrel with a crowbar if the victim is encased in the barrel? My guess is yes." He sounded sad.

"Listen to me again, Auerbach. I know how things are. How there are some scenarios that are not as exhilarating as others. But exhilaration is secondary, isn't it?"

"Yes."

"So when you hear galloping, check for horses before you run around looking for zebras. Mind, the zebra theory is still valid though, okay?"

"Okay."

"You said infrasound bypasses the sensory cells, right?"

"Right."

"And the girls' sensory cells?"

He was silent.

"Auerbach?"

"Disintegrated."

"You've done an incredible job. But keep your pants on."

* * *

That evening, I said to Fitzy, "We've got to figure a way to get to Providence. We need to poke around there. We need to find out who those three sisters tortured. Delby can't get an ID on that boy." I didn't see the percentage in filling him in on the ultrasound theory.

"If a police file on the case exists, it's sealed."

"We'll unseal it."

"We can't get past the Coast Guard. I haven't got a scuba diving certificate."

I did. "Listen, I'm serious. Haven't ships managed to get past military blockades?"

"Not lately. Radar detection is pretty advanced."

"This isn't a military blockade. There aren't that many Coast Guard boats out there. Maybe fifty percent of attempts would succeed today too."

He thought for a minute. Then he looked into my eyes. He grinned. "Poppy, forget it."

"If they ran rum, they could run us."

"Shit."

We found Billy and Mick at the pool table at the Club Soda. When they saw us, they said, "Hey, it's the law."

Fitzy said, "We come to challenge you to a game." He said to me out of the corner of his mouth, "Do you shoot pool, FBI?"

"I shoot everything that needs shooting."

Fitzy and I were good. But they beat us. We bought them a round.

At the bar, lined up on stools, huddled together, we asked if it could be done. Based on the assumption that they hadn't tried all that hard with the tourists.

They hadn't. Mick said, "All the same, tough. Real tough."

"See, we could do it if the sea was calm," Billy said.

"Boat with a real shallow keel, use a trawl engine, minimum noise—"

"Thing is, it would take six or seven hours to get across."

"And we'd have to do it at night. If the wind isn't too bad. Blowing in a good direction to boot."

I said, "Well, it's night. How do we find out if the wind isn't too bad?"

Mick said, "You go down to the beach and squirt into the air."

Oh, joy.

Fitzy said, "You'll have to turn your back, Poppy."

We all went down to the harbor. Billy said, "If it's a go, we'll cut the parking lot lights. A little confusion never hurts. Jake'll do it for us."

I turned my back. So did Fitzy. They tested the wind, zipped back up, and talked fisherman talk. The verdict was no.

Billy felt bad. "Sorry, Poppy. The wind over the water's brisk. It's the open Atlantic out there, not a lake. Maybe tomorrow night, right, Mick?"

"Yeah. We'll try tomorrow." They wanted to do it.

Fitzy said, "Thanks." Then, "Poppy, let's get these boys back to their game. Then I'm going to call in some chits."

Within an hour, Fitzy had clearance to leave. He said to me, "Actually, I'm almost as good with a phone as you are. I just get lazy. I know a lot of secrets, Poppy. It's what I do best—threaten people whose secrets I know. A hell of a lot of people are afraid of me. I swept the mob out of a place where they were more firmly ensconced than they are in Palermo. So just now I've promised a few active chiefs out there that I'm going to back off for a while. 'Course, I was lying. As if I'd back off from anything. I'm always amazed that these goons believe my bullshit. So they called in chits of their own.

Pretty soon, next week probably, someone's going to dip my feet in wet cement and throw me in the drink. But considering what my life has become, it'll be worth it."

"No, it won't."

But he was pacing, raring to go. I drove him to the airport. We waited there for a couple of hours, sitting in the jeep, looking at the stars, listening for the sound of an engine. Fitzy said, "Want to make out?"

I looked over at him. He'd crossed his eyes. I had an uncontrollable laughing fit. So did he. And then we ended up holding hands, saying nothing until the lights on the strip came on just long enough for a plane to come in. Before Fitzy left, during the time we were holding hands, I said, "I was interviewing this guy for a job once. He'd had surgery—it was obvious—for a harelip. It was the first thing that registered when I asked him to sit down. Then I began to notice how he had these great eyebrows that kind of went straight across. Then, as we talked, I became fascinated with his previous work, admiring of what he'd accomplished. And then his personality came through. He was not only cheerful, he was happy, I could tell. And when I saw him the second time, when I got to tell him he was hired, I realized after he'd left the office that I'd forgotten about the harelip. I hadn't noticed it. And until this minute, I realize I've never thought of it since. I'm not aware of it when I see him."

"Poppy, what in God's holy name are you talking about?"

"The girls. I was thinking about them. I was thinking about them without thinking they were fat. I'd forgotten the fat."

He thought for a moment, then said, "I got a call once. Abandoned baby. I'm holding this baby and I'm describing him over the phone and when I was finished

I was asked, 'What race?' I had to look down at him to say, 'Black.' I realized I wasn't thinking *black* the whole time I had him. I was thinking *baby*."

Once Fitzy was gone, I went back to Joe's cottage and waited till morning to call Harry in Atlanta. I didn't need to stir him from his bed for my hypothetical question.

When I asked it, he said, "No, Poppy. No one gets clearance under any circumstances. There is no clearance whatsoever when we issue a travel ban."

"Sorry, my mistake." I hung up. It was fortuitous that Fitzy could accomplish such a thing without Harry's knowing about it. But I'd needed to make sure. Fitzy arrested wouldn't help anything. Rhode Island might be the world's smallest state but it's got politicians who can get whatever they want done, one way or another. Texas can't do that; I don't know about Alaska. Fitzy could take care of himself.

I wouldn't sit around doing nothing. Denying the killer could be one of the volunteers guarding the girls was worse than foolish. He was lurking, and vigilance was the order of the day. I wouldn't even go to the Patio first; I ate two pieces of toast and threw a few things into a bag. Before I got in the ragtop I tried Spike yet again, shook his box of dry cat food. No big orange tail sprang up from the grass. If I left food out for him, every vertebrate and invertebrate on the island would be fighting for it. The gulls, of course, would be the big winners. So I compromised and left a bowl of water. Spike had had a lot of time sharpening his mouse trapping skills. He'd fend.

When I got to the camp, I found chaos. One of the girls was ringing the dinner bell, which happened to be mercilessly discordant. The rest were clumped in circles together on the grass in various stages of despair. The two counselors were trying to bring about some kind of control by screaming at them. Christen spotted me and came running. Her face was red. She blurted out, "It's Stupid!"

I jumped out of the jeep. "What's wrong with her?"

"She's gone!"

"She can't be gone."

"Yes, she is. Because the freaking Cabbage Patch doll is gone too."

"Where's Willa?"

"We had breakfast, and then she went back to her store for supplies. She said she wouldn't be gone long—told the counselors not to let any of us leave. While she was gone, Stupid snuck away. She told us she had to put Elijah Leonard down for his nap. That was half an hour ago. Longer, I think. We just realized she wasn't here now!"

One of the counselors was wringing her hands together. "Everyone was cooperating. We never saw where she went!"

I looked around. The bell was quiet. The girls were stopped in their tracks, staring at me. I said, in my calmest voice, "I'd like to speak with the counselors."

The hand-wringer and another girl stepped up to me. I told them I needed their help. The hand-wringer said, "We're scared."

Christen stalked up to her. "What the hell have *you* got to be scared of? You're not *fat*!"

I put my arm around Christen. I asked the counselor, "Is the van back?"

"Yes. But it's making a funny noise."

"That's all right. As long as it moves. I want you and

three campers to drive to the clinic and tell the doctor about Kate."

"Tell him about who?"

"About Stupid."

I thought of sending the other counselor to Tommy, but he was still making sure the skeleton was left alone and somehow keeping Jake under wraps. I said to her, "I want you to get these girls into groups of four. Each group is to head off in a different direction and call her name. Maybe she misplaced her doll and she's in the bracken or at the beach looking for him." I was trying to sound rational but I knew Kate would have heard the camp bell if she was within half a mile of us. Maybe she was following the route she'd watched Rachel take, hoping to come upon the man with the picnic. "Be sure to go all the way around the point."

I said to them, "She wouldn't have gone off with someone. She knew better. We'll find her. Christen and Samantha, you're coming with me. Let's get moving. Now." But Kate *didn't* know better. She was ten years old.

One counselor grabbed some girls and headed for the van and the other began counting the rest of them off. They formed their groups and hustled away.

Christen and Samantha got in the ragtop with me.

I started it up and took off. The first thing Samantha said was, "She doesn't need food. Her grandfather sent her enough food packages to feed the whole camp. So she's not out looking for the picnic man. And she never lost sight of that doll. Never. She went off with someone. It had to be someone she knew. Someone she trusted. Someone who promised her Drake's Cakes because she's finally out of them."

Christen said, "Maybe that guy from the grocery

store. Willa's husband. He's always nice to us. He's always adding a few Drake's Cakes to her bag when we can get into town. I mean, Stupid is obsessed. So maybe the guy promised her more."

And maybe Esther had heard such a promise. And there wasn't an opportunity to kill Esther via torture because there was no way to entice Esther to wherever he enticed the girls. But *Ernie*? And then I remembered all the Styrofoam boxes piled up on Esther's kitchen table. He'd paid many a visit to her. I said, "We'll start there, then, at the store. We'll ask Ernie if he saw her this morning."

Just Willa was in the store, stocking up for the girls as she'd told them. "What's wrong?"

"Willa, one of the girls left the camp."

"Oh, no!"

"Where's Ernie?"

"He's with Jake. Jake started having some kind of attack or something. Took him to the clinic." Her eyes were wet. "Doc was going to force him to take a Valium. Which girl?"

Christen and Samantha both said, "Stupid."

"Stupid? She said she was going to play cards with you kids."

Christen put her hands to her mouth. "We didn't let her play," she wailed. Her bottom lip began to tremble.

I turned to Willa. "Go get Tommy and Ernie. Maybe the doc's got Jake settled. Get Jim Lane's kid. Get everyone. We have to find her."

I hustled the girls back into the jeep. I could only hope that Kate hadn't died yet. Maybe she was in the throes of whatever it was that killed the other girls. Maybe she could still be saved before he was finished with her.

I drove fast, and for the sake of the girls I stared

hard at the road ahead of me, as if I knew where I was going. I asked myself, Where would the killer dump the body this time? Someplace different. Six islanders were patrolling Rodman's Hollow, and Sandy Point was taken care of. Tommy would have sent someone there if he'd had to leave. So I didn't head toward the long narrow spit of Sandy Point. I would drive to Joe's side of the island, the southwest coast, sparsely populated—to the rocky unused beaches where his cottage perched above the Atlantic—and then I'd head north until the road ran out at the cut into New Harbor.

The road along the western shore was just inland, narrow but paved, high sea grasses on each side. I looked at Joe's map. It was printed in 1953. Joe told me nothing had changed. The road didn't have a name then and it didn't now. Everyone referred to it as the Western Road. There were five unpaved tracks in addition to Joe's that led away from the road to the sea. Once past the track to Joe's, it took me two minutes to reach the one after his, Dickens Bluff. I turned onto it and drove to the shoreline, where it ended at the edge of an eroded clay cliff. There was nothing but a long tumble of charcoal gray dry muck reaching right into the water. The stuff looked like the deep innards of the earth, something no one was ever supposed to glimpse.

The next track was Dory's Cove Avenue. Avenue. Incredible. Maybe a joke on Dory. Wasn't a dory a boat? I took it. There had been a cove, but it was full of the charcoal clay, a sandy beach turned into a muddy ugly flat. Nothing was there.

The next track was unnamed and led to what had been a lifesaving station, swept out to sea by a storm in 1867. The storm had also swept out the beach, and a rocky shoal now jutted out of the water. Joe had shown me the original foundation of the station. He'd wanted to build there. No go, too exposed. I turned the jeep around.

I sped along. The elevation lessened. I could see the ocean glimmering to my left. Two tracks remained. At the end of the next one, Clay Head, the head itself had eased away to sea level. There was a wide beach, big waves. Bikes were parked by the side of the track. At least a dozen people were belly-boarding. Joe and I had gone surf casting there. I put the jeep in reverse.

Christen said, "This is taking so long."

"I know."

I looked at my watch. It just seemed that way. We'd left Willa's less than fifteen minutes ago.

I looked at the map. One track left, Tughole Way. This tughole was abandoned—barren, no more peat. At the corner was the soaring electrical tower, the transformer that directed electricity from the mainland to the island. I jammed the accelerator to the floor, reached the track in another minute, and took a left by the tower. Tughole Way ended in a cleft carved right through the center of another wide beach. The cleft was full of rocks, coated with clinging blackened seaweed. The cleft kept going right into the sea, another rut gouged out by the ancient glacier. It acted as a funnel, sucking in debris, seaweed, mounds of shells and piles of driftwood. A large old piling, ripped from a dock somewhere, ten feet long and two feet around, lay a few feet from the encroaching tide.

Christen said, "I hear something."

We all did, a soft sound intermittent with the crashing of the waves.

"It was a gull, Christen." A ring of them, overhead, were scoping out the beach. I turned off the engine and they came in lower, cawing at one another. We listened carefully and then we heard the sound again, louder.

And longer. It did sound like a gull, one of their more terrible calls. But it came from the other side of the driftwood. I could only imagine the very worst, that the gulls had found her before we had, had completed their diabolical feeding, and that there would be another skeleton behind the length of piling. What had Delby said? An hour and a half.

I leaped over the jeep door and ran, shouting at the girls to stay where they were, but Christen was already out. I couldn't stop her. We left Samantha to extricate herself from the backseat.

I heard a low groan just as I reached the driftwood. A groan is not a noise any gull makes. The groan was human.

On the other side, Kate was on her side, lying still. Her hands were clapped over her ears, her eyes squeezed shut. Her clothes were torn, but she hadn't ripped them off. A gag was wrapped around her mouth. Something had stopped him. He'd brought her to the beach and left her the way you'd abandon a baby, as he'd done with the camper on Sandy Point—Erin, who was already dead.

I threw myself over the log and practically lying on top of her, pulled the gag out of her mouth, off her head. She let out a shocking, bloodcurdling screech, and then so did Christen, staring down at us from the other side of the piling. We were inundated with a horrible chorus of awful screeches from the gulls circling willy-nilly just above our heads. They came together and flew off over the ocean.

Kate began flailing wildly. She was freezing cold. I wrapped my body around hers. I looked up at Christen. "There's a blanket in the back of the jeep. Quick, Christen." She was gone. The blanket would not warm Kate. But it would be the only way we could possibly carry her.

Kate started screaming, "Stop them! Stop them!"

I tried to pull her arms down but I couldn't; her muscles were spasmed.

Christen and Samantha were beside me. Christen let herself fall alongside Kate. She took the girl's face in her hands. She said, "Stupid, it's me. It's Christen. You're with us, with me and Sam."

Kate wrenched herself away. The edge of a wave touched my leg. Whoever left her there had depended on the incoming tide to finish off his miserable deed. He'd thought of the old tughole but it was caved in and grown over. This littered beach, the rising tide, was simpler.

"Please, please, stop them," Kate begged.

I let go of her. "Girls, we've got to wrap her in this blanket. Somehow. We've got to wrap her up as tight as we can and get her to the clinic."

We tried. We couldn't do it. She was swinging back and forth, crashing against us. And then Samantha saw something down the beach. She backed away, stood, went stumbling toward the crevice that cut through the sand, and stopped just shy of the funnel of rocks. She picked up a large wet lump and ran back with it, dropped down beside Kate and pushed Elijah Leonard into the girl's face. "Look, Stupid. It's Elijah Leonard. He's here with you. But he's all wet. We'll have to put him under our hair dryer."

She rubbed the doll against Kate's face. And Kate stopped struggling, though her entire body was shaking uncontrollably.

We laid the blanket out and rolled Kate and her doll onto it. We wrapped her up, tied the ends of the blanket into tight knots. I had Samantha shove her arms under Kate's neck and shoulders, Christen the same beneath her knees. I took the middle of her body. A wave came in and the blanket was saturated.

We couldn't lift her.

"We'll have to drag her."

We each grabbed fistfuls of blanket and pulled. We got her a few inches along the sand. The waves were around our ankles.

Christen wailed, "We can't do it."

"In ten minutes, she'll be under water. We have to at least get her around the driftwood." We pulled. The blanket ripped.

Kate began to struggle again. She started to beg once more. Begging for whatever was happening to her to stop. Her friends had tears streaming down their cheeks. And then we heard the mopeds, three of them. We watched as each came skidding to a stop next to the jeep: three couples in their twenties, all sturdy and strapping, laughing and yanking their helmets off. One by one, their engines were silenced, and one by one they stopped laughing as they caught sight of us.

In front of his clinic, Brisbane injected Kate with a tranquilizer as she lay crushed across her friends' laps in the back of the ragtop. They were holding on to her for dear life. Within seconds she calmed, and then she was asleep. The doc said, "I'll take her in my van to the airstrip. Where's Joe?"

"He's in DC."

"Okay, I'll get a plane from Providence if we don't find one."

Carol was next to him. She said, "Doc, the ban."

I ran into the clinic and called Atlanta. I don't know what I sounded like. I don't know how clearly I spoke. I don't know what threats I tried, but I made Harry understand that we had another victim who was seriously injured; she wasn't dead yet but she'd be dead if someone didn't get out to the island and take her to a hospital.

He asked me if there was an airport.

"A landing strip."

"Get her there."

He told me Kate would be taken to a Federal quarantine unit with medical facilities on Staten Island.

I said to him before I hung up, "I never knew about it."

He said, "No one knows about it."

I wondered if Fitzy knew about it.

We got Kate onto a stretcher and into the back of Brisbane's van. Before he drove off, the doc said to me, "She's just a little girl." Christen and Samantha were looking at him, standing by the side of his driveway, exhausted, their faces completely drained of color. I said, "They're all little girls."

13

Everyone was back at the camp. Willa was there too. They'd heard we'd found Kate and I told them she would soon be in the hospital. I didn't dwell on her condition. Carol had come with me. She would be in charge of the girls in Merlin House, Willa in Arthur, each with a counselor, and me in Lancelot. I would sleep in Kate's bunk. When we arrived, Willa stood with the two counselors in the front of the dining hall where they were having the campers put together pans of lasagna. I told them it was best if they all went back to what they were doing.

Christen was very quiet, disturbed, her friend Samantha now becoming the strong one. Christen had to go right to her bunk. Samantha and I sat with her. Samantha said, "See, Christen, the main thing is that Stupid is in the hospital. A special hospital. Get everything else out of your mind. She'll be all right."

"She'll never be all right."

"Yes, she will. Her grandpa will visit her there, bring

her another suitcase of stuff to eat. Bring her big bags of you-know-what. And . . . she'll get counseling."

"We should have watched her."

"How could we have thought in a million years that Stupid would go off with someone? I mean, she was always hanging on one of us."

"We didn't let her play cards."

"But she was always *dropping* the cards because of Elijah Leonard. Maybe the picnic man was behind one of the Porta-Potties and grabbed her when she went to the bathroom."

"She wouldn't even go to the Porta-Potties alone, and you know it."

The two of them became quiet, contemplating their failure. I told them we should pack up Kate's things so they could be sent to her in the hospital. So they did that, glad to have something to do for her, stacking up her CDs and MP3 players and books. Folding her clothes, laying them in her suitcase.

The air felt heavy, the humidity thick. We heard a rumbling. Rumbling was not uncommon on Block Island. Storm clouds could suddenly cover a blazing sun, only to scuttle away just when you were sure the thunderclaps couldn't get any louder. There was another noise, louder yet, and we all jumped. But it was only Carol coming in, letting the door bang behind her.

"Poppy, Joe is on the phone in Irwin's office. Phone's full of static, but you'll be able to hear him." Then she said to the girls, "Ernie is bringing ice cream later. The lasagna's almost done. Finish up and come to the dining room."

I went with Carol and let them pack the rest. The sky outside was a sickly green. A wind was coming up and the bracken was rustling.

Inside Irwin's office, I picked up the phone. "Hello, Joe."

He didn't say hello, he released a flood of explanation instead. "I was a fool. They're my family. They treat me like I'm a kid. I forget all my problems when I'm on Block Island. They never ask me how I can work for the ATF, how I can go around shooting innocent women and children. They're respectful. I didn't want to be a part of whatever was happening there. I didn't want to imagine that one of those people could be a sociopath.

"Poppy, this morning I went out to Dulles. I didn't know about the travel ban. I couldn't believe it. I called Harry. He refused to help me out. He said an exception was made for the girl only because it was a life-and-death situation and useful to their scenario medically. I said, 'What girl?' I didn't know what he was talking about. He told me about Kate. Jesus God. I called him every name I could come up with, him and his damn travel ban. Didn't do any good, he refused to give me clearance to fly to Block Island. I called the hospital in Staten Island to see how she was."

"What did they say?"

"Right now, she's sedated. Her family is there. Apparently a dozen of them."

"Were her eardrums perforated?"

"No."

That was something. "Was she able to—"

"No. When she speaks, she's incoherent. So I came to Providence to wait it out, met up with Fitzy at the airport. He can get us back over to the Block, ban or no ban—I'll never understand how—but there are storm cells everywhere. Flights are suspended for now anyway. We'll have to wait it out. A few hours, at least, probably more. So Fitzy and I got to talking. He told me about Esther's clippings. About the boy. I thought he'd lost his mind. But he hadn't."

"I know."

"Well, *I* know because Fitzy and I went to the place where they keep the old police files to see what we could find. That's where I am now, some warehouse in downtown Providence. The files are long gone, wasn't a matter of an open case. But as it turned out, we never would have had to look for anything after all. We just told the librarian about it, and he remembered the case. This librarian is quite an old fellow. One of his cousins used to work in Newport, used to take the family's guests fishing. The family of the three sisters. We're looking through a stack of papers now, to see where the psychiatrist went—"

There was a crack of lightning, a roll of thunder, and the line went dead. I stared at it and started pressing all the numbers, and then I smacked the receiver against the desk.

I looked up to see Carol standing in the door. She came over and patted my back. "Christen and Sam are with the others. Come eat with us." She replaced the phone receiver. "I'm surprised the lines held out that long. First thing these electrical storms do is put out the phone system." She turned on a light. "Generator's still going strong. Good for Jake. I had him come over yesterday to hook up something more powerful for the girls. Told Tommy it would give him something to do."

"He could understand what you wanted?"

" 'Course. Jake isn't dumb, just has some screwed-up circuits. Doc thinks he's always playing with wires and stuff because he's trying to get his own wiring in order. Doc's not all bad, Poppy." But she didn't get any sympathy from me. "One of the girls showed Jake her laptop. You should have seen him. He didn't know what it was, but once he did, he liked it! Started doing things on it right away. But then it made a noise and he got scared. The girls felt bad. So they offered him some candy in return for fixing up the generator. Turtles. He took three. I didn't want them to think he was a hog, so I explained to the girls that thing he has about three. Explained it as best I could. I mean, you can imagine how hard it is to explain Jake to anyone. But they understood. Those girls eat in threes themselves. So they gave him three *boxes*. Jake put them under his arm, went running home, smiling ear to ear."

A crackling jumble of lightning veined the sky, a mass of bright white capillaries. Carol ran out to the porch. I followed her. We stood and watched the light show. All the campers were at the windows of the dining hall, taking it in. "Summer storms do this sometimes, Poppy. The cells form up over our waters, and then these thick clouds gather above the bluffs. Sometimes we have a rain of lightning bolts, hitting the water, hitting us. Goes on and on. Then the clouds split open and we get a drenching. We pray for that part, the flooding. We're prepared here for flooding, but not the other, the lightning bolts that touch the ground. Our buildings are very old. The wood is dry as tinder. We can't do much about the flash fires popping up all over. We have to depend on the deluge to put them out."

The entire island lit up. Carol said, "Get ready," and her words were hardly out of her mouth when they were followed by the loudest and longest clap of thunder I'd ever heard. The girls at the windows stepped back. Carol said, "Mother Nature'll distract those kids from their worries."

Huge drops of rain came pelting down. We dashed across the grounds while the sky lit up again. This time there wasn't a thunderclap; instead, a rumble of thunder rolled and rolled, its volume up and down, up and down. We reached the dining hall and stood on the porch. Carol said, "When the bolts hit the ocean close by us, they rebound from wave to wave across the water. Timpani. That's the name for it."

"More like a cymbal player running amok."

"Actually, timpani is good. Means the cells are staying over the sea. Ocean can't catch fire."

"How long will it last?"

"It'll be all around us at least till ten tonight, midnight, a little later maybe; depends on how many cell clusters keep forming. Definitely clear out by dawn, though, just kind of peter out, you'll see. Let's hope a cell doesn't end up zeroing in on these barracks. One stab of lightning—they'll go up in thirty seconds." I had already figured that, considering the warning Joe had given the girls about their candles.

The rain was coming down harder, blowing sideways.

"Carol, can we leave a light on in each of the houses all night?"

"Sure. Jake did a job, I'll tell ya."

My hair blew into my eyes. The bracken was whipping from side to side. Carol said, "We'll be able to keep these kids in tonight, Poppy, for sure. And any drug dealers will stay inside too."

That was, in fact, the first thing I told the girls when we got inside. They looked at one another. Drug dealing was a story they weren't buying anymore. I knew that, but I couldn't bring myself to say *picnic man* and I certainly wasn't going to say *Chinese water torturer*. Then there came a great crack and a brilliant flash. Accompanying the timpani that followed came wide sheets of rain. The noise of the bombardment on the tin-patched roof was ferocious.

The girls had gone back to their tables, and while they ate they watched the rain crashing against the windows. Willa brought Carol and me a couple of plates of lasagna. I had a bite. "Wonderful." It was. I could eat a horse. A moose. I thought of Kate. I ate. So did everyone else, all of us mopping up sauce with huge chunks of bread. The level of chatter expanded and rose, drowning out the storm until the door was thrown open by a great gust of wind and the rain blew in on us. Carol and I had to put all our weight against the door to shut it. Then we sat down and the girls were silent again. The storm that had distracted them now scared them.

We played board games the rest of the afternoon. The girls were competitive.

They put on music after that. We sang. We danced. And we laughed. Carol had brought a record player and a stack of vinyls. She taught us all the dance James Brown had named after himself, and we spun around the floor, dancing and singing all those feeling fine, feeling good lines. I love oldies. I knew the words to all Carol's songs and most of the girls knew the words to a lot of them, but they all knew one particular Frankie Valli hit. They played and sang "Big Girls Don't Cry" three times in honor of Jake. In honor of themselves, I thought.

Carol picked up an album, slid it to the bottom of the pile, and chose another. I caught a glimpse of the one she'd hid. *The Zombies*. They'd had a big hit in 1964: "She's Not There."

The sky outside the windows, already dim with the storm, grew darker still as the late summer dusk set in.

The bare lightbulbs gave off an eerie yellow glow, creating shadowy hulks on the walls. Willa announced we'd have a little supper. She turned us all into an assembly line. She had long loaves of Italian bread, which she spread with mustard and mayonnaise and sprinkled with oil and vinegar. She had us placing six varieties of cold cuts and three kinds of cheese, lettuce, and tomatoes across the open loaves.

The girls were mesmerized by the operation.

"What's that?"

"Mortadella."

"What's mortadella?"

"Fancy bologna."

"What's that?"

"Chopped pimento." She talked while she sprinkled.

"Are those anchovies?" was followed by moans. "Please hold the anchovies."

"Hey, I like anchovies."

"Willa, how about anchovies just on half?" I said.

"Sure." She looked up at me. "I've always loved kids."

"I've never known any until fairly recently."

She cut the heroes into one-foot lengths. The girls helped themselves. Carol and I split one. I said to Willa, "Where's yours?"

"Not that hungry."

Willa looked a little worn. Much more jumpy. Weren't we all?

One of the girls said, "Now *this* is a fat farm!"

They were content because they were all in the same boat, being bad. Eating was always the worst kind of bad for them, and now no one cared. Comfort in numbers. Christen wasn't taking comfort, though. She sat by a window, alone, nibbling the edge of her sandwich. She'd retreated back to wherever she'd been before. The girls had surrounded Sam. They let Christen be,

Samantha told them to. "It's what she wants. She'll come around if we give her some space."

Ernie arrived. He was wearing oilskin, head to toe, and had on a hat with a long brim all but covering his face. An ancient mariner come to make sure the girls knew they were being taken care of, watched over. He would leave in his wake gallons of ice cream, containers of hot fudge, packages of nuts, cans of whipped cream, even jars of maraschino cherries. He had large plastic bowls, spoons, napkins.

The girls began scooping. I said to him, "Ernie, this is perfect. They need to keep their minds off of Kate. They can't stop blaming themselves."

"That was the idea. Wish I could get *my* mind off her, though. Her and her Drake's Cakes. Wish I could stop blaming *myself*."

He went to the door and the girls all sang out, "Thank you!"

He turned and smiled. He looked like some kind of apparition in the pale yellow light. A ghost of a fisherman off a sword boat. A diabolical serial killer? I couldn't think it possible.

He said to me, "I'm going to drive the camp van out onto the road and park it there in case you need to get anything. In case you need to get me. This place is a swamp. The water is collecting and the track to the road is filling up. I'll leave the keys in it for you. We won't have phones back for a long time."

"If I need anything, I can take the jeep."

He said, "That's one antique vehicle, Poppy. All in all, best not to go anywhere." And he was gone. The wind slammed the door behind him.

The rain seemed to let up a little, or maybe we just hoped it would. We decided it was time to make our way back to the bunkhouses. We splashed across the grounds, and minutes after we were inside again the timpani resumed. We sat on the bunks listening to it. Then one after the other, the girls had to use the Porta-Potties so I watched as they'd run out into the storm, come back drenched, and have to change their clothes. Getting soaked to the skin made them laugh. Each girl would give a report on another girl from another house who she'd met up with going to the bathroom. They began gossiping and giggling and then took out books and journals and postcards. Christen lay in her bunk, her back to the rest of us. I knew she could not stop thinking of Kate, could not stop beating up on herself. She would take comfort from no one. Tomorrow, I would force some comfort on her. Tonight she needed to come to terms.

By the time they settled in to sleep, it was almost eleven o'clock. They'd played music and eaten vast quantities of junk food they kept pulling out of suit-cases, from their backpacks, and from under their beds. I finally understood now that children could have addictions just the way adults could and how breaking a food addiction was probably as hard as breaking a craving for gambling—for alcohol, tobacco, or firearms. Joe had told me that acquiring and owning an arsenal of guns was an addiction too.

The storm had calmed, but once the girls were all in their bunks, it stirred up yet again. A few new cells.

It was another half hour before all of us fell asleep to the distant pounding surf far below us, at the base of Mohegan Bluffs where the girl Cass had run from Jake. She hadn't had any trouble getting her parents to come for her. That we could hear the surf above the sound of the rain on the tin roof was incredible. The seas were fierce. I thought of Esther's paintings and wondered what would become of them. Then I drifted off; the rain was as heavy as before, but with just a rare lightning bolt and clap of thunder. More of a typical hard summer thunderstorm.

I woke a short time later. I looked at my watch. It was midnight. I'd awoken from a dream. The dream of a sound. The sound of a motor. Maybe it was just another roll of thunder. There'd been an image of a boat—the dream came back to me—an old schooner tipping over, people aboard screaming though I couldn't hear them. Not infrasound though. The rain and the thunder were what drowned out their cries before the sea would swallow them in a grand finale.

I sat up. I tried to sort out what was a dream and what was not. The thunder and the motor were not.

I got out of my bunk and walked down the aisle between the two rows. At the end of the row, Christen's bunk was empty.

I ran outside. By the time I got to the Porta-Potties, I was soaked. I didn't bother to knock, I just opened each door. I knew she wouldn't be inside.

I went back into the barracks. They were all asleep except Samantha, who was sitting up staring at Christen's empty bunk. She looked at me. She whispered, "Oh my God, Poppy."

I sat on the bed beside her.

"Where did she go?"

"I don't know."

"What did she say?"

"Well, she didn't say she'd look for him *tonight*."

"Look for who?"

Her face crumbled. "I don't *know*."

The other girls were awake, sitting up too. One of them said, "Poppy, she told us she was pretty sure who did it. She said tomorrow she was going to grab a baseball bat and get him."

I stood up. While I changed into a T-shirt and jeans I told them, "Girls, I dreamt I heard the sound of a motor. Christen's taken the van. You all run over to King Arthur and stay with Willa. I'll go after Christen in the jeep." They climbed out of the cots and began pulling slickers out from underneath. They gave me one. It was enormous. It would keep me dry if it didn't just blow right off me.

We went out. The girls ran across the grounds toward the light at Willa's. I got into the ragtop and it started right up. I pressed down on the accelerator, and the jeep went forward two feet before it sank, into the muck that was already clinging to my sneakers, a combination of saturated peat and decomposing foliage and clumped clay. I tried rocking my way out but the jeep sank deeper. And then everyone was out around me, a circle of flapping slickers, Carol, Willa, all the girls. They could have lifted me out of the hole I was in but I still wouldn't make any forward progress.

Carol shouted through the downpour, "Even a jeep won't drive in a swamp!"

I got out. "Are there bikes at the camp?"

They looked at each other. Samantha pointed toward a shed. "Maybe if we look hard enough there'll be one with tires that aren't flat. You better forget about brakes."

They all wanted to go to the shed to help me look. I said, "No, go back to your houses. I'll get a bike myself. You don't want to catch colds. You're going home soon."

There was a soft whisper: *Home.*

Carol said to me, "You can't look for Christen in this storm. You can't *see* anything. You can't hear."

"I'll see her headlights."

Samantha stood in front of me. "Poppy, she probably won't put them on. She's sneaking up on someone, remember?"

Willa said, "She's sneaking up on who?" But the girls didn't know. Then Willa said, "Poppy, how could you have let her out of your sight?"

We all stopped, stood there and let the rain pour down our faces. Samantha said, "Poppy's doing all she can."

Willa looked down. "I'm sorry." Maybe she remembered how she'd let Kate out of her sight.

One of the girls said, "The bikes don't have lights."

I felt around the floor for the flashlight and came up with it.

Carol said, "A flashlight is not going to help in a storm like this one. You have to wait, Poppy."

"Listen, I'll only bike as far as Tommy's. Have him get everyone together again. Hopefully, she's run off the road. I'll find her before she gets to wherever she thinks she's going."

Willa and Carol glanced at each other but they didn't argue further. I climbed out of the jeep. I said to them, "Go inside now. All of you. You're soaked."

I ran across the ground to the shed. My sneakers, squishing, filled with water. I shone the flash inside the door. Bikes were piled in a heap. I did find one with tires intact. I put the flash under my arm and I squeezed the brake handles. There was no resistance at all. I wheeled the bike out to the track and got on. The girls were all at the windows again, Willa and Carol too.

I held the flash against the handlebar with one hand, but just as I wheeled into Lakeside Drive it dimmed and went out. I threw it on the road. Lakeside was uphill. I wouldn't need brakes. When I reached the intersection of Coonymus and Center Street, I could see lights coming from every window of the Pleasant View Inn. Aggie's trapped guests were partying. I passed by the Indian cemetery, past the graves of Dutchy Kitten and Orange, and onto Center Street toward Old Town Road.

The night was a wall of black except when the lightning flashed. Great bolts, longer and more zigzagged than earlier, seemed to be in competition against one another: Which one could be brightest, which could travel the longest route across the sky, which would drive into the ground the deepest. Their glow kept me to the road. I watched a bolt plunge down from directly above me and split a fence post just yards away. The post burst into flames and the sizzling that erupted as the rain put the fire out sounded like static on an old radio.

I pedaled faster. By the time I neared Tommy's house, I'd fallen off the bike three times, the first time because I couldn't avoid the potholes—craters taking up half the road—and the second time because I was flying downhill and could only stop myself by crashing into the roadside shrubbery. I picked myself up, got back on the bike, and kept going. Then I hit something in the road, debris or a rock, and went flying over the handlebars. I kept my chin up. I was a ball player sliding into second on his stomach. I came to a stop. I didn't move for a short moment and then I did what I had to do. I lifted my right arm, bent it, did the same with my left, then I bent my right leg, bent the other leg. Nothing was broken. I stood up. My knees and elbows were bloody, but I was all right. The bike was right next to me. Its front wheel was bent, more an oval than a circle.

I started running down Old Town Road and when I was ten yards from Tommy's house I saw the camp van under a shrub where it had run off the road. Christen must have skidded. The engine was warm. I could only hope she hadn't gotten hurt.

I opened the driver's door. The van was empty. She'd been on her way to get Tommy's help too. She'd run off the road but she'd made it.

I dashed to the house. I could see just one small light and it was coming from Jake's shack. Jake was standing outside, his hands over his ears the way Kate's had been. He was trying to block out the thunder. I shouted, "Please go inside, Jake," but he didn't. Why wasn't Tommy with him? Because Tommy was too old to take responsibility for Jake any longer.

Just as I reached the front porch my foot snagged on something and I fell into the porch steps. I got tangled in the soaking poncho. I freed myself and went up to the door, banged on it, and tried to turn the knob. It was locked. I saw a doorbell. I pressed it. A light flashed on inside the house. Jake had rigged something up with the doorbell.

I waited but nothing happened. No one came. First, I went to the side of the porch and tried to open a window. It was locked, too, or stuck. I turned back toward the porch just as a crack of lightning rent the entire sky, and I saw a wire on the ground. It ran along the edge of Tommy's house in front of the porch and kept going along the ground. The wire was what had snagged my foot when I'd first reached the porch, more of Jake's doing.

I saw a light come on inside the front window. I ran to the door and was about to bang on it again when he opened it. Tommy stood there, his face haggard, his eyes weak with fatigue. I felt a sense of comfort in that tired worn face. A network of lightning infused the sky, surrounding us in a web finer than the network of capillaries I'd watched with Carol, and accompanied by the roll of the timpani and then Jake's piercing scream. Tommy's face was illuminated by the lightning for just a second with such a glaring whiteness that his grizzly whiskers, deep wrinkles, and the bags under his eyes were all erased and his face became as smooth and flawless as a child's. The timpani rolled and rolled as if it were coming at us. Tommy grimaced, and one hand went up to protect his ear. With the other, he grabbed my wrist and yanked me to him, and my eyes were inches from his. I recognized the face of the child in Esther's newspaper clipping.

14

I willed my jangling nerves to be still. I said, "Tommy, I'm hurt."

I held up my arms so he could see the blood running down from my elbows, smeared everywhere because of the rain mixing in. "I fell. My knees are really banged up."

He relaxed his grip and then let go. I slipped out of the poncho. "My knees." They were bleeding harder than my elbows.

He said, "Come."

I followed him into his kitchen. He couldn't have had time to kill Christen. Then where was she? Maybe he had overpowered her with a remote control, with an acoustic laser. Maybe Auerbach was right. Maybe there were zebras. In the kitchen, Tommy turned to me. I smiled at him.

Tommy had me sit at his table. He went to the sink, opened the cupboard beneath, took out a bottle from a cardboard box, and came back to me. It was a gallon jug, three-quarters full of a greenish-yellow liquid. He put it on the table and went to another cupboard and got a basin. He placed the basin on the table and put my elbow into it. Then he poured his green soap down my arm. I yelped. He did the other arm. He didn't hear my yelps. His sensory cells, at least a good number of them, had disintegrated when he was a small boy. He went to the sink and filled an empty bottle with water, came back, and rinsed my arms. He was firm but gentle, just as he was with Jake, whose screams he couldn't hear.

Then he got down on his knees the way he had when he'd studied Dana Ganzi, one of the girls he'd killed, the one I'd found lying in the middle of Coonymus Road.

He said, "Your knees aren't as bad as they look," and he dabbed them with a cloth soaked in his green soap.

There was a bumping sound from overhead. Tommy didn't hear that either. It had to be Christen. She'd heard me yelp.

"Tommy, I came because another girl is missing. We have to find her."

"She can't go anywhere in this weather. She's found shelter."

"Tommy, she must be with the man who killed her friends."

I stood up.

The bumping from above was much louder. Tommy tilted his head. He'd sensed it. He stood too, and he looked into my eyes. He grabbed my wrist again.

Tommy had a grip stronger than any I'd ever been subjected to. He twisted me around so that my back and the arm he'd immobilized were crushed up against his rock-hard chest. His free arm he held tight across my upper body. The pain from my jerked-back shoulder felt worse than the one in my crushed wrist. I did all that I was taught except screaming. Screaming was useless. No one outside would hear me except maybe Jake, and Jake was impotent. So I saved that element of my strength. As ferociously as possible, I alternated between kicking back at his shins and stomping on his feet. But he was wearing boots and I had on soaking wet sneakers. I tried bashing the back of my head against his chest, but he only held me tighter.

He dragged me out of the kitchen. I saw a baseball bat lying in the hallway. The name LANCELOT was painted across it in red. Christen had brought her weapon just as she'd told her friends she would.

Tommy pulled me backward down a hallway. He wilted for just a second when I decided screaming at the top of my lungs couldn't hurt after all. Maybe screaming would make me stronger, a theory some held. The theory was false. But with my screams there came a stronger thumping now, directly above us. He never paused. He hadn't felt it this time, he was concentrating too hard on pulling me across the floor. And then I heard my name called out, muffled. He hadn't heard that either—hadn't heard Christen, secured in the room over our heads, calling my name.

I shouted, "Christen, it's Poppy! Try to get out! Try!" I didn't know if Tommy could make out any of it. I didn't know the extent of his hearing loss. But sometimes, someone who is hard of hearing can't understand the words if they're spoken at a loud pitch.

In the lightning flashes, I could see a painting on the wall. Esther's. He hadn't killed Esther. She was his friend, trying to help him in her own way, trusting him with a picture. The wind was picking up and the rain flew horizontally into his windows as loud as bullets. I stopped struggling. I turned my head to the side, my lips near his ear. I said to him in a normal voice, "Tommy, don't do this. I understand what happened to you. But the girl upstairs isn't the one who did it. The girls from the camp did nothing. They did *nothing*."

He was too involved with getting me through his house to pay attention to what I was saying even if he could hear me. Tommy made the most of my attempt to calm myself, to speak rationally to him. He hauled me through a door. I felt desperate. Now I screamed Jake's name—"*Jake!* "—over and over again, screamed for him to help as Tommy dragged me down a stairway into his cellar. Tommy was the man with the picnic, and Kate thought she had seen another person in the picnicman's truck. It had to have been Jake.

There was light in the cellar, a bare bulb in the ceiling with a string hanging from it just like the one in each of the Camp Guinevere barracks.

I kicked Tommy with a vengeance. I could survive a fall better than he could. Still, he was strong, a big man, and he hung on to me all the way down the rest of the stairs. I was unable to trip him. I threw my head back and caught his chin. He jerked me harder into the vise of his arms and body, and I felt the incredible shock of my shoulder separating. Now I didn't shout deliberately, I screamed in pain indiscriminately.

He'd felt the fight go out of me. He released some of the pressure of his arm across my chest while he pulled back a large bookcase standing against a wall. There was a door in the wall and a small window next to it. Under the window, a console, a board with toggles and switches and wires jury-rigged from the insides of radios. Jake's doing.

He opened the door and pushed me through it. I came down on my knees onto a cement floor. I could make out nothing but the one window where the bit of light came through. No light at all slipped past the outside edge of the door. It was fully sealed. The room was about eight feet square. The walls were poured cement except for the new wall with the door and window, which was lined with soundproofing wallboard, as was the ceiling. There was an open drain in the middle of the cement floor. This was the place where the girls vomited the contents of their stomachs and where he washed it away.

Pain was shooting out in all directions from my shoulder, down my arm, across my back, becoming worse. The one thing I had to do that took precedence over anything else was to fix the shoulder. I cradled my arm, got to my feet, and walked till I was close to the wallboard. Then I took a tight hold of my elbow, grit my teeth, and smashed my injured shoulder into the wall. My head filled with black dots and I went to my knees again in a faint that lasted just a moment; the burden of pain fleeing my shoulder acted like a shot of morphine. I stood up again and right then bright lights came on in the little room.

Tommy's face was in the window. He was looking down at his control panel. Then he looked up at me. His face was as hard as granite. I was in a place he'd intended for Christen, the place where he'd killed the other girls and so harmed Kate.

I smiled at him, the same smile I gave him when I ran into him on the street, at Richard's Patio, and yesterday when I'd asked him for help. Whenever I'd spoken to Tommy he'd looked intently into my face. Now I understood why; he'd been reading my lips. The psychiatrist who raised him must have taught him to do that. I spoke to him slowly and deliberately. "Tommy, I'm Joe's friend. Your friend. You don't want to hurt me. It's too late to hurt me. The little girl with the doll— she's alive. You know that. You know we saved her. She's told the doctors what happened. They *know*." But his gaze had left my lips. He chose not to see what I was saying. He was looking down again.

I went to the window and touched the glass. His face came up, inches from mine. "Tommy, we want to help you. We found out the terrible thing that happened to you when you were just a child."

His eyes glittered and he said something. He pointed up. He was talking about Christen, but I couldn't hear him and I did not know how to read lips. So I guessed.

I said, "No, she's not the one who did it to you." But he cast his eyes down again.

I banged on the glass with my fist. "I'm hurt, Tommy. Please." He raised his eyes and I said it again. "I'm hurt, Tommy."

This time I could tell what he said to me. He said, "I'm sorry."

And the sound of Gershwin's *Rhapsody in Blue* filled the room. No piece has been played by more pop orchestras than this one. A bit of trivia I'd read. After just a few bars, though, the music stopped. It was how he tested the system. That's what he'd used to test his mechanism on Dana, and Rachel, and the girl who'd arrived early—the first girl, Erin—and Kate, too, and maybe Christen, before I interrupted and he'd had to get her up two flights of stairs. Maybe she'd gotten treated with the same diabolical method of torture that I was about to get, only I knew what to expect and she hadn't.

A bell clanged louder than any noise I have ever experienced. It clanged again, louder still, and then it clanged nonstop. I put my hands over my ears and looked up at the amplifier perched in the corner of the ceiling. The loudspeaker sticking out from it seemed to be alive, to become a face, a menacing face, a face from a horror movie taunting me—clanging and clanging and clanging. There were three other amplifiers in the other corners of the room. The second one came alive too, a shattering piercing whistle. I made the same shocked sound I screamed when my shoulder ripped apart.

I went to the door, turned the doorknob, and pushed at it. He had a bolt thrown across the jamb. I threw all my weight against it and all but dislocated my other shoulder. The door frame was reinforced. There was no give at all.

I could see Tommy move a little to his left, and the third amplifier came on. I think the noise was the sound of a train, a helicopter, I couldn't be sure. The pounding inside my head prevented me from being able to differentiate between the noises anymore. I never heard the fourth one come on but it must have. The noise was so insufferable I suppose I did what the girls did. I was against the other wall now, the concrete wall, banging my head into it. Then, without knowing it, I rolled across the floor in some involuntary attempt to get away from the noise. That roll across the floor saved me from losing all reason because another pain struck me—a normal pain coming from the injured shoulder that my roll had caused. I didn't want my muscles to spasm, my eardrums to burst, my lungs to collapse and my heart to give out. I looked at the window. Tommy wasn't watching me. He'd watched the others, I knew, but with me . . . he was sorry.

But then I began to hallucinate. I thought trucks were bearing down on me, crashing into me, big tandem trucks, their enormous wheels crushing my bones. And I could hear the moaning of the foghorns back and forth across the sea too. I began rolling again and my injured shoulder brought me back once more. I was the one who was moaning, not the foghorns.

I forced myself up and over to the window. I banged on it. I tried to speak but I couldn't. I was crying hysterically. I couldn't breathe. I thought my head would explode, and a new pain was coming from my wracked eardrums, an unbearable, excruciating throbbing.

I pulled off my T-shirt. I tried to wrap it around my head. Then I did what the dead girls had done. I ripped off pieces of it with my teeth as they had ripped off pieces of theirs. I stuffed the shreds of the shirt into my ears. Immediately, the sound was muffled. I tried to see, and it took me a moment to understand that I couldn't see because my eyes were squeezed shut. I opened them. The light in the room had dimmed. On the other side of the window, Tommy was moving about frantically, trying to get his power up. The noise had diminished, was now no louder than a smoke alarm. I could bear it. The pieces of the shirt hadn't muffled the noise; it was the storm that had done it.

There had to be a tree somewhere lying across the electric wires leading to Tommy's house. But there were no trees on Block Island. Maybe a branch from one of those scrubby pines I'd seen sprawled across Esther's roof had ripped off and blown into a wire. The branch hadn't broken all the way through the wires though. I thought of Joe's complaints about the frequent Block Island brownouts.

I took off my sneaker. I went to the window and bashed at it. I knew it was futile. It was still a sneaker, not a boot. But Tommy looked up, and when he did I thought maybe he was more than Esther's friend. Now he was watching me. He was not androgynous. I took off my bra. I put my hands on my hips. I felt perspiration trickling down between my breasts. And Tommy stared.

I unzipped my jeans and peeled them off. They were soaked through.

The sounds around me grew a little stronger. So did the light. The power was returning. I slid off my underpants and held out my arms to him. I said, "Tommy. Come and get me out."

The light flared and the din bowled me over. I was down again, rolling, holding my ears, stopped by the wall, banging my head into it. I threw up.

I no longer felt the pain in my shoulder. The hallucinations returned. I was outside in the storm. The thunder and lightning were nonstop, piercing my ears, stabbing at my eyes, right through them and into my brain, filling my head. I was in a boat on the water, tossed up and down, back and forth by the waves. I tried to throw myself into the sea. I did and I went under, under the cruel seas of Esther's paintings—down, down, down to the rocky bottom strewn with bones—and then everything stopped, all the horrendous clanging and whistling and smashing. I was dead.

I was dead and a new sound, a familiar one, came from deep inside me. I listened carefully and then I recognized it. It was the beating of my heart. I had survived the shipwreck, I hadn't drowned. I heard Esther's words, I read her description of the courage of Dutchy Kitten, twelve years old, half dead, frozen, unable to understand what people were saying to her, unable to get them to repeat her name, and so I made the same effort she had once made to crawl out of the surf. I pulled myself along and I felt the tide helping me, the waves washing me onto the shore. All was quiet and still. It was pitch dark. But I knew my eyes were open and then a thought came to me, a rational thought instead of the ones I'd just been having, one that reflected reality. Another pine branch just heavy enough to do more than lean onto a wire had severed it. Or maybe the transformer at the start of Tughole Way had been hit by lightning. Toppled over.

The electric power to Tommy's house was cut off.

My body was shaking so hard, I couldn't move. Instead of the noise of the amplifiers, I heard echoes of that noise reverberating through my skull. The pain in my ears was a dull, deep ache, the terrible throbbing gone. And then I saw a small pinprick of light outside the little window, a steady one that remained on, nothing to do with lightning. Tommy had turned on a flashlight. I could see my bare skin. I snapped my fingers but I couldn't hear the sound. I was deaf. Tommy and I were even.

I willed myself to a spot next to the window and flattened my body up against the wall. He had to be deciding whether to wait it out or get rid of Christen and me now. But he knew what I knew—even if the transformer had burnt out, the islanders didn't mind going without electricity because they all had generators in place. But not a generator strong enough to create the kind of power necessary to run Tommy's torture machine.

He did have a genius, though, at his beck and call—Jake. Jake could probably build a generator to service all of Block Island, but obviously he hadn't. At that moment I felt such a vast hatred for Tommy, for what he'd put Jake up to, I wanted to kill him, to beat his head with a rock, to make his head feel just the way my head had. And then I felt shame.

I remembered Tommy already knew what my head felt like. I didn't want to kill him at all. I wanted to rescue him. I understood now exactly what Tommy had gone through when he was a boy. His injuries had left him with a severe hearing loss, his brain had been damaged, and he had been left with a propensity to madness. But I had to save myself. And I had to get to Christen.

Through the little viewing window, his flashlight's beam roamed the floor of the room and then the walls, but I was huddled under the window and Tommy never saw me. Then the beam disappeared for a few seconds before it reappeared in a long thin line. Tommy had opened the door a crack. I'd never heard the bolt slide or the door open. I could only hear the pounding inside my head.

I slid along the wall until I was behind the door. It opened halfway. The beam of the light came into the room, and behind it a hand I knew was there but couldn't make out. Joe had taken me crabbing once on the Chesapeake Bay. Joe said crabbing was an art. Fingering the line, you can feel when the blue crab begins to tamper with the rotted chicken leg at the other end. You can feel when he takes hold of the bait, settles in to eat, one claw holding fast to the bait, the other forking pieces of the chicken into his mouth. Then you lift him very slowly, just off the bottom, a few inches at a time, stopping each time the line feels slack, continuing when you feel him holding firm again; then, near the surface, you have to guess where he is and scoop swiftly upward with your long-handled net. Took practice, Joe told me, especially the guessing part. I'd practiced until I reached a point where I could feel a crab on my line before Joe could feel one on his, and I would lift the bait, lift the line a half inch at a time, lift just a little bit more, then yank the net up out of the water—always with a glistening wet blue crab struggling inside.

So I deliberated for half a second and guessed as to

where exactly Tommy's wrist was. I made my hand rigid and lifted it high. With all the power I could muster, I sliced down through the air behind the light.

My wounded ears felt the vibrations of a scream. The flashlight hit the floor and went rolling. Tommy was in the light for just a second. In his other hand he held a short metal pipe.

He took a swing at me. The pipe glanced my bad shoulder. I didn't see black dots, I saw flashing stars, so I knew I wouldn't faint. I had the advantage. My shoulder hurt but it was back in position. Tommy's broken wrist would stay broken.

There was no strength in my left hand but at least I could use it. I grabbed at the iron pipe and tried to wrench it away. I couldn't. We both went down. He went for the flashlight, which was not a cheap plastic one but was metal and solid, and he swung it at me. He swung it and swung it, and on his third swing I pulled the pipe from his grip just as the flashlight hit me in the jaw. The blood filling up my mouth gave me what I needed. I felt a rush of adrenaline surge through my veins.

I went for the door, opened it, ran through, and slammed it shut. I threw the bolt just as Tommy flung himself against it. He flung himself at the door again and then again. He had no chance. I spit the blood out and I took a few deep breaths. Icy hands touched my back. I swung around and screamed a scream I couldn't hear.

Christen was in front of me. In the light that came from the flashlight I could see her face; her mouth gagged the way Kate's had been, but she'd managed to loosen it and yell. I got the gag off. She said something to me.

"Christen, I can't hear you."

She yelled into my ear, "My hands are tied!"

She turned around and I untied her wrists.

Tommy was smashing his boot against the window. The window wouldn't be broken. It had to be hurricane glass; it would take a lot of pounding. He stopped and threw his body against the door yet again. Christen yelled into my face, "The bolt is wiggling!"

I said, "Get the bookcase."

She didn't need me to help her; she was a strong girl. She pushed the bookcase back into position. She dragged a workbench across the cellar floor and shoved it up against the bookcase. The lightning was still coming through the crack in the black curtains covering Tommy's cellar windows, not such sharp flashes anymore, distant glows. The storm was moving offshore.

Christen was staring at me. She shouted, "Can you hear me now?"

I could, as though she were talking to me from the hallucinations I'd had just a few minutes earlier. "Yes. I can."

"You're naked."

She pulled off her sweatshirt. I went to put it on but I'd forgotten about my left shoulder. A pain shot through it when I lifted my arm.

Christen said, "Omigod, what's wrong?"

"Nothing. I hurt my shoulder. It's okay."

She said something else.

"Louder, Christen."

"Is your arm broken?"

"No."

"I broke my arm once. It really killed. When I was nine. . . ."

While she shouted the story of falling out of a tree, I eased my sore arm into the sleeve of the sweatshirt, got the other arm in the other sleeve, and pulled it down over my head. The sweatshirt came down to my knees.

She stopped her story. She smiled. "You're warm now, right?"

She'd thought I must have been cold. It was such a childlike voice. But I heard it and that was all that mattered. I wouldn't be deaf forever, like Tommy.

I put my good arm around her. "Don't hug me back, Christen, it'll hurt. What about you, are you okay?"

"Yes. I snuck up to Tommy's house. But I tripped over something. Then he was right there and he grabbed me and tied my wrists. He put me in there, in that room."

Christen looked toward the bookcase, hiding the window with the room behind. She said, "I heard this music and then this really loud bell. *Really, really* loud. But then red lights started flashing outside the window, in the cellar. He came and got me out and made me go upstairs. He was going to hit me with a pipe. He said to me he wanted to watch me just like I'd watched him. I tried to tell him I didn't know what he meant. I never watched him. He really scared me, Poppy."

"I know."

"He locked me in a bedroom and tied me to a hanger screwed in the door. It took me a long time but I ripped it out. I broke down the bedroom door just now."

I sensed a noise, a crack. Christen's eyes went wide. Tommy had cracked the window. "He can't break it, Christen. It's hurricane glass. It'll only crack. You've trapped him. There is no way for him to escape that room. We've got to get out of here and go find someone to come and see to him." She was still as a statue. "Now."

She turned her head just a little bit. "No," she said, "let's not. Let's not tell anyone. Let's let him just stay there until . . . until he *starves* to death."

"Christen, he's ill. Psychotic. He's—"

"I don't care what he is." She whirled around, came

back to me. "Oh, no! Poppy, I can hear the door shaking."

He'd loosened the bolt. "He can't get through that door. We'll get someone here to guard him until the police come."

"But what if he does get out?"

"He won't. Believe me, you've seen to that. Let's go, Christen. Let's go right now."

We went up Tommy's cellar steps, through his kitchen and his living room, and out the front door.

I could hear our footsteps and I could hear Tommy's bashing. The little sensory cells in my ears were rising up again. I could feel it happening because of Auerbach, who'd made it sound so real, so alive. The tiny sensory cells were collecting sound waves once more.

Outside, the storm had lost its violence. Flashes flew in the far black distance. The rain still fell in sheets, but it wasn't flying horizontally. A candle burned in Jake's window. I said, "Christen, I want to see if Jake is all right."

She grabbed me. "Jake will let him out."

"He won't do anything unless he's told to do it." I went into Jake's shack through his unlocked door. Christen was a weight, hanging on to the back of the sweatshirt she'd given me. But Jake wasn't inside. "He's not here, Christen. Let's get the van and drive to the clinic, get the doctor."

"The van's out of gas." She looked up into the sky, the rain pelting her face, a face so innocent, hiding her instinct, her insight.

"Christen?"

"What?"

"How did you know it was Tommy?"

Her face came to mine. "He'd stare at us. He didn't laugh at us, but he stared. He seemed, I don't know, it was like we made him nervous or uncomfortable or something. That's how things are, though, with some people. I figured he just didn't like fat people. Or, you know, judged us. But Stupid would always say, No, he's just very serious. Because he's like a sheriff. Stupid said he reminded her of her grandpa. Her grandpa was gruff but he had a kind heart, she'd say. That's how I knew she would trust the constable." And then she turned her face away again. She was listening to something. "Poppy, what's that?" I tried to hear. She said, "I think there's a plane coming."

I heard it too. "That's Joe's plane."

"How do you know?"

"Because no one else is fool enough to fly in this weather. C'mon, the airstrip is less than half a mile."

"Okay."

We hurried along, past the dead van as we went splashing through the puddles, trying to be careful and not fall. I heard the sound of the plane land. Christen and I went faster, helping each other stay upright. I was getting winded. She wasn't. Christen was capable of enormous endurance. And then the lights of Fitzy's car came at us. Christen began waving wildly. I remembered to wave with my right arm, not my aching left one.

The car had barely stopped before Joe and Fitzy were out of it. They ran toward us. I stopped in my tracks. When they reached us, I said, "Joe, don't touch me."

Christen said, "She's hurt."

He stopped.

"A little. It's nothing. My shoulder . . ."

"Jesus, Poppy, are you all right?"

"Yes."

We all stood facing one another. It was Fitzy who took a step forward. "You stumbled on him."

I couldn't respond. I felt myself blinking back tears, tears of terror—delayed reaction—and I suddenly knew how lucky I was to be alive. Yes, I had stumbled on him.

"And you got him, didn't you?"

Christen was the one to throw her arms around someone. Around Fitzy. She said, "Yes! We got him! We fucking got him."

He pulled her away so he could face her. "Tell me where he is."

"He's—" And right then Christen came back to earth just moments after my own descent. "He's—" What had hit me hit her. She started to cry, and her crying became a wail the way children will wail when they're in total despair, the sound of absolute heartbreak.

Big girls do cry, but it takes a hell of a lot.

Now Fitzy hugged her back, took her into his arms. "You're okay, kid. And your little friend in the hospital's doing a lot better. Her grandfather came. That was all she needed. She doesn't remember anything that happened to her. She'll never remember, either." He looked past Christen and into my eyes. He kept talking. "She asked about you and Sam and all the girls at the camp. The nurses are bringing Elijah Leonard rice pudding. Now you have to try and stop crying so you and Poppy can tell me everything I need to know."

I said, "It was Tommy. That's all there is to know and you already know it."

Fitzy said, "The psychiatrist never worked again. She brought him to Block Island where he'd be safe. Anonymous."

Now Joe had something to say. "I'm sorry."

I was getting really sick of his being sorry.

Fitzy said, "Block Island had been the psychiatrist's home. She was descended from one of the founding fathers. No one questioned her widowhood, which is what she told them. It was the psychiatrist's stuff that was left at Esther's years ago. Esther found the clippings in one of the bags."

Suddenly, something was not right. Christen startled. Fitzy and Joe looked around. Then I was able to hear it—a strange whirring sound. Joe looked over my head toward town. I turned to see what he was staring at. One after the other, the harborside buildings came aglow; one after another the houses and inns in the center of town filled with flickering lights muted by the drizzle—all that was left of the storm. The power was reaching the million-dollar cottages, one at a time in a line coming toward us, electricity passing from one to the next.

Fitzy said, "Well, that should help."

And Joe stared at me. "Poppy, what's the matter?"

Two strips of tiny blue lights came on at the landing strip just as electricity surged through the wires leading to Tommy's house, releasing an enormous cacophany of bells and whistles and infernal crashes that resounded through the night. Tommy had managed to break the window, after all.

Christen stared at me. She put her hands over her ears. We all did. And then Christen smiled and said, "Yes!"

Dogs began to bark, babies were crying, and gulls in great numbers rose from nowhere into the sky. Their screeching could not overpower the noise coming from Tommy's house. We ran to Fitzy's car and were at Tommy's in minutes. I told Christen to stay where she was. She did not protest; she was bent over, her hands still covering her ears.

Joe didn't move. "I'll stay with her."

Fitzy followed me into the house and ran with me across the kitchen, through the hall, and down the cellar stairs. The noise was no less shocking than before, even though it was now dispersed into a much larger space. We pulled at the tool table and then the bookcase, exposing the window and the circuit board beneath. The window was smashed. I stared at the circuit board, a row of little glowing red lights. I began pushing switches. Splinters of glass cut my fingers. Fitzy stepped in front of me, grabbed the entire board and ripped it out. But one wire remained connected. And we listened to all that was left of the deadly recordings—strains of *Rhapsody in Blue*.

In the little window, jagged shards stuck up from its bent frame. We could see Tommy on the floor, rolled into a ball, moaning. There was blood everywhere. He had used a piece of the glass to slice his wrists.

We pulled and pushed at the bookcase until we could get into the room. The bolt on the door had been ripped away, but Tommy hadn't been able to push himself past Christen's barrier.

I sank down beside Tommy, pulled his hands from his ears, and cradled his head in my lap. Fitzy squatted down beside him too, picking up my T-shirt and my underwear from the floor to tie his gushing wrists.

Tommy's face was bone-white and soft, again the ghost of the child he'd been. I brushed a few wisps of hair from his forehead, just the way I had Kate's. His eyes opened. He said something, very softly; Fitzy told me later what it was. He'd said, "I didn't want to hurt you, miss." But I couldn't hear him. I'd responded all the same. I said, "It's all right now, Tommy."

He spoke again, his lips barely moving. Fitzy told

me the rest of what he'd said. "That last one. She was just a little child. I didn't know."

He shut his eyes. I said to him, "Tommy, it's all over now."

It wasn't quite over, though. He said "Jake" before he died. I was able to read that word on his lips.

15

All the storm cells made their way out past the horizon by morning and the air was clear, the sky the color of Rebekah's eyes, the ocean like ink. Mick's forecast had finally come about. It was the kind of day Block Island brochures crow about. So finding Jake didn't take very long. It turned out he had other haunts he enjoyed visiting besides the old South Light, besides the cliff looking east out over the ocean by Joe's cottage, besides the girls who had simply aroused his curiosity. He also liked to sit and gaze upon the electrical tower near the Western Road, at the turnoff to the track called Tughole Way. His body lay on the ground just beneath. He'd succeeded in sabotaging the transformer, but he'd made one mistake and touched a wire, drawing the last volts of electricity to Block Island into his body.

The night before, when Tommy had me crushed up against him and I'd screamed and screamed for Jake to help me, he'd set out to do it.

At Richard's Patio, Mick said, "Matter of throwing a switch if you know where it is. That's why the power got restored so fast. One of the boys just climbed on up there not long after we lost it and got the power goin' again. Too dark to see Jake right then, though."

Willa became hysterical at the news, so Fitzy had to take her to the clinic and have the doc give her a shot. She didn't get to learn all that had happened until later: what Tommy had forced Jake to do; how Jake had somehow figured out that he could rectify what he'd wrought. To find a sense of morality his demons hadn't quite obliterated.

Ernie made us breakfast after they'd all done their best to sympathize with me. Aggie invited me for a cup of tea any time. Then, with that duty out of the way, I listened as they agonized over all of it. Billy said, "It was because we didn't know what we'd do with Jake. How could we take care of him? So now they're both gone. Who'd have thought it?"

I drank my entire cup of coffee. I couldn't make sense of what Billy had said, so I asked Mick to tell me.

"Mick, what did Billy say?"

Mick used almost the exact same words, but not quite. "What would we have done with Jake if it were true?"

Vague little clicks came together in my brain. "Mick, I'm sorry—if what were true?"

Billy explained more carefully. "He means when we figured out it was Tommy. That's when we didn't know what to do. Not that we were *sure* it was him, no, ma'am. Couldn't *prove* anything. But Tommy turning out to be an outsider and all, I guess we should have known even sooner."

Mick said, "Him turning out to be adopted and all."

I must have appeared utterly dense because Mick tried to explain again, kept at the point they were trying to make so I'd understand. "See, we figured we should say something to the authorities. Maybe go to the trooper. But he beat out the ban and was gone. It's like I'm tellin' you, we had no proof. And the thing is, who'd watch Jake? I mean, it's not like the boy took to any of us."

Ernie said, "Willa wanted to. Willa always wanted to. She pressed me. But I'm too old to be feedin' meals to someone in his condition. Tommy had to dress him, bathe him—all that stuff you have to do when someone is—well, you know. When I was at the doc's yesterday trying to help him with Jake, I kept sayin' to him, 'Where the hell's Tommy?' He didn't know. Nobody knew. Then those campers came barrelin' in, told us another one was gone. The little one. That's where Tommy was."

I turned to Joe. "Did you think Tommy was the one?"

"No, of course not."

"Then why did you run away?"

"Because I didn't want to know who they thought might have done it. Our whole community was—"

"Community? *What* whole community? The community is a *lunatic asylum.*"

Jim Lane's kid said, "I'm not a lunatic."

"You will be if you don't get out."

Mick protested. "But Poppy, we saw the girls were watched over. I mean, once he tried to kill the young one. So's he couldn't do it to anyone else until the ban was lifted. That girl who went out in the storm, the one who went after Tommy—we didn't think the girls would figure it out. We thought they would trust the law and stay put at the camp. She didn't stay put."

"What about me?"

Their eyes shifted away. Then Billy brightened. "Well, you're alive, right? Besides, we couldn't've stopped you. Carol tried, said so. Willa did too. Tried to keep you up there at the camp. But that girl, the one who went after Tommy on her own? You were up there with her. How come you couldn't keep her from going out?"

I was on my feet, but just as I'd stood up, the little bell over the door tinkled and my stomach turned over. I felt myself cringe exactly the way Jake had not too many days ago. It was Fitzy. He stopped short at the sight of me. "Now what?"

None of us said anything.

Fitzy said to me, "Just hold that thought, Poppy," and to Ernie, "I need to speak to you."

"Is Willa all right?"

"Come on outside."

They went out the door and I watched the bell bumped by the door and waited for the tinkle, all in slow motion, and when the sound came, it was a tone from hell. Poor, poor Jake. I was hearing the little bell the way he heard it. So sensitive to sound. To the point of agony. He was the only one besides Tommy who had any idea of the suffering Tommy's victims endured. But Jake had fought the demons and beaten them.

Fitzy came back in alone. I was sitting down again, too tired to vent my fury, too depressed to tell Joe what I thought of him. I was completely wrung out. Fitzy pulled up a chair. He said to Jim, to Billy and Mick, to Aggie, and to the taxi brothers that Ernie needed them. "He's in the store."

One by one they left, without so much as a glance my way, except for Jim. Jim Lane's kid hefted his bag of paraphernalia and said to me, "They just didn't know what to do."

I said to Joe, "You tell him."

"They knew what to do, kid. She's right. Get away from here."

He followed the others, one last glance at me over his shoulder.

Joe went behind the counter and brought the pot of coffee over and a cup for Fitzy. He poured out the last of the carafe. He said, "What's going on, Fitzy?"

When he said that, I found I didn't want to know. So maybe it had been a first for Joe, too, like it was for me, right then—not wanting to know. But with me it only lasted a second. It had taken a few days for Joe to come to his senses—when it was too late.

Fitzy downed his whole cup as he was wont to do, put it down, and said, "I just cooked my insides." He helped himself to what was left of my orange juice. Then he said, "I spent the night looking through Esther's stuff. Figured someone had to know it could have been Tommy." I made some kind of noise, sort of like *hah*.

Joe told him what *hah* meant, which was the very thought Fitzy had asked me to hold. Fitzy just shook his head. Then he said, "It was that family tree, Poppy. Tommy had been on an earlier version, but not the one you saw. Esther found out he was not his mother's child but had been adopted. She told everyone too. I know that because she told Willa. I asked Willa about it. She told me that's when they suspected Tommy: when they learned he was an outsider. If you feel any better, Poppy, that's what they based their suspicions on. Wouldn't quite have held up in a court of law in Rhode Island if it had been ours.

"But listen, guess who *is* on that tree? Poppy, remember the blank line?"

"Yes."

"That was for Jake's mother. I kept going through the stuff until I found the papers that legalized Tommy's taking the wardship of Jake from the state. Jake was illegitimate, and even though everyone knew he was a foundling, that he'd been abandoned, they never thought he'd been abandoned by one of *them*. I would guess the psychiatrist, being a medical doctor after all, probably delivered Jake and kept the identity of the mother secret."

I listened. I felt I was in a trance by the time he got to that part. I said, "Fitzy, Willa was standing right over us when we were looking at Esther's clippings. At the picture of Tommy when he was a little boy. We *showed* it to her. She spilled the coffee she was pouring. She'd seen those clippings before. Probably at Esther's. Right when we were sitting here looking at them she probably realized who the boy was. Who he grew up to be."

"Yeah, well, that's moot. Here's the point I'm making. Willa was Jake's mother."

Joe said, "No."

Fitzy said, "Yes."

I told Joe to stop saying no to everything.

Fitzy just ignored him. He said, "Willa told me Tommy hated her when she was a girl." He leaned back in his chair. "But hated her for what? Did he know she was pregnant?"

I said, "Maybe. But I know what she was trying to tell you. She'd attempted to comfort the girls one day—told them she was overweight when she was their age. That's why Tommy hated her."

Fitzy reverted to his usual expression of frustration. "Shit." Then he said, "Willa would not be found out. She would not admit to being Jake's mother. Not then, not ever. The thing is, what would have happened if she had? Would Ernie have beaten her to death, for Christ's sake? Drowned her? Left her? What was she so afraid of that she'd actually go and poison Esther? What century are we living in here?"

We looked to Joe. He hadn't an answer. He said, "I don't know. I don't understand."

Fitzy said, "Me neither. But mine's not to understand. I gotta go. Meet the plane. Take Willa in." He stood up. He put his hand on my shoulder, the injured shoulder. He patted it very gently. "So long, FBI."

I stood up, too, and he put his arms around me. My shoulder protested, but I stayed in his hug for a long while.

I called my favorite shrink on the question Joe couldn't answer. He found it all quite fascinating. "The group of people you have on that island, isolated as islanders are, is probably the closest thing to children of slaves that exists. They've been deprived over generations. And when there's a maelstrom of secrets, collective paranoia, an overreaching umbrella of shame—well, put it together and you can conclude a psychopathy, particularly if you add to the mix the humiliation and guilt connected to a child born of illegitimacy. Born of rape.

"Poppy, your Willa has led a double life. That alone can drive you bonkers. I'll vouch for that myself."

He could vouch for it because he was a noted criminal profiler, a respected psychiatrist who happens to have an acute gambling addiction. I thought, There sure are a goddamn lot of addictions out there, though none could come close to Tommy's. To kill his persecutors.

He said, "Her whole life was a web of secrets. But then it was finally all over. She'd found legitimacy with her husband and, because of Joe's efforts to restore the islanders' property rights, a life she could officially claim. She and her husband owned a home, they had their store, the coffee shop. But Willa also had an irrational terror of losing it all if Ernie found out that Jake was her son. Especially if he found out who the father was. Who *was* the father, Poppy?"

"We don't know."

"You will. You will see the thing that is askew."

I only needed to hear him say it, and I knew what was askew. The blank line on the genealogy for Jake's mother was to protect Willa. There was no blank line for the father, though, because Esther didn't know who he was when she'd drawn the tree.

The shrink listened to my brain whirring, and then he said, "Had to be the killer, I take it."

"Yes." Willa had been the first to trigger Tommy's madness but he stopped short of killing her.

"Why hadn't he killed the girls the year before? When the camp first opened?"

"Not triggered fully. But in anticipating their return, he became uneasy—agitated. At some point last winter, the trigger released and he devised a way to wipe out his tormenters. On the back of that poor fellow, Jake."

"So, Poppy, this Willa knew her place. And I come from a culture of people who thrive on knowing their place. There's nothing new there as far as I'm concerned. The thing is, why would the dead woman want to betray Willa's secret?"

I thought about why Esther would do any such thing.

"Poppy, was she blackmailing Willa?"

"No. Yes. Sort of. Esther—the dead woman—knew Tommy couldn't care for Jake any longer. She figured his mother should. Esther was a hard, judgmental woman. She threatened Willa with exposure if she didn't perform her duty. After all, Jake was one of them. Tommy was the outsider, something she'd recently come to understand. Jake's mother had to take over. It was an empty threat. The genealogy's blank links proved that. Willa didn't bother to take Esther's version of the family tree once she saw that Esther hadn't actually intended to expose her. She left it. How terrible."

"Poppy, harsh judgment is how people are kept in their place. Esther learned that. Still, there may have been a secondary blackmail going on. Esther may have insisted Willa tell her who the father was. If Willa wouldn't take care of Jake, his father should."

I thought about it. Enough to make me shudder. "Yes, she probably threatened Willa. And Willa knew that somehow Esther would find the answer. Maybe thought she already had."

"Then there it is."

16

Back at Joe's cottage, I called Delby to tell her I'd be back late that afternoon.

She said, "Good."

"What's wrong?"

"Nothing. But do you remember that fireman?"

"What fireman?"

"The Irish guy, the one with that sexy accent. The marshal from Boston."

"Oh. Yes, I do."

"Thought you'd remember. Guy's gorgeous."

All firemen are hunks according to the girls of Camp Guinevere. "Delby, what about him?"

"He's left you a couple of frantic messages. I thought they could wait till you checked in. But he called again just now. He's here in town. Drove down from Boston on his day off because he has to see you."

"Tell him I can see him tonight. Arrange something."

"Tonight. Okey-doke. Got a minute to talk to a contrite Auerbach?"

"Sure."

"Now?"

"Put him though."

He was right there on his line. He said to me, "How are your ears?"

"Fine."

"Poppy, it is wonderful that the ear is such an incredible organ. It can survive anything but a direct and prolonged attack. Your hearing is a hundred percent?"

"I believe so."

"Better get checked out."

"Auerbach, I'm grateful for your concern. Now tell me what you want."

"I need to explain to you how it all works. I wanted you to appreciate that the structure and functional design of the ear is so incredibly perfect—beyond perfect, even, because there's the binaural facility of our having *two* of them, one on either side of our head. The organ allows for a huge gathering range and inherent directional finders. So when you were in a place where sound could not escape but only reverberate, in a place with concrete walls, which are the best monolithic nonporous barriers for achieving high airborne sound insulation—and add to that the electrified horn-loaded drivers in the cellar—well, what happened was this: you suffered the *brilliance* of the ear. The *brilliance!*"

Oh. Now I felt so much better.

My hearing was fine. I knew that when I'd heard Spike's meow that morning before Joe did, below the bedroom window. Might have been because I was wide awake, hadn't slept, and Joe was unconscious. I ran to the door to let him in, one bedraggled cat, still fairly soaked, his fine tail now ratlike. I picked him up and hugged him to me. Far more strong a snuggle than he preferred. He squirmed out of my arms and leaped to the floor. The thump was what woke Joe and he came down in time to see me emptying a can of Chicken of the Sea tuna into Spike's bowl instead of his usual Nine Lives.

While I was packing, Spike kept climbing in and out of my suitcase, standing on my clothes. His paws, of course, were muddy. It was nice that he didn't want me to leave, just the way he didn't want to leave himself. I'd told Joe to find an adoptive home on the island for Spike. With Aggie just around the corner. Or Jim Lane's kid or someone else. The cat was a Block Islander. Joe agreed, said I was right.

While Joe packed, he kept telling me we'd talk about all this. I was sure we would.

I picked up the box I'd gotten from Esther's. I took out the little framed pieces of poetry. There was an extra one that I hadn't read. Esther must have put it in the box with the others—a little gift. I stopped packing to read more of John Greenleaf Whittier's lines from "*The Palatine*," the stanzas describing what happened after the ship was lured onto the shoals.

> *O men and brothers! what sights were there!*
> *White upturned faces, hands stretched in prayer!*
> *Where waves had pity, could ye not spare?*

> *In their cruel hearts, as they homeward sped,*
> *"The sea and the rocks are dumb," they said:*
> *"There'll be no reckoning with the dead."*

But they were wrong, Mr. Whittier. Ask my friend Fitzy, he'll tell you. The sea and the rocks will tell all if you stop and listen to them. In the end, you have no choice but to reckon with the dead. And it's my job to see to it that you do.

AUTHOR'S NOTE

Block Island is a place of beauty, serenity, and unforgettable clam rolls. My characters, and a bit of the island's history and geography found herein, are entirely the product of my imagination and bear no relation to actual people and places.

ABOUT THE AUTHOR

M̲ary-Ann Tirone Smith is the author of seven previous novels, including *Love Her Madly*, the first of the Poppy Rice Mysteries, which was chosen as a *People* Magazine Page-Turner of the Week. She has lived all her life in Connecticut except for the two years she served as a Peace Corps Volunteer in Cameroon.

BOOK YOUR PLACE ON OUR WEBSITE AND MAKE THE READING CONNECTION!

We've created a customized website just for our very special readers, where you can get the inside scoop on everything that's going on with Zebra, Pinnacle and Kensington books.

When you come online, you'll have the exciting opportunity to:

- View covers of upcoming books
- Read sample chapters
- Learn about our future publishing schedule (listed by publication month *and author*)
- Find out when your favorite authors will be visiting a city near you
- Search for and order backlist books from our online catalog
- Check out author bios and background information
- Send e-mail to your favorite authors
- Meet the Kensington staff online
- Join us in weekly chats with authors, readers and other guests
- Get writing guidelines
- AND MUCH MORE!

**Visit our website at
http://www.kensingtonbooks.com**